Entangled Realms

Entangled Realms
Madilyn DeRose

Copyright © 2023 Natasha Cox
All rights reserved.
ISBN: 9798862990188
Independently Published

The characters and events portrayed in this book are fictitious. Any similarities to real persons, living or dead, are coincidental and not intended by the author.

No part of this book may be reproduced, or stored in a retrieval system, or transmitted in any form or by any means, electronic, mechanical, photocopying, recording, or otherwise, without express written permission of the author.

Cover design by: Natasha Cox using Canva
Printed in the United States of America

Dedication

We all love enemies to lovers and men who fall first. Make him grovel and beg. Stab him a few times, even.

In the end, it might be his textured dick, split tongue and questionable sense of morality that win you over.

Just enjoy the ride and hold onto those branch-horns for dear life.

Preface

Important Remarks About Content

This book sort of developed a mind of its own. Is it a Beauty & the Beast retelling? Yes, but it's a bunch of other things too. Have so much fun!

This book is meant to be consumed as a work of fiction. The themes and actions depicted are not meant to be recreated and are not in any way examples of healthy relationships, love, or sex. I've done my best to include accurate content warnings. Ultimately, it is your responsibility to determine if this is the right book for you.

Please prioritize yourself and your health.

Trigger Warnings

To ensure the health and safety of all readers, please review the trigger warnings listed here. Use your best judgment to determine if this is a safe book for you to read. I've done my best to determine possible triggers that may be included in the content and themes of this book to varying degrees.

In an effort to avoid getting flagged, I've moved my major warnings to Instagram. A comprehensive list of warnings can be found on my page @madilynderose.author.
Check the links in my bio, navigate to Book Trigger Warnings and find this book in the list.

Please for the love of gods heed the warnings! If you don't know what any of the terms mean, please do your research or reach out to me beforehand.

Table of Contents

Dedication..I
Preface...III
Trigger Warnings V
Chapter 1 1
Chapter 2 9
Chapter 3 16
Chapter 4 26
Chapter 5 33
Chapter 6 43
Chapter 7 49
Chapter 8 55
Chapter 9 60
Chapter 10 67
Chapter 11 75
Chapter 12 81
Chapter 13 85
Chapter 14 93
Chapter 15 98
Chapter 16 105
Chapter 17 115
Chapter 18 122
Chapter 19 128
Chapter 20 135
Chapter 21 143
Chapter 22 150
Chapter 23 158
Chapter 24 162

Chapter 25	168
Chapter 26	177
Chapter 27	184
Chapter 28	191
Chapter 29	199
Chapter 30	206
Chapter 31	214
Chapter 32	221
Chapter 33	228
Chapter 34	237
Chapter 35	243
Chapter 36	253
Chapter 37	260
Chapter 38	269
Chapter 39	277
Chapter 40	283
Chapter 41	291
Chapter 42	299
Chapter 43	305
Chapter 44	313
Chapter 45	319
Chapter 46	324
Chapter 47	330
Chapter 48	337
Chapter 49	343
Chapter 50	351
Chapter 51	357
Chapter 52	361

Chapter 53 368
Chapter 54 374
Chapter 55 382
Chapter 56 391
Chapter 57 397
Chapter 58 405
Chapter 59 411
Chapter 60 416
Chapter 61 421
Epilogue I 426
Epilogue II 429

Madilyn DeRose

Chapter 1

"I took a deep breath and listened to the old brag of my heart. I am, I am, I am."
-Sylvia Plath, The Bell Jar

Kiera

This place was one hundred percent not my vibe. It was dark and there was a lingering scent of alcohol everywhere you went. I didn't even know where they were getting the alcohol, since there wasn't anyone selling it. Maybe they just brought it themselves, which also didn't elicit confidence in the rationality of us coming here.

"Who told you about this place?" I asked.

Eli glanced sidelong at me. "Preston did."

Immediately, I stopped walking. Someone bumped into me from behind and called me a bitch before going around. Eli turned, giving me an exasperated look.

I fixed him with a glare. "Is he going to be here?"

He looped an arm through mine and pulled me along. "Yeah, but it's going to be fun."

"Last time you tricked me into coming on a date with you, I ended up having to Uber home because I couldn't find you guys."

"It's not a date. Plus, do you want me hanging out with a guy I barely know without backup? He could take advantage of me."

I snorted a laugh. "Maybe you shouldn't go to shady places like this, then."

"We'll have a good time. There might even be someone for you here."

Wrinkling my nose, I looked around. I wasn't exactly sure what went on here, but judging by the blocked off section in the middle and the plethora of health code violations, I'd bet my ass it wasn't legal. The light was a dim yellow and the floor was concrete. The longer we were here, the more scents accosted me and I had no interest in spending the time trying to identify them.

"Yeah, nobody here is my type."

"You don't even have a type."

"Of course I do. Tall, growly, and sexy."

"Oh, your type is imaginary men you read about in books."

Throwing him a grin, I shrugged. "If I never find one, I'll spend my life alone, which is perfectly fine with me. It's better than settling for someone mediocre. At least I'll always have you."

"You're a crazy bitch."

Someone appeared behind Eli and my eyes widened. The guy was tall with dark hair and a jaw that might have actually been able to cut glass. Speaking of book boyfriends...

Eli turned around and was immediately wrapped in a very intimate embrace. When the guy kissed him, I saw their tongues meet. Yeah, that was a show I didn't buy a ticket to, but got a free pass to anyway.

After a moment, Eli pulled away and breathed a laugh. "Well, that's one way to greet someone."

The other guy shrugged nonchalantly. "It's better to get the first kiss out of the way early, otherwise everyone's stomach is a mess the whole night."

"I can't say I'm opposed to the idea. Uh, Preston, this is Kiera. Kiera, this is Preston."

Preston offered me his hand and I took it firmly. "I figured, but there was always a chance you were some random guy."

He smiled at me, revealing dimples on either side of his mouth. For the first time in my life, I wished I was a man so that I could have a chance with this beautiful specimen. It looked like Eli was going to be living out my dream.

"Was Eli afraid to meet me by himself?"

"He thinks you'll take advantage of him."

"Okay, introductions are over," Eli interrupted, narrowing his eyes at me.

Coming up to his side, I looped my arm through his and rose on my toes to whisper in his ear. "He's a dream. If you screw this up, I'm choosing him in the breakup."

"Okay, Kiera. Let's not pull out the dramatics this early in the night."

Before I could respond, a bright light turned on in the center of the room. Now that I could see better, I took in the space more fully.

The middle of the room was separated from the rest by a sort of chain link barrier that reached all the way to the ceiling. There was a pathway leading to the far wall, which had a large black door. Above, there was a grated walkway and what resembled stadium seating on one side of the room. Across from that was a smaller seating area with a large, comfortable looking chair and a few modest seats beside it.

It was all very showy and it was hard to believe this was something in real life. My first thought was that it looked like some sort of fight club. Considering we had to be on a mysterious list to get in, that could be exactly what it was. The thought made my stomach flip.

"Is this a fight club?"

Preston grinned at me from around Eli. "It is. Didn't he tell you?"

Eli grimaced when I narrowed my eyes at him. "You wouldn't have come if I told you."

"Of course I wouldn't. It's illegal, for one. Second, I don't want to watch people beat the shit out of each other."

"It'll be fine, Kiera. It's probably all fake anyway."

After grinding my teeth for a moment, I nodded. "If it gets gross, I'm leaving."

I glanced at Preston, who was wearing a little smirk. He turned to look at me, then winked, before returning his attention to Eli.

When I looked up again, the seats were full. My gaze traveled to the other chair, which was more like a throne, and my eyes widened. There was a man there that could probably command a room with a single look. It was hard to tell from here, but he looked huge; both tall and broad.

His hair must have been nearly white and his skin was pale. He was wearing a black button up, but the sleeves were rolled to his elbows, so I could see that there was ink on his arm. I wished I was close enough to see what the art was. With his relaxed posture and his legs stretched out in front of him, he appeared bored.

His head dipped in my direction and I looked away quickly. My heart was racing, but I didn't know why. There were hundreds of spectators here. Even if he was the big head honcho, he wouldn't notice one random person staring at him.

There was shouting from inside the ring. Rising on my toes, I watched as someone was shoved out the black door, then it closed behind them. After trying and failing to open it, they turned around and started to walk slowly toward the center.

Another person was already there, looking more sure of themselves. Both were women and they were wearing similar black outfits; tank tops that ended just above their belly button and tight shorts that didn't leave much to the imagination.

What I found most strange were the masks that covered their faces. They were similar to fukumen masks, leaving their eyes bare, but covering their heads and the lower half of their face. The more confident one was wearing a deep red one, while the other woman's was white.

I assumed they were to conceal their identities, but to me they just looked creepy. Aside from the masks, it was unnerving to see the way the second woman was acting. She was glancing around while she rubbed up and down her arms. If I were to make an inference, it would be that she didn't want to participate in this. Maybe she had cold feet.

The light above them turned green and red mask rushed forward, colliding with white mask, sending them both to the ground. There was a scream as they wrestled with each other, then the crowd drowned out any other sounds. I was grateful for it, considering the intensity of the fight. Red mask was landing blow after blow relentlessly and I wondered how long the other one would hold on before tapping out.

"This is brutal," I called over the cheering.

Eli must not have heard me, so I took a step closer and put a hand on his arm. When I rose on my toes to position my lips at his ear, I was struck by how far I had to reach. An unfamiliar scent reached my nose; it was a strange combination of something similar to peach mixed with what I could only conceptualize as Earl Grey tea. It was a scent I knew well, but had never associated with anything outside of autumn and days spent reading.

Hastily, I pulled my hand back and looked up. My breath caught when I saw a head of bright hair, rather than Eli's tight black curls. Jesus Christ, this fucker was tall up close.

Why the fuck was he so close?

"Sorry," I said quickly.

Entangled Realms

When I took a step back, he took hold of my bicep, keeping me from moving any further. My heart raced as I looked up at him. His head was cocked slightly as he studied me, the completely neutral expression on his face making me feel more unnerved.

"Excuse me." I tugged on my arm and he released me.

"Apologies."

His voice was deep, but not as low as I would've guessed, considering everything else about him. While it wasn't full of ridiculous bass, it was rough in a way that sent a shiver through my body. The worst part was the accent. It wasn't something I could identify, the lilt being incredibly graceful, but making that single word sound like a threat.

Forcing myself out of my spiraling thoughts, I casually glanced around the space. Eli and Preston were nowhere to be found, just like I knew was going to happen. Next time I was going to put all of my trust into the law of probability and skip the weird meet-and-greet.

"Have you lost someone?"

I glanced toward the man, but didn't meet his eyes. "Just looking for my friend. Don't worry about it."

"Perhaps I can help. I had quite a view from up there."

"I'm sure you did, but I doubt you would've noticed him."

He hummed thoughtfully. "What do you find brutal about this?"

My brow furrowed. "I, uh, it's just sort of fucked up. I'm not into fighting."

"Tests of strength have been a pivotal piece of all cultures across humanity's lifespan."

"Pivotal or not, it's barbaric. That girl didn't seem like she wanted to fight at all."

"Perhaps you'd like a closer look to determine if your assertions are correct."

This time, I met his gaze. Even though it was dark in here, I could make out his pale jade eyes. They weren't just green, though. It was like different shades of green had been swirled, the way bakers did with a marble cake. In a way, they reminded me of a moss agate. I wondered if he was wearing contacts.

"A closer look?" I repeated.

"A tour," he said, the corner of his mouth lifting.

"Why would I want that?"

His eyebrows went up for a brief moment before he smoothed his expression.

"For fun?"

"Is that a question?" I laughed.

"You appeared to be very curious before."

"Anybody would be when they're in a new place. Especially one like this."

"You'd be surprised. Many are only here to sate their bloodlust and most cannot take their eyes off the fight, even when the brutality makes them feel ill. It's human nature to be drawn in by the macabre."

"Maybe I'm not human," I joked.

He raised one brow as he dragged his eyes down my body. When he met my gaze again, his lip was curled slightly.

"You're quite mundane."

"Wow. Well, I'm just gonna go."

"What about your friend?"

I held up my phone. "There's a thing called texting. Nice to meet you, uh..."

"Around here, they call me Leander."

Biting my lip, I tried to hold in my laughter. His cheek twitched, but if I'd irritated him, he betrayed no other sign. Deciding it was best to get out while I was ahead, I jabbed my thumb over my shoulder and turned around.

His fingers wrapped around my wrist, stopping me again. I hissed at the static shock from his touch. He stepped in front of me before pulling his hand away.

"You didn't tell me your name."

"Okay."

"It's common courtesy when someone gives you their name, is it not?"

"If we're getting technical, you gave me your moniker, but not your actual name, so I think we're square."

He narrowed his eyes. With a wink, I turned back to the door.

"You can call me Griselda," I called before I rushed off, keeping my arms crossed over my chest so he couldn't grab for me.

Thankfully, I made it outside without any issues. As I headed toward the street, I glanced behind me a couple of times to make sure nobody had followed me. Once I was in an Uber, I sent a mildly irritated text to Eli and let out a long breath.

That place was in my metaphorical rearview mirror and nothing could convince me to return.

Chapter 2

Kiera

"God damnit, Eli," I muttered, ending the fifth call that had gone to voicemail since this morning.

It was just after four and he still hadn't come home. I was all for getting laid, especially when it included someone as scrumptious as Preston. What I didn't like was not knowing when he would be back. Common courtesy would include letting his roommate know that he was holed up in a sex-scented room so that I didn't have to imagine all the places he could be floating belly up.

Taking a deep breath, I slipped my phone into my pocket and leaned my elbows on the counter. There was no need to lose my head. Eli was eccentric, slightly irresponsible, and prone to falling head over heels faster than anyone I'd ever met. He was smart, though, and he wouldn't put himself in a bad situation.

Drumming my fingers on the surface, I contemplated spam calling him until he got pissed off and answered. God, I felt like a mom with a teenager. My parents probably hadn't known how good they had it with me.

Not to jump on the 'not like other girls' train, but I'd rather be reading about mythical worlds than get drunk in a place that wasn't my living room. Drunk while reading about a mythical world was even better. Two birds and all that.

When my phone rang, I fumbled it, barely getting a grip on it before it could end up on the floor.

"Eli, what the fuck?" I nearly shouted.

"Uh, Kiera?" a timid voice asked.

"Oh, sorry. I thought... Nevermind. What's up, Vivian?"

"I didn't want to bother you because I know it's your first day off in a while..."

Resisting the urge to groan, I dropped onto the couch. "Who called out? I will personally skin them alive."

"Eli was supposed to be here at two."

At that, I sat up straight. "He called out?"

That was extremely unlike him. As much as he complained about his job, he had an impeccable work ethic. On top of that, he loved finding fun- and expensive- things to do, so he hated to miss out on making money when he could.

"No, he just didn't show up."

Something curdled in my stomach. "Okay, I'll be there in an hour."

"Thanks, Kiera."

Flipping the phone over repeatedly, I tried not to let myself spiral. Thinking the worst was good when the situation turned out to be catastrophic, but it was too early to make assumptions. Maybe he felt burned out and just needed the day off. He could have forgotten to call in or it might have slipped his mind that he worked at all.

I shouldn't have left that club without trying harder to find him. Even though he creeped me out, that Leander guy might've actually been able to help me. He seemed important, so I wouldn't be surprised if he knew everything that went on in that club.

It wasn't like I could do much about it right now, so I headed into my room to get changed. Apparently, I'd be spending my evening making coffee for people that really didn't need the extra caffeine.

🌷 🌷 🌷 🌷

"Thanks so much," I said, putting on a sweet smile for the man that stuffed a dollar into the tip jar. When he turned around, I glared at the pitiful container of crumpled ones and stray pennies.

"Well, isn't this a beautiful coincidence?"

No, no, no. I couldn't deal with that on top of everything else. I silently pleaded with the universe to transport me into some pocket between realms.

Turning around, I found a man wearing a grin that made me a little nauseous. He was dressed in a red sweater that looked comical in October, but probably cost him a couple hundred dollars. His dark hair was styled neatly with a very purposeful strand positioned over his forehead.

"Grayson," I greeted, barely concealing my disdain.

"Kiera, I didn't know you were working tonight."

He always pronounced my name wrong, even though I'd corrected him on multiple occasions. It wasn't Kee-ra; it was like Sierra, but with a K. I didn't think it was that hard to figure out, but the guy wasn't the sharpest knife in the block.

Sure, he spent an annoying amount of time in this bookstore, but I was pretty sure it was only to hit on women. When he drank his coffee, he'd sit and read the popular smutty books, then he would go on the hunt for someone pretty that was looking at one he was familiar with. It was a great icebreaker, which was the only compliment I'd pay the douchebag.

"I wasn't scheduled, but here I am."

"You close in a few minutes, right?"

"That I do."

He hummed thoughtfully while I prepared myself for the inevitable. No matter how many times he asked and I shot him down, he just kept trying. Maybe he thought I was playing hard to get. A guy like him couldn't fathom how someone wouldn't swoon over his square jaw and muscles that were entirely for show.

"You know," he drawled, leaning his elbows on the counter. He casually flexed his biceps before looking up at me. "There's a movie playing at the theater."

"Isn't there always a movie playing there?"

"Well, I guess, but that's not the point."

"What's the point, Grayson?" I matched his stance, putting our faces a foot away from each other. His eyes blazed, then dropped to my chest.

"Come see a movie with me, Kiera."

I pretended to mull it over. "Nope." Tapping his nose with one finger, I straightened.

"Come on, baby. It's just a movie."

"I don't like movies."

"Who doesn't like movies?"

People who didn't want to think of a better reason to say no.

"It's been a long day and I just want to get home."

"We could watch a movie there."

"Maybe next time."

"Alright. You have my number, right?"

"Yeah," I lied. His name had mysteriously disappeared from my contacts moments after he'd saved it there.

"Alright, beautiful. When do you start tomorrow?"

"Five."

He winked before heading back to his hunting ground. Blowing air through my lips, I started wiping down the equipment.

"I'm out of here, Kiera," Vivian informed me. "When are you here tomorrow?"

"Nine to four."

"Alright, I'll see you when you're heading out. Thanks for covering today. Make sure you give Eli shit for this."

"I will. Goodnight."

She threw a wave over her shoulder before disappearing. Leaning against the counter, I pulled out my phone for the first time in hours. In my experience, someone would respond to you only after you stopped obsessing over it.

My stomach felt acidic when I looked at the empty notification bar. Damnit, Eli. Where the hell could you be?

🌷 🌷 🌷 🌷

"Thanks," I called before shutting the door.

When the car pulled away, my anxiety heightened. This was one hundred percent a bad idea, but I couldn't file a missing person's report until tomorrow according to the rude woman I'd talked to at the station. Going rogue was the decision of dumbasses, so I guess that's what I was tonight.

Zipping up my jacket, I headed down the street, past a couple industrial buildings. As I drew closer, I heard people talking and a moment later, the entrance to the club came into view. It might've been because I was alone this time, but it looked more foreboding than I remembered.

A movement drew my gaze to a second floor window. Squinting my eyes, I tried to spot something, but it was empty. Shaking my head, I joined the line, looking around warily as I waited.

When it was my turn, I realized that I didn't have an invitation this time. I opened my mouth to speak, but the woman waved for me to go through.

"Uh, sorry," I stammered. "My name is-"

"You're good to go in, sweetie."

"But, I...:

She tapped her wrist, then diverted her attention to the next person. I stared at her arm, but didn't see what she was referring to. Not knowing what else to do, I stepped through the doorway, the same scents from before assaulting my senses.

The center light was already on and there was cheering coming from the crowd. Switching on my phone's flashlight, I kept to the walls, casually strolling through. I didn't know what I should be looking for. Clues? Signs of a struggle? I couldn't imagine he'd be here again tonight and nobody here was likely to remember him.

I made it to the other side of the fighting ring with nothing to show for my progress. Biting my lip, I looked at the seating above the fight. Leander was sitting on his throne with his legs crossed, the fingers of his left hand tapping on his armrest. As if he sensed my stare, he looked down, immediately making eye contact.

Swearing under my breath, I dropped my gaze. I hated that he'd noticed me both times I was here and I feared he'd come down and bother me again. The last thing I needed to do was catch the eye of someone like that.

"Kiera."

My skin prickled at the sound of my name. I turned to a short, golden-haired man. He had a kind face and a soft smile, but I didn't trust him. How did he know my name?

"You're Kiera, right?"

"Um, do I know you?"

"No, ma'am. I'm Chester."

"Okay."

He stared at me expectantly for a moment, then breathed a laugh.

"I apologize. My boss sent me down here to escort you upstairs."

A high-pitched laugh escaped me and I covered my mouth. "Sorry. I don't have any interest in going up there."

He frowned, looking so disappointed that I almost backtracked. Instead, I looked up at the dickwad on his throne. His head dipped slightly in my direction, but he didn't turn.

"If I go up there, am I going to be locked up?"

"Excuse me, I don't understand."

With a sigh, I looked at Chester. "I'm looking for someone. Can he help me?"

"If anyone knows what happens in this place, it is him."

"Fine. Lead the way, I guess."

He held an arm out to me, like we were in some period drama. I stuffed my hands in my pockets and nodded for him to lead the way. He led me over to the wall and opened a door I hadn't seen before. As I stepped through, I glanced behind me one more time, feeling like I was somehow stepping into another world.

Be brave, Kiera. He was just some undoubtedly rich asshole that ran a shady fight club. There was nothing to be afraid of, really.

Chapter 3

Kiera

By the time I reached the top of the stairs, my heart was beating like I'd just run a mile. I wanted to blame it on exertion, but it was really just cowardice.

In my opinion, people weren't actually courageous. Bravery was a façade we built to not only convince others that we were strong, but also ourselves. All I could do was put on a brave face, as they said, and try to keep my voice from wobbling like a bobblehead on a dashboard.

Chester opened a set of double doors that let out onto the second floor seating area. To the left were the casual seats and to the right was the pretentious throne. He motioned for me to follow him in that direction. Even though I knew it was where we were going, my stomach lurched.

Once we reached Leander, Chester inclined his head and walked away. I looked at him, pleading with my eyes, but he just smiled reassuringly before leaving through the doors. If I wasn't freaking out up to this point, I sure was now.

Leander didn't look at me, instead staring studiously down at the fight. I followed his gaze, feeling slightly nauseous at the amount of blood on the concrete. I wondered how many fights they had every night. What did the winners receive as a prize? It was probably money. People would put themselves in all sorts of terrible situations if they needed the cash.

A startled sound escaped my lips when Leander latched onto my wrist and pulled me closer. I landed in his lap and I was certain my stomach was going to evict itself straight through my esophagus. Situating me so I was sitting sideways, he twirled a strand of my hair around his finger.

When I tried to get free, he tightened his grip on my thigh. "Let's watch the fight, Kiera."

"Actually, I forgot to feed my snake, so I'll just be going."

His hold on me was firm, not letting me even adjust my position. It was extremely awkward like this and I had this crippling fear that I was sitting on his dick. My gaze dropped for a brief moment, then I stared studiously at the far wall.

"I would very much appreciate it if you let me go."

He chuckled, which just intensified my fear. "You came here seeking answers, did you not?"

"Sure, but this doesn't seem like it'll solve my problems."

"On the contrary, I think it can solve many things."

My nose wrinkled. "So, I was right."

"About what?"

"That you're a creep."

"Your opinions of me are inconsequential."

"Right. How the hell did you figure out my name?"

He finally looked at me, the varying green tones of his eyes seeming to shift, like they were liquid. Whoever made his contacts, I wanted their number. I definitely couldn't afford them, but a girl could dream. That shit was terrifying.

Entangled Realms

"I have my methods and I'm certain you would not approve."

"Well, great. Go ahead and do your illegal little activities, but I'd like to stay out of it."

"You're the one who came to my domain."

"Your domain?" I laughed. "Jesus. That's quite a god complex you have."

"If you were me, you would as well."

"Alright, Leander. I'm just here to see if I can find information about my friend. If you can't help me with that, I'd like to go home. I work in the morning."

"You haven't asked."

Narrowing my eyes, I studied him. Much to my annoyance, his expression betrayed absolutely nothing. As I continued to stare, the green of his eyes seemed to grow brighter. He blinked and they returned to normal.

"Do you know what happened to my friend the other night?"

"Who is your friend?"

"Eli. He was with me last time. Black, curly hair. A few inches taller than me. Blue sweater. A smile that lights up the room."

"Very descriptive. Anything else?"

"Uh, he was with another guy. The picture of tall, dark, and handsome. His name was Preston."

"That's all I need."

"Okay."

We continued to sit there in silence. He stared down at the fight, even though I wasn't sure he was actually watching it. My fingers tapped on my thigh as I waited for him to say something. After what felt like an eternity, I huffed.

"What was that about?" he asked disinterestedly.

"I'm waiting for you to tell me if you know anything."

"Right. I know where your friend is."

My heart leapt. "That's great. Tell me."

"You asked if I know what happened to him. I do."

"Uh, one would assume this is when you share that information with me."

"That wasn't part of the agreement, Kiera. You'll have to compel that information from me in a new way."

"I'm so freaking confused. What do you want me to do? I'm broke as hell, unless I can pay you in ramen noodles or thrift books. If you're looking for something spicier than that, you're even crazier than I thought."

"Christ, you tend to ramble without actually saying anything useful."

Narrowing my eyes, I grabbed the hand that was on my thigh and shoved it away as hard as I could. He didn't stop me when I stood and started marching toward the double doors. This entire thing was a waste of my time and I'd gotten nothing out of it, whereas he got to feel my ass on his dick and found some sick amusement in my plight.

"Go a round in the ring."

I stopped just short of the doors. "Excuse me?"

"Fight in the ring. If you do that, I will give your friend to you."

"Give my friend to me?" I repeated, the gears turning in my head. "What are you saying?"

He put his chin in his hand and watched me. "He is due to fight on Friday. You may take his place, so that he may return home."

Swallowing, I reached behind me to grasp the door handle. "Are you telling me you're... keeping him here?"

The corner of his mouth lifted. "You appear to be quite intelligent, Kiera."

Glancing down at the two people in the ring, I tried to wrap my head around it. The woman that didn't want to fight the last time I was here. The secretive nature of this place. The invite only system.

"You can't just force people to fight for you."

He laughed loudly. "Look around you, Kiera."

I really hated that he was using my name. Every time he said it, I felt like it meant more. Having my name gave him a piece of me that I hadn't offered freely. I was pissed about it.

Shaking my head, I pushed down on the door handle. "This is ridiculous."

Turning back to the fight, he sunk a little deeper into his chair. "Have it your way." When I stepped through the door, his voice carried to me. "Remember that they may fight to the death if they so choose. Let's hope his competitor is kind."

Without waiting for him to throw out more unnerving information, I pivoted and sprinted down the stairs, nearly tripping over myself. I didn't stop in the main room or even when I made it outside. Only when I was a few blocks away did I allow myself a moment to breathe, not that it mattered. It didn't feel like the oxygen was actually benefiting me in any way.

Putting my hands on top of my head, I paced along the sidewalk. All of this was ridiculous. There was no way Leander was holding Eli captive in that place. If everyone there was being forced to fight, how were they getting away with it? It was asinine to think that the people frequenting the place knew about it.

He'd let me leave, even after admitting his crimes to me. Either he was very confident I'd choose to take him up on his offer or he didn't fear me. The third option was that he intended to have me killed before I could rat him out. That thought had me spinning in a circle, eyeing the shadows carefully.

There was really only one logical thing for me to do. I didn't care what the woman on the phone told me. The last time I heard from Eli was over forty-eight hours ago, which meant they couldn't tell me no. I would park my ass in that station until they gave me what I wanted.

🌹 🌹 🌹

It had been two days since I filed that missing person's report and they still had nothing to tell me. I knew these things took time and I couldn't expect something right away, but I'd given them a very solid lead. It was ridiculous that they weren't on top of it immediately.

My fingers tapped rapidly along the counter as I stared at the date on my phone. Tomorrow was Friday and I hadn't heard anything from Eli or the police. If they still had nothing when it came time for his alleged fight, I had no idea what I was supposed to do.

"Vivian, can you cover me for a minute?"

"Of course."

I slipped out the back door into the alley and brought the phone to my ear. By the time it passed the third ring, I was sure my lunch was going to come back up.

"Los Angeles Police Department," a gravelly woman's voice answered.

"Hi. My name is Kiera Beaufort. I filed a missing person's report about my friend, Elijah Baker. I was hoping you had an update."

"One moment, kiddo... It looks like nothing has been discovered yet."

I huffed, leaning my head back against the brick. "I gave them a lead to look into. Do you know if that has been investigated yet?"

"They checked it out and found nothing to go on."

"Excuse me? That's not possible. The guy literally told me he was holding Eli hostage."

"The place was clean, ma'am. That's all I know. The guy was probably just toying with you."

"Okay. Thanks."

Without waiting for a response, I ended the call. It took a healthy amount of self-control to keep from throwing the phone at the wall. There was no way they looked into the place without finding anything suspicious. He literally ran an illegal fight ring there and if he was keeping people locked up, there would absolutely be something for them to find.

Feeling depressed and wondering if I was going crazy, I returned to my place behind the counter and started wiping some things down to occupy myself.

Entangled Realms

"Kiera!"

"God damnit," I muttered. The guy had a sixth sense for when I was in a bad mood.

"You didn't text me," Grayson scolded playfully. "I was waiting by my phone for the past three days."

"I'm sure you were. My, uh, phone is broken."

The traitorous thing chimed in my pocket and I grimaced. He narrowed his eyes momentarily, then waved a dismissive hand.

"Have you read any good books lately?"

"None that you'd be interested in."

"Try me, baby."

"I just started one about a self-absorbed man that is a massive twat-"

"Sounds boring," he interrupted. "The one I'm reading is about a guy with a twelve inch-"

"Excuse me," a deep, musical voice cut in.

Alarm bells went off in my head immediately. Cautiously, I looked over Grayson's shoulder and met green pools. In proper lighting, he looked like something out of a magical realm. His hair was so devoid of color and he was so tall that he appeared out of place in the little coffee shop.

Grayson's mouth dropped open. Ignoring him, Leander stepped around him and placed a hand on the counter. In just a black t-shirt, his ink was on full display. The tattoos were like vines twining around his arms. They morphed from plain to brightly flowered to thorny and dangerous.

"Um, coffee?" I asked lamely.

He smiled slightly. "Alright. Surprise me."

I hated that answer. Most of the time, the person wouldn't like what I chose, even though they were the ones that wanted to take the chance. I had no doubt Leander would be the same way even if he did like the drink just because he was an asshole.

As I began to prepare a toasted almond latte, Grayson stepped up to the counter.

"So, like I was saying. Twelve-inch dick. Isn't that incredible?"

"Sure."

"If you want to find out what it's like, we could- Ah, fuck."

He must've squeezed his cup too hard while spinning that bullshit pickup line. Coffee covered the front of his white sweater, leaving him a disgruntled, soggy mess.

"Damnit. I have to go change. You'll still be here, right?"

"Yeah."

He stared at me a little too long before turning toward the exit. Thankfully, I was off in twenty minutes, so I wouldn't be subject to whatever ugly sweater he came back in.

I set Leander's coffee on the counter and motioned toward it. As he brought it to his lips, I leaned back against the wall and watched him. His eyebrows raised slightly, then he stared down at the cup like it would bite him.

"Go ahead and tell me it's terrible so that I can make you a new one. I'm sure you have very important, illegal things to do."

"You're right."

With a sigh, I grabbed another cup. "What do you want?"

"The coffee is fine. I just have very important, illegal things to do."

"Oh." Resuming my position at the wall, I dropped my gaze to the floor. I didn't know what to do with my hands, so I just shoved them in my pockets.

"Will I see you tomorrow?"

I scoffed. "Is this when you ask me out or something?"

His lip curled. "That's a leap. Tomorrow is Friday."

"Yeah, I know. Tell me how you tricked the police."

His smile made me want to throw hot coffee in his face. "I have no idea what you're talking about, Kiera."

"Stop calling me that."

"But it's your name."

"My name that you acquired through nefarious deeds. It's not really fair."

"Should I call you Griselda?"

"Sure, since I have to use your made-up name."

Humming thoughtfully, he leaned his elbows on the counter. It was such a casual thing to do, yet he still looked mildly ethereal. I wondered if he was Northern European or something. He struck me as someone that would come from Iceland or Sweden.

"Tell me your name."

He breathed a laugh before taking another sip. "That's funny."

"I'm serious. If you do, I'll consider your stupid proposal."

He narrowed his eyes at me. "What game are you playing?"

"I'm just a morbidly curious person. I promise I won't tell anyone your secret."

When I winked at him, he looked more suspicious.

"You are a very stubborn and methodical woman."

"Am I supposed to immediately agree to participate in a fight to the death? Come on. Who actually does shit like this?"

"So, you will leave Eli to do it."

"You could just be a decent person and not force people to fight."

"That sounds very mundane."

"Why do you want me to take his place anyway?"

"I believe you would be better suited to it."

"You could just force me like you do with the others." The thought alone made panic rise in my chest.

"I could, but that's boring. My strength is enough to force anyone to be my slave. It's much more interesting to best a person's mind. Winning brings more satisfaction that way."

"If I win, what happens?"

His head cocked slightly. "Then you live."

"Tell me the rules."

"There are none."

Nodding slowly, I let myself consider the idea. There wasn't any part of me that wanted to do it, but at this point, I had to believe that he was telling the truth about Eli. The question was whether I was the type of person that would sacrifice myself for someone else. I'd never had to consider it before and I wished I could've stayed ignorant of what this felt like.

Clearly, the police weren't going to be of any use here. Somehow, he had a way to keep them from the truth. I didn't have an army or a secret weapon I could use to break him out, nor would I know where to start. If he could outsmart the police, I was sure I couldn't get anywhere close to finding where he kept his prisoners.

Prisoners. That was such a ridiculous notion. I got dragged to some underground fight club and now I was pondering the best way to save my best friend from what could possibly be his death, at the expense of myself.

There was a chance I could win the fight, of course. I didn't have any useful physical skills, but it was unlikely that the people Leander captured did either. He said there were no rules, which could give me an advantage considering I had time to prepare, unlike the others.

"Okay," I said, raising my gaze from the floor.

My brow furrowed at the empty space in front of me. He was gone, only the fifty on the counter betraying that he had been here at all. Picking up the bill, I saw there was something written on it.

Reynaeros.

Fuck that guy and his overdramatic personality. If I miraculously made it through this whole situation, I would seriously consider finding a way to assassinate him and end his entire sketchy business.

It was 2023. We no longer enslaved people, thank you very much.

Chapter 4

Reynaeros

Flicking my wrist, I unlocked the door to the shitty little room I'd thrown the weak one into. He was huddled on the bed with his knees to his chest. The way he was shaking reminded me of those tiny dogs I'd seen barking endlessly on the Internet.

"I come bearing great news for you," I announced.

He looked up and I saw him swallow hard. "You're letting me go?"

Shaking my head, I laughed. "We'll see about that. I just saw your friend and I've got a feeling she'll come to your rescue."

"What happens if she does?"

"She takes your place, remember? That is what you agreed to when you sold her out."

"You just asked for her name and where to find her. I-I didn't want you to make her fight."

"Do you think I care what you want, Elijah? She's simply a better candidate than you are. Look at yourself.

You wouldn't last thirty seconds in a fight against a toddler."

"You don't have to do this."

"Au contraire, this is the only thing I have to do. You'd better hope she is more useful to me than you have been."

"Please don't hurt her."

When I appeared beside the bed, he shrieked. Latching onto his throat, I pulled him closer, wrinkling my nose at the smell of him.

"Oh, she will be hurt. If she survives the round, it will be worse for her. See, sometimes death is the mercy. I hope you can live with whatever happens tomorrow."

"God," he cried. "I'm sorry. I'm so sorry. Just let me fight. I'll do it."

Releasing him, I headed toward the door. "It's too late for bravery now, human. You have handed me a rose and I'm very interested to see how sharp her thorns are."

He was still crying when I shut the door. It was laughable that he would try to feign nobility now. If I threatened his life again, he would quickly return to offering others to fight in his stead.

Truthfully, I didn't know why I made him give me her name. It pissed me off that she refused to tell me herself. Not everyone was susceptible to my influence, but it was something I didn't often run into here.

Nobody in this place was clever or percipient. All I had to do was speak to them and they'd be interested in what I had to say. They would follow me easily, not knowing that they were being led to the last place they'd ever see.

She wasn't so easily persuaded. Even when I threatened her friend's life, she took time to ponder her next move. She took so damn long that I had to seek her out myself, which was even more infuriating than her keeping her name to herself. Going out was the last thing I ever wanted to do.

Tomorrow, she would show up to replace Elijah. I was certain of it from the resigned expression that had come over her in the coffee shop. Once she came to the decision, her eyes changed. The resilience there further solidified my belief that she was a good choice.

Fighting wasn't always about brawn or agility. Often, one could best an opponent simply because they were smarter than them. A methodical fighter would determine how they could use the environment to their advantage. They would identify the strengths and weaknesses of their counterpart, then compare them to their own.

It had been ages since someone capable had walked into my domain. She would quickly regret coming into this place and capturing my attention. Her inquisitive stare was the thing that would ultimately be her downfall.

For the first time in longer than I could remember, I was excited to watch a fight. I prayed to the gods that she wouldn't disappoint me or I might have to turn this place upside down to sate my rage.

Looking at the doors in the hallway, I decided on one to the left. As soon as I opened it, the person began to cry. They were so weak, it was a mercy I gave them a meaningful death in this place.

🌹 🌹 🌹 🌹

Even though I was confident she'd show up, I couldn't stop pacing. I'd ensured that nobody could see me on the upper deck at the moment, so they wouldn't witness my weakness. After so long without a worthy fighter, I could not quiet my mind.

My hands buzzed with my rising agitation. Straightening my fingers, I tried to quell the energy, then I relaxed them again.

"Reynaeros," Chester said from the door. I turned to him, raising a brow. "The girl is here."

My heart felt like it leapt in my chest. "Good. Have her meet me in front of Elijah's room."

"Of course, my lord."

After taking a moment to roll up my sleeves, I headed down the stairs. The door into the hall appeared before me and I marched through it, feeling excitement rise with every step I took. I was nearly bouncing from the feeling while I waited for them to join me.

Finally, I smelled jasmine and rose. I leaned back against the wall, planting one foot against it. They turned the corner and Kiera's gaze immediately landed on me, her eyes widening for only a moment before she hid her expression. She was good at it, but it was the miniscule changes in her face that nobody would catch that gave her away.

I couldn't help trailing my eyes down her body. Unlike the fighters I put in the ring, she was almost entirely covered. Even so, the skin tight black leggings she wore didn't leave much to the imagination, although I was imagining what lay underneath. She wore a black sweatshirt and her hair was pulled into a neat bun, making her cheekbones look sharper.

"Kiera," I greeted.

A flush rose on her neck. "Leander."

I smiled at her use of the moniker. The way she said it now sounded mysterious, as if she was keeping some sort of secret. Giving my name to her might have been impulsive. Only those closest to me knew my true name and even they sometimes referred to me by the one I'd chosen long ago.

"That door..." She trailed off, biting her cheek. "I didn't see it last time."

"You must be terribly unobservant."

Pushing off the wall, I shifted the door lock and led her inside. Behind me, she gasped and her footsteps stopped. I continued until I was beside the bed where Elijah was sitting. When he saw her, he looked like he might cry again.

"Eli," she said, her voice cracking.

She rushed forward and threw her arms around his neck. He held her around the waist tightly and both their shoulders began to shake. I glanced sidelong at Chester. There was compassion in his eyes as he watched their interaction.

Regardless of the respect I had for him, there was no denying that he was too soft. He was loyal to a fault, though, and I would trust him with my life.

When he saw me watching him, he cleared his throat and ran a hand through his hair. The other one was shoved into his pocket, as it usually was when he was around anyone.

"This is tiresome," I drawled. "Let's move on to business."

Still clinging to his arm, Kiera turned and glared at me. The fierceness in her eyes made me more excited to get her in the ring.

"Let him go," she demanded.

"You may ask as many times as you wish and I will say no. Nobody leaves for free."

"I'm here for your stupid fight. That's the price, right?"

I smiled. "Yes, little rose. That is the price."

"Then let him go."

"Once you fulfill your part of the bargain, he will be free to leave."

"Kiera, don't do it," Elijah insisted, taking her hands.

"I have to, Eli. He'll just keep you here if I don't."

"No, I'll fight. It's okay."

"You could die."

"So could you. Please, just leave while you have the chance."

She tapped her fingers on her thigh, appearing lost in her thoughts. After a while, she shook her head.

"I've already decided and I'm prepared. You look like you could barely stand."

"Please. He's a monster."

I couldn't help but laugh. When she narrowed her eyes at me, I motioned for her to continue their back and forth game. At this point, I wouldn't let her leave, even if I had to threaten everyone in her life. It wouldn't be the first time I'd acquired someone's acquiescence through subterfuge.

She brushed his cheekbone with her thumb, then kissed his forehead. Straightening, she turned to me, setting her jaw.

"May I safely assume that you've made your decision?"

"Yeah."

"Great. Let's go."

When I turned, I sensed her movements. She went for something in her pocket, then quickly rushed forward. I sidestepped, receiving only a small cut on my side. Before she could attack me again, I pivoted, wrapping my fingers around her throat. The force of being slammed into the wall caused her to drop the knife, the loud clatter making me grit my teeth.

"Where does bravery end and stupidity begin, Kiera?"

Her mouth opened, but nothing came out. Tightening my grip, I lifted her a few inches off the ground. There was an intense fear in her eyes that made me want to snuff out the last of the light in them.

"Stop!" Elijah shouted.

He dove for the blade, but it disappeared before he could grab it.

"What the hell?"

Chester stepped in and tossed him across the room. Kiera clawed at my hand, drawing blood. I released her and she hit the ground on her knees, letting out a pained cry. She coughed in between her wheezing breaths.

"Perhaps I would have been kind to you, Kiera. It's unlikely, but now it's unimaginable." After touching my side, I looked at the red staining my fingers. "Where I'm from, drawing blood is a declaration of war between two people. Do you truly want me as your enemy?"

She rubbed at her throat and shook her head. "I'm sorry."

"Good. Chester, put her in the ring."

He grabbed her arm, helping her to her feet roughly. The softness from earlier seemed to have been replaced by an irritation similar to my own. As I said, he was loyal to a fault.

"I do hope you fare better against your next opponent," I called as I stepped into the hallway.

Her infuriating attack had almost been enough for my control to slip. The last thing I needed was for the imbecile to have more tales to spin when I threw him out of this place. Most likely, everyone would just consider him crazy, but it was still an irritant I didn't want to deal with.

Fucking humans. They were ridiculous creatures, yet they had the audacity to call me a beast.

Madilyn DeRose

Chapter 5

Kiera

Plan A had been a failure, which I was ninety-nine percent sure would be the case before I executed it. It would've been remiss of me not to try, though. From the ferocity of his rage, it was clear that I was lucky to have survived the encounter. Well, lucky was relative, considering I would likely get beaten to death in this match.

As I walked toward the circular ring, the cheering of the crowd raged in my ears. It all sounded hazy and I was more than a little bit overwhelmed. The light above was significantly brighter from this position and made it hard to see the opponent that stood on the other side.

Before I even had a chance to get my bearings, the light turned green and a body was getting closer at an alarming rate. Swearing, I leapt to the side, landing on my knees. The concrete hurt my skin through my thin leggings, but I did my best to ignore the pain as I got to my feet.

The woman took a few slow steps to the side, as if she was evaluating her approach. I used the opportunity to pull my hoodie over my head. Tossing it to the side, I quickly glanced up at the asshole sitting on his throne. After a moment, he straightened, his hands gripping the armrests.

I snickered, readjusting my homemade masterpiece. After my shift yesterday, I'd picked up a plain, black jersey and some art supplies. I wasn't that great with my hands, but I'd managed to make it look pretty nice.

That name of his was a mouthful and I didn't know how to correctly pronounce it, but he'd given me the spelling, which was all I needed. The front of the jersey read, 'Say no to Reynaeros.' On the back, it said, 'Bow to no one. Fuck Reynaeros.'

Judging by the look on his face, he was not happy that I was advertising his name to the whole place. Good. I wasn't happy that he choked me out and dodged my attack. I'd at least hoped to give him a better stab wound, but he was annoyingly perceptive, apparently.

Thankfully, I had the foresight to come prepared. As my opponent rushed toward me again, I freed my knife from underneath my shirt and gripped it tightly. At the last moment, she saw it and pivoted, ramming her shoulder into my side. I hit the ground hard, sending a jolt of pain through my ankle.

She straddled me, locking her hands around my neck. That was an experience I didn't want to repeat. I lodged the blade in her side, making her shriek. Using her grip on me, she raised me off the ground slightly, then slammed me back down. My head felt like it'd been scrambled and I had to blink a few times to get my bearings.

Her fist connected with the side of my face. I'd never thought too long about how much that would hurt, but it was a lot worse than I'd expected. My skin, my bones, and everything else that made up my head were simultaneously throbbing and stinging.

Before she could continue the assault, I reached for the handle and pulled it out of her side. Blood spurted out, the wet splash beside my ear making me gag a little. Even though I really didn't want to, I thrust the blade into her again.

I didn't know if it was a crazed bloodlust ignited by my intense desire to live, but I stabbed and pulled it out repeatedly until she swayed. As soon as she fell off of me, I scrambled backward, putting my back against the fence. Someone grabbed me through the gaps and I shrieked, thrashing to dislodge them.

Their touch disappeared and I smelled something sweet like flowers. Chester grabbed my arms and pulled me to my feet, quickly ushering me down the walkway and through the black door. Once it shut behind me, I stumbled and ran into a wall. Deciding to just go with it, I slid down to the ground, continuing until I was lying flat on my back, staring up at the white ceiling.

Things weren't spinning, per say, but they didn't look all that stable or corporeal. Maybe it was the blood that had no doubt splashed into my eyes. It was like I'd opened my eyes underwater and was staring at the refracted, wobbly light from under the surface.

"What the fuck is this?"

I rolled my head toward the voice and recoiled when I saw Reynaeros' pale hair. The sight of it made me laugh. Bringing my hand to my mouth, I tried to stop, but it seemed to only get worse. His brows went up as he watched me, then they furrowed when it had been an embarrassing amount of time.

"Can you walk?" he asked briskly.

"Who knows," I drawled.

Using the wall, I got to my knees, then planted my feet on the floor. As soon as I managed to stand straight, my legs buckled. I prepared myself to hit the ground, but I was suddenly floating. No, not floating.

"Why are you carrying me?"

"Because you're clearly too damaged to handle yourself and Chester is too proper to touch you like this without feeling like he's intruding."

"I'd rather he intrude on me than you."

"That's too bad. If you don't get sleep and a medical evaluation, you could die before you even get a chance to celebrate your victory."

"Victory," I repeated with a scoff. "I killed someone."

"Yes. That's what I said."

"I don't want to see your janky doctor. I'll go after I leave here."

"That's not going to happen."

"You don't even know me, so don't assume I won't go."

If I was being honest, I probably wouldn't go unless it got bad enough for me to think I could actually die. I'd heard you weren't supposed to sleep with a concussion, but that was exactly what I wanted to do. Climbing under fresh, cold blankets sounded incredible after the day I had and it was suddenly all that mattered.

"I need to go home."

"Just rest your thorns, little rose."

"That's stupid."

His chest rumbled a little. My head felt like shit and the bright lights were only making it worse. Leaning against his chest, I let out a contented sound. He was tense, but didn't throw me on the floor, so that was good at least.

At a certain point, the pressure around my body disappeared and I felt something soft under my fingers. I didn't open my eyes, fearing this comfortable feeling was part of a dream I didn't want to lose.

🌹 🌹 🌹 🌹

The smell of roses was strong when I woke up. It was comforting, like the time my parents took me on a trip to the French countryside. We stayed at a quaint bed and breakfast that drew a bath for you in the morning and brought breakfast to your room on a tray. It was like being in a fairytale.

A wave of emotions came over me and I pushed the memory away quickly. When I opened my eyes, they felt heavy and crusty. Everything was blurry, but my room seemed bright, so it must have been morning.

When did I go to bed last night? It felt like I hadn't slept at all. If I got drunk, I should've remembered the first couple drinks at least. The last thing I could recall was...

Oh, shit. I sat up quickly, groaning at the sharp pain behind my eyes. It sure felt like a hangover, but I wasn't so lucky.

After rubbing my eyes and clearing away some of the grit, I looked around the room. It was bigger than mine, with ornate furniture and heavy curtains that were open, letting in way too much sunlight. The bed was one of those classic four-poster ones like a princess would have. The blanket I clung to was thick and heavy; if I wasn't currently freaking out, I would've snuggled under it again.

There was a door to my right and one to my left. I headed to the latter one, my eyes widening when I saw the claw foot tub. On the other side of the bathroom there was a walk-in shower with a glass door that opened outward. Why the hell had that asshole put me in a place like this?

The pounding in my head reminded me that I'd taken a solid whack to the concrete and he'd told me to rest. A wave of nausea twisted my stomach as I thought about the fight. I wanted to play ignorant and hope the woman wasn't dead, but there was no questioning it. I'd done what I had to do in order to survive and free Eli, but that didn't make me feel less guilty about it.

Exiting the bathroom, I nearly had a heart attack. There was a woman standing beside the bed, setting what looked like a mug of coffee on the nightstand. She was young and pretty, with soft blonde hair that curled in a way that reminded me of the fifties. The smile she gave me calmed my nerves slightly, but I remained by the far wall, crossing my arms over my chest.

"Where am I?"

"In your room, ma'am."

"Uh, gross. My name is Kiera."

"Of course. Sorry."

"What's your name?"

"It's Portia. I brought you some coffee. The caffeine might help with your head."

Tentatively, I rounded the bed and took a sip of the hot liquid. It had a nutty flavor that reminded me of autumn. With a moan, I took a longer drink, not caring about it burning my tongue.

"Here are some clothes for you."

She put some items on the bed and stepped back. My brow furrowed as I stared at the simple pair of jeans and a black t-shirt, neither of which belonged to me. Glancing down at myself, I realized I was still wearing my blood-splattered leggings and jersey. The memory of Reynaeros' furious expression brought a smile to my face.

Not caring about the company, I stripped and began pulling on the new clothes. I was dying to take a shower, but I didn't want to linger any longer than was necessary. He struck me as the type of person that would demand recompense for his kindness and I had no interest in being indebted to him.

"Well, I appreciate it. Can you point me in the direction of the exit?"

Her eyes widened slightly. "That door leads into the hall. I can give you a tour-"

"I don't need a tour. I don't know what time it is, but I have a shift at noon. Unfortunately, I don't have this type of expendable income, so I can't miss it."

"Are you confused? You did hit your head quite hard."

"Portia," I said a little too firmly. "You're sweet and all, but I don't think I'm being unclear. If you can't show me where to go, I'll just go wandering around by myself and I'm pretty sure your boss wouldn't want me sticking my nose in his secretive exploits."

She chewed on her lip, looking more distressed than made sense. Either she was missing something or I was. Something was curdling in my stomach the longer she stood there.

"Alright. I'm off to find my own way. Wish me luck."

After searching the room for a few minutes, I determined that my phone wasn't here. That pissed me off, especially since I didn't have the cash to get a new one, but there were more important things right now. If I had to walk all the way back to the apartment, that's what I would do.

As I stepped into the hall, I was struck with another wave of panic. I hadn't seen Eli after the fight, nor had I been given any information about him. Reynaeros was supposed to release him, but I wasn't exactly inclined to trust his word. I needed to make sure that he'd gotten home and was safe.

The hallway was unnecessarily long with doors on each side. They all looked the same, except for the numbers on them. It was like some weird hotel. I wondered if this was where he kept his prisoners. If so, it was nicer than where he'd thrown Eli.

When I reached the end, I huffed and turned around. I threw open one of the doors, only to find a room similar to the one I'd woken up in. It was slightly smaller with less fancy furniture, but it was still nice.

A woman came out of the bathroom with wide eyes, clutching the towel she had wrapped around herself.

"Shit. I'm sorry."

I shut the door quickly and rushed back the way I'd come. Curious, I opened another random door and found someone sitting on the bed. She gasped and scrambled backward, then relaxed slightly when she saw me.

"Who are you?"

"I, uh, I'm looking for the exit."

Her brow furrowed. "Exit?"

"Yeah. I'm trying to go home."

"I don't understand."

Swallowing hard, I backed up. This wasn't right. Why were there so many rooms here? Did every one of these doors lead to a bedroom with a mysterious, frightened woman?

I reached the door I'd come from and veered left down a similar hallway. There was a set of double doors and my heart leapt. When I pushed through, I found what looked like a cafeteria with circular tables. There was a bar style table set with various trays of food and a few women looked up curiously at my entrance.

"What the fuck?" I muttered.

Spinning around, I tried to fight the stinging in my eyes. Another door led to a room with some couches and a television. It was like a prison in here. A sanitorium was also a fitting depiction.

Thrusting my hands through my hair, I did a circle in the hallway, staring at each of the doors. There had to be an exit around here. He'd brought me into this place, so I was willing to bet there was some secret door I hadn't noticed, like the one that led to Eli's hallway before.

I frantically opened every door, barely peering inside before moving to the next. Almost every one of them was occupied by women in various stages of fright. Some appeared more curious than afraid, while others looked like they were moments away from having a heart attack.

Portia found me as I threw open another door, making the person inside scream. She grabbed my arm, pulling me back into the hallway. I shoved her away, making her hit the wall. Right now, I couldn't even worry that she was hurt. As far as I was concerned, she was a guilty part of this little horror show.

"Fuck," I shouted. Running my hands over the walls, I felt for something- anything- that would betray some sort of hidden door.

"Kiera."

No. Absolutely not. I ignored the voice, continuing to rub, tap, and pound on the walls.

Fingers locked around my bicep. I spun around with an angry scream and immediately punched him in the face. Terror erupted in my chest at the contact, but I couldn't focus on it too much. There were worse things than him killing me for my assault.

He narrowed his eyes, then tightened his grip and dragged me down the hall. I fought against him, thrashing and striking at him. When we reached my room, he thrust me onto the bed, my teeth clashing with the force. The door slammed shut, seemingly on its own, and my eyes began to burn again.

"Calm down."

"Let me out of here."

"That's not how this works."

Jumping to my feet, I advanced on him. He didn't attempt to stop me as I slammed my hands into his chest. He might as well have been a brick wall for how much it affected him. Still, I continued, drawing the smallest amount of comfort from it.

"If you hit me one more time, you will regret it."

Setting my jaw, I threw myself at him again. Even though he didn't move, I was pushed back until I was lying on the bed. He appeared above me, planting a knee on the mattress.

"Let me go," I repeated, barely containing my terrified whimper.

"No."

"This wasn't our deal."

"Oh, but it was."

He grabbed my wrist and held it in front of me. There was a shock where he touched me, then a shape began to appear on my skin. It was like a scar, raised and slightly paler than the rest.

"What is that?"

"It is our contract, Kiera. You willingly participated in my fight and now you belong to me."

"No," I whispered.

A dangerous smile curled his lips. He straightened, adjusting his shirt as he stepped back.

"Get comfortable, my little rose. You might just be my new favorite."

With that, he retreated into the hallway, the door clicking shut behind him. I looked at the mark on my wrist, running my fingers over it. I had no idea when or how he'd put it there and it didn't look new. There was no inflammation or any sign that it had been put there at all.

I'd never really wanted a tattoo and whatever this weird scarification thing was didn't appeal to me either. If I was going to be branded, though, at least it was something as pretty as a rose.

Chapter 6

Kiera

Damsel in distress was something I never wanted to be. Even though I'd cried until the sun was low in the sky, I told myself it was warranted and didn't make me weak. After what had happened since I got here, I deserved a few moments to lose my absolute shit.

Now, I was just pissed. It was laughable that he thought he could get away with this. Someone would report me missing and the police would see the report I made about Eli. At that point, they'd put it together. They would have to look into this place again and, hopefully, do a better job of it.

If Reynaeros did follow through on his end and released Eli, he would fight for me. My best friend was as stubborn as a mule and he had no qualms about turning the situation into a massive problem. He'd whip out his phone and go live, relentlessly calling the police department out for their inadequacy.

It was more likely that he hadn't been released, though. In that case, Vivian would make a report. Two employees

Entangled Realms

disappearing shortly after the other was suspicious, especially since we lived together.

Either way, this whole thing would get sorted out. Reynaeros wasn't a god, no matter how much money and reach he had. This place existed somewhere and it was impossible to completely hide it.

There was a soft knock at the door, then Portia popped her head in. She looked wary as she carried a mug and plate of food over to me. After setting it down on the nightstand, she stared at me.

"It's not so bad," she said.

I let out a dry laugh. "I'm a prisoner. How is that anything but bad?"

"You get three meals a day and even dessert. Your room is nice and the waterfall shower is wonderful. There are worse ways to be a captive."

"Are you stuck here too?"

"In a way, perhaps. I choose to work for him, though."

"In my book, that makes you just as bad as he is."

"You see so little in your short life. At a certain point, you learn that all things are relative."

"You're, what, twenty-five?"

She smiled, lifting the mug and passing it to me. It smelled like tea, which only made me want a nice book to curl up with. There was a window bench in my room and it made the atmosphere feel perfect if I was ever able to forget that I'd been kidnapped.

From what I could see out the window, we were in the same area as the fighting ring. There was a view of the water and I thought we might only be a few buildings down. Maybe there was some passageway that led here. It would help to explain how the police hadn't found anything when they checked it out. Soon enough, someone would come looking. I just had to make it until then.

"If I may offer some advice, Kiera."

Looking at Portia, I took a long drink of the tea and raised my brows. "Sure. It can't hurt."

She nodded toward the tea. "Drink all of that. It's much easier that way."

Narrowing my eyes, I looked at the drink, then back to her. I set the mug down and settled back against the headboard, crossing my ankles.

"I have no idea what that means."

"Just trust me. It's always hardest the first time."

"Well, I don't trust you, so maybe you should just leave."

She hesitated before inclining her head and backing out of the room. Alone, it felt eerily quiet in this place. I had never thought about how much I would miss music or the sound of traffic. Whatever military grade glass they had here, it blocked out every single sound. Even as I watched the water flow and boats pass, I couldn't hear a single thing.

Grabbing the mug, I brought it into the bathroom and dumped the rest of it. Portia's words unnerved me, but I didn't think it was a good idea to listen to her alleged advice. She was willingly a part of this thing, which meant I couldn't trust her, even if she did sound genuine.

Whatever was coming, I was going to face it head-on. If Reynaeros didn't like that, he could get fucked.

My eyes felt heavy, so I laid down and pulled the covers up to my chin. Within moments, I felt myself drifting off, my body feeling like it was floating on a cloud.

🌷 🌷 🌷 🌷

Everything felt off when I started returning to consciousness. For one, it was hard to determine if I was even awake. This could have easily been a dream, considering how groggy I was.

Opening my eyes, I found mostly darkness. There was just enough moonlight for me to see the shapes in the room. When I noticed someone standing by the window, I sucked in a sharp breath. He turned, cocking his head.

"Hm. I assume you didn't drink all of your tea, then."

I opened my mouth, but couldn't form words. If I was breaking the whole thing down correctly, that bitch had drugged me. I would have been glad that I poured the rest down the drain, except that it had done enough to keep me conscious while remaining mostly immobile.

With great effort, I lifted my head to see him better. I could hear my own breaths cutting through the silence and they came faster when he approached. There was the slightest smirk on his face as he stood over me.

"Do you remember what I said about bravery and stupidity, little rose? You're really beginning to resemble the latter."

"Fuck you," I gritted out. The words scraped like glass in my throat.

"It doesn't matter to me. Portia just hates to hear the screaming and I have to admit, it's much easier to get through when your mind is muddled."

He pulled his t-shirt over his head, the paleness of his skin standing out in the darkness. His body was lean and muscular, matching the ethereal beauty of the rest of him. Right now, it was only making me nauseous.

"What... are you..."

"Shh. Your voice isn't pleasing to me."

When he unzipped his pants, I whimpered. As he began to pull them down, I turned away the best I could, choosing to stare at the ceiling instead. The decision I'd previously thought was so strong now weighed on me heavily, taking away the last of my hope. Even if I got out of this place, it was clear I would be taking a piece of it with me. A piece that I'd never be able to rid myself of.

My view was obscured when he climbed onto the bed, planting his knees between my legs and forcing them open. I realized that I wasn't wearing any clothes, which must've happened at some point while I was sleeping. One of his hands gripped my thigh hard, his touch making that uncomfortable electricity crawl over my skin.

Unable to just do nothing, I lifted my arm, weakly pushing at his chest. He grabbed my wrist, forcing it down to the mattress. When he lowered himself further, I felt something brush against my entrance. Tears began to spill onto my cheeks, a desperation rising in my chest. There was no way for me to fight him. I was powerless, completely at his mercy.

"Do me a favor and try not to squirm too much."

"Please," I whispered.

He cocked his head. "The begging has never done much for me before, but I wouldn't mind hearing you do more of it."

I watched as he reached down to stroke his dick. With the dim light, I couldn't see too much of it, but I could tell it was big. I'd only been with one person and it was a couple of years ago. It might not have helped, even if I had more experience with it, but maybe I could have been a little bit more prepared.

As soon as he touched my entrance with it, I knew it was going to hurt. He must've used lube because it was wet, but even that didn't do much against the sting as he breached me. Dropping my head back, I let out a little cry and fisted the sheets.

Once the head was inside, he thrust the rest of the way in. I gritted my teeth, all of my muscles tensing with the invasion. It burned and ached at the same time. He was so large, I felt him sitting deeper than I'd ever gone.

Bracing one hand beside my head, he let out a breath. "That was the easy part."

That was foreboding as fuck. I looked at him, even though it made me feel worse. He didn't return my stare. Instead, he closed his eyes and pursed his lips.

"What-"

My words halted abruptly as pain erupted inside me. It was excruciating, unimaginable. The drug still had my body too immobile for me to try fighting him off. All I could do was flail the slightest bit, but he grabbed both my wrists and held them above my head, hovering over me as he drew in slow breaths.

"Stop," I screamed when the sharp pain reached deeper.

It felt like I was being stabbed from the inside. Whatever it was must've been ripping me apart. The sounds coming from me were far away as my head swam.

After what felt like an eternity, he began to move inside of me again. It amplified the pain to a point that I didn't know if I would make it through. I prayed to an unknown deity, begging for it to be over or at least for me to lose consciousness.

"What are you doing to me?" I wailed.

Releasing my wrists, he sat up straighter, thrusting deeper. I was shaking so violently, he had to hold onto my thighs while he fucked me.

"You're not the only one with thorns, little rose."

His eyes closed again just before his mouth dropped open. Burying himself deep, he stopped his movements, a shudder traveling across his body. His cum was abnormally warm and there must have been a lot because I could already feel it beginning to seep out of me.

The things impaling me retracted, then he pulled out. The warmth inside me spread, igniting a burn everywhere it touched.

As he dressed, my insides began to numb. The relief was so great, I wept harder. I wanted to roll over onto my side, but my body was still too heavy.

"It'll get easier," he said casually. "Until next time, Kiera."

A million colorful insults came to mind, but I held them back, simply watching him leave. I didn't want him to linger any longer than he already had and the idea of there being a next time made me wish I could leap out of that window.

Madilyn DeRose

Chapter 7

Kiera

The sun was up and I was still crying, although it was more of a pathetic whimper at this point. There weren't any tears left. My cheeks were stiff and itchy from the ones that had dried there. I hadn't stopped trembling since he left and I wondered if I ever would.

When the door creaked open, my stomach lurched. I'd regained enough control to retreat to the other side of the bed, even though I knew it wouldn't help. If I tried to fight him, recovered or not, I would lose every time. He was not only strong; there was something that wasn't right about him. Something inhuman.

Portia entered the room with what I assumed was breakfast. Putting anything in my stomach was a recipe for disaster, so I just shook my head. Her eyes softened as she sat on the edge of the bed.

"I told you to drink the tea, Kiera."

"You knew and you just let it happen. Is that what everyone here has to endure?"

"Just the first time. His seed will heal the wounds, leaving just the imprint for him to use next time."

"I don't know what any of that means," I cried.

"It is how the bodies become compatible. The barbs keep you connected during the act. Now that he's made the marks, they will remain, so that he does not have to pierce you again."

"This is so fucked up."

"To you, perhaps it seems that way. You will acclimate, just like the rest do."

"I don't want to acclimate. I want to go home."

She nodded toward the rose on my wrist. "You entered into a binding agreement."

"Well, I wasn't presented with the terms and conditions."

"It is not required. All that must happen is for you to agree to participate."

"Did he... Can you tell me if he released my friend?"

"Of course. It binds him as much as it does you."

"Is that part of it too? Someone has to trade themselves."

"No. He simply enjoys the game. Determining what it takes for someone to risk themselves. Sometimes it's money. Other times it's honor or simply the thrill of the fight."

"Why?"

"It's not my place to say, Kiera. If I offer you another piece of advice, will you listen this time?"

I shrugged, avoiding her gaze. If she wanted to give me tea when he came to my room, I'd drink it in its entirety every time. Anything to drown out what he was doing to me. In fact, I'd prefer to remain asleep until I was granted the reprieve of death.

"Don't make it hard. He will fuck you and you will fight for him, but at all other times, you are free to do as you please in this place."

"That's hardly encouraging."

"The more you fight him, the worse it will be for you. It is not wise to anger him."

When I didn't say anything, she sighed.

"Make friends, Kiera. Enjoy the food, learn new skills. Nearly everywhere you can go is open to you."

"Nearly?"

She stood and brushed her hands down her pants. "Take a bath. It will help."

With that, she left me alone again. I hated how eerily silent it was. The quiet had always been comforting to me, but I didn't realize it was never truly silent. Here, I was starting to understand how it could be deafening, overwhelming.

With a groan, I stood and headed for the bathroom. I was sore and it burned when I peed. The inflammation made getting into the hot water uncomfortable until I adjusted to it. Once I was situated, though, I decided I wanted to spend the rest of my life in that tub. Drowning myself in it was also sounding like a viable option, but I knew my survival instinct would kick in and make me come up for air.

Portia assured me that Reynaeros- fuck that name, I was going to start calling him Reyn and hope it pissed him off- had held up his end of the bargain. Even so, I couldn't bring myself to believe them. It didn't seem like too much to ask him to provide proof. That would require me to speak to him, though.

At some point, I was going to have to decide how I was going to proceed with my situation. I could simply acquiesce like everyone else seemed to. It was arguably the only option, but it felt cowardly. Even if it made things worse for me, I wanted to be the biggest problem he'd ever dealt with. Maybe he'd release me because of it or maybe he'd kill me. I could live with both options.

After my bath, I stepped into the walk-in closet and came to an abrupt stop. All of my clothes were in here; everything that I owned. This motherfucker really went to my apartment and gathered up my stuff. I didn't know why that pissed me off, but it did. They didn't belong in this hell hole.

Wearing some soft shorts and a t-shirt, I ventured into the hallway. There was nobody around, so I headed into the cafeteria to see if there was anything decent to eat that wouldn't make me sick. Crackers, maybe.

As I loaded up a plate with some mild fruits, I glanced around the space. There were a couple other people in here, most of them sitting alone. I didn't want to make any friends, but they could be useful in other ways, so I sat across from a woman with copper hair and pasted on a smile.

"I'm Kiera."

She looked up, pulling her lip between her teeth. I raised my brows as I waited for her to respond.

"This is Collette," someone else announced before dropping into the seat beside her. She draped an arm over the other girl's shoulders and grinned at me.

"Lucy," Collette hissed.

"Calm down. She's new and probably freaking out."

"I am," I agreed. "Maybe you can fill me in on everything this nightmare entails."

"Well, Kiera, I'm Lucia, but you can call me Lucy. Collie here is timid and afraid to anger the beast, as if he gives a shit what we do when he's not around."

"I don't want to piss him off," Collie muttered. "Amanda did that and now she's gone."

"Did he kill her?" I asked.

Lucy laughed, but it sounded forced. "Don't be ridiculous. He's not that bad."

"Considering what he did last night, I'm inclined to disagree with you."

"Damn. I remember that first time. Did you drink all the tea?"

"No."

"God. You poor thing. It won't be as bad next time."

"Why does there have to be a next time?"

She shrugged. "That's just how it is."

I eyed her for a moment, taking in her shimmering golden hair and lithe frame. She looked like she would have been the popular girl in high school. Maybe a cheerleader. She was bubbly, but she struck me as genuine, so I decided to put a little bit of trust in her.

"You seem completely okay with the whole thing," I noted.

"I'm not, but at a certain point you have to accept it. After that, it doesn't feel quite as bad."

"And what about you, Collie?"

Collie ducked her head, turning a piece of celery over in her fingers. "She's right, but she somehow deals with it a lot better than anyone else. If you ask me, the nights he chooses you don't get any better, even if the pain stops."

The despondency in her voice made my chest ache. They both had accepted it, but in completely separate ways. They couldn't be more different, yet they seemed very close. Maybe that was what really held them together.

I didn't want to become like either of them. Even though they had figured out a way to deal with it, they'd given up. There was no more fight in them and to me, that was the worst way to live. Collie chose apathy and Lucy lived in a state of delusion. It wouldn't be me.

"What is he?" I asked as casually as I could before popping a piece of cantaloupe into my mouth.

"Nobody knows," Lucy replied. "Not human, that's for sure."

"What can he... do?"

"Uh, it's hard to explain. I've seen things move around him when he wasn't touching them."

"He uses plants, I think," Collie chimed in so softly I almost didn't catch it.

"So, he's some sort of witch," I mused. "At least, he can use magic."

Lucy hummed thoughtfully. "Maybe. It doesn't really matter."

"How do you figure?"

"Well, no matter what he is or what he can do, he's stronger than all of us combined. If you're trying to figure out how to escape, just shelve that idea right now."

"I'm not-"

"You are and it's normal, but the longer you fight against it, the harder it'll be for you. Listen to those that have been here a while and if Portia offers you any advice, always take it. I think you learned that the hard way."

Gritting my teeth, I nodded. The two of them started talking about something that seemed inconsequential considering what was going on. Maybe they'd developed Stockholm Syndrome. It would make sense.

"How long have you been here?"

"A few years," Lucy answered. "Collie got here just after I did. We went through the worst of it together and that's how we became best friends."

"I see. Is there anything interesting to do in this place?"

"There's the game room. Puzzles. Art supplies if you like that sort of thing."

"I'm not creative in that way. I prefer books."

"Lee has a library, but he doesn't let anyone go in there, so you might be out of luck."

"He lets you call him that?" I asked with a laugh.

"No, but if you don't say it to his face, what's the harm?"

"Chester can sneak a book to you," Collie chimed in.

Lucy giggled. "Maybe just for you, Collie."

Her cheeks pinked. "Shut up."

"Well, I think I'll go explore. Maybe I'll find some secret passageway to worlds unknown."

"Don't take the red door."

Pausing, I met Collie's gaze. "What red door?"

"Just... If you do find it, don't go inside. One of the others did and Lee lost it."

"I've never seen him that angry," Lucy agreed.

"Thanks for the advice."

As I left the cafeteria, I pondered what she'd said. Red door. If I found it- no, when I found it- I would absolutely be uncovering its secrets. If it was enough to make Reyn lose his shit, it must have been serious. Maybe it would help me figure out his weakness. He had to have one, inhuman or not.

My two pieces of advice today were not to piss him off and not to go inside the red door. Bet.

Chapter 8

Reynaeros

As I sat above the fighting ring, I could hardly pay attention to the spectacle below. It wasn't uncommon for me to retreat inside my head during these, but today I was even more distant. I felt tired, which was a rare occurrence for me. My body didn't suffer that sort of weakness unless something was wrong. Perhaps it was a malady of the mind that had invaded my sleep.

Something felt different than it had just a few days ago, but I couldn't place my finger on it. Reaching out with my mind, I ensured that my domain remained intact. There wasn't a single thing wrong with it and everybody seemed to be faring as they usually were.

One signature was new, which felt odd, as it usually did when I added someone to the building. It didn't help that she was fucking loud. Negative energy was rolling off of her at an alarming rate. If it continued, I'd have to find a way to subdue it before she started affecting the others.

If it was anyone else, I might have just rid myself of her early on. This one was special, though. In her first fight, she came out the victor in record time. She'd brought a knife with her, but I did tell her there were no rules.

She was lucky I saw potential in her because as soon as I saw that damned jersey, my fingers had twitched with the desire to rip it off of her. It was petty and an annoying attempt at a power move. From the smile on her face, I knew she'd noticed my reaction, so I guess she won that round, but it wouldn't happen again.

Now that she was here, she couldn't pull any more stunts like that. When I wanted her to fight, she would fight. When I wanted to fuck her, I would fuck her. If she got out of line, perhaps I would fuck her again until she learned exactly what her purpose here was.

"Reynaeros," Chester said from my left side.

I turned to him, noting the pinched look on his face. "Has something happened?"

"Not necessarily."

"Then why do you look like you haven't shit in a month?"

"It's just that Portia is a bit worried about your new competitor."

I raised a brow. "Kiera is stubborn and unruly, but there's not much she can do in her wing. What is your sister concerned about exactly?"

"She's wandering the halls relentlessly, opening everyone's doors and tapping on the walls."

"She is trying to find a way out. Eventually, she will give up."

"In the cafeteria, she met Lucia and Collette."

My lip curled. Those were the last two people that needed to befriend Kiera.

"What happened?"

"One of them mentioned the red door, sir."

My fingers tightened on the armrest. After a deep breath, I released the tension. Pieces of wood fell to the floor, leaving the remaining part jagged.

"Those bitches and their big mouths. It's no matter. She won't find any way out of her wing unless someone that knows the way shows it to her. I trust that none of you will do that."

"Of course. I just thought you should know what's going on."

"Thank you, Chester. Have Portia continue to keep an eye on her. Perhaps you could pay Kiera a visit as well. She seemed to take kindly to you."

"If you think it'll help."

"It might be wise to grant her access to the gold room."

His eyes widened slightly. "Do you think so?"

"I'll determine it after her next fight."

He turned and headed back toward the doors. I dropped my gaze, watching the two women wrestling on the ground. Tori was one of my more experienced fighters and it was already clear that she would overpower Maria. I lost the most competitors in their first fight, which at least saved me the trouble of trying to decide if they were worth my time.

Soon, I would have to put Kiera back in the ring to see what else she could do. If my instincts were correct, she might actually make it to the top.

Before I could get my hopes up, I reminded myself that it might not mean anything. Being able to win against her own was important, but it was highly unlikely she'd have any significant effect in the end. I would just have to test her.

🌹 🌹 🌹 🌹

As I slipped through the door, I glanced around the room. Judging by the lump in the bed, I assumed she was asleep. That meant I got to see the initial terror in her eyes when she woke and realized what was happening.

Stripping out of my clothes, I rounded the bed and knelt on the empty side. Reaching under the blankets, I hooked my fingers in the waistband of her shorts and pulled them down. Her body jerked, then she blinked rapidly.

"No," she cried, trying to move away from me.

"I heard you were causing problems today."

"That's not true."

Tutting at her, I moved between her legs, pushing them open. She didn't fight me like some of the others. She knew it would only make things worse.

"Your tongue is loose, Collette. For all your worrying, you don't know how to stop yourself from doing things that will earn my ire."

"I'm sorry."

As I stroked my dick, my barbs began to push through the surface. I spread the wetness they excreted, moaning a little at the sensation. When I lined myself up, she let out a long breath in preparation.

Gripping the tops of her thighs, I thrust all the way inside in one motion. A whimper left her lips as my barbs locked into the notches I'd created.

Pulling out to the tip, I felt them stretching to accommodate the distance. They wouldn't disconnect until I retracted them; a way to ensure my kind procreated. Since human bodies weren't compatible with my seed, it was simply a guarantee that they could not escape me until I was finished.

The first time, I'd been alarmed and concerned. Our females were more malleable. When we had sex for the first time, we created the holds for our barbs, but it didn't pain them quite as much as the humans. They also didn't bleed as profusely.

I thought my dick would be the death of the first one, but just like with our females, my seed mended the wounds without allowing them to close. They just had to endure it the first time. If Kiera had simply listened to Portia, she wouldn't have suffered as greatly, but it seemed she was determined to be a thorn in my side.

It didn't matter. After I'd fucked her a few more times and made her fight, she would be as easy as the rest of them. There was nothing better to do in this god forsaken place besides keep them as pets for my entertainment and my pleasure.

Why should I care if they enjoyed it? Many of their own kind treated them far worse, yet here I was giving them luxurious bedrooms, food, and anything else they might want, save for freedom. I didn't have that luxury, so neither would they.

Gripping Collette more tightly, I sped up. I would've paid Lucia a visit as well, but I couldn't stand dealing with her. I hadn't even fucked her in close to a year, simply because I hated to hear her voice. She was fucking annoying.

When I finished, I quickly stepped back into my clothes and headed for the door, stopping at the threshold.

"Do not cause more problems, Collette. I don't want that one's curiosity fed by anyone."

"They're always curious when they first arrive. What's different about this one?"

"Nothing," I said immediately.

I ground my teeth together for a moment before closing the door behind me. In the dark, it was peaceful and quiet. I found myself standing there for a long moment, just staring down the hallway. When I realized I was looking directly at Kiera's door, I turned and marched the other way.

"Nothing," I repeated.

Chapter 9

Kiera

Collie must have been smoking something. I'd touched every inch of wall that I could reach in the past two days and hadn't found anything resembling a secret door. There was no hollow space to indicate anything out of the ordinary, there wasn't a little button to make the wall swing inward. There was *nothing*.

It begged the question of how anyone got in and out of this corridor. Did they turn into bats and fly? Oh god, if they were vampires, I was going to be so pissed.

With a frustrated scream, I threw my plate. It collided with my closed door, shattering into a hundred tiny pieces. As I stared at the mess on the floor, I realized the tantrum might have actually worked in my favor. Before anyone could come to investigate, I grabbed the two biggest pieces and shoved them under my mattress.

As if on cue, there was a knock on the door. I ignored it and a moment later it opened. I was expecting Portia, but a different blonde head peered inside, his eyes widening when he saw the shattered plate.

"Well, I was going to ask how things are going, but it seems I've already got my answer."

"What do you want, Chester?"

"Like I said, I wanted to see how you're doing."

I gestured around the room dramatically. "It's like a vacation in Buckingham Palace. Gold star. Couldn't ask for anything more, except maybe freedom. I'd also take a bullet to the brain."

He frowned as he closed the door. "You're quite negative."

"Wouldn't you be negative if you were forced to stay in a place you didn't belong?"

The corner of his lip lifted slightly. "Well, I can understand where you're coming from."

"Right. I don't need you to come lecture me about the proper way to be a prisoner, so you can just go tell your master that I'm fine."

"He doesn't particularly care how you are, but I do, so let's talk."

"No."

He rolled his eyes, the gesture making him appear young. He couldn't have been older than twenty-five, if that. Now that I was looking at him, I realized he bore very familiar features.

"Are you and Portia related?"

"We're twins," he said with a grin that betrayed his fondness for her.

"So, she's the one that sent you."

"You keep assuming that I'm here on anyone's whim but my own."

"All of you speak like you're from the seventeen hundreds. Are you vampires?"

"Vampires," he repeated with a laugh. "No, we are not vampires, but we have existed for that long."

My eyes widened. "Wait, are you serious?"

"Deadly."

"What are you?"

"It doesn't matter."

"I think it does."

"Mm. Perhaps one of us will tell you someday. Right now, I'm here to inquire about your habit of banging on walls."

Setting my jaw, I turned away from him. I knew he'd been sent here for some reason. Everyone here seemed to have ulterior motives or they just acted shady. Even Collie would barely look at me since that first day and it made me feel alone, even though I hadn't wanted to make friends from the start.

"Do you have a favorite food, Kiera?"

"Everyone has a favorite food," I replied, keeping my gaze fixed on the wall.

"Your comfort food. What is it?"

My jaw was beginning to hurt from how hard I was grinding my teeth, so I forced myself to stop. With a heavy sigh, I clasped my hands together.

"A giant blueberry muffin from the café on the corner of fifth. I could put back a dozen of them on a particularly bad day."

The bed dipped and I turned to look at him. He was sitting on the edge and in his hand was a brown box. I grabbed it, setting it down and flinging the lid open.

"What the hell?"

Inside, there were six of the exact muffins I'd been talking about. They smelled incredible and my mouth began to water.

"Are they real?"

"Of course they're real."

Taking one out, I put my nose up to it and inhaled deeply before breaking a piece off. My moan was embarrassing, but god damn, these things were good. The food in this place was arguably fantastic, but it had nothing on one of these bad boys.

"How?" I asked around a mouthful.

"What you might call magic, I suppose."

"What else can you do?"

He hummed thoughtfully. After a moment, he smiled and put his hand behind his back. When he brought it around again, he was holding a long-stemmed rose. He laid it gently on the bed, brushing a finger over one of the thorns.

"So you guys can conjure things."

"We all do different things. I didn't create the muffins, only moved them from one place to another. It's nothing special."

"I beg to differ. This is incredible."

"That's kind."

From the look on his face, it didn't seem like he agreed. I wanted to pry, but I was struck by the reminder that he was the enemy. Or, at least, he was in the enemy's counsel. The same went for his sister, no matter how sweet they both appeared.

"Why are you really here?"

He met my gaze, the blue of his eyes shifting in that same liquid way that Reyn's did.

"I was being honest before, but I also came to tell you that you will fight tonight."

The swirling in my stomach made me suddenly regret eating that entire muffin. Pushing the box away, I folded my legs underneath me.

"I don't want to."

"It's of no consequence. I know that your adjustment has been difficult-"

"It's not an adjustment. It's literal kidnapping."

"Kiera-"

"I'd like you to leave."

He gave me an exasperated look. "I'm trying to be helpful."

"No, you're trying to keep me from being a problem. I'm not an idiot. You and your sister don't have me fooled."

"There's no need to question the nobility of our actions. If you are upset with Reynaeros, then so be it. My sister and I have not earned your ire."

I snorted. "Being complacent does not make you innocent, Chester."

His brow furrowed. After staring at me for a moment, he shook his head and stood.

"Portia will collect you when it is time."

He waved his hand and a folded outfit appeared on the bed. A moment later, he was gone. Picking up the items, I recognized the same clothes the fighters had worn before. There was a white mask along with it and some basic black sneakers.

Round two, I guess. It wasn't like I had a choice in the matter.

🌹 🌹 🌹 🌹

As I stood in the ring waiting for my opponent, I scanned the crowd. With the bright light in here and the dimness out there, it was impossible to determine if I recognized anyone. The only person I could imagine showing up here was Eli, but I hoped he chose to stay away. I didn't trust that Reyn wouldn't capture him again and this time, there was nobody to save him.

I tried not to be bitter about the fact that Eli hadn't found a way to rescue me. Maybe he'd tried. It wasn't like I'd know, considering I was locked away in a metaphorical tower to be used as some magic-wielding monster's sex slave.

Now that I knew they had unknown powers, I had very little confidence in the police being able to do anything. He probably had some sort of spell that kept them from seeing anything suspicious. At this point, I had to come to terms with the very depressing idea that I was well and truly stuck here.

The black door opened and a woman was shoved through it. With the mask, it was impossible to determine if I knew her or not. Either way, she was my competition while we were in this cage, which meant it was kill or be killed, so to speak. Reyn didn't say it had to be to the death, so maybe I could find a way to knock her out.

Entangled Realms

When the light turned green, neither of us moved. Her shoulders were shaking and her eyes were glistening. It just made it harder for me to consider making the first move. I slowly walked up to her, making her tense, then I held up a hand.

"Hey, relax. I don't want to kill you."

"Y-you don't?"

"No, but we have to fight, so maybe we can work together."

"I don't understand."

"We can tussle a little, put on a good show, then I'll knock you out."

She whimpered. "I don't want to do any of this."

"Do you think I want this?"

Raising my gaze, I looked at Reyn. He was leaning back casually in his seat, but was looking directly at me. As he watched me, he tilted his head and cupped his jaw.

"What's your name?" I whispered.

"Olga."

"I'm Kiera. You can trust me, okay?"

After a long moment, she nodded. Without wasting any more time, I grabbed her biceps and forced her to the ground. She made a startled sound and tried to fight me off, landing a solid kick to my chest. I swore and stumbled backward, struggling to regain my footing.

"Oh my god. I'm sorry."

I shook my head. "This is good. Now, let's just do a little more of that, then I'll knock you out."

"Will it hurt?"

"I mean, probably. Just don't think about it."

She threw a weak punch at my stomach. While she focused on aiming another, I kicked out at her knee, making her drop to the ground. I straddled her and the crowd began to roar. Grabbing her by either side of the head, I gritted my teeth and slammed her against the concrete.

Her eyes didn't open, so I decided it was good enough. There wasn't blood pooling or anything, which hopefully meant I hadn't fucked up and killed her. If she was lucky, she wouldn't have too bad of a concussion.

Leaving her on the ground, I headed straight for the black door. It opened, letting me into the corridor.

Round two was finished and I just had to hope I had some time before the next one, otherwise my mental state would go down the drain very quickly.

Chapter 10

Kiera

Putting a hand to my chest, I rubbed the spot where Olga had kicked me. That would undoubtedly leave an ugly and painful bruise.

"Clever," a deep voice reverberated down the hallway.

Dropping my head back, I groaned. "Is it not enough that I had to see your ugly face up on your throne? Now I have to tolerate you after my fight when all I want to do is go to bed."

"Fight? That's hardly what I would call it."

"Well, there are no rules, your majesty." I bowed dramatically before walking past him.

He grabbed my wrist, igniting that little shock. I yanked it away, ripping my mask off so he could see the glare I sent his way.

"Your insolence is enough to drive a man mad."

"Tell me if you see one, Reyn."

"Excuse me?"

"I said tell me if you see one."

"What the fuck did you call me, Kiera?"

I smiled at him. "Don't you like it? It's what we humans call a nickname."

"You've chosen to call me by something that falls from the clouds?"

"Sure. It's better than that nightmare of a name."

"Do you take issue with the name Reynaeros?" he asked with barely concealed rage.

"Oh, is that how you say it? I thought it sounded more like rhinoceros."

Pinching the bridge of his nose, he closed his eyes tightly. "You may call me Reynaeros or Leander. Perhaps 'my lord' would suffice. Those are your options."

Crossing my arms, I hummed thoughtfully. "I hear you, Reyn. I do. However, I'm going to opt for door number four, which leads to my bed. Peace."

Before I got far, he latched onto my arm again. I fought against him as he pulled me down the hall. He didn't give me much choice unless I wanted to literally be dragged across the floor, so eventually I trodded along after him.

"You seem to think there are loopholes, Kiera. I assure you, there are not."

I followed him up a flight of stairs that led to a hallway that looked identical to all the others. We came to a set of gold double doors and stopped.

"This room will be accessible to you from this point on."

"And what, pray tell, is in this room, Reyn?"

His teeth ground together aggressively for a moment. "It is where you may train."

"For what?"

"For your fights, clearly."

"Why am I just now hearing about this place?"

"You are the only one that will be allowed to come here."

My brow furrowed. "I don't understand."

"You don't need to. All you must do is come here every day. I'd prefer you to spend the majority of your time here, in fact."

"I don't even know how to get out of my own hallway. The door Portia brought me through today wasn't there before."

"It is there. You were just unaware of it. Now that you know it's there, you may use it and come to this hallway."

Nothing in this place made a lick of sense. For one, there were magic doors that existed, but you didn't know existed unless you were aware of them. That was a whole clusterfuck of senseless information. Two, I was supposed to be training to fight every day, but I was the only one, even though everybody held here had to fight.

What the hell was going on?

"I need a stiff drink," I sighed.

"Pity."

He pushed open the doors and stepped inside. I took in the large space, from the floor that felt both firm and foamy, to the dark walls and beams high up in the ceiling. There was a rope hanging from one of them, offering a way to get up there, not that I was anywhere near strong enough to manage it.

Along the walls were various weapons. On the other side, there was a giant rock wall that looked far more intimidating than any I'd seen before. If I didn't know better, I'd say it was a real cliff face.

To my right, there was a glass door, through which I could see a pool. Weight benches were set up throughout and there were even a couple of treadmills. It was all sorts of ridiculous.

When I was done surveying the outer edges of the room, I focused on the center. Olga was sitting there with a man and a woman beside her, looking like they were standing guard. She was trembling as she watched us approach.

"What's going on?" she cried.

"We're finishing the round," Reyn announced.

"But we did finish it," I pointed out. "I won."

"Sure, but it was subterfuge and you know it."

"There are no rules. You said so yourself."

"True, but I found it a bit boring, so I've decided to extend the round. An encore, if you will."

"I'm not going to fight her again."

"Good thing I didn't expect you to."

He grabbed Olga by the hair and thrust her onto her back. She cried out, trying to dislodge his hand, but he held firm.

"Stop!" I shouted.

"Here is how things work, little rose. You fight for me, you get fucked by me, and you don't continually try to undermine me. You will not gain the upper hand and it's simply an annoyance when you try."

"Fine. Whatever. Lesson learned, now let her go."

"If you do not kill your opponent, they return to their room and await their next fight. They get thrown into the running. So, since you chose not to kill this one, she becomes the newest addition."

Bile rose in my throat when he unzipped his pants. Olga screamed, resuming her thrashing. Putting a hand over my forehead, I stepped back.

"You can't be serious."

"Can't I? This is my domain and I rule it as I see fit. You..." He laughed, shaking his head. "You are a human with a bad attitude. If you weren't useful, I'd dispense with you immediately. Instead, I'm giving you a choice."

"A choice?"

"She can become one of you or you can finish the round."

My breath got caught in my throat. When I collected myself, I realized what game he was playing and I hated him for it.

"This is cruel."

"What have I done since you've met me that makes you think I care?"

Looking at Olga, I tried to think about what I would want in her position. She was weak and I was certain that she would die quickly in the fights. The only thing I could do was ensure she went out with a piece of her still intact.

Entangled Realms

Rushing forward, I grabbed the hilt of a dagger at Reyn's hip. One of the guards stepped forward, but stopped when he shook his head. Without allowing myself time to second guess it, I jammed the blade into Olga's chest where I estimated her heart to be. Her eyes widened and a pained sound came from her lips, then her eyes began to roll back.

Straightening, I stared at her for another moment. She was my second kill since coming here. I reached inside myself, searching for a sense of apathy to drape myself in so that I wouldn't have to feel it so wholly.

Turning to Reyn, I set my jaw and let the dagger fall to the ground in front of him. He watched me intently, even as I walked away. I could feel that stare like it was a corporeal thing digging into my back.

He could stare all he wanted. There was no scenario in his little game where he didn't win. If nothing else, I refused to give him the opportunity to gloat about it.

Since that first night with Reyn, I had been sleeping lightly. With how quiet the room always was, I woke immediately to the soft sound of shuffling. I sat up, immediately spotting the dark figure leaning against the bedpost. He had his arms crossed casually over his chest as he returned my stare.

"What do you want?" I asked curtly.

"That's a stupid question."

"Don't you have a whole harem to choose from?"

"All of them have learned their place. You, on the other hand, are still just as sharp as the day you arrived."

"So, you want to break me. How unoriginal. I played your stupid game earlier, now leave me alone."

Faster than I could track, he was hovering over me on the bed. My breath caught, but I clenched my teeth tightly, refusing to back down from his stare. One corner of his mouth lifted slightly.

"You make it so fun to win, little rose."

"Stop calling me that."

"But you're so..." He hooked his fingers over my shorts and yanked them down roughly. "Sharp."

Closing my legs tightly, I shoved at his chest. He grabbed my wrists and I wrestled free. When my foot connected with his stomach, he growled.

"I see we're back to that stupidity you love so much."

"Leave me alone," I shrieked, continuing to strike at him.

"You do realize I could just..."

He released my wrists, yet I still couldn't move them. Strong bonds kept me pinned to the mattress, at his mercy all over again like the first time. This time, though, my mind wasn't hazy. I was far too clear-headed.

"That's better," he drawled.

He freed his dick and began to stroke it. My nose wrinkled at the sight of it. The moonlight was brighter than before, allowing me a better view of the disgusting thing. It looked much like a normal dick, except for what looked like four tiny thorns; two on each side. They barely protruded from the skin, but as he continued to stimulate himself, they began to grow.

A thick liquid appeared at the tips of the barbs, as Portia had called them. When he'd spread it over his length, he thrust inside of me, not giving me a moment to adjust to his size. I cried out at the sudden pressure that triggered an uncomfortable ache.

I felt the barbs grow, brushing against my walls. Tensing, I waited for the pain. They burrowed themselves deep and there was a sting as they gripped me inside the little cavities he'd made the first time. With each passing second, I expected to feel them ripping me apart, but nothing else happened.

He pulled back slowly and I felt the motion tug at the barbs. It only caused a slight pressure, but it didn't hurt. That wasn't to say it was comfortable. This entire experience was horrifying and even though I wasn't in excruciating pain this time, every muscle in my body was tense with the need to reject his intrusion.

His hand settled on the mattress beside my head as he moved rhythmically. Staring up at the ceiling, I bit down on my lip to keep him from seeing the way it trembled.

"You look incredibly uncomfortable, little rose."

Refraining from looking at him, I bit down harder. I didn't want to play his baiting game. It would only lead to me saying something that would make it worse.

I whimpered when he gripped my jaw tightly, forcing me to look at him. Tears pooled in my eyes and my nostrils flared with my emotions. The amusement was evident in his expression.

"Perhaps I'll set aside every night for you until it becomes clear that you do not have power."

A tear broke free, traveling down my cheek. He jerked his hand back, his lip curling. His thrusts became harder, each one making the headboard slam against the wall.

Squeezing my eyes shut, I started playing through what I could remember of The Princess Bride. It was my most watched movie and I could remember quite a bit of it. It took until she got captured by Vizzini for him to jerk inside me, filling me with warmth.

His weight disappeared and so did the pressure holding my wrists. Immediately, I rolled onto my side facing the bathroom.

"You are to start training after breakfast."

I ignored him, counting the panes on the door. There were nine of them, which annoyed me. It would've been better to have eight or ten.

"Kiera." His voice was firm, the annoyance clear in his tone. "Do you understand?"

"Yes," I whispered.

A moment later, the door shut hard. If I was getting on his nerves, it was far less than he deserved. I should've been trying harder to placate him, but that was the thing about apathy. My self-preservation instincts weren't fully intact at the moment. I couldn't decide if I wanted to settle into this state permanently, but that was something I could deal with later.

Right now, I just wanted to sleep. I was so fucking tired.

Chapter 11

Reynaeros

Putting a hand over my mouth, I yawned for what felt like an eternity. It kept happening and it was infuriating. I turned the page, feeling another one coming on.

By the time I'd read a few more, I couldn't stand it anymore. The book itself was captivating enough. Something about the act must have been making me tired. Maybe I was bored. Unfortunately, there was hardly anything entertaining in this place.

Checking in with the energy, I felt a wave of annoyance. Kiera was just as pissy as ever. Worse, even. She was skewing everything with her foul moods. Whereas my usual captives felt copious amounts of pain and despair, she was a flaming ball of rage at all times.

Slamming the book closed, I headed toward the training room. If there was anywhere that could help her work off her anger, it would be there, but somehow she maintained it regardless of the circumstances.

Even last night, she stubbornly held onto that emotion. When her tears touched my skin, I expected to taste her desperation, but instead they'd been laced with her fury. Hate. A burning desire for retribution. I would not stand for it.

I threw the doors open and looked around. There wasn't a single person here. Peering through the door to the pool, I confirmed that it was also empty.

Now I was the one filled with rage. As I marched down her corridor, a few women scurried into their rooms, sensing my mood. It felt like it rolled off of me in waves, threatening my control.

I forced the door open before I reached it. She looked up from her place on the bed for only a moment before pulling her knees up and resting her chin on them. I slammed the door behind me, staring at her as she watched a boat traveling on the water.

"You're supposed to be in the training room."

She shrugged. "I decided not to go."

"That's not an option. I told you after breakfast-"

"I didn't eat breakfast."

Letting out a dry laugh, I moved over to the window and drew the curtains closed, casting the room in shadow. Without the view, she laid on her side and pulled the blanket over her head.

"Get the fuck out of bed."

She didn't respond or move an inch. Dropping my head back, I stared at the ceiling for a few seconds. When I'd centered myself, I grabbed the blanket and threw it to the floor. She made a disgruntled sound and curled up tighter.

"What the hell is wrong with you?"

"I'm depressed," she muttered.

"And what do you expect me to do about that?"

"Got any dopamine?"

"I have no idea what you're on about."

"Does your little magical head not get all screwed up when life sucks?"

"My 'magical head' is clearly far more evolved than your human one."

"So, you're not human."

Huffing, I grabbed her ankle and dragged her to the foot of the bed. She kicked out at me, connecting with my stomach. Latching onto her other leg, I yanked hard. She landed on her ass on the floor, releasing an extremely colorful slew of words. The rage rolling off of her felt like it could knock me over.

Leaning against the footboard, she looked up at me with a fierce glare. "That was extremely uncalled for."

"Your entire existence is uncalled for. Now get up and follow me."

I walked off, then paused at the door. When she didn't even make an effort to get moving, I felt my skin begin to buzz.

"I swear to the gods, Kiera..."

"Funny. I didn't take you for the religious type, Reyn."

"You are going to be the death of me. I'm really questioning my decision not to kill you."

"You might as well. There are a dozen other sources of entertainment for you around here."

"If that was all you were, it is exactly what I would do."

She narrowed her eyes. "What do you want me for?"

"That will become clear when it is time. Right now, you need to get off of your ass."

"I'm comfortable where I'm at."

"Stop being weak, Kiera."

When she got to her feet, I felt incredibly relieved. That feeling quickly dissipated when she marched up to me and slapped me across the face. Her anger and my own combined with the contact, stripping me of my careful control. Her eyes widened momentarily before I regained my composure.

"Do not attack me."

Her intention was clear before her hands connected with my chest. I latched onto her wrists and backed her up to the bed.

"Let me guess. You're going to show me I'm powerless."

"If that's what it takes."

She rose on her toes, getting close to my face. "You can fuck me into submission, beat me, force me to fight for your sick entertainment. I'll never bow to you, Reyn."

My chest rose and fell rapidly, even as I tried to control my breathing. She continued to stare directly into my eyes, making me feel unnerved. Nobody ever dared to look for so long. I felt my irises shifting and blinked quickly.

I shoved her backward onto the bed, then turned on my heel.

"Eat something and go to the training room before I decide to move on to cruder methods."

"I'm not eating."

"Then fucking starve!" I shouted before the door slammed behind me. The force of it made the wall shudder and someone screamed.

Was this meant to be my undoing? Maybe that was the point of this goddamn curse. I was beginning to wonder if it'd be better to throw in the towel and drown her in the tub. It might be worth it if this was only about me.

🌹 🌹 🌹 🌹

Settling on the rocks at the bank of the river, I dipped my feet into the water. My eyes fell shut as the gentle current pushed against my skin. There was a certain purity to its energy, even if it wasn't nearly as clean and unsullied as what I'd once been used to.

In this century, there was so much pollution, it choked everything it touched. The trees felt the burn of gasoline and the rot of a hundred thousand pounds of garbage. Plastic contaminated the oceans, making an imprint that the life there wouldn't be free of for hundreds of years after the last humans faded away.

Despite the depressing nature of this world, I could still feel its life. This deep in the woods, there was hardly a trace of the negativity that permeated the air in the city. Once in a while, there would be campers or teenagers

Entangled Realms

looking for a place to commit acts that would make their parents gasp, but overall it was peaceful.

Leaning back on my hands, I dug my fingers into the dirt, relishing the hum that traveled over my skin. Moonlight filtered through the trees, bringing with it a different sort of energy. Being out here like this was almost enough to dispel all of the stress from the past week.

When I sensed another presence, I straightened. I was on my feet in an instant, harnessing an energy I'd latched onto when I was connected to the soil. A soft laugh came from the trees.

"Come on, Reynaeros. You're always so quick to attack."

"That's what one does when they are threatened."

I released the branches that held her and a moment later she stepped out from behind the tree. Her crimson cloak stood out starkly among the dark forest. She dropped her hood, revealing long silver hair that contrasted starkly with the black protrusions on her head. They were wimpy, just as she was.

"What are you doing here, Riniya?"

"Visiting. It's been a while."

"Wonderful. Now that we've said hello, you can return home."

She rolled her eyes and stepped closer. My hands clenched at my sides. Her brow raised as she looked at them.

"You're just dying to strike me, aren't you?"

"Speak plainly before I lose my patience."

"You know better than that, but I'll comply. See, I had a chat with Lyndis about your little predicament."

"Is that so?"

"There doesn't seem to be much time. I'm sure you're aware of this."

"I don't suppose you're offering me a solution."

"Of course not. I simply thought it would be best to see you before I lost my chance entirely."

"Essentially, you came to gloat."

She smiled, revealing her sharp white teeth. "You think so ill of me."

"That is because I loathe you. Perhaps you should leave, lest you lose the opportunity."

"You would only damn yourself."

"If I'm nearly out of time, what have I got to lose?"

Her eyes narrowed, but she took a small step back. Even in her position, she knew she did not have the advantage. My fingers twitched with the desire to end this entire thing right here. If she was correct, it might be worth it.

It was possible that I was close, though. I owed it to everyone to keep trying. If that meant I had to swallow this desire for vengeance, I would have to do it.

Relaxing my hands, I dipped my head slightly. "Thanks for the visit, Riniya. Let me be candid before I leave. I may be letting you go this time, but if you dare to return, I will not hesitate to immortalize you in the ground on this world. It would be worth it."

Her lip curled, making me smile as I turned around. I felt her irritation, but also the fear that lurked just under the surface. She couldn't hide it from me. She never could. It was why she'd orchestrated all of this. I just wished I had the perspicacity to see it back then.

Hindsight was a bitch, as the people of this world would say.

Chapter 12

Reynaeros

With a roar, I flung one of the tables across the library. It hit the wall, shattering into a mess of splinters. I looked at a particularly sharp one, imagining embedding it in that bitch's chest for continuing to defy me.

For the second day in a row, she was refusing to eat or train. Whatever fucked up genetics she bore had shaped her into an unruly, stubborn little monster. Nothing persuaded her, even threats of violence.

When I considered fucking her, the force of the rage rolling off of her made me reconsider. I hated the caress of it, especially so close. Sadness and pain awoke something in me; they made me feel something. Anger was just uncomfortable, like a rough material rubbing on my skin.

It made no sense. I knew that she was afraid. I'd felt it a few times; when Chester brought her up to the viewing floor, when she walked into her first fight, and when I took her for the first time. It was never pure, though. She tucked it away, somehow choosing to feel something different. She wore that anger like a cloak and I hadn't figured out how to strip her bare.

I would figure it out. Everyone had a weakness and through that crack in their defenses was their breaking point. Once I found that fissure, I could rip her wide open.

"Goodness," Portia said from the doorway.

Chester stepped inside first, eyeing the broken furniture. He breathed a laugh as he shook his head.

"What has you so worked up?"

"Besides a visit from Riniya last night?"

His eyes widened. "What the hell could she want after all this time?"

"To gloat, it seems."

Portia hopped up on a table, swinging her legs idly. "I feel it."

"We all do," Chester agreed.

"There's still time," I said curtly. "It could take a century yet. There's no telling."

They shared a brief glance that made me roll my eyes. In my opinion, twins were the worst. It was like they always had a secret. It didn't help that those two could actually communicate between their minds.

"What truly has you so worked up?" Portia asked.

"I don't know what you mean."

"Come on, Reynaeros. That tiny-branched whore has never burrowed under your skin in this way."

Pacing over to the window, I stared out at the water. The weather was poor today, the wind making the river choppy. I'd come to enjoy gray days like this one. There was a certain beauty to them that most people didn't see. Everyone preferred sunshine.

"It's the girl, isn't it?"

I glared at Chester. "She's infuriating, but I'll find a way to break her."

"If you're so sure, why are you destroying your favorite room?"

Thrusting my hands through my hair, I growled. "Nothing I do seems to work. She's always angry. What am

I supposed to do with that? It's not malleable. I can't shape it or control it. It's just... It's just fucking there."

"Perhaps you need a different approach," Portia offered unhelpfully.

"I'd prefer to approach it by throwing her into the river during a nasty storm."

"Oh, calm down. Matching anger with anger doesn't do any good."

Chester snorted a laugh. "He doesn't know what else to do. It has always worked for him because his ire makes them fearful."

"That's precisely the problem. She doesn't fear me."

"Like my sister said. Try a different approach."

Drumming my fingers on the table, I mulled it over. "Should I torture her?"

He gave me an exasperated look. "No, you shouldn't torture her."

"It sounds like as good a plan as any."

"You've become a grump in your old age," Portia said, shaking her head.

"I haven't heard you two offer anything remotely helpful."

"The girl is different, Reynaeros. She will respond to your anger with a ferocity of her own because it is how she defends herself. If you wish for her to react differently, you must approach her without anger."

My lip curled. "I don't know how to do that."

"You once did."

"I once spent my mornings bathing in a hot spring untouched by the pollution of this world. Things are not as they once were, Portia."

"That's precisely the point. You want that life again, as we all do, so this is what you must do."

"Fuck," I groaned. "Am I to ask her favorite color or some ridiculous thing like that?"

"Just be kind to her," Chester suggested. "I gave her muffins and a rose. It was enough to make her have an amiable conversation with me."

"Muffins and roses sound easy enough." I held my hand out, letting one sprout from my skin.

"Well, maybe find your own version of it and don't grow things from your body. It might freak her out."

"That's asinine. She clearly fears nothing."

"She fears much," Portia disagreed. "It's simply that she conceals it. The goal here is to make her see past some of your more monstrous qualities so that she will work with you instead of actively trying to work against everything you say. She doesn't have to like you and you don't have to like her."

"Good. I can't stand the mere thought of her."

They shared another look and I narrowed my eyes. With a smile, Portia hopped off the table and kissed her brother's cheek. She came up to me and I bent down so she could do the same.

"Quit being such a curmudgeon. You'll get wrinkles."

"I'm not a fucking curmudgeon," I muttered as she exited the room.

Chester raised a brow. "Should we ask the rest of the court?"

"Perhaps we should just move on with our respective days."

"Wise choice, cousin. I'm very interested to see how this whole thing plays out."

I was not at all interested, but apparently I had no choice. Be kind. I could manage that.

Chapter 13

Kiera

Flopping onto my back, I tried to ignore the pain in my stomach. It had been two days since Reyn came in here throwing a toddler-sized tantrum. Sure, I'd provoked him and continued to poke the bear, but that was beside the point.

Whether this was part of apathy regarding my well-being or some short-sighted rebellion wasn't clear. Realistically, I knew it would end badly. Most likely, he'd give in to his desire to kill me. From what he said, though, he wanted me for something else. I might go so far as to say that he needed me. That tipped the scales slightly in my direction.

Since my purpose remained unclear, I was doubling down on being a stubborn bitch, even at the expense of my stomach. It made no sense that having an empty stomach for two days made you feel like throwing up, but I'd reached that state a little while ago. Now I was having some pretty solid waves of pain in my gut.

If any of the experiences in my books were correct, I could last a while without food. As long as I stayed hydrated, I might be able to give Reyn an aneurysm before I kicked the bucket. I was under no delusion that I'd be able to keep starving myself until I died, but I intended to milk this for as long as I could bear it.

I made the mistake of looking toward the dresser, where a box of blueberry muffins had mysteriously appeared while I was showering earlier. I wanted to commend myself for my own self-control. Not long ago, I was certain those fuckers were actually calling my name, like an ethereal voice on the wind. Maybe it was one of their magical abilities.

Lying around was incredibly boring, which only made me feel more hungry, so I meandered into my closet and began going through my clothes. Most of them hadn't been worn in years, but I had trouble getting rid of things. Everything had a memory attached to it, no matter how big or small. How was I supposed to part with something that held a piece of my life?

I determined that I would try them on and get rid of anything that didn't fit. Stripping out of my clothes, I began to bring the items into the room, laying them on the bed. Balancing a few pairs of shoes in my arms, I stepped out of the closet.

A figure beside the bed made me scream. The shoes flew in three different directions, then made a cacophony of thuds as they hit the floor at different times.

"What the hell?" I screeched.

Reyn raised a brow. "That was dramatic."

"You scared me." Realizing I was in my bra and underwear, I put an arm over my chest and hurriedly grabbed something to wear from the bed.

"I have seen your body and I do not care about it."

"I don't want you to see it in any context, least of all when it's daytime."

"It's not impressive. I'm not looking."

Entangled Realms

After pulling on a shirt, I glared at him. "Did you come here to insult me?"

"Of course not. I'm just telling you that I don't find human bodies attractive."

"All of you look human, aside from your weird, milky eyes."

The corner of his mouth lifted. "You have not seen our bodies, Kiera."

I almost mentioned that I had seen his, but it just made me nauseous to think about. Aside from his barbed dick and ethereal sort of beauty, he looked human to me. The other day when I'd pissed him off, I could have sworn his teeth looked different- sharper, maybe. It must've been my imagination because as soon as I blinked, everything looked normal.

"Well, as much as I've enjoyed this visit, *Reyn*, I'd like to get back to what I was doing."

His jaw ticked. "Stop shortening my name."

"Then stop intruding on my privacy."

It looked like he wanted to argue. Instead, he came over to my side of the bed. I backed up until I hit the wall, my heart rate spiking. I was overcome with the urge to beg him not to touch me, but I shoved it down and met his eyes.

He stopped a foot away from me. "I see you're still subscribing to your starvation diet. Even the muffins didn't deter you from it."

"That was you?" I asked incredulously.

His fingers tapped against his leg rhythmically. "You should have one so you don't pass out in the training room. Humans are quite frail."

"If you're so turned off by us, maybe you should leave us alone."

"Then I'd be bored and nobody wins in that scenario."

"You could screw one of your own kind. Like Portia."

"She is married and we do not fuck our cousins."

"You're related?"

"Would you like to see my family tree, little rose?"

He held his hand out in front of him. I watched as the skin split open and a vine sprung from it. A red bud sprouted at the end, then unfurled into a rose. He plucked it and the surface smoothed over.

I put a hand over my mouth. "That was disgusting. Were you trying to make a joke?"

He hesitated, twirling the rose between his fingers. "No."

"Jokes are not in our arsenal of allowed interactions. Either yell at me or get out of my room."

Brushing past him, I started to pick up the shoes. Vines suddenly appeared and lifted them off the ground. When they soared toward the bed, I swore, jumping out of the way before one could hit me in the shoulder.

"Can you stop with your weird magic?"

"I was helping you."

Putting my hands over my face, I groaned. "Please just leave."

"Not until you agree to my demands."

"Your demands mean nothing to me."

He grabbed my arm, pivoting us so he could push me onto the edge of the bed. My body began to react to the threat and I struggled to keep my breaths even.

"I am trying to be kind, Kiera. Stop being so difficult."

"Kind," I scoffed. "You can't be serious."

"I'm not joking, if that's what you think."

"What I think," I said firmly, shoving at his chest. He stepped back, his hands fisting at his sides. "Is that you're stupider than I thought. After everything I've gone through since you took me prisoner, you think that you can come in here and put on some bullshit façade to get me to agree? Fuck you, Reyn."

"God damnit. This is impossible."

With a frustrated shriek, I shoved at him again, He continued backing up without stopping me. When he hit the wall, he grabbed my wrists and flipped us around. His hand came up to my throat, gripping it tightly enough that it was an effort to draw in a full breath.

"Why the fuck are you so angry all the time?"

My lip trembled. "You don't deserve anything but my anger."

He shook his head. "You've been angry since the moment I saw you in the club."

"You don't know anything about me or what I feel."

"It assaulted me that night as soon as your attention was on me and it has not stopped for a single moment. I *feel* you, Kiera, even when I'm trying to sleep. While everyone else lies peacefully in their beds, you sink deeper into whatever it is that antagonizes you. When you should be afraid, you are angry. When you should give up, you're angry. When you are starving by your own hand, you are *angry*. I cannot stand it."

"Then get rid of me."

With a huff, he released me and paced toward the window. "What'll it take?"

"To what?"

"For you to agree. I am not asking for a lot."

"To be fair, I don't even know what you're asking for. You want me to train, but for what?"

"To fight, of course."

"Nobody else is doing it."

"That's because they are no match for what I need you to fight."

I was sure a dozen different expressions passed over my face because that was how many emotions were fighting for dominance in my head. One thing I knew for certain was that I didn't like the sound of that statement.

"Is it a Rancor?"

"I have no idea what that is."

"Of course you don't. Uncultured."

"Be serious, Kiera. Tell me what it'll take."

"If I say freedom..."

"No."

I made a disgruntled sound, dropping my head back against the wall. "You don't get to fuck me."

"Also out of the question."

"Then I fail to see how this benefits me at all."

"There must be something else that will bring you a modicum of joy."

I narrowed my eyes at him. "You have to let me call you Reyn."

He ground his teeth audibly. "Fine."

The barely concealed rage in his tone made me smile. "I don't want to fight."

"You have to fight."

"No. Not in the ring. You want me to do battle with some mysterious thing that for some reason you can't go up against. I'll spend my time training, but I don't want to fight anyone."

He rolled his eyes. "Alright. Is that all?"

"I heard you have a dope library."

The green pools of his eyes seemed to move more rapidly. He blinked a couple of times and they returned to normal. I wanted so badly to ask about them, but refrained.

"I'm going to kill those bitches."

"Come on. It's just a library."

"It's not just a library. It's my library."

"Hm. Never learned to share, huh? I'm assuming you're an only child."

A murderous look came over his face. "No to the library."

"Then no to the training."

He growled, thrusting his hands through his hair. The gesture forced some of the strands loose from his bun. They came down to frame his face, making him appear more youthful. If he ever removed that scowl from his face, maybe he'd even be desirable.

"Once a week."

"Whenever I want."

Holding a hand over his face, his shoulders shook. I thought he might be crying, which freaked me out more than most other things that had happened. When he uncovered his face, though, I realized he was laughing.

Great. I'd driven him to madness. Deserved, if you asked me.

"Fuck it. Sure. Have the library. Take my fucking throne while you're at it. There is a bed large enough for four in my room."

"Ew. Why would I want anything from your room?"

"Because clearly you wish to take everything from me. Is that your final request?"

As I stared at him, I almost felt like a greedy asshole. Then I reminded myself of all the horrible things the guy had done and continued to do.

"Uh, that's it."

"Good. This was me being kind. Can I be done with it now?"

"What if I say no?"

"Then I truly will kill you this time."

"Hm."

"What are you doing?"

"Pondering."

"What the fuck are you pondering, Kiera?"

"Which option I prefer."

He paused, staring at me like I'd grown a second head. "Are you joking right now? You are considering choosing death in this scenario."

"As an alternative to spending my days with you? Absolutely."

"Dear god. I... I can't."

He marched over to the door. It opened before he'd even reached it, which seemed like a lazy use for magic.

"Meet me up there tomorrow or don't. Remaining here is stealing years from my life."

"How old are you anyway?"

"Old enough to consider you a petulant toddler."

"So, that's what's up with the white hair."

He turned with his mouth slightly open. "I do not have white hair because I'm old."

"Only old people have white hair."

"Or your race's genetics are very unimaginative."

The door slammed shut behind him. The entire room seemed to shudder from the force. Wrapping my arms around myself, I sat criss cross on the bed.

It felt like I'd gained a lot from this, but in the end, I was still his prisoner. He acted like allowing me to use the library was the most generous thing he could do.

I wondered if he'd ever faced any true difficulties in his life. If he had, I would've thought he'd have more of a capacity for empathy. Maybe that was a human trait that didn't exist in his weird, magic-capable head.

Well, if I was going to endure a day in the training room tomorrow, I wouldn't feel guilty about eating all of those muffins.

Chapter 14

Reynaeros

"She insulted my fucking hair," I grumbled.

Chester laughed, making me consider aiming this knife at him. I tested its weight before throwing it at a dummy. Even though I could hit my mark every time, there was a sense of satisfaction that came with it.

"Are you offended by a human's opinion about your appearance?"

"Don't be ridiculous. Of all creatures, they are the last that should be able to mock the traits of others. They all look so similar that it took me a century to begin noticing their differences."

"She's quite pretty for one of them, don't you think?"

Taking another knife from the wall, I threw it at the dummy against the far wall. The force of it made it fall onto its back.

"Reynaeros?"

"No, I do not think she is pretty. Her hair and eyes are brown, which is the least imaginative shade their kind possesses."

"It is the color of tree bark."

"If you find her so alluring, perhaps you should fuck her. You may have better luck with her."

"Would you not kill me if I tried?"

His teasing tone grated on my nerves. It was true that I did not let others fuck the women I kept, but if Chester asked, I may allow it. He was my closest friend, regardless of our blood relation.

"She's late," I noted.

"I think you will have to adjust your expectations. If she comes at all, it should be counted as a win."

"Then she will think that she has power over this situation. The more I allow, the more she will take. That is her nature."

"Maybe."

"What does that mean?"

"Nothing. I haven't known her long enough to understand what goes on inside her head."

"Chaos. That is all I'm certain of."

There were footsteps in the hallway and the force of her emotions was palpable. I could taste the bitterness of her frustration. She was warring with herself as she paced back and forth in front of the door.

I made the doors open and she sucked in a startled breath. As soon as she laid eyes on me, her familiar glare slipped into place.

"I feel incredibly honored that you decided to come," I said.

"Yeah, yeah. Give me a sword so I can turn you into a kebab."

"Good luck," Chester muttered before heading toward the door. Her expression softened as they passed each other. A smile even made a quick appearance before her scowl replaced it.

"Did you eat breakfast?" I asked.

"No."

My hand dropped from the weapon rack. "Are you back to protesting by way of starvation?"

"I'm not a breakfast person."

"What is a 'breakfast person?'"

"Someone that eats breakfast. It makes me feel sick."

That sounded like something she'd just made up on the spot, but I wasn't going to argue with her about it. There was sure to be enough of that throughout the entirety of this day.

"So, what are we doing?" she asked.

"Training."

"Jesus. You're insufferable to converse with."

"Good thing we won't be holding a conversation. Grab something to fight with."

Her teeth worried at her lip as she perused the weapons. It was clear she had no idea what half of them were and I would bet my entire fortune on her not knowing how to use a single one. Humans rarely did, especially in this century.

Her fingers stopped on a claymore. I had to cover my mouth to smother my laughter when she nearly dropped it. With both hands, she lifted it unsteadily, planting her feet so she didn't fall over.

"Perhaps we should begin with strength training."

"Fuck you. Why is this thing so heavy?"

"It's not. It's simply long, which upsets the balance. That and you are pathetically weak."

The sword hit the ground just before she turned around and marched for the door.

"Where are you going?"

"Anywhere but here."

"We had an agreement."

"And I'm going back on it. I don't see a new scar, so I'm assuming this one isn't binding in any way."

Reaching out with a hand, I secured the doors with a winding branch between the handles. She grabbed both of them, yanking with all her strength, but they didn't budge. When she didn't return, I wrapped a vine around her wrist and tugged her toward me.

She shrieked, swatting at it. "Get your creepy plant shit off of me, you nymph."

Once she was in front of me again, I released her. "I am not a nymph."

"Fine. An elf."

"Laughable."

"Some sort of Fae."

My nose scrunched up. "Stop trying to conceptualize me using your world's ridiculous stories."

"Well, spill the beans then."

"No. Pick up your sword."

It looked like she was going to argue, but I was pleasantly surprised when she obliged. She weighed it in her hand and adjusted her grip to accommodate it.

"Do you have a cool healing factor like Spiderman?"

"I can mend my body if I need to."

"Hm."

She thrust the sword forward, burying the blade in my stomach. I swore and thrust her backward. She hit the far wall and fell to the ground in a crumpled heap. Her duplicitous heart was still pumping and I hadn't decided if I was glad for it or not.

Grasping the blade, I pulled it free and put a hand over my stomach. I dropped to the floor and rested my elbows on my knees.

This fucking bitch.

As I began to patch the damage, I stared at her unmoving form. Threats didn't work, nor did kindness. If I couldn't find a way to make her agreeable, it was very likely we were doomed. The longer I knew her, the more sure I felt about her role in all of this. I didn't have any idea how or why it was her. Perhaps it was punishment for all of my misdeeds over the centuries.

If I could kill Riniya simply for subjecting me to this torture, I would do it in a heartbeat. I should have just done it the other night, consequences be damned. There were too many unknowns, though, and I couldn't bring myself to endanger those I had a responsibility to protect. They were my court. My friends, even.

There was nothing better to do, so I got to my feet, groaning when the movement tugged at the wound. It would take hours to fully heal and I was not prone to forgiveness. If she would not be reasonable, I would make her life hell until she could no longer muster up a fight.

Kiera would rue the day she dared walk into my club and brought her negative fucking energy with her.

Chapter 15

Kiera

My back hurt. My head hurt. Even my goddamn ass hurt. I guess that was to be expected when you were literally thrown against a wall by some pissy elf man.

The asshole had left me there, likely not caring if he'd killed me. To be fair, I did stick a sword through his gut. I did, however, verify that he was able to heal himself beforehand. There was a small chance I would get lucky and kill him, which had obviously not been the case. Worth a shot.

I shoved an orange slice into my mouth a little bit too aggressively, judging by the way Lucy's eyes widened. Collie was still being weird and distant. One would think I'd taken a shit in her favorite pair of shoes.

"You're moodier than usual," Lucy pointed out casually.

"Are you saying that I'm usually moody?"

"Yes."

"Well, I'm sorry that I'm not happily settling into this life of captivity. Somebody has to hold onto a shred of self-respect around here."

"You don't have to lash out at us."

"I'm not," I sighed, dropping the slice I was about to eat. I hadn't even tasted any of them so far, so it was pointless.

Now that I thought about it, I hadn't seen any meat here. Paying attention to the food hadn't been high on my list of priorities, then I had that starvation stint. Maybe that was part of what was making me so irritated today.

"Is it too much to give us steak once in a while?" I grumbled.

Lucy laughed lightly. "They don't eat meat."

"I didn't ask them to eat it."

"Maybe they have something against it," Collie chimed in softly.

When I met her gaze, she looked away quickly. "Did I do something to you?"

"What do you mean?"

"You've been acting cold toward me ever since the day we met. I thought you were nice before."

"She's very nice," Lucy said, looking offended.

"Nothing in this place makes sense. All of you are in various stages of acceptance, the non-humans are willfully mysterious, and there are magic doors that you can only see when you know they're there."

Collie looked up abruptly. "Don't tell me you found it. I told you not to look for it."

"Found what?"

"The red... Nevermind."

"No. I've scoured this entire corridor and the other one I'm allowed into. There's no red door."

"Good."

"Not good. I'd very much like to figure out what he's hiding in there."

"You're just going to get yourself killed," Lucy pointed out, pointing her fork at me.

"If I could be so lucky. For some reason, Reyn is adamant about keeping me alive."

"Reyn?"

"It's his name. Well, part of it. His full name is nearly as bad as that one from Twilight."

"I thought Leander was his real name. It's weird he'd tell you that."

"He likes her."

We both looked at Collie with matching expressions of disbelief. She pursed her lips and stared down at her food as if it was a man with a six pack and a strong jaw.

"That's hilarious. He literally threw me into a wall yesterday."

"I just mean that there's something different about you," Collie went on. "He took you out of the fights and is training you. He wouldn't do that if you didn't matter to him in some way."

"I'm a means to an end. He's being very hush-hush about the details, but there's something I'm supposed to defeat for him. It makes no sense, considering he's a million times stronger than me and does weird shit with his mind."

"Wait." Lucy turned to Collie with a furrowed brow. "Where are you getting your information from? I didn't know she was pulled from the fights."

Collie shrugged. "Just gossip."

"Oh my god."

"Lucy, don't."

"You were talking to him, weren't you?"

"Just in passing."

Lucy squealed. "Look at you commanding men's hearts."

"It's not like that. Besides, he's one of them."

"Collie, we're stuck here until we die. They're literally our only option unless you want to start munching-"

"I'm full." Collie pushed out her chair, the loud scraping making me cringe. She scurried away, disappearing through the door in record time.

Entangled Realms

Lucy looked at me with amusement written all over her face. "She's so timid. I wish she'd just make a move on him."

"Is that even allowed?"

"I don't know. She should find out, though."

The thought of her having a crush on one of those creatures should have made me feel a little gross, but I liked Chester. It was possible he was just as fucked up underneath his soft outer shell, but I wanted to believe he and his sister were good. The only thing I could fault them for was being involved in this little operation, which was arguably a pretty massive fault.

Lucy rounded the table and held her hand out to me. I eyed it suspiciously, which made her roll her eyes. Not waiting for me to agree, she latched onto me and dragged me out of my seat.

"Where are we going?"

She held a finger up to her lips. I looked around the room, but only saw one girl in here, so I wasn't sure what she meant by the secrecy. Shit. I'd never stopped to wonder if they had cameras in this place. Maybe it was a magical security system.

When she put her hand on the wall, I felt even more confused.

"Look," she whispered.

As I stared, it pushed inward. Once I realized it was a door, I saw the entirety of it. This one was silver, like one that would lead into an industrial kitchen. That was exactly where we ended up and the sight of it made my mouth drop open.

It didn't really look industrial, though. In a way, it reminded me of what they might have in a really old mansion. The appliances were new, but there was also a big fireplace with a hook to hang a pot. The counters resembled butcher block and there was exposed brick throughout.

The whole thing was both cottage core and extravagant. I didn't want to be impressed, but it was impossible not to be.

"This is where they cook everything? It's so clean."

"That's because they don't use it."

"Why not?"

"They don't need to. The food comes from somewhere else."

"Right. Magic."

She grinned. "Brooks!"

"Why are you yelling? You're going to get us in trouble."

"I thought you were all about stirring the pot, Kiera."

Reluctantly, I leaned against the counter and crossed my ankles. A door I hadn't seen opened and a young guy with a mustache waltzed through. I had to purse my lips to keep from laughing out loud. He was everything I'd expect from some fancy chef, even though he apparently didn't even cook.

"Lucia," he exclaimed, pulling her into his arms. He lifted her off the ground, making her squeal, then cupped her face. "It's been weeks, dear. Where have you been?"

"Oh, you know." She looked down at her feet as she kicked at the ground absently.

"Mm. I see." He trailed his eyes down her body. "Come. I'll prepare your favorite."

Her spirits lifted as she took a seat at the island. I followed suit, watching the entire scene with interest. Brooks grabbed a clean rag and ran it over the counter. When he held his hands over the surface, I thought I felt something change in the air, like it was full of static.

Lucy giggled beside me. My eyes widened when I saw some of her hair rising in front of her. Looking down, I realized mine was doing the same.

The scent of something rich permeated the air. I looked over at the fireplace and noticed a large pot hanging there. Whatever was bubbling inside smelled better than anything I'd eaten this week.

Entangled Realms

A spread appeared before us, complete with cured meats and cheeses that must've cost what I made in a day at my job. I immediately reached for the Swiss, popping a few cubes into my mouth and moaning. Next, I snagged a few slices of prosciutto. It was my favorite, but I could never justify spending the money on it.

"What happened to being against meat?"

Brooks smiled softly. Like with Chester and Portia, I found myself trusting him. He had a warmth that matched theirs. I was starting to wonder if Reyn was the only of their kind that was a complete dickwad.

"We do not eat such things, but these already existed in your world, so the crime was already committed. You waste so much of what these creatures offer and I figure I might be ensuring some of it doesn't get thrown out."

"That sounds so noble."

"I tend to think that it is simply normal and what you consider commonplace is cruel."

If that was meant as an insult, he'd made it impossible to disagree or defend humans. I would never stop eating meat, but I understood where he was coming from. It seemed pointless to mention that his boss literally pitted living beings against each other, especially since the guy was feeding us.

Brooks glanced at Lucy and rolled his lips. Taking a piece of meat and cheese, he rolled them together and held it out to her. When she hesitated, he narrowed his eyes slightly. With a huff, she took it and began to nibble on it. He looked satisfied as he went back to what he was doing.

Three glasses of wine appeared in front of us. I didn't hesitate to take a long drink. This was exactly what I needed right now. Every time I set it down, it refilled, making it impossible to determine how much I'd consumed.

By the time Brooks set a plate in front of us, I had a solid buzz going. I stared down at the heaping pile of mashed potatoes covered in a thick gravy-like substance with large chunks of meat in it.

"This is incredible," I commended after taking my first bite.

"All I did was bring it from one place to another."

"Still. I'd almost say that's more impressive."

"That's only because you have no special abilities." When my brows drew down, he laughed. "Save your ire for the big man. I heard he has been in a mood all day."

"Probably because of the new hole I put in his body."

His eyes widened. "You attacked him?"

"Yeah. I stabbed him."

Leaning his elbows on the counter, he whistled. "You are lucky to still be breathing."

I shrugged as I drained my wine glass. I was going to say something else, but Brooks was staring at Lucy with obvious concern. She was swirling her spoon through the potatoes, but it didn't look like she'd eaten a single bite.

She met his eyes and whatever was passing between them seemed personal, so I turned away. Since my glass was refilled, I went for it. It wasn't like there was anything better to do in this damn place besides eat and get drunk when the opportunity presented itself.

When my head was swimming, I leaned my elbows on the counter and nibbled on more cheese. It somehow tasted better than it had before. I was grazing for so long, I started to get tired. Just as my eyes began to close, there was a loud bang that made me jump.

"Shit," Brooks muttered.

He touched the counter and everything disappeared. It was too late, though. The man standing in the doorway looked none too happy about what he was seeing.

With how pale his skin was, the flush on his face was stark. If he was a cartoon character, there would be steam coming out of his ears. The thought made me laugh. Once it started, I couldn't stop it. I leaned forward in my chair, bracing myself on my knees.

Entangled Realms

Oh, I was definitely going to get thrown into a wall again.

Chapter 16

Reynaeros

"Where the hell is Kiera?" I asked, leaning against the doorframe to Chester's room.

He ran a stone over the edge of his dagger, barely looking up at me. "I'm not sure. Why?"

"I have news for her."

His movements stopped. "I have a feeling this will not be in line with our kindness plan."

"Fuck kindness. It works even less than my threats."

"Maybe because it was not genuine."

"That's not something I can remedy, so I will simply have to break her."

He sighed as he continued sharpening the blade. Both of his hands were uncovered, which I knew wasn't something he'd allow around anyone besides me and Portia. The two missing fingers on his left one might have made the task difficult for others, but he'd become an expert at finding ways to accommodate it.

"Do you have something to say, Chester?"

"I just think you should try harder."

"I tried very hard. I got her muffins, which she did not care about. I granted her every request, even the library. There's no greater kindness I can offer."

"To her, those are just things."

"Explain."

"If you handed her a million dollars, that would be an extraordinary gift, right?"

"Sure."

"If you have a billion dollars to your name, that gift hardly affects you. Now, consider that someone else offered her five hundred thousand. Who do you think she'd be more grateful to?"

"The former, obviously."

"No because the latter only had five hundred thousand to his name."

"But she would have double the money on the one hand."

"True, but we're not talking about material things. The second person gave her everything he had, while the first gave her pocket change in comparison. If she only cared about the money, that might mean something to her, but she's not greedy."

"Might I point out that offering access to my library is essentially the same as what the second man did."

"But she doesn't know that," he said firmly. "It's just a library to her."

Tapping my fingers on my leg, I tried to think of what to say in return. He'd overcomplicated the entire situation. Kiera wouldn't care about the things that mattered to me, so attempting to tell her would be pointless. She would immediately jump at the opportunity to take my most prized possession from me.

"I have to find her."

"Don't make her fight, Reynaeros."

Ignoring him, I made my way down to her corridor. Her bedroom was still empty and there was nothing to indicate that she'd returned at all. I checked some of the public rooms, drawing frightened gasps from the women there.

When I entered the cafeteria, I thought I sensed her energy, but it wasn't in its usual state. Whereas it was always tumultuous, ready to thrash like the ocean in a storm, this time it was calmer. There was a lightness to it that began to ease my own distress.

As I approached the kitchen door, I smelled meat. It disgusted and infuriated me. I thrust the door open, catching Brooks entertaining Lucy and Kiera over a meal. The scent of wine was overwhelming when it was mixed with the humans' blood.

Kiera looked at me with wide eyes. When she devolved into laughter, I was dumbfounded. Nobody had told a joke, nor did I think this situation was funny.

She composed herself and put a hand to her chest. As soon as she looked at me again, she went right back to it.

"Brooks, I expect you and Lucia to be gone before I decide to turn this entire place upside down."

He took her by the elbow and led her through the back door. The way he protected her struck me as odd. I knew they spoke sometimes, but there was an energy that passed between them when he touched her skin. I'd have to deal with that later. I couldn't have my people going soft. Not right now.

Coming to stand beside Kiera, I tried to study her without appearing what she might deem as threatening. She met my gaze, even though her eyes were unfocused.

"Come on," I sighed, taking her by the arm.

She jerked away forcefully. "Stop touching me."

"Don't start this shit right now. You're quite drunk."

"I'm perfectly fine, thank you."

She slid off the stool, barely managing to stand up straight when she touched the floor. I watched her teeter all the way to the door, hoping she would fall on her face so I could gloat. The thought brought a smile to my face, so I discreetly planted something in front of her foot.

"Fuck," she shrieked. She hit the floor on her hands and knees, the sound of her bones on the surface making me cringe.

"Perhaps you'll stop being needlessly stubborn now."

Putting her hand against the wall, she rose from the ground, immediately stumbling again. As she made her way to the door, she kept hold of the wall. From the way she kept swallowing and touching her stomach, I thought she might end up vomiting.

God damnit. She was in no condition to fight a dawdling toddler, let alone someone that would attempt to kill her. Part of me felt angry that she'd drank so much, but I refrained from starting an argument. I could piss her off when she was less inebriated.

This ridiculous journey was taking too damn long. With a frustrated growl, I swept her into my arms. She tried to strike me as usual. It was so common when I was around her that I easily evaded her fist.

"Calm down."

"Put me down."

"If you could move faster than a grandma, I would."

"Takes one to know one."

The corner of my mouth twitched. "That didn't make any sense."

She waved her hand toward me. "You know. Because of the hair or whatever. I don't know."

"Mm. We're back to that."

"Fuck you, rhinoceros. Just put me in bed and leave me alone before your face makes me throw up."

"Jesus. You're far worse to deal with when you're drunk. I'll have to make sure Brooks doesn't supply you with alcohol again."

She made a disgruntled sound. It reminded me of how young she was. She was intelligent, but immature. By the time she outgrew it, she'd be halfway to her death. I couldn't imagine living such a short life.

Every person we passed stared like it was some spectacle. When I glared at them, they scurried away quickly.

"Oh, power moves," Kiera giggled.

She leaned her head against my chest, making my lip curl. The verdict was in and it determined that I hated her even more in this state. Her emotions were all over the place, even as she appeared relatively level on the outside. With her touching me, she was essentially attempting to force them inside my body.

I stepped into her room and let the door close behind me.

"What the fuck?" she growled when I dropped her on the bed.

"You've made it back to your room without ending up on the floor a second time. You're welcome. As you can see, kindness is my new thing."

"Get the hell out."

Narrowing my eyes at her, I leaned back against the door, slipping my hands into my pockets. I barely ducked out of the way in time to avoid a pillow to the face. My skin prickled in reaction to the attack and the feeling intensified when she poised to throw another.

"It's very unwise to attack me, little rose."

"I'm not a fucking rose," she shouted, throwing the pillow.

A large thorn burst from my hand, slicing it down the middle in midair. Her eyes widened for a quick moment before she plastered on a blank expression. Brushing bits of fluff from my shirt, I stepped toward her.

"I treat you like everyone else and you think me a beast. I go against my nature and treat you with kindness and your opinion remains the same."

"That's because it's exactly what you are. A few fake niceties don't change what's on the inside."

"And what, pray tell, is inside of me, Kiera?"

"My best guess would be fairy dust."

I reared back. "Fairy dust?"

Entangled Realms

"Yeah. Clearly, the best thing I can compare you to is a fairy. Magic. Immortality. A nasty bite."

Grabbing her by the throat, I thrust her backward onto the mattress. She set her jaw and held my gaze. Leaning down, my lips barely brushed hers. I could taste the fury that surged beneath her skin and I could feel its heat.

"I was going to let you sleep off your wine-induced ineptitude, but I've changed my mind. I'd much rather stick to my original plan."

"Let me guess. You're going to fuck me."

Cocking my head, I studied her eyes. They were just brown. There was no life in them like my kind had. With most humans, it made them easier to read, but she was infuriatingly blank. Perhaps I was wrong about her and she was actually incredibly dense.

"That wasn't even on my mind."

"Oh."

She relaxed slightly. It wasn't a submission, but my body interpreted it as one. Pressing my hips down, I relished the way her breath hitched.

"Since you've vexed me, we can start here."

"No, wait."

When I unbuttoned her pants, she closed her legs tightly. Instead of fighting with her, I tore the material, leaving it in two strips on either side of her. Sliding my hands up her thighs, I trailed my thumbs in the creases at the tops of them.

Her legs trembled more with each of my touches. The alcohol clouded her mind, made her emotions act abnormally. There was fear radiating through her, more than she'd displayed since I'd met her. I tightened my grip, basking in it for a moment.

While my eyes were closed, her palm connected with my face. Shaking my head, I couldn't help but laugh.

"You're incapable of giving up, aren't you?"

"It's the twenty-first century. You can't expect women to bow to you because you have a dick."

"You're right. I don't expect women to bow. I expect everyone to bow and it has nothing to do with my sex, little rose. It has to do with this."

My index and middle fingers lengthened, the texture becoming rougher and the color changing to resemble that of her eyes. When they joined together into one long protrusion, I brushed her lips with the tip of it. She clenched her teeth, a pathetic whimper setting in.

"Power, little rose. You know nothing of it, nor will you ever."

If she was beginning to regret her stupidity, it was too late. I had her in a place I hadn't previously been able to push her to. A single tear sprung from the corner of her eye and I watched until it dropped onto the mattress.

Freeing my dick, I spread my lubrication across it and moved forward. Once I'd maneuvered the head inside of her, I gripped her jaw tightly, squeezing until she was forced to unclench her teeth. Before she could slam them again, I thrust the two morphed fingers inside, hitting the back of her throat and making her choke.

As I held it there, her gags became stronger. Only when she was nearly at the point of throwing up did I pull it back. She sucked in a shuddering breath, then coughed. There was red on the jagged parts of the wood, so I dragged my tongue over it, tasting the unique flavor of her human blood mixed with the wine that laced it.

I positioned it at her lips again. She shook her head, then winced when a splinter cut her lip.

"Have you learned nothing?"

I thrust forward, burying myself inside of her. She cried out, gripping the sheets tightly. When she turned her head away, I hooked two fingers around the inside of her cheek and yanked on her so she was looking at me.

Pushing my fingers in further, I watched her eyes begin to shutter, hiding that fear from me once more. Leaning down, I trailed my tongue over the blood on her lip, then pulled her up by my grip on her cheek. She planted her hands on the bed to relieve the tension and her nostrils flared.

"Are you angry?"

Unable to speak around my fingers, she nodded. I pushed forward again, groaning at the way her pussy gripped me. My barbs tightened with the wave of pleasure, trying to ensure that I would finish what I started. I had every intention to.

She grabbed at my wrist in an attempt to remove my hand. Her nails dug into my skin, drawing blood. The smell of it mixed with hers made heat course through my veins. A shock in the place she touched me made her jerk back.

Bringing my wrist to my mouth, I collected the blood on my tongue, then fisted her hair, tipping her head toward me. When I shoved it into her mouth, she resumed her struggling. After I'd brushed the liquid onto her tongue, I straightened and gripped her hips tightly.

She was staring up at me with a look of utter fury. If she had the ability, she would not hesitate to strike me down. Even when I thrust into her roughly, she continued to stare, only the tight set of her jaw betraying how uncomfortable this was for her.

I tried to ignore her as I chased my pleasure, but she might as well have been screaming at me for how loud her glare was. Forcing the barbs to retract, I pulled free of her. She looked relieved until I flipped her onto her stomach.

Pressing my weight down on her, I reentered her from behind, the new angle forcing the barbs to position themselves differently. She cried out at the pain, but it didn't last as long as the first time. Once she quieted to a whimper, I resumed my rhythm.

Her forehead fell against the mattress as she finally accepted what was happening. For the first time this week, I was able to draw in a full breath.

Deciding I wanted her to suffer a little more tonight, I lengthened one of the thorns at the base of my shaft, rounding out its tip and growing it into a thicker vine. As essentially an extension of my dick, I had nearly as much feeling in it and I wondered why I hadn't done this before. I guess nobody had pissed me off enough to make me think of it. I'd never even fucked a woman in this position, but I was enjoying it quite a lot.

When I spread my lubricant over her asshole, she went rigid. She peered at me over her shoulder with wide eyes. I could smell her fear and it drove me on. With a wink, I slid the tip of the protrusion inside of her.

Her hands fisted as she dropped her head forward again. The entirety of her body was trembling and I had to grip her hip to steady her. Her cries were muffled by the mattress, but she couldn't hide them from me.

Slowly, I pushed further in, making sure to keep the barbs tucked inside of me. Once I was fully seated, I pulsed it a little, expanding, then reducing it to help stretch her out before I started to fuck her. Even so, the first few thrusts made her scream.

With the combined sensations, I felt blinded by the pleasure. Her pussy wrapped snugly around my cock while her ass gripped me like a vice. I pulled nearly all the way out, shuddering when I felt that tightness on my tip, then relished the way it traveled to the base as I buried myself deep. It was a new sort of bliss unique to this act.

In her defiance, Kiera had introduced me to an experience I would be employing with her more often. It seemed to subdue her better than anything else I'd tried. I had no qualms about repeating this.

My fingers would no doubt bruise her with how hard I held onto her hips as I came. When the power of it began to subside, I found myself gasping. Getting to my feet, I adjusted my clothes and took a moment to compose myself.

"Change quickly."

She hadn't moved from the position on her stomach. Her shoulders were visibly shuddering and I could smell her fresh tears.

"Kiera," I said through gritted teeth.

"Go away." Her voice was gravelly, barely recognizable as one that belonged to her.

"Let's not do this again. I literally just finished cumming in you."

"I-I d-don't want you h-here."

Rolling my eyes at her weakness, I grabbed her arm to help her up. She screamed and thrashed like a madwoman. Getting a grip on her other wrist, I flipped her onto her back and held her down so she couldn't hurt herself.

"Kiera."

"Let me go," she sobbed, the fierceness of her emotions traveling in waves over my body.

"Quit with the dramatics. My cock in your ass won't kill you. There is a fight to be won tonight."

She quieted a little, her lip quivering pathetically as she stared at me. "No, I can't."

"You can and you will."

"But we had a deal."

"One which you defaulted on. Very forcefully, I might add. It's very difficult to simultaneously heal my body and keep control of... Just get yourself together so I don't have to come back and drag you out of here."

Leaving her there looking like a threatened chihuahua, I headed toward my room to get myself cleaned up. Maybe I'd even go for the whisky because of the ridiculous evening I was having. At least it had resulted in a win for once. Gods know I needed it.

Chapter 17

Kiera

As I stepped into the ring, I was in so much pain that I could barely process anything going on around me. It didn't help that my head was still swimming from the wine and a migraine had set in just after Reyn left me in my room.

After that, I'd thrown up viciously, only finding reprieve from it when my stomach was empty. I'd vomited up bile, then dry heaved before reaching a half-awake state on the floor. Portia had found me like that and helped me get ready for the fight. I was simply flying on autopilot at this point.

The bright light above made me squint as I glanced up at Reyn's throne. He wasn't looking at me, instead staring off at the far wall. I wondered what went through a beast's mind after stealing a woman's body from her. He appeared perfectly unbothered; content, even.

Swallowing, I grimaced at the sharp sting from the wood he'd shoved down my throat. His fingers had morphed into tree bark right before my eyes. That wasn't nearly as unnerving as whatever second dick he must've grown. I didn't get a look at it, but it felt much like the first one and I hated the idea of him having a second weapon to hurt me with.

The woman across from me didn't look frightened like the last one. Her mask was green, which I now knew meant something. In her case, she'd won three fights. With just two under my belt, my own covering was yellow.

She stood confidently, holding my gaze. I didn't have the strength for power moves, so I turned away, scanning the crowd. The faces staring back at me looked hungry. As I watched them, I felt fury rising in my chest. Rage began to overpower all of the other emotions; the pain, the despair, the humiliation and feeling of worthlessness that was setting in.

Fuck all of that.

Reyn may have broken me today, but he didn't get to win. I didn't roll over and give up. I'd been through bad things in my life. Maybe they weren't as bad as this or maybe they were just different, but I knew that I could find a way through this.

As soon as the light turned green, I sprinted to the other side of the cage. The woman dove away and I used her unstable footing to my advantage, kicking out at the side of her knee. She cried out, but didn't fall.

Rushing forward, she grabbed hold of my biceps. We both tried to get the upper hand, but it was like tug of war with evenly matched opponents. Neither of us made much headway before the other gained some traction.

Using your head in a situation like this was always the best way to go, which was why I did just that. Pain erupted across my skull when it collided with hers. Both of us stumbled back and tried to get our bearings. She recovered first and managed to wrestle me to the ground.

With her on top of me, I was at a disadvantage. I was taller than average and not built all that thin, but I was far from strong. Using that training room to my advantage was starting to sound like a better idea. Maybe I could make

Reyn think I was in there for his purposes and get back in his fake good graces. It might buy me some time without some horrific punishment at least.

I thrust my knee upward with as much force as I could. She grunted, but kept her position. Panic rose in my chest when she got her hands around my neck. My nails sliced through her skin and tears were pooling in her eyes, but she still didn't relent.

This was bad. I couldn't overpower her and the longer I went without breath, the weaker I became.

"Stop," I whispered. "I yield."

She shook her head. "There's no yielding."

No, no, no. I didn't want to go out this way. There was still so much for me to do. I refused to die as a captive in some illegal fighting ring run by fairies. Losing to this bitch was the last way I would've imagined it happening. At the top of my list was having my neck snapped by the beast upstairs.

As my eyes began to feel heavy, I looked up at him. His fingers were tight on the armrests of his chair and he looked furious. After all that talk about me fighting some mysterious creature for him, it must have made him feel like an idiot to see that he was wrong.

Something cold touched my fingers. I grabbed the object, not taking too long to ponder where the hell it had come from. With all of the strength I could muster, I lodged it into her side. Her grip loosened enough for me to draw in a deep breath.

Before she could try to collect herself, I kicked her in the stomach. She fell onto her back and I dropped down to straddle her. I would have felt bad about embedding the blade in her trachea if she hadn't been so ruthless when I'd asked her for mercy.

The wet sound made me gag. My empty stomach hurt so badly, I wasn't sure if I could stand. In the end, I wouldn't get the chance to find out. Everything got extremely blurry, the scene in front of me melding into one giant amalgamation of colors.

Entangled Realms

The last thing I saw was pale hair, then I was cradled against something warm. Too bad I'd dropped the knife. It might have been the perfect opportunity to lodge it into his heart. I guaranteed he couldn't heal from that wound.

🌹 🌹 🌹 🌹

"Are you sure you want to stay in here?" a woman's voice reached my ears.

"Yeah," I said, though I didn't remember where I was agreeing to stay. My room, I assumed, but if that was the case, where was she going?

"Promise me you'll be safe here. I don't want you wandering."

"I told you it's just a migraine. It'll pass. If it goes away soon, I'll meet you there."

"Alright. You call me if you want us to come get you."

Wait. No. Take me with you. I don't want to stay here.

"Just go," I laughed. "Get all that gross, cutesy shit out of your system so I don't have to see it later. That's probably why I have the migraine."

Please. It's just a migraine. It'll pass. Just bring me with you.

"I love you, ma belle fleur."

There was a smile in her tone, but I couldn't see it. In fact, I couldn't see anything. There was only darkness to accompany that voice and it felt infinite, just like the time since I'd last heard her speak to me.

I love you, ma belle fleur.

I hadn't even said it back because I was trying to be playful and flippant. Even though the migraine had felt like it was splitting apart my head, I hadn't wanted her to be concerned while she was out. She always worried herself sick.

Slowly, I began to recognize the feel of my own body. With consciousness came pain. My ass still hurt, which pissed me off. My back was sore and there was a throbbing in my head, but I'd grown used to it. The worst of it all was the burn in my throat. It felt like I'd swallowed gravel and when I tried to wet it, I found my mouth too dry.

"She's trembling."

The voice made me jump. I opened my eyes and was met with a jumbled blur of shapes and colors. I winced as I pulled crust from my eyelashes, then blinked away the bleariness.

The room was dark, save for the bit of sunlight streaming in from the closed curtains. Even that ignited a sharper pain behind my eyes. When I held my hand up to block it, someone whispered.

After removing my hand, I found barely enough light to see Portia. Another shape came up beside her, making me shrink back. He crouched beside the bed and reached out. I was ready to throw a punch at his face, but then I noticed his softer features and hair that was a few shades darker than Reyn's.

"What's going on?" I asked, noticing the way my words slurred slightly.

"Nothing." Portia assured me. "We're just making sure you'll be alright."

"You should've let me die."

Chester frowned and grasped my hand. "There was no reason for you to die."

"I don't want to do this," I admitted in a whisper.

He glanced at his sister, who nodded and retreated from the room. Now that we were alone, I felt awkward. I wasn't uncomfortable, surprisingly. I just didn't know what to expect.

"Are you going to hurt me?" I asked, grimacing when the words came out.

"Of course not. Why would I hurt you?"

"He does."

He let out a long sigh before sitting on the edge of the bed. "He's..."

"What?"

"He's a fucking idiot."

"Well, at least we can agree on something, though I'd use a much stronger expletive."

"He doesn't know what to do with you."

"Maybe he should treat me like everyone else and just bother me once in a while."

"But you're not like them."

"Right. I'm supposed to fight something for him. If he can't beat it, how the hell does he expect me to?"

"Reynaeros can't fight it."

My brow furrowed. "Why not?"

"It has to be someone else."

"Who made that stupid rule?"

"It's not my place to disclose the details."

He held out a muffin and I couldn't help but smile. My stomach was feeling questionable and the migraine wasn't helping, but neither would not eating, so I started picking at it slowly.

"If you agree to train with him, it will be better."

It was an effort not to roll my eyes. "I'm not sure I believe that."

"It's your choice."

"It's not, though. Really, it's just choosing how much I want to suffer."

He rolled his lips. "I'll talk to him."

My eyes widened. "You would do that?"

"I like you, Kiera. That's part of why I couldn't let you die in that ring."

"That was you? Wait, did you carry me out of there too?"

"I did."

Tears pricked my eyes and I blinked them away quickly. In this place, an act of kindness felt like a small miracle.

"I can't imagine he's too thrilled about what you did."

He shrugged. "This thing isn't only about him."

I wanted to ask what he meant by that, but he stood and headed for the door, smiling at me before he stepped into the hall. When the door shut behind him, I set the rest of the muffin on the nightstand, taking deep breaths to dispel the nausea.

It didn't work, so I decided to lie back down and try to sleep. I was so tired, I wished I could just stay in my bed for days.

Chapter 18

Kiera

"Well, color me surprised."

Ignoring him, I aimed another knife at the dummy. It hit the thing in the chest, but not with the blade. I frowned when it clattered to the floor beside the other ten.

"Knife throwing is clearly not your specialty."

Grabbing another, I pulled it over my shoulder, but quickly pivoted before I released it. He barely stepped out of the way in time to avoid a new hole in his face. From the look he gave me, I figured he was imagining using something sharp to open me up and pull out my insides.

"Oops," I offered, pasting on a sweet smile.

"Are your parents actually demons? It's the only explanation for what you are."

Gritting my teeth, I threw another knife and growled when it hit the dummy hilt-first. He snickered behind me and I went back to ignoring him, throwing a few more that didn't hit their mark.

"Alright, this is just pathetic at this point. Let me show you."

"No."

"The point is for me to train you.'

"No. It's for me to train. Nobody said it has to be you."

"I'm the only one that could possibly have a chance of making you worthy of this battle."

"Jesus. Do you have a god complex on top of being a massive dick?"

He grabbed my wrist and I immediately tried to pull away.

"Don't fucking touch me."

He pulled it back over my shoulder, then pushed the hilt of a knife into my hand. Relaxing slightly, I allowed him to move my arm through the motion of throwing it.

"You need to release it at the right time and in the correct way. This one's handle is heavier than the blade, so you hold it there. If you choose one with a heavier blade, you would flip it around."

"Well, that's what I've been doing, but it doesn't work."

"Learn to throw it the same way every time. Once you can do that, you can determine the distance you should be from your target. In a real battle, you won't always be able to be in that perfect position, but for now, we'll work based on ideal scenarios. Now, let me see you throw it again."

I did, only to fail. Grinding my teeth, I shook my head.

"This is impossible."

The corner of his mouth twitched. He took me by the shoulders and pushed me back a step, then turned me just slightly.

"Go again."

"It's not going to help."

"Shut the fuck up and go again."

I took the knife he offered and focused on throwing it the same way I had before. When it sunk into the dummy's stomach, I squealed, rising up on my toes. I repeated the throw a few times, making one of them, which was better than I'd been doing before at least.

"See? You're not completely useless."

"Was that a compliment?"

"No. It clearly only applies under my direction. Alone, you're nothing more than the average human."

"You know, if you train me to be a big, badass fighter, maybe I'll just use those skills to kill you."

"Maybe you will, but it's doubtful."

"What next, fairy boy?"

He dropped his head back and stared at the ceiling. I watched his hands fist at his sides and was torn between being amused and terrified of what he'd do. After a minute, his fingers relaxed and he motioned for me to follow him.

We made it to the other side of the room and he grabbed the rope hanging from the rafters. I looked up, feeling queasy at how high it was.

"Don't ask me to climb that."

"I'm not asking."

"Fuck. I can't."

"If you're afraid of heights, you'll have to move past it."

"I don't understand what this has to do with training. I'm not having a race with your mysterious monster."

"No, but if you can't even make it to the other end of this rope, you have no chance. An effective warrior learns to use everything at their disposal, including their environment. You can't utilize the things around you if you're too weak to use them."

"So, essentially, if I can climb up to the rafters, I can perform a better flying elbow leap on the enemy."

He raised a brow and his cheek twitched. Deciding it was better to avoid pissing him off too much, I took the rope and situated my hands. I pulled myself up, my arms immediately shaking with the effort. As soon as I removed one hand to reach higher, I lost my grip and dropped to the floor.

"Don't say a damn word," I warned, resuming my position.

"Fine. I'll leave you to it. Perhaps we'll be able to move onto the next lesson sometime before your human body gives out and dies."

"You won't have to wait very long," I muttered, grunting as I got my feet off the floor.

"Your dramatics are tiresome."

"Then leave."

He didn't reply and when I fell back to the ground, I realized that he was gone. Good. The last thing I needed was someone watching me fail repeatedly. Everything was harder to accomplish when there was an audience.

🌷 🌷 🌷 🌷

Climbing ropes was a pointless, ridiculous exercise. If I was able to do it, I might have felt differently, but for the last week I'd been trying and failing. Every day, I was more sore, which made it harder. I'd even been doing some weight training in an attempt to get stronger.

Clearly, Reyn was impatient and didn't know how the human body worked because he kept finding me and asking if I'd accomplished it yet, then he would insult me for being weak. I was constantly questioning why I was doing this shit. The fact that it would somehow benefit him would have been enough for me to continue refusing, but from what Chester had said, I assumed it was something that would help them too. I liked them enough to allow myself to care a little bit.

Reyn had been holding up his end of our previous bargain and he hadn't subjected me to his freaky dick since the night of my last fight, so that was a win in my book. The one thing he hadn't fulfilled yet was showing me the library. Every time I tried to bring it up, he brushed past it or walked away entirely. It was fucking annoying.

When I left my room, blueberry muffin in hand, I saw Portia walking down the hallway. I rushed to catch up with her and touched her arm.

"Oh, Kiera. How are you?"

"Fine. I wanted to ask you something."

She shifted on her feet. "You can ask."

"Can you show me where the library is?"

Her eyes widened. "No."

Entangled Realms

"No? But it's part of my deal with Reyn and he's being a bitch about it."

"That's between the two of you. I have no desire to anger him."

"You could just show me the door. I'm super curious what it looks like."

She gave me a pointed look and began walking again. I followed, staring at her the whole time, hoping she would get annoyed enough to simply oblige.

"Stop following me," she demanded when we were on the next floor.

"Come on. He wouldn't even know it was you."

"He would know it was either me or my brother."

"What's he gonna do? Throw a tantrum?"

She glanced sidelong at me before shaking her head. "You should be focusing on your training."

"I'd like to read a damn book so I can escape into a world significantly better than this one. A horror book, for example."

"Kiera, I won't help you. Now, I need you to stop following me."

"Maybe I'm interested in finding whatever secret door you're heading to."

She raised a hand and something sprung from it. I swore when it felt like dust got in my eyes. By the time I managed to clear them, she was nowhere to be found.

I really hated magic.

Approaching footsteps made me tense. They sounded like they were just around the corner, so I rushed through the first door I found. Before I closed it, I caught a glimpse of a broom and some shelves, then it was pitch black. I pressed an ear to the door, trying to control my breathing.

I wasn't sure why I was hiding. The training room was on this floor, so I was allowed here. It wasn't as if I could find my way into anywhere he didn't want me to go.

The person passed by the door and I released a breath. Cracking it, I caught a glimpse of Reyn's white hair before he turned the corner.

It occurred to me that tempting his ire was a very bad idea. Not once had it worked out for me and he had no qualms about upping the ante. Regardless, I slipped out of my shoes and silently went in the same direction. For all I knew, he could be heading to the library. I'd never gone this long without reading and it was really affecting my mental state. If I could just have this one thing, it might make everything slightly more bearable.

When I turned the corner, I saw him stepping through a green door. It closed behind him and now that I knew it existed, I could still see it if I focused my eyes just right. I waited a few moments to be safe, then cautiously went inside.

This corridor was different from the others. There was a buzzing in the air, like it was electrically charged. It reminded me of what passed between us sometimes when Reyn touched me, though it was significantly milder.

On top of that, it was short, more like a foyer than a hallway. My bare feet were met with soft grass that was a darker, deeper shade of green than I'd seen before. Ivy climbed up the walls, which looked like they were made of stone. From the ceiling hung various types of vines, some with flowers growing from them and others with deadly-looking thorns that dripped a milky liquid.

There was the click of a door shutting at the end of the hall on the left. I saw the handle release at the last second, which gave me just enough knowledge of the location for me to see it.

This one was harder for me to focus on. As I stared at it, the surface wobbled, the appearance resembling a heat mirage. Every time it solidified, it began to do it again.

Its strange state was the least interesting part of it. My heart raced madly as I stared at it, a mixture of fear and excitement coursing through me. The blood red door had officially been added to my list of known places. The question was: What would I do with the information?

Chapter 19

Reynaeros

My god, she was weak. It had been eight days and she could hardly make it halfway up the rope. It was pathetic, even for a human. Their kind truly had not won the genetic lottery.

Her arms began to tremble more fiercely, then she lost her grip. I took a step back, watching her land on her ass with a pained cry. The flooring absorbed much of the impact, yet she still acted dramatic about it. When she glared up at me, I raised a brow.

"Maybe I'd get this down faster if you caught me or something. My tail bone might never recover."

"If I made it more tolerable when you fell, you'd be less motivated to avoid it."

"I think you just like seeing me in pain."

With a smile, I strode over to the far side of the room and started throwing knives. She joined me, her throws far less skilled, but better than they were the first day. At least, she stuck a blade into the dummy about half the time, even though she generally failed to hit anywhere vital.

Her ineptitude made me feel conflicted about my original sentiment. There was something about her that made me think I was right, but I didn't see how it could be possible. If I wanted to, I could kill her in less than a second and she would be powerless to stop me. What was it about her that made her the one?

It was entirely possible I'd developed poor judgment in my old age. That or I was simply desperate and seeing things where they didn't actually exist. If she was the contender, I shouldn't have even needed to train her. It felt like that defeated the purpose.

I loathed curses and not only because they'd put me in this position. They were always ambiguous, shaped into some sort of riddle. It may have been straight forward or we could have completely misunderstood its meaning. The only thing we could do was take a chance and try. It certainly couldn't make anything worse.

She'd stopped throwing, so I looked over at her. Her face was pale as she stood with a hand on her chest. Her eyes were closed and she was breathing heavily, but slowly.

"Try climbing again," I instructed.

When she opened her eyes, she narrowed them at me. "I've done it enough times today."

"It's enough when I say it is."

"Just let me work on throwing knives."

"You aren't even doing that."

"I just needed a second."

"It's not a tiring activity."

She huffed and threw another one. When it missed, her face turned red. I felt her anger rising, rolling off of her in waves.

"You need to stop being so goddamn touchy."

"Touchy?" she repeated, her tone annoyingly high-pitched.

"Yes. It's a wonder you haven't exploded."

"If I could self-detonate right now, I'd do it in a heartbeat, simply because you're in my blast radius."

"You hate me, but it's no reason to have such foul energy. It's insufferable."

"Maybe not everything is about the great Rhinoceros," she nearly shouted as she yanked the blades free from the dummy.

Shaping my energy, I positioned a taut vine behind her. When she turned around, her ankle ran into it, making her fall forward. The knives clattered to the floor and she barely put her hands out in time to catch herself.

"You know, you look quite a bit more tolerable when you're kneeling."

When she looked up at me, her eyes were shining, but she had that now familiar look of defiance on her face. I despised it and I'd hoped we were past this, but clearly she had forgotten her place. Crouching in front of her, I grabbed her jaw and forced her to look at me.

"Little rose, you're not very good at self-preservation."

"Just..." Something in her expression changed and she was biting the inside of her cheek. After a deep breath, she shook her head. "Please just let me throw the knives."

The softness of her voice surprised me. Whatever game she was playing, I wouldn't fall for it.

"I'll give you a choice. The first option is climbing the rope until you're so tired that you cannot move."

"And the second?"

"You can throw knives, go to sleep, cry in a corner, or whatever else you do. I'm just going to fuck you first."

She set her jaw and averted her gaze. As I waited for her to decide, I tried to quell my impatience. It was difficult when I could read nothing in her eyes.

"Why are you even giving me a choice? It's not like you have any other time."

"You chose to be a pain in my ass, which directly led to two of the instances, so I beg to differ."

She put two fingers to her temple, rubbing it firmly. "Fine. Let's get it over with."

It was difficult to hide my surprise. I was completely unnerved when she readily began to remove her shorts. I followed suit with my own pants, trying not to become too annoyed when her lip curled as she looked at my dick.

I moved toward her, but she held up a hand. Ignoring her, I put my hands on her thighs, trying to push them apart.

"Jesus. Stop."

"That's not how this works, Kiera."

"Right now, it works the way I want it to. I've agreed to suffer through this horrible thing, so you can chill the fuck out on the whole getting turned on by rape thing."

I opened my mouth to argue and she put her hand over it. My teeth sharpened and just when I was about to bite her for daring to do such a thing, she touched my dick. Sucking in a sharp breath, I grabbed both her wrists, pulling them away from me.

She wrestled against my hold, making me laugh at her weakness. Using my grip, I pushed her onto her back and hovered over her.

"Reyn," she warned.

I resisted voicing how much I despised it when she called me that. It was part of this ridiculous bargain I'd been forced to make with her.

"Why are you holding me down?" she asked, her voice hitching.

"Because you're playing a game."

"No, I'm not."

"You touched me."

"You want to get off. That's what I'm doing."

"I don't understand what you're going on about."

Her thrashing stopped, the intensity of her gaze making me grit my teeth. I felt my eyes shifting and blinked a few times.

"Have you never been with someone without forcing them?"

"Kiera, we have a deal."

"Just fucking hold on for a second."

Huffing, I released her and leaned back on my heels. "Having a conversation is unnecessary."

"I'm a very curious person and it's possible I'm about to change your life."

"This sounds like one of your dramatic antics."

"Just answer the question."

"It's not possible."

"Why?"

"Humans are not interested in something they do not understand. Now, I'm done answering your pointless questions."

She rubbed her temple again, then looked down at my dick. I was considering blindfolding her or turning her onto her stomach again. When she scooted forward, I narrowed my eyes, trying to determine what her mode of attack would be.

"Can you control the, uh, barbs?"

"Yes, if I wish, but I do not."

"Alright, look... I'm going to do this so we can get this shit over with and I can go back to my room and consider drowning myself in the tub. You have to keep those things under the skin, though."

"Kiera-"

"Lie back."

"No."

She gave me an exasperated look. "Just do it."

This new game was convoluted. She didn't appear to be backing down and while I could simply force her to stay put, I decided to see where this would go. As soon as she attacked, I could have something wrapped around her neck or embed a thorn in her side.

When I was on my back, she planted her knees on either side of my thighs. She grasped my shaft and I swore.

"What language was that?"

I dipped my chin to look at her. "Mine."

Bending down, she brought her mouth closer to my dick. I immediately reached out to stop her. If biting it off was her new game, I wouldn't hesitate to kill her, regardless of the damned curse.

She caught my wrists and pinned them to the ground. Thorns poked at her skin, ready to pierce through her palm.

"Chill out. Haven't you been here long enough to know what a blow job is?"

The word was familiar to me and I had a vague idea of what it meant, but I didn't understand the point. Why would I want someone to put my dick in their mouth like it was food? I'd much rather fuck them.

Her tongue touched the head and my hips moved upward on their own. She released my wrists and put her hands on my thighs, trailing her tongue down the underside of my shaft. My barbs twitched under the skin, wanting to latch onto something, but I kept them firmly rooted.

Her lips closed around me, enveloping me in the heat of her mouth. My senses felt like they were overloaded as her tongue circled my head. She slowly took more of me in her mouth, then her eyes raised to meet mine. What I saw there, combined with her energy, made it extremely clear she wasn't happy to be doing this, but that didn't matter. For some reason, she preferred to do this than to have me fuck her today, and I couldn't be upset about it if I tried.

She looked away from me before moving further down. My fingers pressed into the floor, the force making them ache. I was itching to do something with them, but I didn't know what.

It took her a few moments to work me all the way inside of her. The feeling of her throat bobbing, tightening around my tip, made my lips part. I continued watching her as she pulled back to the tip, then buried me again. It had only been a couple of minutes when I felt myself nearing my orgasm. It was ridiculous; it didn't make any sense that this had so much power over me.

She increased her pace and my hands fisted. Various plants burst from the ground around us. Saplings, thorny bushes, flowers that could kill a human with a single touch. Her movements stopped and she looked up at me again.

"I'm not going to hurt you right now," I assured her, making the ones closest to her wither.

There was a certain amount of fear laced with her energy, but she resumed what she was doing. My hips arched up to meet her movements and my breaths quickened. A slew of words in my own language were coming from my mouth. I just couldn't keep them at bay, even though I hadn't uttered anything in this tongue for nearly a century.

When I couldn't take any more, I clenched my teeth and let the pleasure take me. I inadvertently thrust a hand through her soft hair, gripping it tightly at the roots and not caring if it pained her. She grunted as I came in her mouth, then swallowed a few times. I didn't know how I felt about her drinking my cum, yet it ignited a strange feeling in my stomach.

She quickly moved back and I released her hair, my hand hovering in the air for a moment. Without a word, she pulled her shorts back on and rushed out of the training room. I watched her go, unable to turn away until the door closed behind her.

Fuck. I had an intense fear that I'd just inadvertently given her a modicum of power. From the beginning I told her that was something she'd never have. From that smug look she'd given me before she started, I knew that this move had been very deliberate. She was playing a game alright and I had been too blind to see its true direction.

Madilyn DeRose

Chapter 20

Kiera

As I threw up the last of what was in my stomach, I put a hand over my forehead and tried to hold back my tears. My body was trembling and I felt far too warm, despite the cool temperature of the tile. I didn't feel good and I hadn't since the other day in the training room. Longer than that, but it was worse right now.

Sucking Reyn's dick was something I'd never wanted to do, but at the time it had seemed better than letting him fuck me. I'd been in pain and didn't think I could endure whatever he might feel like doing that day. When I learned that he didn't even understand the concept, I knew it would be a quicker and slightly less horrific experience right then.

It was clear it had blown his mind, which both unnerved me and gave me a sense of power over him. He'd lost control of his magic for a moment and even though it had rightfully made me fear him, it was the first time he'd told me he wouldn't hurt me. It was also the first time anything he'd done that was remotely nice had been genuine.

If I wanted to gain the upper hand in any situation with him, I could probably start using that to my advantage. I hadn't seen him in the training room since, but I was sure he'd show up soon. Apparently the only time he would be slightly agreeable was when I was giving him new, mind-altering experiences. If I was willing to drop to my knees when he was being particularly gruesome, I could save myself some pain.

The idea made me nauseous all over again, but there was nothing for me to expel from my stomach. I braced a hand on the counter and used it to get to my feet, trying to ignore the throbbing in my muscles. This training regimen might kill me before anything else could.

I brushed my teeth, then headed out into the hallway. I found Lucy and Collie in the game room putting together a puzzle with a lion on it, looking content in a way I hadn't known for a while. Maybe their acceptance of this made it easier, but to me it felt like the phrase 'ignorance is bliss.' I thought I'd rather be miserable and true to myself than delusional.

"Hey," I greeted, sitting on the floor in front of the couch.

"Hi Kiera," Lucy replied cheerily.

Collie muttered a greeting while she scrutinized a puzzle piece. There was a nasty bruise on her face that I tried to not to stare at. I didn't know how the fighting schedule worked and I hadn't thought to ask, since it didn't affect me right now.

Up until this point, I hadn't even thought about what the other girls would think about that, but from the stares and whispers since I'd walked in here, it struck me that they might have an opinion about it.

"You don't look good," Lucy noted.

"Thanks."

"I'm not being hostile, I swear. You just look tired."

"I've barely slept since coming here and I've been working too hard, but I'll be okay. Anything exciting happening around here while I've been busy?"

"Not really. Things don't really change."

"Leander has been down here a lot more," Collie said.

My nose wrinkled. "I haven't seen him."

"Then you're lucky. He's been extra... rough."

"That's terrible. I'm sorry you guys have to deal with that dickwad."

"He doesn't bother me," Lucy shrugged.

"Why not?"

"He hates me. I'm a good fighter, though, so he keeps me around for that."

I almost wanted to laugh at the fact that he didn't use her that way because he didn't like her. I could imagine her annoying the hell out of him. Honestly, good for her. Fighting still sucked, but silver linings or whatever.

Her comment had me thinking about this mysterious foe, though. It was clear as day that I wasn't the best fighter here. I didn't have the most potential and I wasn't bloodthirsty. There was no reason for him to pick me for this special fight. I couldn't even climb a damn rope.

"You should use the training room with me," I suggested. "I bet you could teach me a lot."

Her eyes widened. "Leander would kill us both if you brought someone else with you."

"Well, he can suck my dick."

She snorted a laugh, her eyes lighting up. "You're a troublemaker, Kiera. Anyone else would have been dead by now."

"That's what happens when you're his special little whore."

All three of us looked at the woman in the corner. She didn't seem to be paying attention to us while she sketched something on a pad.

"Don't be a bitch, Vera," Lucy scolded, her tone sharp. From the way she glared at her, I assumed they weren't buddies.

Entangled Realms

"It's only true. She clearly has him under some spell. I bet she lets him stick it in her ass."

I set my jaw, trying to keep my lip from trembling at her comment. Collie sat forward, setting the puzzle piece on the table.

"She's helping him with something. Don't start a problem."

Two other women came up beside Vera, looking at me with barely concealed disdain.

"She doesn't have to fight," one of them sneered. "She hasn't been subjected to his angry fucking the past few days. Every day, she has fancy muffins and there are always fresh roses in her room."

"You've been in my room?"

"You never know what's going on down here while you're gone for hours with the monster."

I got to my feet, taking a step toward them. They stood their ground, their stances threatening. When Collie and Lucy moved to stand beside me, I felt a little better, but the last thing I wanted to do was get into a fight. There was enough of that going on here already.

"Back off," Lucy warned when one of them stepped forward.

"What are you gonna do? All I have to do is throw an apple at you and you'll be cowering in fear."

The other girls laughed, which just pissed me off. Lucy grabbed my elbow and tugged me backward, shaking her head.

"Come on."

Hesitating, I glanced at the girls again. They looked smug about the whole situation. It was infuriating, wrong. Deciding she was right, though, I followed her into the hall.

"I hate them," Collie muttered.

"You'd think we would all want to stick together in this place," I noted.

Lucy looped her arm through my elbow, leading me further down the hall. "It's human nature to form hierarchies. They hate me because he doesn't fuck me, but you can't let it get to you. They're just bitter and have nothing better to do."

"It makes me feel bad. It doesn't seem fair."

"Who cares? We're all suffering in our own ways in this place."

It was the first time she'd so clearly expressed how bad this place was. I wasn't sure what part she was referring to, considering she didn't seem all that pressed about the fights and she didn't endure the rape like everyone else. I didn't think I had a right to ask something so personal.

"Just steer clear of them," she went on. "They beat the shit out of someone a few months ago."

"Jesus. What for?"

"Entertainment maybe. I don't really know. They're not good people."

"There seems to be no shortage of those around here."

"You've got us." She grinned at me, tugging me into her bedroom. "Now, you're going to spill the beans. I've been dying to know what secret mission you're a part of."

🌷 🌷 🌷

"That wasn't all that impressive."

Groaning, I twisted around from my place on the floor to glare at Chester. He was standing just inside the training room, looking at me with amusement.

"Did you come to add to Reyn's arsenal of insults?"

"No. I'm here to train you."

"Oh. I haven't seen him for a few days. Did I finally convince him to give up on me?"

He chuckled, but there was something in his eyes that made me wonder what the true answer was. When he made it over to me, he grabbed the rope and began climbing up with an agility I couldn't dream of. Within a minute, he pulled himself onto the rafter and looked down at me.

"It's easy."

"Well, you have an unknown level of magical ability and god knows what else. I'm not inclined to think a comparison is fair."

"Your head is holding you back."

"No. It's literally my wimpy muscles."

Something hurtled toward me at an alarming speed. I screamed, trying to leap out of the way, but it wrapped around my waist and lifted me off the ground. Clawing at it didn't help one bit and only made my fingers hurt.

The cord was replaced by an arm around my waist, steadying me when I was set gently on the rafter. I looked down and immediately felt dizzy.

"I told you. The idea of getting too high scares you because at a certain point, the fall becomes deadly for you."

"And how does this help?"

"Here's how."

His grip disappeared from around me so suddenly, I lost my footing. My arms flailed, but I couldn't find purchase on anything. The next second, I was no longer standing on anything solid and the floor was approaching at an alarming rate.

This was it. My naivety would be the death of me in the end. Chester had soft features and an award winning smile, so I'd placed my trust in him. Now, I was about to become goo on the training room floor for some sort of sick entertainment.

I closed my eyes tightly, not wanting to know exactly when it was going to happen. Something soft touched me, spreading across my body. There was no pain or jarring impact at least, which was more than I could've hoped for. I wondered if this was a cloud I was now floating on like a little cherubim. If I had to learn how to play the harp, I was going to be pissed.

"Stop being afraid, Kiera."

My eyes flew open. I gasped when I found myself just above the floor. There was some sort of bush that was almost cradling me, its vines soft, yet firm around me. It slowly sunk back into the ground, leaving me safely on the floor with no trace of anything strange ever happening.

Chester swung down on a vine, which withered and disappeared after he released it. I looked from him to the rafter, then to the floor, trying to wrap my head around what was going on.

"You're not going to get hurt in here."

"How?"

"It was made by us. Its very bones are alive and if your fall is going to be fatal, it'll reach out to alleviate the danger."

"That's insane. What's with the plants? Are you guys actually fairies?"

"No," he laughed. "If you need to conceptualize it, I guess we'd be closest to what your world knows as a Dryad. We're significantly better, though."

"Isn't that technically a branch of fairies?"

He pursed his lips, making me laugh.

"Don't tell Reynaeros I told you and especially don't call him a fairy."

"I already have been."

"No wonder he's been in a mood."

"He deserves to have his comfortable little life rocked a little bit."

The amusement drained from Chester's face and he averted his gaze. Clearing his throat, he motioned toward the rope.

"You might still struggle with it because your body isn't used to it, but conquering the mind removes a massive barrier to your success."

"Why wouldn't he tell me about this if he wanted me to accomplish it so badly?"

"He wanted you to figure it out on your own. It means he thinks you're smart enough, so don't take it as an insult."

"I'm assuming that means you disagree about my intelligence."

Entangled Realms

The smile returned to his face. "No, I simply don't think it matters how you get there, just that you do. Perhaps I'm impatient and not quite as stubborn as he is."

"Thank you," I said sincerely.

He put a hand on my shoulder and squeezed it. "This is important to all of us, even if you can't understand it. Regardless of your disdain for each other, I know that he has a certain amount of respect for you."

"I doubt that."

"You challenge him and he hates that. You know what I think, though?"

"What?"

"You should keep fucking with him. It's quite entertaining to see him knocked off his pedestal. He's been on it for a few centuries too long."

I couldn't help but smile. Making his life hell was one hundred percent part of my long-term plan if I was going to be forced to live here. I didn't know how long-term it would be, but I'd keep at it nonetheless.

As I looked up at the rafter again, I took a deep breath. There was an ache settling in behind my eyes, but I grabbed onto the rope and tried to dispel the fear that had held me back before. Even if I didn't get it on the first try, I felt more confident that I eventually would.

Chapter 21

Reynaeros

Gripping my jaw, I paced in front of the door to the training room. Kiera hadn't been on her floor, so I had to assume she was in here. I'd been avoiding her for nearly a week and I didn't know why. She was tiresome, for one. Annoying and infuriating were also fitting.

Focusing on the room, I reached out to feel her energy. It was angry, as usual, but not as volatile as previous encounters with her. I was sure that would change as soon as I walked through the door.

"Fuck!"

I rushed inside, looking around for her and fully expecting to find her impaled on a sword due to her ineptitude. She wasn't anywhere to be found, though. There was no visible blood, nor did I smell any. Her energy hadn't shifted to pain, but to something lighter with a sort of vibration to it.

She laughed, the sound coming from above. My eyes widened when I saw her on the rafter, hands on her hips and staring up at the ceiling. Her chest was rising and falling rapidly and when her head dipped to look at the floor, there was a huge smile on her face.

I stared at her, noting the way it made her eyes crinkle at the corners and made two little indents appear on the sides of her mouth. When she saw me there, her lips immediately thinned, though the brightness in her eyes remained.

"If I leap from here, I won't die, right?"

"No."

She hesitated for only a moment before shrugging and stepping over the edge. I knew the room would catch her, but something made me reach out with my own hammock of twining branches to catch her halfway in the air. I lowered her to the floor, then withdrew them back into my body.

"That's kind of gross," she said, wrinkling her nose in my direction.

I couldn't help but laugh. "Gross?"

"Yeah. Nasty. Odious. Repulsive. It gave me the ick."

"Yes, I understand the meaning of the word. I do speak English."

"You didn't know about blowjobs, so forgive me if I didn't know."

My stomach felt uncomfortable at her words. Shaking it off, I looked up at the rafter.

"It's about time you made it up there. I thought I'd have to rid myself of you and search for someone new."

"Mm. Right. From what I've gathered, there's no one as dope as I am."

"I think I preferred you when there was nothing but rage inside of you."

She rolled her eyes. "You know, I was thinking that Lucy might be able to help train me."

"Absolutely not," I said immediately.

"Why not?"

"What would she be able to do?"

"She's the best fighter you have. Honestly, I don't see how she's not the better option-"

"This isn't so simple as being a good fighter. If that were the case, I would have kidnapped every professional in existence."

"Then give me the details."

"It's unnecessary."

"I beg to differ. If you want me to help you and your people with whatever the fuck sort of beast is threatening you, most definitely at the cost of my life, I want details."

With a groan, I motioned to the rope. "Show me you can do it again."

"That's not-"

"For fuck's sake, Kiera. Show me."

Her anger heightened and she narrowed her eyes, but grabbed the rope and began pulling herself up. She was shaking the entire time and releasing annoying little grunts, but I could already tell she was considerably better than she had been a week ago. As she pulled herself onto the rafter, I wrapped a vine around it and let it bring me to the top.

"That's cheating," she said.

"Using every tool in one's arsenal cannot be considered cheating."

"Alright, fairy boy. It's your game, so your rules, I guess."

Taking a deep breath, I refrained from kicking her from the beam. It wouldn't kill her anyway, but it didn't serve my purposes right now. I stepped toward her, taking in her appearance.

There was sweat on her forehead and her skin was flushed. Behind the coloring, she looked quite pale from her time stuck inside. Some strands had escaped from her bun and I reached out to wrap one around my finger. She swatted my hand away, moving back.

The corner of my mouth lifted as I watched her try to retreat. I advanced on her quickly, nearly making her tumble over the edge. Wrapping an arm around her waist, I steadied her, then backed her into the wall.

Entangled Realms

"What are you doing?" she asked, her voice strong and slightly threatening. It was amusing to see her put on the façade that made her feel powerful.

"It's been a week since I've had you, little rose, and it seems that there is a reason to celebrate today."

"Celebrating would be not having to endure your touch. Besides, I heard you've been on a sexual rampage, so I'm sure your dick is just fine without stealing from me."

"Things are very stressful," I mused. "Fucking happens to be the most effective outlet."

"Then go pick one of your other harem girls."

"No."

Her rage practically slapped me in the face. I felt it so wholly, it made me feel angry along with her. Pushing a hand into the front of her pants, I lengthened my middle finger and thrust it inside of her. She hissed, trying to close her legs against me.

Removing my hand, I held it up in front of me. "I'm curious about something."

"Then Google it."

"You tasted me. Is that a normal thing for humans to do?"

She pursed her lips and I thought she might have been trying to smother a smile.

"Do not mock me."

"Why not? You're basically a teenage boy learning about sex."

"I do not need to learn about it. I am nearly as old as your species."

Her eyes widened. "That's disgusting."

"Does it work the same way?" I asked, ignoring her insults.

"Does what work the same way?"

"Does a man... taste a woman?"

"Uh, sure. If they give a shit about their pleasure."

"Hmm."

Tentatively, I brought my finger to my lips. I could smell her on it and it wasn't repulsive, but I still failed to see the point of this. Allowing her to have such power over me was unacceptable, though, and if I could regain that power, I would do it.

When I closed my lips around it, her lip curled. I, on the other hand, was... confused. It was not what I expected, nor was it unpleasant. Having it in my mouth was not like tasting food. This didn't ignite a physical sort of hunger, but I found myself intrigued and possibly aroused by it.

While I wanted to take control from her, I actually had very little understanding of how female human anatomy worked. None of the women I'd fucked seemed to particularly enjoy it. Of course, I did not give a shit about that and forcing them clearly erased any pleasure they might have taken from the act. Admitting my ignorance was unacceptable, so I'd simply have to learn before attempting it with her.

When I pushed her leggings down, she started to fight me, as she always did. I freed my dick before locking my fingers around her throat. I felt her swallow hard, but she betrayed no other signs of distress. If she thought she'd somehow come out on top again, she was sorely mistaken.

Sliding my dick along her a few times, I waited for it to sufficiently lubricate her. I took one of her legs under the thigh and lifted it around my hip to give me better access. I pushed inside of her, making her whimper a little and drop her head back against the wall.

Satisfied that the fight had gone out of her, I began to thrust into her hard. I tightened my grip on her, something about this position bringing me a more powerful sense of pleasure. After a few minutes, her eyes opened and she locked her gaze on me intently.

Looking down at where we were connected, I tried to ignore her. It was difficult when she was radiating fucking rage. I couldn't stand being around it so much. Even when I avoided her, I could feel the shifts, the moments she felt it more powerfully. It made me want to find her so that I could do something to make it stop. Throw her from a high branch perhaps.

I nearly jumped out of my skin when she put a hand under my shirt. Her touch traveled up to my chest, then the other hand followed. My muscles tensed beneath her palms and I gritted my teeth.

"Stop it."

"Why?" she asked, cocking her head as she continued to stare.

"I don't enjoy this."

"Are you sure? Maybe this is one of those things you just don't understand yet."

"Kiera, remove your hands from my body."

"Mm. No."

Despite her words, she did as I asked. Before I could feel too relieved, she went for the buttons, quickly undoing each of them. With my free hand, I grabbed one of her wrists, but she still managed with just the one. When my shirt was open in the front, she leaned forward and licked up my chest.

My breath hitched, making her breathe a laugh. With a growl, I gripped her thigh hard enough to make her swear. Narrowing her eyes, she wound her arm around my neck, making my skin prickle. She tightened her grip, then lifted her other leg off the floor.

Before she could fall, I released her wrist and grabbed onto her thigh. Holding her like that against the wall, I reached deeper inside of her and had better control of my movements. It felt so good, I dropped my head against the side of her neck, my lips parting as I tried to regain control of myself.

Ivy spread outward from the tips of my fingers, wrapping around her legs. She made an alarmed sound and tried to squirm out of my hold, so I tightened my grip.

"Stop being a coward, little rose."

"Fuck you," she said through gritted teeth.

"You're maddening."

"Yeah, well, you're insufferable and disgusting."

The plant winding around her body cinched tighter, tiny thorns appearing along its vines. She sucked in a sharp breath as they pricked her, the smell of her blood reminding me that she didn't have any true power here. I could crush her in an instant.

Moving my lips to her ear, I let the sharpened tips scratch her skin. "You can insult me, attack me, try in vain to gain the upper hand. Never forget that no matter what you do, you will be full of my cum whenever I desire it." The vines traveled up to her neck, wrapping around it. "Your very breath belongs to me, little rose."

She pushed her fingers through my hair, ripping the tie free. I gritted my teeth when it tugged on the strands. Tightening her grip, she tipped my face toward her. I met her gaze, meeting the challenge that lay there.

"You're wrong," she whispered before dragging her tongue over my lower lip.

When my mouth opened, she took it between her teeth, tugging it outward and applying pressure. I was still watching those eyes as pleasure rippled down my spine. I had no control over the orgasm that nearly whited out my vision. An unfettered sound came from my throat and when the feeling passed, my body was trembling.

She dropped her legs and removed her arms from around my neck. After quickly adjusting her clothes, she leapt straight off the rafter. I watched her leave, feeling a sense of déjà vu as the door closed behind her.

Sitting on the rafter, I let my legs hang over the edge. What the hell had just happened and how had I lost control of the situation so quickly?

Chapter 22

Kiera

Reyn seemed to be avoiding me again, which I found hilarious. I'd felt even more satisfaction making him fall apart this time. The look on his face was a mixture of shock and absolute confusion. It was laughable that he'd been alive for such a long time and was as ignorant as a virgin without internet access.

It didn't even take much. I was incredibly inexperienced, but I'd found a way to bend him to my will, at least in a certain regard. Could I get him to show me the library or end this whole underground harem fighting ring? Absolutely not. Taking away his sense of power was enough for me.

I left the cafeteria carrying a plate of fruit I intended to eat in my room. It was too bright and loud in there right now, since it was dinnertime. Plus, Lucy and Collie weren't at our table and I had no desire to sit there awkwardly.

As I passed a few of the other girls, they eyed me suspiciously. One even seemed to snarl. The whole thing was ridiculous. It wasn't as if I'd been given a better lot than them. At least they probably had good lives before this and fond memories to look back on when they were feeling down. Some of us could never shake the cloud that cast shadows over our past.

Regardless of how they felt or what their lives had been like, there was no doubt we'd all die here. I certainly wouldn't live a long and healthy life and neither would they because one day they would lose a fight. That would be it for them. Whether they considered that a mercy was up to them.

Settling on my bed with my ankles crossed, I slowly started to eat my fruit. It was light enough that I hoped I could stomach it. As long as that asshole didn't come crawling in here looking for some action, I thought I'd be okay.

Now that I'd conquered the climbing rope, I wasn't exactly sure what I was meant to be doing. Chester had joined me in the training room a couple times and worked with me on throwing knives, but I didn't know what the point was. Nobody had given me any information about this mysterious villain and I had no idea what was expected of me.

The longer I did this, the more ridiculous I felt. It was like some book with an unlikely hero. The thing was, I didn't fit that persona. I wasn't strong or significantly smarter than anyone else. In reality, my body was weak and there was no telling how long it would even hold out.

Shaking my head, I put my empty plate on the nightstand and sunk further down. I was so tired that my eyes quickly became heavy. I wasn't sure how long I dozed for or if I even fully sank into sleep.

It was the shivering that woke me up and set off alarm bells in my head. This place was always the perfect temperature somehow; I'd never been cold like this. I was going to pull the covers over me, but I felt a breeze.

Looking at the window, my heart rate sped up when I saw that it had been shattered. The curtains were swaying with the wind, which brought a bitter chill inside.

Cautiously, I set my feet on the floor and approached it, stopping at the end of the bed when I realized there was glass in my path.

Taking a step back, I intended to head for the door, but I bumped into something. Before I could turn around, fingers locked around my biceps firmly. I flailed and let out a scream. When my elbow connected with something, a man swore.

He shoved me forward and the glass cut into my feet, making me fall forward. My skin burned with the slices the shards made on my hands and knees. I tried to get up, but putting more weight on any part of my body just made them dig in further.

An arm wrapped around my waist and lifted me completely off the ground. A moment later, I was thrown onto the bed on my back. It took me a second to focus my eyes, but when I did, I was filled with a visceral terror.

The person standing at the side of the bed wasn't someone that I recognized. He had a mask covering the bottom half of his face and dark eyes stared at me intently. When a second man joined him, I couldn't contain my whimper.

"What do you want?"

The first man chuckled menacingly. "We're here to take care of a problem, little girl."

"A problem?"

"You."

He put a knee on the mattress and nausea rose in my throat. I tried to move back, but the second man grabbed onto my ankles to keep me in place.

"Please, I don't know what I did."

"We want information on the beast."

"I don't understand. Are you talking about Rey- uh, about Leander?"

"Look, Paul, she has a brain cell. I do love the intelligent ones. They tend to fight harder."

"I don't know anything," I insisted.

"Of course you do. You've been in his lair, little girl. Spending time with him. Getting in his good graces."

"I'm not. He hates me. There's nothing I can tell you."

"That's too bad. We'll just have to find another way to bring this place down."

"You're trying to rescue everyone?"

He laughed. "No. Just a couple."

"Then why don't you just do that? Their rooms are somewhere in this corridor."

He grabbed my wrist and held it up so that I was looking at the rose. "This is like a lock. He'll always be able to find you."

The idea of that made my stomach constrict, but not as much as it did when I heard a belt unbuckling. Panic rose in my chest, making my breaths ragged.

"I didn't do anything to you. Please."

"See, my sister doesn't like you. That means I don't. Since you're that freak's special little whore, that makes me even more interested in ruining you."

"How do you know anything about me?"

"We have our ways of exchanging information, whore."

"This isn't going to help you against him. M-maybe I can do some recon. Get information for you."

"You said yourself that he hates you."

"But I can change that."

He snorted. "Nice try. I'd much rather desecrate his plaything so that he throws you away. He'll be disgusted by the state of you."

I struck out at him, but it was pointless. He easily gathered both my wrists in one hand and thrust them above my head while he pushed his pants down. He groaned as he stroked his dick and tears began to fall from my eyes.

"When we're done with you, you'll be so used up, you won't be able to breathe without feeling all the ways we fucked you."

The second guy got on the bed, settling closer to my head. He had his dick in his hand and smiled as he looked

Entangled Realms

down at me. When he brought it to my lips, I turned away, but he fisted my hair and forced me into the position he wanted.

With his other hand, he gripped my jaw tightly, forcing me to open my mouth. I screamed, then it was cut off when he thrust all the way inside. Pain flared between my legs when the other man invaded me.

With my hands secured and my head held in place, I was completely at their mercy. Powerless. A fuck toy to two men that thrived on my pain in a way beyond what Reyn had ever done to me.

They thoroughly used me in every way. They struck every part of my body except my face, claiming that they didn't want Reyn to see my shame until he undressed me. They continually emphasized how disgusting he would find me and how he'd dispose of me in horrific ways for being a whore to more than just him.

By the time they left, I was in a state of complete apathy. The emotions were there, they'd just been so overused for hours that I didn't feel them right now. I'd run out of tears, but my body still shook violently with sobs, mostly because of the pain. It was excruciating.

Eventually, I managed to drag myself to the bathroom where I sat on the bench in the shower for hours, cleaning myself slowly. The water had run cold, but I didn't care. I didn't even really feel it anymore.

After getting out, I saw a glimpse of myself in the mirror and almost screamed with the anger and humiliation I was overcome with. Nearly every inch of my skin was covered in bruises that were still darkening. There were cuts, scratches, and bite marks deep enough that I feared they'd never fade.

I pulled on a sweatshirt and leggings, making sure I was covered up to my neck. The window had somehow repaired itself, seemingly for the same reason the training room did weird shit. Magic or whatever. There was no indication that anything horrific had happened in this place and I didn't know if that made it better or worse.

The door flung open and I jumped, wincing when the sudden movement pained me. Reyn stood there, his chest rising and falling rapidly. His gaze landed on me and his brow furrowed.

"What's going on?" he demanded.

"I don't know what you mean."

My voice was hoarse, gravelly. It hurt to speak and I had to work hard not to cough from the scratchiness.

"Are you bleeding?"

"It's just my, uh, period."

He approached me and I reared back, pressing my back against the wall. The way he cocked his head made my blood run cold. It was as if he was sizing me up, deciding whether or not he would take a bite out of me.

The men's words from the night before came back with full force. I was utterly terrified of what would happen if he found out. If he even touched me, he'd know something was wrong. He'd kill me right then and there. Dying in this place was inevitable, but staring it in the face right now with no control over it frightened me to my core.

"You're afraid," he said, sounding surprised.

"No."

"I can feel it, Kiera. What's going on?"

"I d-don't want you here. Please just leave."

"Is it me you're afraid of right now?"

"Yes."

His mouth opened, then closed again. There seemed to be a war going on in his mind, but I had no idea who the contenders were. He set his jaw and took another step forward. I closed my eyes, planting my palms flat against the wall as I waited for him to hurt me.

I felt him brush his fingers over my cheekbone and I couldn't contain my pathetic whimper. At this point, it was taking every ounce of strength I had left to hold myself together as well as I was.

"If it's because of the fight, I will find someone else."

My eyes opened and I flinched at how close he was. "Fight?"

"Yes. For Vera since she's sick. She told Chester you volunteered to take her place."

"Oh."

"Is that not what you want?"

Staring past him, I chewed on the inside of my cheek. The attack made a little bit more sense now. I hadn't thought too much about it when they were speaking to me last night, but obviously it was that bitch. She had some balls, that was for sure.

"Who is the fight against?"

"Tori. Kiera, something feels like it isn't adding up. What is going on?"

"Nothing," I assured him quickly.

I knew Tori was one of the girls that had been with Vera in the room when they confronted me, but I couldn't remember which one. It didn't really matter. Either I'd get the honor of killing her or she'd end my life. At least I could say I'd given it my all.

I doubted they'd leave me alone for a second, especially if Reyn let me out of the fight. It would only intensify their feeling that he was favoring me somehow. He simply didn't want to lose the person that was allegedly supposed to help him, but I wasn't allowed to give them those details. If I could kill Tori, maybe they'd back off a little.

"Lucy will take your place," he said, turning toward the door.

Latching onto his wrist, I stopped him. "No. I just woke up from a nap and was sort of groggy. I'm happy to take Vera's place."

His jaw worked as he thought about it. "I can't risk you losing. You have a purpose."

"If I lose, then obviously I wasn't the one you were looking for. Besides, I've been training, which isn't something anyone else has been able to do. I'll kick her ass in five seconds flat."

He seemed to relax just slightly. "Fine. If you die, I'm going to be vexed."

"I'll make sure not to die. I'm sure you'll throw my body in the dumpster and that just sounds like a grotesque resting place."

"That's terrible."

"What?"

"Living things should always return to the Earth."

"Oh. Okay."

"You have until six."

Without another word, he retreated from the room and I let out a heavy breath bordering on a sob. He hadn't found out. If I could just keep him at bay until my body healed, maybe I'd be okay. I just had to get through this fight somehow.

Chapter 23

Kiera

After telling Portia I was having bad cramps, she gave me something that helped a lot with my pain. I didn't know if it was magic or some good prescription, but my wounds had settled into more of a dull ache. Even though it got worse with movement, I thought I might have a chance out there. Just in case, I'd pocketed one of my plate shards, which I intended to lodge directly into her neck.

The sound of the crowd grew unbearably loud as soon as I opened the door into the ring. My head pounded incessantly, breaking straight through the efforts of the medication. Shaking it off, I squared my shoulders and marched as confidently as I could into the circle.

My opponent was watching me closely. If I could see her face, I was sure she'd be smiling. From the color of her eyes, I recognized her as the one that had bitched about my muffins. Undeserved, if you asked me. Those things might as well have been made by god himself and were often the only things I could tolerate when my stomach was feeling iffy.

Turning away from her, I scanned the crowd. Tears pricked my eyes when I saw a head of curly black hair. The face below it wasn't Eli's, but I wished it was. I wondered if he was okay. I couldn't imagine he would be, but there was nothing for him to do except move on. He was smart enough to realize that.

As much as it pained me, that was what I wanted to happen. Otherwise, my sacrifice and everything I'd endured since would be in vain. I couldn't stand the thought of that. This hell I was experiencing had to have some sort of purpose or I would completely lose myself to this desperation that was settling in my bones.

While I was lost in my head, I didn't notice that the light had turned green. Something slammed into my side, then I hit the ground. I heard a crunch before I felt the fiery pain in my wrist. When my brain processed it, I screamed, clutching at it.

What sort of Karma had I earned to be subjected to all of these horrors in succession?

A few people in the crowd made sounds of disgust, but they were quickly followed by laughter. My agony was a game to them, a sick form of entertainment, just as it was to Reyn and those men last night.

I'd seen Reyn's interest every time my strength began to fail, when I couldn't hold back my tears any longer. He enjoyed it every time. In fact, he sought it. When he sensed my intense emotions earlier, he'd run to witness the spectacle. It was probably going to become the most played memory in his spank bank.

When I looked up, I met his green eyes. The color was bright, even from here. I had no doubt he was getting enjoyment out of my screams.

Giving up was something I prided myself on avoiding for most of my life. There'd been a short time where I'd considered it, but I made it through that. I liked to think I could make it through this as well, but whereas my turmoil had felt endless back then, this one actually was.

Scanning the crowd again, I let myself accept that I would never see Eli again. I would never see Vivian or the annoying neighbor across from us that let her cat wander the hall, which made it smell like piss. Even fucking Grayson would make it on my visitor list if I had the choice.

No, this was my future. I'd given Olga an out and maybe that was the best option. If I lost this round, it would be merciful because I just didn't know how much more I could take from Reyn or this entire goddamn place.

I'd tried so hard. Coming out here wasn't meant to be a way to give up, but I was starting to see no other option. There was no way I could heal from what had been done to me. Not emotionally. It wasn't like I'd receive any support here. I wouldn't even be able to close my eyes again.

The desperation I was hit with was visceral. It invaded my entire body, felt like it was pumping through my veins. After what happened to my parents, I'd been in a horrible state and spent hours on the floor crying. That was the sort of breakdown that was raw, that rattled you to your core and never truly let go of you, no matter how many years had passed.

That was how I felt now, but I didn't have the luxury of curling up in a ball. In truth, I didn't want to go through the horrible process of healing. I didn't want to live through the same experience over and over, day in and day out. Never again.

Rolling onto my knees, I looked up at my opponent. She had her fists raised, ready to fend off an attack. Instead, I met Reyn's eyes again. His brow furrowed and he sat up straighter in his seat, resting his elbows on his thighs as he watched me.

I shrugged at him, then put my hands flat on the ground. Tori was hesitating, probably thinking this was some sort of trap. It could be a smart move if I utilized the makeshift blade in my pocket. Instead, I remained unmoving, my head drooping as I waited for the inevitable.

When a couple minutes passed, I looked up at her. She was glancing around warily, then she waved at someone in the upper seats.

"Come on," I growled.

She met my eyes, her brow furrowing. "I'm confused."

"Come on, you fucking bitch! End it. Please."

My voice cracked on the last word and I felt my emotions rising. She needed to do it now, before I humiliated myself in front of hundreds of people. I wanted to go out with a modicum of self-respect.

Finally, she started forward. I let out a relieved breath, but I didn't get what I wanted. She came to a sudden stop, her mouth opening. There was a rattle coming from her throat, then blood began to pour over her lips.

She hit the ground on her knees, staring at me with so much pain in her eyes that I couldn't help but pity her. When she flopped onto her back, she convulsed a couple times, then stilled completely. I peered down at her, trying to understand what had happened.

It looked like there was something in her throat, pushing at the skin from the inside. Through her open mouth, I saw something in the back. It was too dark to tell what it was, but whatever had caused it had taken away my chance to make things easy.

There was a plan B, though.

Pulling the shard from my pocket, I clutched it tightly. Curling in on myself, I tried to even out my breathing as I prepared myself.

I didn't know what waited for me beyond, but it had to be better than this. At least, it couldn't be worse. There were people waiting for me somewhere on the other side. I'd give anything to see them again, to hear their voices. I guess the thing I had to give was my life.

Straightening my arm, I gathered as much momentum as I could and aimed for the side of my throat.

Chapter 24

Reynaeros

As I stared down at the fight, I was filled with complete and utter confusion. At first, Kiera appeared determined and I'd been confident she would succeed. Now, with her wrist very likely broken, she looked defeated.

I was sure it was extraordinarily painful, but she wasn't even trying to fight anymore. She had to have some sort of plan. Maybe there was a strategy behind this, like an animal that played dead.

She looked up at me, her brown eyes looking darker and glossy. When she shrugged, it felt like my stomach was trying to flee my body.

"Come on," she said after a few minutes.

Tori looked up at where Chester was standing by the upstairs doors and raised her hands in a confused gesture. He glanced at me, but I didn't have any clue what to do.

"Come on, you fucking bitch! End it."

She said the last word so quietly that I didn't catch it, but there was such emotion in her voice that I knew exactly what she was doing. She was giving up. Absolutely fucking not.

When neither of us responded, Tori started forward. Before she took more than two steps, I reached out to the life energy in her heart and twisted it into something that matched my own. It took root, traveling through her tissues and growing inside of her. As it pushed its way through her throat, blood poured from her mouth. Within a minute, she was dead on the floor.

I thought that was the end of it, but Kiera pulled something from her pocket. Some foreign sense of desperation erupted in my chest when I saw a shard in her hand. Releasing some of the hold on my form, I had a firmer grasp on my abilities. I leapt down from the upper floor, wrapping my feet in a spongy wood to absorb the impact.

As she began to bring the shard toward her neck, I reached out, my arm shifting into a branch, allowing it to grow and make it the ten feet to her, knocking the weapon from her hand. Gasps erupted from the crowd, whose presence just pissed me the fuck off right now.

Thrusting my arms out to the sides, I shot spores in every direction. They settled along the walls, growing into thick, durable vines that crossed over each other until all the exits were blocked off. Chester landed beside me and released his own, which traveled into the lungs of the humans, choking them.

"Dispose of them," I ordered.

Kiera was on her knees, hunched over and crying. It was a heartbreaking sound, something I'd never expect to hear from her. This was the sound of despair, loss so powerful it changed you forever. It didn't belong to her. It couldn't.

Grabbing her arm, I tried to pull her up, but she cried out as if in pain. It wasn't the one with the injured wrist, so I didn't understand. Crouching beside her, I pushed up the sleeve of her shirt. I hadn't thought much about her attire previously, but it wasn't what was usually worn during the fights.

Her skin was mottled with various colors: yellow, blue, purple. My heart rate spiked at the sight and I had the sudden urge to search the rest of her and to demand where these had come from.

Ignoring her cries of protest, I picked her up, cradling her as gently as I could against my chest. Even the slightest movement seemed to pain her. I grew vines as soft as feathers that wrapped around her, securing her to me and absorbing as much shock as was possible so that she didn't feel jostled as much.

I didn't want the others to see her like this, so I went to the only other place I could think of. After closing the door to my room, I adjusted my appearance so as not to frighten her, then climbed onto the bed with her in my arms.

The wrappings fell away, revealing just how much she was trembling. She was shaking violently, the sounds coming from her making me concerned.

"Kiera," I said softly.

"No," she cried, pushing on me.

I set her carefully beside me, unsure what I was supposed to do.

"What happened?"

"Leave me alone."

"I can't do that."

"Leave me alone!" she screamed, sitting up to shove at my chest.

The anger inside her grew exponentially more volatile. This wasn't her usual state. It was more; terrifying, unfettered, and frankly, it was heartbreaking. This wasn't the sort of anger someone had access to unless they'd been severely broken.

Ever since I'd met her, I wondered about it, but it wasn't until now that I really recognized it. I thought it was nearly impossible to draw out her fear and her pain, but that was exactly what this was. She was constantly afraid and in pain and she was *angry about it.*

What sort of thing could break a person this way?

"Kiera," I repeated as softly as I could.

She continued to beat at my chest, screaming and crying. I wasn't sure if she was entirely present or if she was so lost to what was happening in her mind that she was simply reacting on instinct.

I caught her wrists, afraid she would hurt herself. The left one was swelling and it must have been painful. Even so, she thrashed, trying to get out of my hold.

"Stop," I demanded.

When she didn't, I considered just tossing her back in her room to deal with her fraught emotional state alone. I shouldn't have even brought her in here to begin with. If she was intent on hurting herself, I could have Portia remain in her room with her. She was more than capable, but I needed to get to the bottom of this.

Pushing her back onto the bed, I tried to get her shirt off so I could see what was going on. Her screaming intensified and tears poured more quickly from her eyes.

"Jesus, Kiera."

"Don't touch me!"

"What the fuck is going on?"

"Please," she sobbed. "Don't touch me."

Gritting my teeth, I sat back on my heels. "Show me."

She shook her head. Her breaths were shaky, a little hiccup occurring with every other one.

"Show me," I repeated. "Or I will strip you bare regardless of your protests."

Her head drooped. I watched a tear hit the blanket, darkening the green. Taking her chin as gently as I could, I lifted her face, then used my other hand to brush away a strand of hair that had become stuck to her cheek.

"Why are you hiding yourself? It's weak."

"I know I am."

"No. That is why I'm confused. You are always strong, standing up to me even when it is likely to get you into a nasty situation."

Finally, she met my eyes. What I saw there was enough for me to decide that whatever had caused such darkness and agony would meet a very unpleasant death. I would destroy not only them, but their entire bloodline. Not a trace of them would exist in this world or any other for the rest of eternity.

Blinking, I pushed away the strange intensity that had my eyes shifting.

"Tell me."

Her chin wobbled and I gripped it tighter.

"Please."

"You'll kill me."

"I have no desire to kill you at the moment, but every second you hold to this stubbornness, the more I question that decision."

"Do you promise?"

"Would you trust me if I did?"

"No."

"Regardless, yes. I promise I won't kill you. Today, at least."

Nodding, she grabbed the hem of her shirt, grimacing as she began to pull it over her head. I helped her get her arms out of it, then froze completely.

She was... ruined. Her body was covered in those marks in various colors. Bruises, I thought they were called. One on her abdomen was an ugly black and purple color and bigger than my palm. She had cuts across her abdomen and over her shoulders. There was one on the side of her neck that was bleeding a little.

Swallowing, I reached for her legs, pausing before I touched her. She hesitated for a few moments, then allowed me to help her out of her pants.

The skin looked much the same. On her thighs, there were bruises that appeared to be in the shape of fingers, further confirming what I'd feared from the moment she removed her shirt. On her hip there was a tattoo of words that I hadn't paid enough attention to her body to notice. There was a cut through the middle of the words that made it slightly misshapen, but it was still legible. *I am. I am. I am.*

Trailing my eyes over her again, I saw a purple mark that wrapped around her throat. I thought about the way her voice sounded right now. When I'd first heard it in her room, it had alarmed me, but I allowed myself to believe she was simply dehydrated or feeling ill.

At a certain point last night, I'd woken up and been filled with terror. After analyzing the energy in the building, I'd found an intense negativity coming from her hallway, but I'd tried to brush it off. It had barely allowed me any rest for the remainder of the night, so I'd left to spend time in the woods by the river. When I got back, I could still sense it, so I went to investigate.

While I was in her corridor, I didn't feel anything as intense as before. As I was about to leave, it had reignited; not as powerfully, but enough for me to recognize. Sure enough, it was coming from Kiera. She'd been fresh from the shower and I wanted to blame her sweet rose scent for my failure to recognize how terribly wrong things were.

My mind had been too distracted lately. I shouldn't have ignored it last night. If I'd just taken a minute to check...

Shaking my head, I stood and headed out of the room. Outside of fixing her current state, I needed to learn exactly what had happened. I wasn't sure how much I would get out of her right now, but I would make sure she told me eventually. I just hoped it wouldn't take too long.

Vengeance was on my mind, anger flowing through my veins. I'd claimed Kiera when I marked her. It was the way of things in my world. She bore my imprint, which meant nobody would dare touch her unless I explicitly allowed it. When I found the person that had done this, I would bring her his head.

I liked to think I would do the same for any of the women I'd claimed. It just happened to be her in this situation this time, which meant I'd be tapping into the beast inside of me for a woman that aggravated me to no end.

Madilyn DeRose

Chapter 25

Kiera

Reyn promised he wouldn't kill me, which didn't do much good when I couldn't trust a word he said. So far, I was still alive, but he'd left me here without saying anything. That made me feel uncertain about my future.

It wasn't a new feeling for me, but I still hated it. If I wasn't in an extraordinary amount of pain right now, I would try to find my way back to my own room. For now, though, I had to stay here because I barely had the strength to sit up.

At first, I hadn't known where he'd brought me. I was distraught, lost to my madness. Once I'd made the decision that I didn't want to live, everything else blurred, giving me a sort of hyper focus on my end goal. Now that I'd mostly come out of that state, I simply felt lost.

Looking around, I took in the space. The room was big, but not extravagantly so, as I would've thought. In my head, I pictured fixtures made of pure gold and a mirror on the ceiling so he could admire himself. Instead, I was met with something extraordinarily comforting.

The walls, floor, and ceiling were a dark green that I at first mistook for black. The entire wall to my right was a giant window with a door set into the middle to match. With only the moonlight, I could see a patio, but not any details. He had a beautiful view of the water that was higher up than mine was.

The bed itself was at least king-sized, with a silky blanket and more pillows than were necessary. It sat just a couple feet above the ground and had a fancy frame that made it look like it was simply floating in midair.

My favorite part was the décor. Ivy climbed up the walls, as well as other vines with various flowers; some I recognized and others that I didn't. Plants were hanging from the ceilings, making the room feel fresh and tranquil.

Beside the giant window was what resembled a bonsai tree. Its roots must have gone straight through the floor, but I didn't see any raised areas like those on a sidewalk when tree roots started to push them upward.

For lack of a better word, it was magical in here. I hated to appreciate anything that belonged to Reyn, but it would be pointless to claim that this wasn't incredible.

The door opened and I sucked in a breath, shrinking back against the headboard. When I saw that it was him, I relaxed slightly. There wasn't any part of me that trusted him as a whole, but I had a feeling that he wasn't going to hurt me right now. I was certain he would do it later, but that was a problem for future me.

He resumed his previous position on the bed and set some items down. They looked like medical supplies, which made my stomach feel acidic.

"What are you doing?"

He barely glanced at me. "Your human body is inadequate when it comes to, well, everything, but it's particularly bad at healing itself. This is the best I can do."

"I don't need you to do anything. Actually, I'd prefer it if you didn't."

"Shut the fuck up, Kiera."

"Excuse me?"

Moving onto his knees, he grabbed my chin again. I had the urge to punch him in his sharp-jawed face, but it would take too much energy.

"You're of no use to me in such a state and I'm not interested in more suicide attempts, so I will try to help heal your body and you will focus on healing your mind."

Gritting my teeth, I cast my eyes to the side and nodded. He released me and grabbed something that looked like a cross between a cotton ball and a towel. When he squirted some liquid on it and reached for me, I reared back.

"What is that?"

"It's to clean the wounds."

"Cool. That's not what I asked."

He gave me an exasperated look. "This comes from a plant in my world. It will help transfer the solution into your skin while drawing out any toxins."

"That sounds made up."

"In this world, perhaps."

This time when he brought it forward, I let him press it to the wound at my neck, hissing when it burned. It had opened up at some point and had been throbbing intensely. That was probably a bad sign. Whatever fancy thing this plant sponge did, it hurt like a bitch.

"You're trembling," he noted.

"Tell me more about where you're from. I need a distraction."

I thought he would refuse, but after a moment he smiled a little.

"It's very beautiful. Similar to this world before your kind poisoned it."

"Yeah, we're the greatest plague to exist on this planet."

"You are."

Jokes weren't always the guy's forte. He understood most things, but there were some qualities that aged him. I assumed he didn't spend much time on the Internet.

"How does the magic work?"

"It's not really magic. It's an energy that we share with living things. The link allows us to trade it, so that we can harness many different forms."

"Is it just plants?"

"I can use energy from any living thing, but I'm only able to manifest it that way because that is the shape of my energy."

"Did you kill Tori?"

"Yes."

"Why?"

He pulled the sponge away, then it dissolved. Picking up another, he moved onto the next cut.

"You're of no use to me dead."

"Then why let me fight at all?"

"You could have won if you didn't succumb to your weakness. It was not something I expected to happen."

I stared down at the cut he was cleaning on my thigh. It was a deep one and the sting brought tears to my eyes. There was no doubt I'd have scars from them; permanent fixtures that would forever remind me of what happened, regardless of how much I tried to forget.

When I focused my eyes, I found him staring at me.

"What?"

"You need to tell me what happened."

My heart started hammering. "No."

"It's not optional."

"It doesn't matter. I just want to forget."

"That's weak."

"You don't get to tell me how to deal with it," I snapped. "You're no better than they are."

His jaw worked for a moment. "There was more than one?"

Pulling my knees up, I scooted a little bit away from him. "Two."

"How did they get in?"

"They broke my window."

He said something in what I assumed was his language. I'd heard it before and I couldn't help but be intrigued.

When he used it, his voice didn't sound the same. It took on some ethereal quality, like words floating in on the wind. It was both creepy and beautiful.

"I don't see how that's possible. Not if they were human."

"Well, that's what happened."

His brow was still furrowed and his thoughts seemed far away. After a moment, he shook his head. "Tell me how to find them."

"I don't know," I said softly.

He narrowed his eyes. "I can see through your lies."

"Just let it go. That's all I want to do."

"No."

"What would you even do?"

"I intend to relieve them of their cocks, followed by each of their organs."

"Why?"

"Because they touched you."

The ferocity of his statement made me shrink back. Wrapping my arms around my knees, I perched my chin on them. I didn't know if it was the events of the night or what he'd just said that was making me nauseous. I didn't like belonging to someone, as if this was some primitive time when women were property.

Reyn could defile me repeatedly and in horrific ways, but when someone else did it, he suddenly tried to claim the moral high ground. It was disgusting.

Even so, the idea of those men being gone, unable to hurt me ever again, brought me the barest sense of peace. I already had one beast to fear under this roof. If I could rid myself of further threats, I would be stupid to refuse.

"I think one of them is Vera's brother," I whispered.

He balled his fists in his lap. His skin seemed to ripple for a moment, then returned to normal. As if nothing had happened, he opened his palm and grew what looked like a tiny, pale green tree. He plucked it from his skin and I stifled a gag.

"Do I disgust you?" he asked as he peeled a layer of bark from it.

"Yes."

His gaze raised to mine for a moment before he went back to his task.

"It's not as if human bodies are beautiful. You're quite grotesque, if I'm being honest."

I snorted. "I don't care what you think about humans. You have no issue with taking advantage of them when it suits you."

"What else is there to do in this fucking place?"

"If you hate it so much, then go home."

He peeled another layer from the little trunk, then held it over a cup the size of a shot glass. When it was full, the tree disintegrated and he held the liquid out to me.

"For pain," he said curtly before I could ask.

When he looked at me again, he appeared angry. With a small shake of his head, he stood and left the room, the door slamming shut behind him.

I had no idea what I'd done to piss him off this time, nor did I particularly care. He could go stick his dick in a tree and work off his frustrations. The last thing I wanted to do was stay here, but after drinking the weird plant juice, my eyes grew heavier. As soon as I laid back on the pile of pillows, I knew there was no way I'd be getting up for a while.

🌷 🌷 🌷 🌷

It took me an embarrassing amount of time, but eventually I made it down to the cafeteria. I had no idea what time it was or how long I'd slept. Judging by the horrible grogginess and the pounding in my head, I'd say it wasn't long enough.

My stomach was painfully empty after throwing up so much yesterday. Reyn hadn't returned after his little fit, so my only option was fending for myself. Somehow, each door that was visible to me led me in this direction, which seemed more than coincidental. He was likely waiting around impatiently for me to get out of his space.

As I was putting some random things on a plate, the door to the cafeteria opened.

"Oh my god," Lucy exclaimed.

She rushed over to me and wrapped her arms around me, making me whimper. Pulling back, she looked me up and down.

"Are you okay?"

"Uh, fine. Why?"

Her eyes widened. Taking my plate from me, she led me over to a table.

"After what happened this morning, I was worried. Then I couldn't find you..."

"I don't understand. What happened?"

"You don't know?"

I shook my head. "I've been... sleeping."

"Oh my god. Leander came down here and dragged Vera out of her room, demanding she tell him about her brother or something. He flew into a rage."

"Jesus. Is she okay?"

The look on her face made my stomach curdle. Dropping the cracker I was about to bite into, I folded my hands in my lap and waited.

"He killed her."

Covering my eyes with my palm, I took a deep breath. "God damnit."

"What is it?"

"It's my fault."

"How?"

"She, uh... It doesn't matter. She made a move against me and I got hurt, but I'm fine."

"Wait. You're saying he did all of this to defend you?"

"No," I said, breathing a laugh. "I'd say he's trying to restore order, get people in line. That's my best guess, at least."

"He's never stepped in when the women fight."

"Well, this was pretty bad."

She stared at me for a while, making me shift in my seat. "Are you sure you're okay?"

"Yeah. Don't worry about it. So, I bet everyone is in a panic now."

She chewed on her lip, glancing toward the door, then back at me.

"Maybe you should see for yourself."

I was going to ask her to clarify, but she started toward the exit. Getting up as quickly as I could, I followed her. In the hallway, she turned left, opening a door I hadn't known was there. It looked like I'd added another to my list of discovered locations, which was cool, I guess.

This one opened up straight into a staircase. She headed up, continuing for a few floors. I thought my body was going to give out from the exertion when we finally reached another door. Sunlight streamed straight into my eyes when she opened it.

Stepping through, I squinted and looked around. I felt a wave of emotion as I stood in the sun for the first time in weeks. It was chilly and a little overcast, but it was absolutely gorgeous.

We were standing inside a greenhouse on the roof. It was filled with various plants all in full bloom, even though it was autumn. I rushed through the door onto the exposed part of the roof and spun in a circle, throwing my arms wide.

"This is incredible," I exclaimed. A laugh bubbled out of me and it felt so good, I could have cried.

When I looked at Lucy, she wasn't smiling. She was standing on the edge, looking down at something. I cautiously joined her, feeling queasy when I saw how high we were.

"There."

She was pointing down and I really didn't want to look, but I followed the direction she was gesturing toward. As soon as I saw it, my hand came up to cover my mouth.

Below us there was a large tree, the top of it ending a couple floors down. There were dark green vines wrapped around a high branch and on the ends of them hung heads. Not full bodies. Just heads.

Vera was in the middle, her jaw slack and her skin a sickly gray. On either side of her were the two men from the other night. Just the sight of them made me feel ill, the memories beginning to resurface.

Shifting my gaze, I took in the rest of the heads hanging from the same branch.

"Who are they?"

"Her entire family," Lucy replied softly.

"What? Everyone?"

"In the city, yeah."

I swallowed hard, feeling thankful that I hadn't eaten much. A couple of the people looked young. They could have barely been teenagers. It was sick; twisted in a way I wouldn't have been able to fathom prior to seeing it.

Lucy was looking somewhere else, so I followed her gaze to a branch on the other side of the tree. Jesus Christ.

It wasn't just Vera he'd gone after. He'd killed them all. Every woman that had been in this place was hanging from the tree, save for me, Lucy, and Collie.

"Why'd he spare you and Collie?"

"He said he knew we weren't involved. That we're your friends."

I never should have told him anything. This was my fault. Dozens of deaths were on my hands. Guilty. Innocent. The elderly. The children.

Every day it felt like I had more trauma I'd have to recover from. If I even got the chance.

Chapter 26

Reynaeros

Pacing the length of the library, I rubbed my jaw repeatedly. I didn't know what else to do. For the past few days, I'd felt bored. Even reading wasn't capturing my attention.

The door opened and I looked up as Chester strode through.

"How is she?" I asked immediately.

He stopped, pursing his lips on a smile. "Why don't you go see for yourself, rather than wearing a path in the grass?"

I looked down, frowning when I realized he was correct. Waving a hand, I returned it to its healthy state and resumed my pacing.

"I have no need to see for myself. I'm simply asking after her well-being, as any decent person would do."

"Are you a decent person?"

"Would you like to have your head used as a holiday ornament as well?"

He breathed a laugh as he returned a book to its shelf. I narrowed my eyes, but didn't comment. I knew he'd been borrowing them under the pretense that he was reading them, but secretly let Collie have them instead. It was annoying, but for some reason it seemed to bring him satisfaction.

"She's just as you would expect, I think. I don't really know how she should be acting."

I hummed thoughtfully. "If she's acting normal, she should be full of rage and immature sarcasm."

"To be fair, that's mostly when you're around, so you'll just have to grace her with your presence to see how she reacts."

"No. I have other things to do."

He raised a brow. "Like actively avoiding her."

"She irks me and her energy tastes foul."

"I don't feel it as strongly as you seem to. Are you sure you're not simply becoming attuned to it?"

"Of course not. It's just fucking loud. Tangible."

"Mm."

With a growl, I dropped into a lounge chair, stretching my legs out in front of me and pressing my fingers against my forehead.

"Has sleep escaped you recently, Chester?"

"Not more than usual. Do you have a concern?"

"I don't know. It looks the same, but something feels different. Every night, I cannot stop worrying."

"It doesn't do any good to agonize over it, Reynaeros. We just need to act soon if you think she's the one."

"That's the problem. It makes less sense to me all the time. How could it be her?"

"I've always wondered how it could be any human. It's just impossible if I'm being candid."

"I know. It was simple to keep telling myself that it would make sense someday, but now we've come this far and I feel as lost as the day we arrived."

"Have you thought about telling her what she's meant to be doing?"

Dropping my hand, I tapped absently on the armrest. "I've considered it, but I don't know if it will help or worsen the situation. Right now, I don't know what I can even ask of her."

He leaned back against my desk, looking lost in thought. His brows pulled down, then he met my gaze.

"She needs to trust us. All of us."

"She despises me, so clearly that won't happen."

"You need to change your approach with her."

"I don't know what you expect me to do."

"Reynaeros, she's been through hell. And... May I be candid?"

"Of course."

"It's not entirely what happened just recently. You've done the same to her."

"It's different."

"How?"

Turning to the shelf in front of me, I scanned the rows of books. I'd amassed a great many over the years, both in my realm and this one. Seeing them nestled amongst each other felt both strange and fitting. I pondered whether I would keep the library the same when I returned home.

"Reynaeros."

"What?" I asked curtly.

"This is not a problem you can ignore and wish will disappear."

"I'm aware of that."

"Then cut the power play bullshit you have going on and take this seriously."

"I've taken it very seriously. I made a ridiculous bargain with her to make her amenable and I've kept her from death on multiple occasions. Just three days ago, I destroyed all but two of the women in this place because of her."

"For her."

"What?"

"You did it for her. Frankly, I'm growing tired of your stubbornness on this issue. You're fond of her and you have been from the start."

"I was intrigued by her," I disagreed.

"You kidnapped her friend and made false threats to throw him in the ring in order to get her here."

"She required extra persuasion."

With a sigh, he came to sit in the chair across from me, leaning forward to perch his elbows on his knees.

"Things are happening that we don't understand. We are missing something and it could easily be the reason we fail. Between Kiera's arrival here, Riniya paying you a visit, and this strange feeling you have, the last thing I want is to be caught off guard."

"I know," I sighed. "We may need to reevaluate everything. There must be something we're missing."

"Do you still trust me to advise you?"

"Always. You are the one who will acquire my throne someday."

He smiled slightly, then looked at me seriously. "You need to fix it. I haven't spoken ill on your actions thus far because I understand what pains you. Now, it matters. I don't care if it involves groveling and humiliating yourself. It's time for you to remember who the fuck you are because no matter what it takes, we are beating this thing. You need to get ready to be who you were meant to be, not this beast you've become. One day soon, we will breathe the Aerranata air and it will cure every pain of the past seven centuries."

🌷 🌷 🌷 🌷

Everything Chester said this afternoon was correct and I agreed with his assessment. That did not, however, make it easy. Perhaps it was from so many centuries causing pain or it could be because I still found Kiera infuriating. I had no idea how to approach the situation and every time I thought about it, I felt slightly nauseous.

There was this lingering image in my head of her pushing me away if I tried to check on her. Worse, she could fear me. If I was meant to be gaining her trust, I couldn't allow that emotion to take root, no matter how much I'd craved it before.

Until I could find the resolve to confront her, I needed a way to make sure she was okay. Asking after her had become embarrassing at this point, so I decided on another approach. She'd probably hate me even more for it, but she wouldn't know.

Standing outside her door, I felt for her, confirming that she wasn't as volatile right now and her energy was at rest. It was still uneasy and fearful, but it always was.

As quietly as possible, I opened her door just enough for me to slip through. White spores flowed from my hand, floating over to her. As soon as she breathed them in, her signature calmed even further, showing that she'd sunk into a deeper sleep. Maybe it would help her be less grumpy if I decided to pay her a visit tomorrow.

Heading over to the dresser, I set up the plant I'd brought. It was a nice succulent that didn't require her to fuss with it, so I hoped she would leave it alone. I made sure to angle it just right, then stepped back and admired it. It's energy was healthy and vibrant, easing my own nerves slightly.

Satisfied, I returned to the door, putting a hand on the knob. Rolling my lips, I hesitated, then glanced at Kiera. She was lying on her side with her head resting on one hand. In sleep, there was a softness to her features that didn't exist when she was scowling at me constantly.

Aside from the absence of her murderous expressions, I noticed other differences. Her jaw, which was usually tense, was relaxed and her lips were slightly parted. The tightness in her brow was gone and her hair was loose, fanning over the pillow.

I didn't realize I'd moved until I was standing above her. My fingers twitched at my side and my heart rate had somehow spiked. I rushed out of the room, not allowing myself to look back.

After shutting the door, I turned around and swore when I almost ran straight into Lucia. She was staring up at me with her arms over her chest, a cross look on her face. God, I hated this woman.

"What are you doing?" she demanded in a harsh whisper.

Brushing past her, I tried to ignore the footsteps that followed. When she grabbed my wrist, thorns burst from my skin and she yanked her hand back, staring at the blood welling on her fingers.

"Do not presume that you can make demands of me simply because I spared your life. I would make you your own little tree to hang from in a heartbeat. Something dreadful and smelly, perhaps."

"But Kiera would never forgive you."

"That's of no consequence to me."

She snorted. "Is that why you're snooping in her room? You may not know much about humans, but that's considered creepy."

"Lucia, I hope you're not implying that you would say something to her."

"No," she muttered, rolling her eyes. "I'm not that stupid. I'm worried about her, though."

"For good reason. She's been through a lot."

"Haven't we all?"

"Mm."

"So, are the fights over?"

"No."

"You're going to bring more people here?"

"I didn't say that either."

"Then I'm confused."

With a sigh, I leaned against the wall. "People will fight, but they won't be kept."

"Interesting. Does that mean I don't have to participate?"

"I couldn't care less. Go frolic with Brooks to pass the time if you wish."

Her mouth dropped open. "I, uh, what?"

"While you're at it, tell Collette to make a move on Chester already. It's ridiculous that he thinks I don't see his infatuation."

"You're not going to... Use her anymore?"

Tapping my fingers against the wall, I shrugged. "She has grown boring."

"Right. Well, I'm gonna go to sleep. This whole conversation has made me feel super weird."

"Lucia," I said before she closed her door. "Since I've been so generous, perhaps you could help me with something." My gaze drifted to Kiera's door. "Without your loose tongue running off with it."

She contemplated for a moment, then shrugged and opened her door wider. God, this was going to be a chore, but I needed this from her. At this point, she was my best option.

Chapter 27

Kiera

As I stood by my window, I stared at the creepy purple vines that crawled up the sides. Apparently they were like an eviler Venus Fly Trap that would spring into action if anything came through. Portia had excitedly explained that they'd digest a full human adult in about two hours, bones and all.

Basically, they were a serial killer's wet dream and my intrusive thoughts were working overtime trying to convince me to provoke one of them. Maybe they were under orders not to attack me. Did I care enough to risk it?

Yeah, considering what I'd gone through four days ago and my current, volatile emotional state, it was probably not the time to be entertaining that idea. Even though I was still horribly depressed, accosted by crippling flashbacks, and my body wasn't healed yet, I was doing a little bit better. I wasn't actively seeking a way to end it, at least.

Being stuck in my room wasn't helping one bit and remaining stagnant only ignited a pain in my head, so I ventured out into the hallway for the first time in what felt like ages. It was eerily quiet in this place now and I thought I would've preferred it before, even with the bitchy bullies.

No. Don't think about them. Or their brothers. Or their heads.

Holding a hand over my mouth, I focused on walking in a straight line down the corridor. Every time I blinked, I saw one of them. It didn't matter which one because now they were all connected by some fucked up web in my head. If I thought of the other girls, it made me think of the tree, which made Vera pop into my head and in turn brought her brothers to the forefront of my mind. Then I would spiral.

Since I'd failed to stop my train of thought, I hit my knees on the staircase, my chest heaving. I managed to hold back the tears, instead being racked by a dry sob. It shook my shoulders and pain flared in my chest from the tight breaths that were a struggle to pull in.

When I'd reined my emotions back in, I gripped the banister and got to my feet. I was almost there. If I couldn't make it to the training room, I was just a sad, useless lump.

I pushed through the door into the upper hallway, holding my stomach as it roiled. When I collided with something solid, I nearly tumbled backward down the stairs. An arm wrapped around my waist, steadying me, and I looked up into wide, deep green eyes.

"Kiera. Are you alright?"

"I would've been fine if you hadn't attacked me."

"That wasn't what I was doing."

"You've been on this Earth long enough to understand sarcasm. Maybe learn to recognize it."

Shoving his arm away, I continued toward my destination. My skin prickled where he'd touched me, so I started replaying the Princess Bride in my head to keep my thoughts straight. Having a breakdown in front of him would be worse than tumbling down those stairs.

He caught up to me, walking at my side the entire way. When we made it to the door, he sped up and pushed through it, holding it open for me. My nose wrinkled at the gesture, but I refrained from saying something derogatory.

"You look better," he noted.

"Do I?"

"Yes. I think so."

"Coming from someone that thinks I'm repulsive and unattractive, I'm not sure how much of a compliment that is."

"It's... a compliment."

Rolling my eyes, I grabbed a knife and threw it at the furthest dummy. It fell short, just as the next four did. Before, I'd been able to hit it most of the time, even if it didn't always embed itself. I swear, I couldn't have one thing.

Something touched my arm from behind and I sucked in a breath, immediately turning with the knife raised. Reyn swore when it lodged in his shoulder. He pulled it free and I took a step back, staring at the blood rushing down his chest. My vision got blurry, then my legs gave out.

On my knees, I stared down at my hands, expecting tears to be dripping onto them, but my eyes were dry. Blinking, I cleared the haze that had come over me and took a deep breath.

Reyn crouched in front of me, seeming to study me. After a moment, he moved a little further back.

"I'm sorry."

I let out a dry laugh. "For what? I stabbed you."

"It was insensitive of me not to think about your space. I didn't mean to make you afraid."

"I'm not afraid," I snapped. "Not of them or this place and least of all, of you."

"Alright. The knife to the shoulder and your position on the floor say otherwise, but I'll take your word for it."

There was a slight lift to the corner of his mouth that made me want to stab him again. It'd be much more satisfying if I did it intentionally. I mean, who mocked someone in this position? Well, people like him would be a fair guess.

"May I help you up?"

He held out a hand and I just glared at it. With a huff, he straightened and took a step back.

"Oh, am I frustrating you?"

"Yes," he admitted more harshly. "I'm trying to be civil and you shoot down my every attempt at niceties."

"If you somehow got the impression that I want to have some sort of easygoing, buddy-buddy relationship with you, it's probably best that you seek therapy for your delusions."

"You haven't given that impression, but I'm trying to show you that's what I want."

Staring up at him, I studied the tightness of his jaw and the way his eyes appeared wider than usual. He was staring at me intensely with what I assumed was anger he tried to conceal.

"Your effort to feign concern for my well-being is noted, but I don't need it."

"I'm being genuine. You were fucking raped, Kiera."

Getting to my feet, I approached him quickly. He stood his ground, only the tick in his cheek giving away any of his emotions. Stopping in front of him, I stood up straight and met his eyes.

"You have no right to patronize me."

"That's not-"

"What's next? Are you going to give me a big speech about how it wasn't my fault? Are you going to tell me how brave I am and that this will make me stronger?"

"That would be ridiculous."

"You're right. It would be because I already know whose fault it is."

"I know you do. You're intelligent and you'd never let someone like me tell you how to feel, so I won't even attempt it. All I want to do is apologize."

Blinking a few times, I cycled through a multitude of emotions. Eventually, I caught up with the tornado that was my thought process and I started laughing. His brows lowered as he watched me and he stepped forward, but I held up a hand, putting the other over my mouth to compose myself.

"That's the most ridiculous thing I've ever heard. It was a good effort, though. Was it Chester that coached you on what to say?"

"Nobody told me what to say. I'm being sincere when I say that I'm sorry. Things are becoming clearer to me and I see that I wronged you."

All traces of humor had dissipated, allowing me to settle into a more familiar state of mind. He seemed to feel whatever was coursing through me. His expression softened into something pitying, which just infuriated me more.

I stepped forward so our chests were nearly touching.

"I don't forgive you."

"Kiera-"

"Never," I interrupted. "It's actually insulting you would even try this because I'll never be able to forgive you no matter how many nice deeds you do. This is your fault, Reyn. All of it. You hurt me first, raped me, humiliated me. You imprisoned me here. You put me in this situation."

"I get it."

"If I was home, none of this would've happened. I could have lived the rest of my days being somewhat happy. It'd be peaceful. The way I fucking wanted."

He opened his mouth to respond, but I shook my head and walked around him. He didn't deserve the chance to respond and he especially didn't deserve to hear my truth.

I was even more pissed because I'd actually wanted to spend my time training today. It could have been a good outlet, plus I didn't want to lose any of my progress. As usual, fucking Rhinoceros stomped in there to ruin the day.

Entangled Realms

A knock on my bedroom door made me want to groan. Everyone had been super clingy this week and it was unbearable. I appreciated that they cared about me, but I was starting to feel like a spectacle. There was also this lingering, uncomfortable feeling that the nonhumans were only interested in what I might potentially help them with. The big ol' mystery that I still wasn't privy to.

"Come in," I called, not looking up from the notepad I'd been writing in.

After a minute, I glanced around, but there was nobody here. The door was still closed, so I walked over to it. When my hand was on the knob, I hesitated.

If it was someone nefarious, it was doubtful they'd knock. It was even more ridiculous to think they wouldn't come in when I invited them. I drew in a deep breath and opened it, prepared for something to jump out at me. There was only an empty hallway, though.

Just as I was about to close the door, my eye caught on something resting on the floor. I picked it up and ran my hand over the material it was wrapped in. It looked and felt like ultra-thin tree bark, but it was softer, close to paper. There was a little poof of what looked like moss in the middle, making it look like a birthday present.

I couldn't decide if it was pretentious or kind of cool.

There was a travel mug on the ground, which I identified as housing Earl Grey based on the smell.

Sitting on the bed, I carefully unwrapped the package, feeling like an asshole for tearing the beautiful material. When it fell away, my mouth dropped open. Having a book in my hand might have been considered a religious experience after going so long without reading.

More shocking was the title. The Bell Jar. It was one of my favorites and always brought me comfort, even though it was pretty depressing.

How had he known to drop off this book? Maybe it was a wild coincidence. More likely, he'd learned through nefarious deeds, just like he had with my name. My stomach felt acidic when I thought about him kidnapping someone else, but nobody I knew would be able to tell him my favorite book.

There was a little note tucked between the pages. I pulled it out with shaky fingers, turning it over to look at the elegant, loopy scrawl.

Little rose,

This lingering bite in my shoulder won't let me forget about you and your penchant for stabbing me. This is three times now, not that I'm counting. I've heard these things can bring humans relaxation, so I thought it was worth a shot. If you still feel inclined to stab me, I'll just have to stop wearing my good shirts around you.

Reyn

It appeared he was still trying to make bullshit reparations. I didn't know why he tried. I'd already agreed to do what I could to help with their mystery battle.

Whatever his goal was and what weird magic he'd used, it brought me a wonderful contentment to bring the book over to the window bench and settle in with my tea and a blanket.

Chapter 28

Kiera

Training yesterday had been a shitshow. I wanted to try again today, but if he showed his face, I wasn't sure how I'd react. I didn't want to feel all of the dark emotions his presence elicited. Healing meant I had to work through things, but around him I just felt more volatile.

I'd been going up and down the stairs for a while. My legs and ass hurt from the exercise, but it was the only thing keeping me sane. Sitting around allowed me too much time to stew in my negative shit-filled brain. It made me antsy, like bees were buzzing around in my veins.

One of the doors creaked open, but I couldn't figure out which one. I froze, trying to make a decision. Up or down. Up or down. Silently swearing, I dashed up the stairs, then screamed when someone stepped around the corner.

Something was pressing against my back, which ignited panic inside me. The guy was a couple steps in front of me, which meant somebody else was here. Had they been trying to trap me by coming from both sides?

I whirled around, my fist connecting with something hard. "Fuck!"

When I stepped back, I ran into the guy and spun around again. I was confused, angry, and unnerved. He moved away from me and held up his hands.

"Jesus. Relax."

"Who the hell are you?" I demanded, cradling my hand.

It was the same one that bitch damaged in the ring. Thankfully, it hadn't been broken, but a sprain still hurt, especially after punching a wall of wood that appeared out of nowhere.

"I could ask you the same thing, though by your attitude, I can make an educated guess."

Narrowing my eyes, I looked him up and down. His appearance was striking and not just because he was beautiful. His skin was pale, but had a blue tint to it, as well as the twining, vine-like tattoos Reyn had. His hair was white, with the same blue tint as his skin. The vivid blue eyes I was mesmerized by moved similarly to the way I'd seen Reyn's shift, but it was smooth, like a gentle current.

When I noticed the horns on his head, I reared back, nearly falling down the stairs, but his wood wall saved me from an untimely death. I looked closer, realizing that they looked more like branches than horns. They must've been a foot tall, with tips that split into a couple of smaller protrusions.

"It's rude to stare, you know."

"Shit," I muttered, looking at his face again.

"Let's not make it weird."

Through his slightly parted lips I noticed the sharp points of his top teeth. His accent wasn't as strong as Reyn and the others, but it was noticeable.

"Uh, so who are you?"

"Rath."

"Rath? As in..." I swung my arm as if I was holding a sword, which made him purse his lips on a smile.

"Yes, Kiera. Like that, but not. You're human, though, so I won't give you too much shit for it."

"That's more than I've gotten from other people around here, so that's good."

"Well, now that introductions are finished, I'll continue on my way."

"Wait."

I grabbed his wrist without thinking about it and he tore it away from me. His nostrils flared and the color of his eyes became more intense.

"Sorry," he said quickly. "I don't usually let humans touch me."

"Oh, so I've found another bigoted fairy."

To my surprise, he laughed. "Don't apply your human conventions to me. No, I'm not a bigot."

"Then why do you hate our touch?"

He licked his lips, trailing his eyes down, then up my body. "You're an inquisitive thing. Do you not fear us?"

"Why would I?"

He gestured at himself. "This isn't exactly something you walk past on the street. Additionally, I'm sure you haven't been treated... kindly."

I was unable to hide my grimace. His eyes softened, the waves dying down to a gentle movement that was barely noticeable.

"You're more interesting than most people I come across. Will you follow me and I'll answer your questions?"

I hesitated, pulling my lip between my teeth. I'd never met this guy and there was a chance he was more like Reyn than Chester and Portia.

"I'm not him. I won't hurt you. Here." He pulled out an intricate dagger with a curved blade and held it out to me. "Now I'm unarmed and you're not."

Swallowing, I nodded and took the blade, motioning for him to lead the way. He smiled in a way that lit up his face, then the wood barrier crumbled. I cautiously trailed behind him, hoping I wasn't being led to my death. Or worse.

❦ ❦ ❦ ❦

Color me surprised as hell. Rath had led me out of the building, which I didn't know was possible, and brought me into a forest that sat a mile away. We stopped at a stream, where he kicked off his shoes and sat on the rocks. When he slid his feet into the water, I couldn't help but laugh.

"Instead of laughing at me, you should join. It's refreshing."

"It's November and it's cold."

He rolled his eyes and patted the spot beside him. Grudgingly, I lowered myself to the ground, struggling to find a comfortable position. Deciding it was hopeless, I simply removed my shoes and did as he said.

"Jesus," I nearly screeched, pulling my legs back. "That's ice cold."

He laughed, making me glare at him. After a moment, he held up a placating hand and composed himself.

"Alright, sorry. I had to fuck with you a little."

"I don't understand how it's that cold. It has to be in the fifties right now."

With a wink, he inclined his fingers toward the water. "Go again."

"Forgive me if I don't trust you anymore."

"Humor me, you little asshole."

Grumbling under my breath, I dipped a single toe in the water. I gasped when I found it as warm as bathwater. Sinking both my feet into it, I moaned at the sensation.

"See? We're not all bad."

"Chester and Portia are nice. It's only Rhinoceros that's on my bad side."

His laugh seemed to fill the entire space. "Please tell me you've called him that to his face."

The corner of my mouth lifted. "He hated it."

"From what the others have said, you're ruining his life."

"Others? I didn't realize there were more."

"You thought Reynaeros' court was made up of only a few?"

"Let's be real here. I didn't even know this was a court."

He hummed thoughtfully. "He hasn't told you anything, has he?"

"Only that I'm supposed to fight some mysterious thing he can't for some reason."

"I'm not surprised. His social skills need some serious work."

"Maybe you'll tell me," I tried, giving him a sweet smile.

"I'd rather not be imprisoned inside one of his trees."

"Is that something he does?"

"I've seen it, but it was well-deserved. Unfortunately, he's quicker to exact punishment these days."

"He's a monster."

Rath's head cocked slightly as he stared at the water. It began to move differently, winding one way, then the other. I was so intrigued by it, I didn't realize he was staring at me until he cleared his throat.

"The water," I said. "How does it work?"

"It has life. A form of energy my body is attuned to."

"Can you all do that?"

"No. We're all different in certain ways. While I can grow a great many things, Reynaeros has a mastery over all things that come from the ground. Chester and Portia are able to break things down to their basest level and reform them."

"That's how he got me my muffins."

"Muffins," he repeated with a laugh. "Yeah, it's a pretty useless ability."

My brow furrowed. "It seems like the best out of the bunch."

"In our realm, there's hardly a use for it. We survive on things that grow. We live in them, eat them, we are them. I don't need to transport anything to another place because I can simply grow another one."

"Maybe you're all just unimaginative."

"Maybe," he agreed with a soft smile. "What about you?"

"I have no magical Earth powers."

"No, what's special about you? Reynaeros appears certain of your place in this, but I don't see how."

"Are you saying I'm not capable?"

He leaned back on his hands. "I'm sure you're capable of many things, ma belle, but this is not one that I believe anything in your world is capable of."

My heart hammered in my chest and I had to close my eyes to reorient myself. When I opened them, he was staring at me curiously.

"Why'd you call me that?"

"It's just an endearment. I spend most of my days in France. Does it offend you?"

"No, it's just... Someone else used to call me that."

"Someone who is gone now?"

I nodded. "It's fine."

"I can call you by your name if you'd like."

"No, I don't mind. I just haven't heard it in a while. At least, not outside of my head."

"If you're sure."

"So, are you going to tell me who you are in this mysterious 'court' that Reyn has?"

He smiled, revealing his row of sharp teeth. "I'm surprised you want to know, given your poor experiences with my kind."

"You're surprisingly pleasant to be around."

"Well, I'm glad to-"

"Rathiain," a familiar stern, gravelly voice said.

Rath dropped his head back to stare at the sky. "We've been caught, ma belle."

Footsteps crunched behind me, making the skin on my neck prickle. Suddenly, water leapt from the river, soaring over my head. A few drops landed in my hair, letting me know that they were icy cold. The angry shout of my arch nemesis was worth the chill a thousand times over.

Rath jumped to his feet, dancing out of the way of some sharp stakes that burst from the ground. I scrambled out of the way, not trusting him to keep me out of the crossfire.

"Relax, Reynaeros," Rath drawled. "You don't need to be angry because I got a woman wet when you've never managed it."

It was impossible not to laugh. When Reyn's angry expression shifted to me, I schooled my face into a glower befitting someone like him. He took a deep breath, wiping away some of the emotion on his face.

"Come, Kiera. We're going back inside."

"She's not doing any harm out here," Rath argued.

"You've been home for all of an hour and you're already causing problems. Perhaps you should return to your villa with your wine and human women."

"Oh, come now. I don't discriminate."

"I don't care. I'm just ready to be rid of you."

"It's tempting. I probably would have left, but I've made a friend. Aren't you proud of me?"

Reyn put two fingers to his forehead, clearly struggling to keep his composure. "Rathiain, I swear-"

"Stop being a dick, Reyn," I said, rolling my eyes and getting to my feet. As I swatted the dirt off of my pants, they both stared at me. "I'll go back to my cell. The last thing I want is you two destroying the forest over some stupid disagreement."

"At least somebody can be agreeable."

"That's what happens when you traumatize someone," Rath muttered.

Reyn growled, but didn't respond. When he held a hand out to me, I walked past him, drawing a laugh from

Rath. Someone swore and made a pained sound, but I didn't check to see which one.

I could hear them following close behind me and it unnerved me. My hands were balled into fists and it was difficult to force myself to unclench my jaw. Suddenly, someone came up beside me, making my body tense.

"Relax," Rath said softly. "If it makes you feel better, I don't believe he's going to hurt you."

"It doesn't, but thanks."

"Trust me. He's beating himself up internally. Maybe that will help you to smile when we get back inside."

"I doubt it. It's all a façade."

He hummed thoughtfully, glancing behind us. "I don't know. Now that I've seen him with you, I can tell something is different."

My nose wrinkled. "Yeah, he hasn't gotten laid since he got rid of his little harem. It's sure to weigh on a guy."

"Yeah, I saw his little decorative piece. Quite a spectacle."

"It's disgusting."

Rath walked ahead of me to hold the door open. I smiled at him as I walked through. He stayed by my side all the way to my room, which was an odd sort of comfort. Reyn had disappeared soon after we'd returned, thankfully.

"Are you sticking around?" I asked, stopping in the doorway.

He leaned against it, crossing his arms. "If I do, am I likely to receive a stab wound?"

"No," I said with a dramatic eye roll. "You seem like much better company than Rhinoceros, and the twins aren't around very much."

"It sounds like you're saying you want to hang out with me, ma belle."

"Well, there are few options in prison, so 'not a complete dickwad' is where I've set the bar for new acquaintances."

He chuckled before stepping back. "I don't know how long, but yeah. I'll be here."

"Cool. It won't bring his wrath down on you, will it?"

He continued to walk backward, flashing me a grin. "He'll get pissy, I'm sure, but I'm not afraid of him. He's many things, but my brother isn't that petty."

Before I could respond, he turned around, leaving me staring after him with my jaw on the floor. Fuck me.

Chapter 29

Reynaeros

Even after giving her the book, she refused to speak to me. Using my little spy plant, I'd watched her open it. She'd even smiled. Then, she sat down beside the window and read the whole thing, looking more content than she'd ever been in my presence.

I'd been finding reasons to go down to her corridor and when we'd run into each other, she would walk away without even looking at me. It was completely maddening.

I knew she was going through something that had broken her, but she was acting normal with everybody else. She'd always been cold to me, but before it had been laced with insults and jokes, sarcasm and feistiness. Now she wasn't giving me anything.

Seeing her conversing easily with Rathiain both infuriated and intrigued me. When I'd first seen them on that bank, she'd been smiling. There was nothing that would betray her recent state of mind. She was open, free. As soon as she'd heard my voice, all of that had melted away.

Entangled Realms

Really, it made no sense to me. Sure, I'd wronged her, but I'd also saved her multiple times now. I annihilated every threat to her in this place. Their heads still hung outside on the tree I'd grown specially for her. Wasn't there such a thing as balancing one's wrongs? Karma or something.

With a sigh, I determined that I would have to go see Lucia again. Probably tonight. There was nobody else and I was in no position to get anywhere with Kiera, obviously. She'd made that exceptionally clear.

I came to a stop in the hallway when I saw something sitting outside of her door. Glancing around to make sure nobody was around, I crouched down to pick it up. My brow furrowed as I tried to understand why she'd put it here.

Something was barely sticking out of the top and I plucked it out, unable to conceal my smile when I read the note.

Rhinoceros,
This lingering hatred in my soul won't let me forget about you either- particularly your penchant for acting like a beast. Seriously, my window has an up-close view of your little art project and it's disgusting. There are flies constantly propelling themselves against my window.

See attached art. I've heard this can be quite perilous for weird, wood fairy people. If you still feel inclined to inconvenience me with your attention, at least send more books. You owe me a whole library trip, but I've yet to find you agreeable, so this will have to suffice.

Kiera – NOT a rose
P.S. Do you have wings you're concealing somewhere? I bet they're pink.

Her handwriting made me laugh a little. She was intelligent- that much I'd known from the moment I met her- and she was eloquent when she wanted to be, but her scrawl was childish and large. The picture she'd drawn was even worse. It appeared to be a man- me, presumably- with wings and branches for arms. Her demented little drawing had me engulfed in flames.

When I realized I was still smiling, I folded the note and tucked it into my pocket, putting the book back in front of the door in case she wanted to reread it.

She wanted more books, but I didn't know what she liked to read, aside from that one. I thought about cheating and going to her old apartment in the hopes that her possessions were still there. This felt like an exciting challenge, though, and I wasn't one to back down. I would just have to take the time to figure it out.

I knocked on Lucia's door quickly, glad that there weren't many people left to see me. They would surely gossip, especially since I hadn't sought her out in a long time. The quiet was actually peaceful. I didn't have a whole selection of women to fuck anymore, but that didn't upset me as much as I might've expected.

They were always just a pastime for me, never actually making me feel anything. I fed on their intense emotions and took basic pleasure from their bodies. That was the extent of it.

My cock throbbed as the memory with Kiera on the rafter appeared in my mind. It was just sex, the same act I'd completed thousands of times. Why the hell had it felt so fucking extraordinary?

Lucia opened the door and groaned. "We aren't friends, Leander."

My nose scrunched up. "I would sooner burn myself to ash."

"Lovely. What do you want?"

"You know what."

"Do I?"

"Don't make me say it, Lucia. Right now, I'm considering using your body as fertilizer for my garden."

"Okay, okay. I just want you to say please."

"Absolutely not."

"Hey, if you want to win Kiera over, you're going to have to start being nice."

"I'm not trying to win her over. I simply need her to be more agreeable with me. Maybe consider me an acquaintance."

"It's presumptuous to assume she'd be capable of that, considering what you've done."

"I did the same to you," I pointed out. "And you're capable of holding a conversation without stabbing me."

She put a hand over her mouth as she laughed. "Come on. Even you have to know that you deserve it."

"Sure. If only it helped her move past her anger."

"Look, Leander. She isn't me and I'm not her. Just because we're both human doesn't mean we're the same. I've endured worse at the hands of men viler than you. At least you limit yourself to adults."

My lip curled at what she was implying. And they called me a beast. Maybe I was, but there was clearly a scale and I was not at the very top.

"Do you think me at all redeemable, Lucia?"

"Is that what you're going for?"

"With thoughts of home at the forefront of my mind, I've come to realize just how much I may have changed. I would never claim to be a good person, but I've fallen, if that makes sense. It is in our nature to care for living things, though we are not always a peaceful people. I suppose I only want to ensure that I'm worthy of what I'll have to take on when I return."

"And that is..."

"Well, the realm, of course."

"Of course," she repeated uncertainly before scooting to the side to allow me in.

🌷 🌷 🌷

As I made my way through the door, I looked down at the book I was holding. I couldn't be sure this was one she liked, but it was as good a guess as any. I was sure I'd get some wrong before I figured her out. This one was my favorite and I felt slightly nervous to be giving it to her.

Closing the door behind me, I glanced around. My heart rate spiked at the sight before me.

Three roses had fallen from the bush without warning. They hadn't begun to wither or sicken. Yesterday, they were in perfect health and now we'd lost them.

I quickly counted the remainder. Nine. That was a good amount, considering it had taken between one and three decades to lose a single one in the past. Now, though, the entire future was in question. We couldn't even begin to estimate how much time we had left.

"Oh, Reynaeros," a whiny voice said from behind me.

Gripping the book tighter, I turned to Riniya. She was wearing a tight, red and black corset and dark pants meant for fighting. The ensemble didn't make sense as a whole, but then, she wasn't a sensible person.

"Your gardening skills need work."

"What are you doing here, Riniya?" I spat her name like a curse, making her lip curl.

"Checking in, clearly."

"Twice in the span of two weeks when you haven't been here in two hundred years. Do you think me an imbecile?"

She smiled, revealing her sharp teeth. It may have been a comfort at one time, but now it was a threat. Always a threat.

Her hair, the same color as mine save for the streaks of brown, was tied in a long braid and looped over her shoulder. That and her pale, orange-tinted skin stood out starkly from her dark armor.

The only one that walked around here without concealment was Rathiain and he'd hardly been around for three hundred years. After blending in with this world for so long, her appearance was almost jarring to me, while also igniting a fierce homesickness that settled deep in my gut.

Entangled Realms

"Lyndis sensed something strange in your realm, so naturally, I came to check on you. Now I can see what's wrong." She gestured toward the fallen flowers.

"This is not my realm," I said through gritted teeth.

"Isn't it, though?"

She circled me and I turned my head to the side, tracking her movements. I didn't feel threatened by her, simply because she didn't have a reason to attack me. The only advantage she had over me was that I couldn't kill her. It was a significant advantage, but it wasn't because I lacked the ability, so I refused to count it against myself.

"You are different," she noted when she returned to my front.

"That tends to happen when one is locked out of their home for close to a millennium."

"Different since we last saw each other. It's in your energy."

"Hm."

Her eyes widened just as her lips curled upward. "You think you've found her."

"No. It is the same as always here."

"Can I meet her?"

I narrowed my eyes. "You need to leave."

"Come on. It won't hurt."

"Riniya, you set this match. If my turn does come around, you cannot interfere. This works both ways."

She huffed. "Fine. I'm just so curious. After all this time, I'm finding it hard to imagine what she must be like. Special, obviously. Beautiful, perhaps."

She studied me intently, but I betrayed nothing.

"Perhaps you should be more fearful," I pointed out.

She laughed delicately. "Regardless of the terms, I can't see a scenario where a human would stand a chance, much less a woman."

"It is clear about the circumstances."

"Sure, but success is never guaranteed in these sorts of things. It doesn't matter if you have found her. Even with all the time in the world, you could not make her a worthy contender because all one has to do is..."

She snapped her fingers and the floor split open. Thick black vines burst from it, their thorns dripping a grotesque, shimmering liquid. They reached to the ceiling, latching on with their tiny barbs, and spread across it.

"It's pointless to get your hopes up, dear brother. I hate to see you so disappointed."

With that, her body shifted, roots moving under her skin. Her form dissipated, leaving only her accursed plants and the scent of rot. Waving a hand, I summoned my own vines to wrap around hers, choking them quickly and forcing them to biodegrade.

After spreading thick-wound branches over the floor to patch it, I looked at the rosebush again. Nine flowers were still attached. With the timeline all fucked up, I couldn't begin to guess how much time that gave us.

Nine years. Nine months. Nine days. Hell, it could be nine hours.

Tucking the book under my arm, I rushed off to deliver it. It would be a bad day to linger and I was certain she wouldn't want me to anyway. Unfortunately, I couldn't give her space forever. We were running out of time.

Chapter 30

Kiera

"What do you mean I don't have a choice?" I nearly shrieked.

Reyn stood in my doorway with his arms crossed and a stern look on his face. "I need to test you today so I can determine our next steps. Let's go."

I spluttered for a second, looking back at the reading bench where I'd been nearly finished with the book he dropped off last night. It was one of my favorites. A Tale of Two Cities. I didn't know how he'd guessed correctly twice, but at least I got something good out of it.

God, that sounded like some Stockholm bullshit. Here I was, acting like he'd really done something nice because he brought me two books. Forget all about the prison, the fighting, the rape, and the annihilation of my autonomy.

"Please," he implored when I didn't answer.

"Fine."

He held an arm out, which I ignored. My body felt a bit better today, though it was still tight and achy. I was pleasantly surprised when I made it through the training doors without feeling winded.

"So, what do we have going on today, boss?"

"I'm not your boss... Oh. Sarcasm."

"Wow, look at you. You're moving out of the clueless toddler stage. Is this when you grow your wings?"

"I told you I don't have wings."

"Well, I don't believe you. You're hiding something under all of that beyond branch horns." I gestured up and down his body with a grimace.

"And you're hiding something inside your head, little rose. We all have our secrets."

"Touché."

"I'll share one if you do." He had a mischievous look on his face that seemed out of place on him. I had a feeling his game would end in a way that gave me nightmares.

"Nope."

"Come on. I've been giving you books."

"You were supposed to let me use the library."

He took his lower lip between his teeth. My eyes widened when I saw how sharp they were, like Rath's had been. I'd seen Reyn smile before and they'd been normal, which made me wonder how their concealment worked. To me, the teeth just confirmed the fairy idea.

When he saw me looking, he quickly released the lip and looked around casually. "Fine. Soon. First, we have to see where you're at."

"I guarantee it's not monster fighting level."

"You'll get there."

"Oh, god. You didn't deny that it's a monster."

With a sigh, he grabbed a knife and tossed it in the air, then caught the handle like it was the easiest thing in the world.

"Pick a weapon and fight me."

"Okay. What sort of fight are we having and what are the rules?"

"None of that is established in a real battle, little rose."

Rolling my eyes, I grabbed the claymore I'd practiced with a few times. This time, I didn't drop it and it felt a bit more natural in my grip. Trailing my eyes over his body, I wondered how much he could actually heal himself from.

"I see that murderous look in your eye," he noted, swiping his dagger through the air a couple of times. With it, he looked menacing and undeniably capable of having me on my back in a pool of blood within five seconds.

"What can I say? You make me want to stab things."

"By things, you mean me."

"Obviously. Let's just get this over with, fairy boy."

His jaw clenched for a moment before he took two steps forward. I swore and sidestepped, pivoting so that he stayed in my sights. A vine came out of nowhere, shooting between my feet and attempting to wrap around me. I stomped it with one foot and jumped over it.

"Magic isn't allowed."

"Everything is allowed. It needs to be as realistic as possible."

I threw one hand in the air. "This is ridiculous. There's no way I can stand against something that can do all of this."

"Not something, little rose. Someone."

"Oh, god damnit."

Before I could go on about the senselessness of this whole thing, he rushed toward me. I tried to step out of the way, but he clipped my shoulder, knocking me off my feet. His arm came around me before I hit the ground and he laid me down gently.

Putting a hand on his chest, I pushed him away, then stood. Picking up my dropped sword, I immediately swung it at him. He leapt backward, a short trunk appearing under his foot, which he used to propel himself further away from me.

I grabbed a few throwing knives from the table and tucked them into my belt. He smiled as he watched me, somehow making it look dangerous, even though his teeth had returned to normal- well, my normal.

"Are you gonna keep your distance like a little bitch?" I asked.

"I thought you preferred for me to be far away from you."

"Sure, but not when I'm trying to kill you."

He winked, then his eyes dropped briefly to the floor. I immediately moved three steps back, narrowly avoiding the thorny vines that appeared to grab me. Grabbing one of the knives, I threw it toward him. It missed by a yard, instead hitting the wall. He turned to look at it and I used the opportunity to throw another.

Seeing it just in time, he put an arm in front of him, the skin turning a smoky green. The knife sunk into it, then it seemed to be pushed out from the inside. The skin returned to normal with barely a scratch on it.

"If you were smart, you'd have thrown another just after the second. I may not have been quick enough to block both."

"I'll remember that next time."

"Good."

Moving closer to him, I reevaluated my approach. Rath told me that Reyn could summon anything that grew from the ground. That was a lot of things, especially since it didn't appear they had to follow the rules of nature. Unfair advantage, if you asked me.

I heard the next one before it sprung from the ground. With a wide swing, I managed to cut it in half. One wrapped around my ankle from behind, pulling me to the ground. Grabbing a knife from my belt, I stabbed it at the base, which made it loosen its hold.

"Okay, I need more information."

"What would you like to know, little rose?"

"Can these things feel?"

"No, but I do."

"So, hurting them hurts you."

"They are created from my energy and their life force is connected to me. We essentially have a reciprocal relationship."

"That's why stabbing that one made it weaken. It pained you and you lost your hold on it."

He smiled as he stepped toward me, looking like a predator. "This is why you may have a chance."

"That's assuming the monster has the same powers that you do."

"He does."

My brow furrowed. Before I could ask my next question, four thin tree trunks burst out of the ground, boxing me in. Their branches quickly lengthened, creating a sort of cage. I brought the sword down on one of the barriers. It quivered, but stayed put. Changing direction, I thrust the blade straight through one of the trees. When the branch began to sag, I hurtled over it.

Since I'd been focusing on the plants, I didn't notice Reyn's location. He grabbed me from behind, wrapping an arm around my neck tightly, but not taking away my breath. The position made panic begin to ignite in my chest. My breaths quickened as I fended off the attacks in my mind.

His grip loosened a little and he planted a palm against my collarbone. "I'm not going to hurt you, Kiera."

Slipping my last knife out of my belt, I thrust it backward. He released me with a growl and I took a few steps away from him before turning around.

"Maybe your weakness is being distracted by the female form."

Pulling his hand away from his stomach, he looked down at the red with a grimace. "I was not distracted by your body."

"A distraction is a distraction. Does this mean I win?"

"Not unless I yield."

"Then yield."

He laughed dryly. "No."

Chewing on the inside of my lip, I closed the distance between us. He looked at me warily as I put a hand to his stomach.

"How do you heal yourself?"

When he pulled the t-shirt over his head, I wanted to move away, but I stayed in place. As I watched, the skin around the wound turned that pale, smoky green color. The edges of it seemed to reach out, twining with the skin on the other side. It looked like they were weaving together like when someone was knitting a scarf.

"Hm. Neat. Is that the color of your skin?"

His gaze raised to me, then dropped. "Yes."

Nodding, I tightened my grip on the hilt of my dagger. "Can you actually die?"

"Of course. Every creature has a fatal location on their body."

"Like the heart. Is that fatal for you?"

"Yes."

Reaching up with my free hand, I touched his chest with the tips of my fingers, exactly where his heart was. His muscles tensed at the same time that he sucked in a breath. I trailed down to his hip, then moved closer to the middle.

"Kiera."

"Yes?"

I looked up at him through my lashes. He was staring down at me intently, his brows tight, almost as if he was confused. When I licked my lips, he tracked the movement. He startled me by putting a hand at the side of my neck and I almost stepped back.

"Stop being a coward, little rose. Where are those thorns?"

His thumb stroked across my jaw gently and his gaze fell to my mouth again. I kept my expression neutral as he dipped his head a little. When his lips barely brushed mine, his breaths quickened.

My fingers moved over his abdomen, stopping just underneath his wound. Just as he began to close that last bit of distance, I shoved two fingers into the hole. Before he had a chance to stop me, I brought the blade up and sunk it into his chest.

He stumbled back and dropped to the ground, still holding onto me. I landed on top of him, keeping the knife

Entangled Realms

embedded in his skin. His lip curled and a growl rumbled in his chest. I couldn't wipe the smile off my face.

"Distracted, Reyn?"

Sliding his hand to my throat, he tightened his grip. I gritted my teeth and twisted the knife, relishing the pained expression on his face. Hooking his leg around mine, he flipped us over so I was on my back. I held onto the handle as tightly as I could, unwilling to give up my advantage. There was no way he could last much longer.

Leaning down, he brushed his lips over mine. I latched onto his lower one, biting as hard as I could. His blood dripped into my mouth and I released him.

My eyes widened when I saw his teeth had reverted to their shark state. Pressing his face against my neck, he grazed me with them, making goosebumps travel across my skin.

"It was a smart move."

"Thanks," I replied dryly.

"But you don't know your opponent, little rose."

"Oh, yeah? Go on."

Grabbing my wrist, he forced it to the ground, taking the knife with it. Blood poured from the wound, but as I watched, he started to heal it slowly.

"To stab a person in the heart, you have to know how to find it."

"You've got to be kidding."

He chuckled darkly. "Should we go another round?"

"Fuck you. Get off of me."

After waiting an annoyingly long time, he got to his feet and offered me his hand. I ignored it, pushing off the ground with a groan.

"Where is it then?"

"That's a secret my kind doesn't reveal to anyone."

"Right. My guess is you don't have one. I should've figured that was the case before I tried it."

Something pounded in my head, making me grimace.

"Are you hungry, Kiera?"

"No. I'm going to, uh, go to my room."

"It's early."

"You interrupted my reading," I replied simply before heading to the door.

As soon as I was in the hallway, I sped up. The walk to my room took too long and I nearly didn't make it to the bathroom before pain gripped my stomach. Dropping to my knees, I grabbed the sides of the toilet seat and threw up the little I'd eaten today.

It was quick, but it made me feel tired. I crawled into bed, pulling the covers up to my chin, and closed my eyes, hoping I'd have good dreams for once. I didn't know how much more darkness I could handle behind my eyes.

Chapter 31

Kiera

Little rose,

You've been avoiding me for two days. Let's not forget that you are the one that injured me— quite badly, I might add. Yet here I am bringing you another book. If I let you do it a few more times, will you finally start to tolerate me? I'll give you three more well-aimed blows. Any more than that is just greedy.

Reyn

Did he think he was funny? I wasn't amused. Unless he let me cut off his dick, I wouldn't tolerate him for a second.

"Love note?"

Putting a hand over my chest, I glared at Rath. He smiled, then rolled his lips, painting on an apologetic expression. Shaking my head, I ripped the note in half a few times, letting the pieces fall to the floor.

"Just your brother being his usual self."

"Ah, so he's being a dick."

Raising my brows in agreement, I opened the door wider so he could come in. I left it slightly open and went over to the window seat. He joined me on the other end of it and looked around curiously.

"You got the nice room."

"Apparently, I'm special."

"I guess as far as humans go, you're not too bad."

"Did you and your brother fall from completely different trees?"

He laughed. "Considering he'd probably be offended by that joke, that might be the case." His expression cleared and he turned his body toward me. "He's not terrible, you know. I give him shit and he does the same. Over the years, he's just changed. We all have."

"It seems like you turned out fine. So did Chester and Portia."

"We each found ways to deal with it, Kiera. Seven centuries is a very long time to be miserable."

"How'd you deal with it?"

"I spent a good eighty years drunk and high. Eventually, I began traveling. I spend most of my time in France. I have a vineyard, an art studio, and a home with a vast amount of land filled with nature."

"That sounds lovely."

"It is, but it'll never be home."

There was such a forlorn look on his face, I felt my chest constrict. Reaching out, I took his hand and squeezed it. He tensed for a moment, then gripped me back. I was thrown off by the texture of his skin, but not in a bad way. It felt like it was tough, but still soft.

"And the others?"

"There are many of us and most did not stick around after the first century. They gave up, understandably. Chester and Portia acquiesced, I suppose. They chose human names and spend much of their time around your kind."

"What made you leave?"

"In truth, I do not wish anyone to die. Being here, I could not escape it. It pained me."

"What do you mean?"

"I feel it. Their energy, their fear and agony."

"Does he not?"

"He does. More than most of us. It's why he continues this."

"But you said it's uncomfortable."

"In this world... We have existed here for quite a long time. The monotony can become insufferable. A human's pain is strong and though it feels like a knife to the soul, it can become addictive."

"You become addicted to the pain."

"Yes. At first, I think it was a way to punish himself. Then, it became almost a relief. Feeling something is better than nothing and sometimes, another person's worst pain is more bearable than that which we hold inside ourselves. There is only one emotion that matches the power of someone's pain."

"What's that?"

"Anger."

"Is that why he makes sure to piss me off constantly?"

"It is why he wanted to rid you of it by breaking you. He cannot bear your anger. It's affecting him greatly."

Looking out at the tree, I tried to wrap my head around that. "Shouldn't it feel similar to sadness?"

"Pain has a certain sweetness to it. Those that have been touched by the worst sort of agony find a certain comfort in it. That's what it's like. Contrarily, anger is chaotic. There's no controlling it or choosing how to use it. It is not pain, even if it's rooted in it. It's a lack of control. It shapes everything into something ugly and unrecognizable. Our kind does not stay angry long if we can help it. We're quick to forgive and holding onto resentment can twist our energy into something grotesque. Rotten."

"At one point, Reyn was different, then?"

"Yes and no. All the worst parts of him have become the cloak he wears to hide all the ugly things beneath. Like the anger you hide behind."

Pursing my lips, I tried to shake off the thoughts trying to rise to the surface. Rath and his brother seemed to be similarly perceptive in a way that made it difficult to hide the things they didn't need to see. My weaknesses.

"What could someone like Reyn have to hide from?"

"Reynaeros... He's strong, there's no doubt about that. The thing is, the most frightening beast is one you can't always face. Your failures. Your weaknesses. Your insecurities and the secrets you've never let taste the open air. The thing we hide from more than anything else. Ourselves."

He breathed a sigh and looked out the window. To my relief, the heads had been removed, but the tree still remained.

"That doesn't make me want to forgive him."

"I know and I wouldn't ask you to. To accomplish this, you don't necessarily have to, at least as far as we know. Unfortunately, we actually know precious little."

Taking his hand again, I implored him with my eyes. "Please tell me what I'm supposed to be doing here. I can't do this if I don't know what I'm supposed to be fighting."

He pulled away and got to his feet. I was filled with disappointment when he strode toward the door. He looked at the plant on my dresser, cocking his head, then took it from its place. Without turning, he stopped in the doorway.

"Kiera, there's a curse on our court that traps us in your world. To beat it, he has to find the person that could contend with the one thing he cannot fight himself. We can return home when you bring him to his knees."

The door clicked closed behind him and, just like the last time he walked away from me, I was left completely dumbfounded.

🌷 🌷 🌷 🌷

"Hey, Collie," I greeted, setting my plate down.

She smiled at me, then looked at my food with a frown. "Aren't you hungry?"

"That's why I have the food."

"I'd hardly call that enough with how much you've been training."

I shrugged. "My stomach has been iffy since coming here."

"This isn't like Lucy's thing, is it?"

"No. Just a sensitive stomach."

"Alright."

"Speaking of Lucy, where is she?"

She glanced around the room. "I'm not sure. She's been distant lately."

"That doesn't sound like her. Should I be worried?"

"Probably not. Although..."

"What is it?"

"It's probably nothing, but since the rest of the girls are gone now, it makes me wonder."

"Collie, we're friends. Don't hide whatever it is, please."

"The other night, I saw Lee go into her room."

Something felt like it curdled in my stomach. "I thought he didn't like her."

"He doesn't, but who else is there?"

"Both of us. Not that I want that to happen, obviously."

"He's being careful with you and Lucy told me he basically gave Chester and I permission to see each other. I don't understand why he'd do that, though."

"Maybe because he cares about him."

"Yeah..."

"I'm gonna go find her and make sure she's okay."

"Do you want me to come?"

"No. I want to see if she'll talk to me without feeling like we're ganging up on her. If he's hurting her after this long, I don't know how she'll be feeling."

"Okay, Kiera. You're a good person, you know."

I forced a smile. "Just doing what any decent person would do."

Leaving my food behind, I headed into the hallway, making a beeline for her door. I knocked a few times, then tapped my foot while I waited. If she wasn't in here, I wasn't sure where else to look.

After what felt like an eternity, she cracked it and peered out at me. Her eyes widened and she tried to school her features, but I could see the panic there.

"Kiera," she said tightly. "Uh, what's up?"

"I just wanted to check on you. It's been a few days since we talked."

"Yeah, I've been busy."

"What is there to be busy with in this place?"

Her eyes darted to the side for a brief second. "Just working on my art skills now that I have all this free time."

Chewing on the inside of my cheek, I considered barging into the room and seeing for myself. The way she was blocking the small gap in the door made me feel suspicious. I felt something akin to fear at the thought of her being hurt because of what Reyn did. It would be my fault.

Stepping closer to her, I dropped my voice. "Lucy, tell me what's going on."

"Nothing is going on."

"I don't know if I believe you. Is someone in there?"

Her eyes drifted to the side again. "No."

Gritting my teeth, I put a hand on the doorframe. "I'll kill him if he's touching you."

"Kiera," she said, a note of hostility lacing the word. "Just because you can attack Lee without being punished for it doesn't mean you can come around like you deserve to know everything."

My eyes widened, but before I could respond, she shut the door. I yearned to knock again, but I didn't know what to say. Apologize, maybe, though I didn't think I'd done anything wrong by worrying about her wellbeing. It occurred to me that I just didn't know either of my friends very well and she may be right. I didn't have a right to demand anything from her.

That didn't mean I was okay with what was happening. If she wouldn't talk to me, I'd have to confront the root of the problem.

Chapter 32

Reynaeros

The image I'd been subjected to was enough to make me murderous. Between Kiera's duplicitous antics and my brother's attempts to undermine me, I was inclined to just burn this entire place to the ground and start over.

Ever since she'd come here, things had taken a turn for the worst. The fights weren't as interesting with new contenders every night, I didn't have a group of women to choose from when I was feeling ornery, and every time I was in her vicinity, I had to be prepared for her to stab me. It was a fucking nightmare.

Dropping onto my back, I stared up at the ceiling. With my foul mood, the plants growing from my ceiling began to shift, some of them growing thorns and others darkening. I breathed, trying to get a grip on my anger before it started to infect my mind.

When I tried to find something nice to focus on, Kiera's face swam behind my eyes. The smell of rot assaulted me as my anger multiplied. Just the thought of her and her unnecessarily volatile energy made it spread to me. If I could get rid of her right now, I would do exactly that. Considering how broken she appeared, it would be a mercy.

Now she was avoiding me, as if I was the one that had wronged her. She had stabbed me in the chest with the intention of killing me. Perhaps she was right when she told me I was weak.

If she could so easily land a blow like that, she might actually have a chance of bringing me to my knees, but she'd made a mistake. She did not land a killing blow and now I wouldn't allow myself to let my guard down. In the back of my mind, I'd known she was playing a game, but I'd still fallen into her trap. Why the hell did she have any sort of effect on me?

It was what she'd done to my body. Now that I didn't have my harem, it was nearly impossible to work off my frustrations and my body craved the release. With her closeness and her trickery, I'd been weak for but a moment. It wouldn't happen again.

Even as I decided it, I remembered the smell of her. It shouldn't have been pleasant. It was sweat, the lingering scent of her soap, and the unique signature of her energy. Just lying here, I could taste it if I reached out.

My cock stirred in my pants, making me grit my teeth. Doing that would be a bad idea. As long as I didn't think about her, though, there was no harm.

Pulling it out, I stroked it a few times, a shiver running down my spine at the sensation. My barbs pushed at my skin and I allowed them to poke out. Without the concealment on it, I had more feeling in it, the texture and ridges so sensitive I was nearly overwhelmed.

I imagined a faceless body before me, naked and bared to me. While there was nothing special about humans, I'd been fucking them so long that I was able to see their bodies as a source of pleasure. Their pussies were warm and not completely smooth, the subtle ridges inside making them all the more pleasurable.

Our females didn't lubricate the way they did in this world. With my own sap, it wasn't necessary and I'd never thought much about it. The memory of Kiera's wetness on my tongue made my breaths speed up. The body in my mind quickly morphed, the quote tattooed on her skin making it impossible to deny who it was.

Flipping onto my knees, I held onto the headboard with one hand and stroked my cock with the other. Now that she'd invaded my fantasy, it was her face I saw below me. My hips moved, thrusting into my hand, and I remembered our days in the training room, her pussy gripping me up on the rafter, her mouth sucking on me.

With a groan, I moved faster. Fuck, I could just imagine how incredible she would feel right now. I wanted to smell her, taste her, fucking own her. For the first time, I was interested in the sounds someone else would make while consumed by pleasure.

My grip on the headboard tightened, the wood beginning to splinter. It cut into my skin, making my senses heighten. My mouth dropped open as pleasure radiated down my spine.

"Fuck, little rose," I groaned as my pleasure hit its peak. Sweating, panting, and feeling extremely unsure of what had just happened, I dropped onto my back to stare at the ceiling.

It was enough to get it out of my system. I was certain of it.

🌷 🌷 🌷 🌷

At the bottom of the stairs, I stopped, trying to decide if I was being an idiot. Frankly, I'd felt like more of one every day for a while now. There were more important things to focus on, but Rathiain, the little shit that he was, had removed my plant from Kiera's room, so I had no idea how she'd been for over twenty-four hours.

After what happened earlier today, I should have been avoiding her like the plague. Instead, I found myself entering her corridor. It was silent here in an almost unnerving way.

As I made my way toward her room at the end of the hall, I saw light coming from inside. Her door was cracked and soft voices were coming from inside. I couldn't identify them and I feared it would be Lucia and Collette. That would only make this situation more awkward.

Stopping in front of the door, I discreetly peered through the gap. Kiera's laugh reached my ears, followed by a deeper one. A sort of rage twisted my gut when I saw Rathiain sitting on the bench with her. They both had their knees up and their feet were planted in front of them as they faced each other. He reached forward to tuck a strand of hair behind her ear with a soft smile on his face.

Pushing the door open, I crossed my arms and leaned against the frame. They both looked up, one with an expression of shock and the other with unconcealed amusement. Kiera's face quickly morphed into something between disgust and annoyance as she regarded me.

"What do you want?" she drawled. "I've been training with Rath, but if you'd like another blade to the chest, I'm happy to oblige."

"You're supposed to be training with me," I pointed out.

"I don't think it's wise to take lessons from the person I have to fight against someday."

When I narrowed my eyes at my brother, he shrugged. "You should learn that honesty goes a long way, especially with those you've wronged."

"Get out."

Kiera scoffed. "You can't just go around telling everybody what to do."

"Actually, I can. That's what one does when they are king."

She rolled her eyes. "From where I'm sitting, you have no crown." She cocked her head. "No realm, either. What exactly are you king of, Reyn?"

Dropping my head back, I laughed dryly. Rathiain said something quietly to her and it sounded like she was arguing with him. When I returned my gaze to them, he was standing.

"Both of you clearly need to have some candid conversations, lest one of you ends up killing the other. Then nobody gets to return home."

"Perhaps Riniya will allow you back if I'm gone," I mused. "Next time she visits, I'll call for you."

His eyes widened. "She's been here?"

"Yes and you would know that if you ever gave a damn about what went on here."

"Forgive me I'm tired of waiting around when nothing ever happens."

"Things are happening now, Rathiain," I bellowed, making him shrink back a little.

Kiera pulled her knees in tighter, watching our interaction closely. There wasn't fear rolling off of her, but her anger had dissipated slightly.

Taking a deep breath, I swiped a hand down my face. "Can I talk to you?"

He nodded and joined me in the hall, shutting the door behind him. After walking a little further away, I turned to him, resisting the urge to wrap something around his neck.

"What are you doing?"

"You'll have to be more specific."

"Why are you getting close to her?" I asked through gritted teeth.

His brow furrowed. "She is a kind person, Reynaeros, and she has been through a lot. She deserves someone to talk to."

"She has friends here."

Breathing a dry laugh, he leaned against the wall and shoved his hands in his pockets. "You're blind to so much. You want her to help us, but all you do is attack her, whether physically or emotionally. Forgive me if I actually want a chance of returning home."

"So, you are using her." The thought made my head feel hot.

"No. As I said, she is a kind person and I like her." When I narrowed my eyes, he rolled his, the blue looking calmer than mine felt. "I am not pursuing her, Reynaeros. The fact that it would bother you means you should take a harder look at yourself."

"She is a means to an end. She will help us, then she will return to her life and we will go home to ours. I will not consider her anything else."

"And that's exactly why you will continue to fail. She is not dense and your ruse will not fool her. There is something inside her that I know you have felt and I have a feeling that it will have some sort of impact on how this plays out."

"Then find out what it is."

"I won't be your pawn, regardless of your title. Long ago, I made it clear that I have no interest in that cursed throne, yet my connection to it still landed me here. Fix this."

He brushed past me and I fisted my hands. His footsteps paused, making me turn to him.

"You can live in denial inside your own mind, but that spy plant really worked against you. If only your, uh, little rose knew what you fantasized about in the dark."

With that, he continued on his way. I watched him until he disappeared through the stairwell. My rage and humiliation were warring inside of me, making me feel more conflicted than ever.

"Fucking bastard," I muttered before returning to Kiera's room.

She was in the same place, but had a blanket thrown over her lap and her book perched on her knees. It looked like she was nearly done with it, which gave me an idea.

"Follow me, little rose."

"No," she replied simply without turning from her book.

"I swear you'll like where I'm taking you."

Her jaw clenched before she set the book aside. "Fine, but I'm bringing a dagger."

"I'd expect nothing less."

She marched past me into the hall, even though she didn't know the way we were going. Pursing my lips, I refused to allow myself to be amused. Today I had two goals and they didn't revolve around being nice or groveling. None of that would work and I had no intention of humiliating myself.

I was going to piss her off and regain control of this situation.

Chapter 33

Kiera

Reynaeros passed me on the stairs, setting a pace that didn't accommodate my shorter legs. I scrambled after him, not sure if he was trying to be agreeable or storming off like a toddler. It wouldn't be the first time he'd thrown a little fit. Then again, I hadn't been much better since coming here. I'd acted petty quite a few times, but I'd earned the right, in my opinion.

My heart started beating faster when we went through the door that led into the plant-filled foyer with the red door. He didn't go left, though, instead opening a green set of double doors on the right. I kept my eyes firmly away from the other one that felt like a beacon. He couldn't know that I was aware of it.

Once I stepped inside, my jaw dropped. It legitimately might have been on the ground.

The ceiling was domed and significantly higher than the training room. It had art on it, like the Sistine Chapel, but this was nature and sunlight, the forest and moonlight.

Each piece of it was distinct, yet flowed into the other like they were actually shifting right before my eyes.

Bookshelves lined the walls in the rectangular room, rising so high that there were those cool sliding ladders. I'd always wanted one of those. This was a far cry from my off-balance, waist-level bookshelf in my bedroom.

There was a large wooden desk at the other end of the room. It was connected to two trees on either side of it, as if it was a part of them and had been carved like that. It probably had been now that I thought about it.

The tops of the trees nearly brushed the ceiling and their branches arched outward. Curtains of what looked like cherry blossoms reached all the way to the floor, blocking out some of the light from the window.

Three comfortable-looking chairs were stationed in front of a large stone fireplace between the shelves on one wall. On the opposite one, there was a window that overlooked the river. As I continued further, I couldn't stop taking it all in. If a library could make someone orgasm, this would be the one. I now understood why he didn't want to share it.

Running my hand over the desk, I marveled at how soft the wood felt. It was dark, like espresso, but I didn't think it was stained, judging by the matching color of the trees it was connected to. Once I crossed through the blossom curtain, I stopped.

Whatever was outside the window was not the industrial park or the river. There wasn't a single part of it that looked familiar. It was an explosion of color, from the grass that was nearly dark enough to be black and the flowers blooming on all the trees. The trunks of some were the palest green, almost white, with black speckles.

It looked like... Well, not to beat a dead horse, but it looked like some sort of fairy land. I realized that I was smiling as I stared, but how could I not? It was gorgeous and it was decidedly not part of this world.

"Is this an illusion?" I asked.

"No."

Reyn's voice was close behind me and I gritted my teeth, feeling proud of myself for not jumping. Or stabbing.

He took a step to the side, putting some distance between us. I glanced sidelong at him, then returned my gaze to the window. It didn't look cold there, like it was here right now. I could imagine running through the grass with no shoes and lying in the sun. Eli would love it.

"Are you sad?"

I blinked and felt something roll down my cheek. I swiped it away quickly.

"No. It's just pretty. What is it?"

"It's home." There was an intense longing in his voice, which matched what I saw in his eyes. The pale green appeared to move like a mirage, darker colors joining and swirling.

"I don't understand."

With a sigh, he moved to stand beside the window, staring down at the scene. I joined him, keeping a few feet of distance between us.

"This wing is not a part of your realm. As this exists here, it also exists there."

"How?"

"My library is not just wood and paper. The very essence of it is made of me. Everything here, aside from the books, was born of my own body, grown and nurtured by my energy. It has a certain connection to me that I was able to latch onto through the space between our worlds. It is the only piece I have not lost."

My chest constricted. Looking around, I again felt the intensity of its beauty. Nothing I would ever lay eyes on again would be as powerful as this. In a way, this place was alive. I wondered if it would continue to exist if Reyn were to die. If so, I'd be claiming it if I ever found a way to kill him.

"Pick a book," he instructed.

I couldn't help but laugh. "There are so many. How am I supposed to choose?"

He hummed thoughtfully, stepping through the curtain and looking one way, then the other. After a moment, he gestured for me to follow him to the left. He reached one of the ladders and looked up.

"On the eighth shelf, there is a book with a gold spine."

"Then get it."

When he gave me an exasperated look, I sighed. I'd climbed up that rope, so this should be easy enough. So long as he didn't start shaking the ladder or something. I wouldn't put it past him.

In the end, I made it up to the shelf without issue. Running my fingers over the spines, I smiled at the feeling of them. I'd never seen so many books in one place.

"Have you read all of these?" I called.

"Kiera, I have been alive for a millennium. Yes, I have read them."

Pulling out the gold book, I started climbing down. When I was a few steps from the ground, he took either side of my waist and set me on the ground.

"Sit."

"I-"

"For once, will you not argue with me? Sit and read the fucking book."

"Fine," I muttered, picking the chair directly in front of the fireplace. It was so cozy, I imagined tucking my feet underneath me and drinking hot cocoa while I refused to leave this spot for an entire day.

The book wasn't one I recognized, but it felt old. The writing style was dated in a beautiful way that made me think of stormy moors and angsty, forbidden love. I quickly got lost in it, unable to bear leaving the characters' heads for a moment. It was just as I imagined, but better. There was such a beautiful sort of melancholy to it and I found tears pricking my eyes multiple times.

"Are you enjoying it?" Reyn asked from his place standing by the fireplace. The way he leaned one hand on the mantle made him look like he belonged in the world I was reading about.

"It's wonderful. I can't believe I haven't read it before."

"It was never actually published."

"That's crazy. I would do anything to meet this person."

As I turned the page, I began to chew on my lip. I was in that state where I wanted to know what was going to happen immediately, but I was also enjoying the story so much that I never wanted it to end.

When something touched the tops of my legs, my stomach lurched. Reyn's palms flattened, his fingers spreading over the curve of my thighs. I tried to kick out at him, but his grip tightened. He dropped to his knees and trailed further up.

"Reyn," I warned.

"Go ahead. Tell me all of the nasty, violent things you plan on doing to me."

"Stop."

"Keep reading."

"I have no interest in being your fuck toy. You don't get to keep hurting us."

"Us?"

"I've heard about your little escapades with Lucy. It's disgusting that you would go back to ruining her just because you disposed of your other toys."

When he laughed, my lip curled. "I am not fucking Lucia."

"Oh? What else would have you making late night house calls?"

"Let me show you."

Once his fingers hooked over the waistband of my shorts, my heart started to hammer madly. My breaths quickened and tears pricked my eyes. Resuming my attempts to kick him, I started thinking of all the ways this could go.

I'd been so stupid to follow him here. Nobody would hear me scream, no matter how much he hurt me. I didn't even know how many people knew the way here. He could keep me here for days.

He managed to get my shorts off, then wrapped his arms around my thighs, keeping me firmly in place. I struck out at him, but twining vines appeared in front of me, creating a sort of barrier between us. They were sparse enough for me to see him, but I couldn't break through.

His gaze raised to meet mine and the green pools were thrashing. "Read."

I shook my head. "Please stop."

"Stop being weak, Kiera."

"Reyn," I cried, the first tears falling from my eyes.

His lips pulled to the side as he stared at me. "Am I frightening you?"

"No. Just stop."

"Mm. You can't lie to me. I'm learning how to read your strange energy."

He brushed a thumb along my slit slowly, staring down at me with a curious expression. I was uncomfortable, scared, and feeling self-conscious. Whatever he was doing here didn't make sense and I couldn't figure out what the game was.

"Please, Reyn. Just... Just give me a little longer."

"No."

"D-don't hurt me."

"Actually, I intend to do the opposite. Your body may have been taken from you, but that doesn't mean you can let them keep it."

"I don't understand."

Settling a thumb over my clit, he gently made a circle around it. I clenched my teeth, forcing myself to stay still. The sensitive little traitor didn't seem to care much about my circumstances. The idea of this made me more nauseous than him simply using me.

"Shutting down is weak. I'm going to give you pleasure and you're going to claim it."

"No. I don't want that."

"It literally will not hurt you and I will do it anyway."

He inserted a finger, curling it as he brought it back out. Closing his lips around it, something akin to a growl rumbled in his chest. When he opened his eyes and met mine, they were continuously rippling outward, like wind traveling over water.

"You might as well allow yourself to enjoy it, little rose."

The flat of his tongue settled over my clit, applying slight pressure. I pursed my lips, my teeth indenting them painfully when his finger slid inside me again. I tried breaking through the vines again, but it was useless. It didn't matter how much I fought or protested. I was stuck and this was happening.

He inserted a second finger, moving them so expertly that my toes curled. Shaking my head, I squeezed my eyes shut. I started playing The Princess Bride, hoping I could focus on it enough to get through this. He would stop eventually.

The tip of his tongue flicked my clit, forcing out a little huff of air. No. Princess Buttercup and her gross fiancé. That was what I needed to think about. I tried replacing his face with Reyn's, but the way he suddenly sucked on my clit shattered the image.

His tongue seemed to widen, the pressure moving outward. When it pressed against my clit from both sides, I gasped. Looking down at him, I realized he'd split the damn thing in two like some demonic, serpentine creature.

Moving the two sides back and forth, he stroked me in a way that had me whimpering. It was indirect enough not to overwhelm me, but left absolutely no way for me to ignore the sensations it brought.

His grip on my thigh tightened before he lifted my leg higher and perched it over his shoulder. When he groaned, I felt the vibration against me. He met my eyes, then the vine wall fell away. I held his gaze, a dozen thoughts rushing into my head.

He pulled his fingers free, then sunk his tongue inside of me. Swearing, I instinctively reached forward, tangling my hands in his hair. A fire burned in his eyes and whatever control he had over his concealment began to slip.

I gasped as branches began to extend from his head, similar to Rath's, but larger. They were a creamy white color with green lines swirling around them that looked like they'd been etched there. While they were about the same height as his brother's they curved to the side, then back like I'd seen with horns.

"Fuck," he muttered, pulling back.

Grabbing onto the branches, I held him to me. His eyes widened as he stared at me. After a minute, he dragged his tongues up the length of me and settled them on either side of my clit again. Once he inserted his fingers, I tightened my grip on him.

Heat was spreading from my core and my legs were trembling violently. I could no longer control the sounds he was ripping from my throat, so I stopped trying. We'd come this far and I was aching for release.

I felt his stare, but I dropped my head back, looking up at the ceiling as my muscles contracted. My thighs squeezed his head and I thought I might actually rip the branches from his head. I was pretty sure they were the only things holding me to this plane.

An unfettered cry echoed in the room as my body convulsed. Reyn pushed his tongue inside of me briefly and tightened his grip on my leg. He didn't release me as I recovered and I could feel him looking at me, but I continued to ignore him.

Gasping for breath, I stared up at the artwork on the ceiling. Everything was beginning to settle and I was far from ready to face what had just happened. Or why it had happened.

As I sat there, I began to feel angry. This was a different sort of shame I hadn't experienced yet and it was the last thing I'd needed. It was clear he was trying to confuse me or bend me to his will. Sexual acts might have been enough to make him come undone, but that wouldn't be me.

"Jesus," he said through gritted teeth, releasing me. "What happened? You're fucking explosive all of a sudden."

Grabbing my shorts, I stepped into them quickly, then headed for the door. At least I knew where the library was now. It didn't do me much good, considering I couldn't spend a significant amount of time in here. I assumed that was what Reyn did and I had no desire to be in this place with him again.

Every time I thought I might actually be able to tolerate him just enough to get through this, I was reminded why that couldn't be the case. Hopefully we could get that damn fight out of the way soon. Either I'd be able to kill him or he'd kill me. Escaping him in any way was better than being his prisoner.

I needed to start training harder and more often. The quicker we got this over with, the sooner I could be done with him. There wasn't enough time to dawdle. It was time to get serious.

Chapter 34

Kiera

In the interest of learning everything I could and possibly gaining the upper hand, I decided I needed to follow through on one of my original plans. The red door. It was starting to sound portentous.

He could have another harem behind it. Maybe they were his favorites. That didn't make much sense, though. I couldn't imagine he had the time for all of that.

Before stepping into the foyer, I stared down the hallway for a long minute. I didn't hear or see anything, so I pushed through the door. I looked at the one on the right, wondering if he was in there.

An image of holding onto branches came to my mind and I shook my head, rushing toward the red door. Not giving myself a moment to second guess it, I swung it inward, then hurriedly closed it behind me. Leaning back against it, I listened for an angry, giant fairy man, but the coast was clear.

Looking around the room, I felt an incredible amount of confusion. It was mostly dark, the only light coming from some glowing plants on the ceiling. Most strange was that it was empty, save for a rose bush that lined three of the walls. Most of it was dead with only eight flowers attached to it.

Why the hell was there a giant rosebush in here and how was this the big secret? Were they special somehow?

Stepping forward, I studied them. This close, I felt that strange electricity that sometimes happened when Reyn used his magic, but other than that it seemed normal. Well, this wasn't at all helpful.

When I turned to leave, my heart thumped hard and I came to an abrupt halt. I was not alone in this room. It was more unnerving because the room was small and I wouldn't have missed a whole person standing beside the door.

She stepped forward, her silver hair shimmering in the glowing light. Her skin was pale with reddish tones and there were two short wooden stubs protruding from her head. Her eyes were nearly black, rippling outward without pause. Her attire... Well, she looked like something out of a cheesy DND cosplay event.

"Who are you?" I demanded, looking around as if I might find something to protect myself with. Forgoing the dagger had clearly been a mistake.

"Are you her?" Her voice was whiny, with a similar grit to it that Reyn had.

"I don't know who you're looking for, but I doubt it's me. Excuse me."

When I tried to move past her, a black vine shot out, blocking my path. It smelled like veggies that had started to go bad in the fridge and I had to stifle my gag.

"Tell me your name," she demanded.

"Griselda."

"Hm. It's not very pretty."

"Yeah, I'm not all that special. I really have to take a piss, so if you could just..."

"We should have a conversation, Griselda."

"I'd really rather not."

"I'm not giving you a choice."

"I figured as much."

She latched onto my arm firmly, making me cry out. Things moved under her skin, making it bulge and roll. My body felt like it was being split apart and there was a pounding in my head like a drum. When it finally settled, I opened my eyes and nearly screamed.

We weren't in the room anymore. I was ninety nine percent sure we weren't even on Earth. This place was similar to what I'd seen from the library window. There were colorful plants everywhere, dark green grass, and a sky that was such a bright blue, I wondered if it gave off its own light.

There was nothing around us except for trees and plants. We were in a little circular section, like a meadow, and there was a rosebush that mirrored the one we'd just left, except it was full of flowers.

"What the hell?" I asked in a shaky voice. "Take me back right now."

She sighed dramatically. "I can't kill you, so you have nothing to worry about."

"That's hardly reassuring. Who the fuck are you?"

"I am Riniya. This is my realm."

"Your realm?" My brow furrowed as I tried to put everything together. "You're ruling while Reyn is away."

"Reyn?"

"Reynaeros."

She snorted. "Pet names. How funny. To answer your question, I am not ruling in his stead. This place belongs to me and I won't have it returned to him."

"Why?"

"I don't think that's any concern of yours."

"Considering I can supposedly break the curse, I think it should be."

She studied me with narrowed eyes. "What has he told you?"

"Not much," I admitted. "There's a curse. I have to defeat him in battle somehow. Basically, it's futile."

"Hm. At least you have brains."

"Wait." I held up a hand, looking her up and down. "It was you, wasn't it?"

"It was."

"You look like them. Are you related?"

"I am their sister. As such, there is none more qualified to determine that neither of them is the best person to rule."

"Okay, Reyn is a dick, but you'll have to give me more than that."

"Griselda, may I tell you a truth that weighs heavily on me?"

"Uh, sure."

She came closer and took a lock of my hair, twirling it in her fingers. I stepped away from her touch and crossed my arms.

"You know of my brother's wrongs. You are one of his women and you bear his imprint."

"His imprint?" When it hit me, my nose wrinkled.

She looked at me sadly. "I would like for you to trust me. Is that something you can do?"

"I don't know."

"If you want your freedom from Reynaeros, I am offering a solution."

Holding out a hand, she waited for me to take it. I chewed on the inside of my cheek, feeling more than a little conflicted. Eventually, I put my hand in hers and she smiled. An electricity passed between us where we touched and I tried to pull away, but she held tight.

"We have a connection, Griselda. You bear his imprint because he is a beast that forced it on you. I, too, bear his imprint."

My lips parted and something curdled in my stomach. Yanking my hand away, I paced to the edge of the circle, then back.

"He..."

"Yes," she said so I didn't have to. "He was much the same person back then as he is now. It's just that nobody saw it. I had to get rid of him so he could not have so much power when our father passed."

"Why the curse? Wouldn't someone believe you?"

"No. Even between realms, we have much the same difficulties as women. I could have challenged him for the throne, but he is stronger than I am. Rathiain knew of what happened and would have sided with Reynaeros."

"Rath is good."

"They fight and bicker, but in the end they will always side together. It is something you should be aware of when you return."

"So, what's the point of this? You're going to send me back to, what, accuse him of raping his sister so that he'll kill me?"

"No," she said quickly. "Do not tell him what I've told you, otherwise you're of no use to me. I put this curse in place and the time has almost run out. If he does not accomplish his side of things, the bridge between our realms will disintegrate entirely."

"You want me to stall."

"That's too risky. He will not allow you to defy him, as I'm sure you're well aware."

"Then what do you want me to do?"

"I want you to kill him."

A laugh burst out of me. "I've tried and failed."

"Child, you must kill the root. His heart."

"I don't know where that is."

She smiled at me and I suddenly felt like an idiot.

"You know."

"Of course. It is here." She put a hand over her sternum. "Housed in a protective cage that is difficult to break through. He funnels energy into the wood, keeping it strong and intact. You must find the perfect opening so that your blow is both precise and strong enough to pierce through it."

"I guess that sounds easy enough."

"It would be, except he cannot be in his human form. Every part of his concealment must be stripped away first."

"That's not something I can manage. He always has it in place."

"You are smart, Griselda. That much I know, otherwise you would not be the one capable of freeing him. In the end, I do hope you'll be the one that frees me instead."

"Why should I do this? You could be lying."

She raised a brow, her cheek twitching. "I do not appreciate being disrespected in such a way. Has he proven himself to be anything but what I've described?"

Grinding my teeth, I struggled to come up with an answer. There was no defense for him, even if I did try to play devil's advocate. Maybe she was lying, but either way, she'd given me the key to my own prison. I knew how to kill him and I didn't really care if it helped Riniya. It would free me.

"What about the others?"

She cocked her head. "His court?"

"Yes. I don't want them to be hurt."

"Hm. When he is dead, I will offer them a choice to return and serve me or remain in your realm forever. Does that please you?"

I nodded. "That's fair."

"Good. You may use this to deal his killing blow. It is sharp enough to cut through even his strongest plants."

I took the dagger she offered me. It had a straight blade ending in a tip sharp enough to make me wary of touching it. There was an emerald at the end of the hilt and the cross guard resembled twining vines.

"What if I fail?" I whispered.

She held her palm up and one of her black vines sprung to the surface. It slowly made its way toward me and I forced myself to stay still as it brushed over my skin.

"Hm. My plants like you, Griselda. They taste their own sort of darkness. I have a feeling that, even if you fail, you will not be losing much by departing this world."

My eyes closed at her words, a wave of emotions swimming through my head. Pain erupted in my body again and when I looked around, I was back in the rose room. Alone.

Chapter 35

Reynaeros

Had I regained control of the situation? I hated that I wasn't sure. When she put her mouth on me and gave me pleasure, she had momentarily taken my power from me. For some unknown reason, this felt the same. It was impossible that two opposite things had the same result.

Every time I thought about the way my body had begun to revert, I felt her hands on my branches. She'd looked at me, not with fear or anger for once, but with an open sort of curiosity. She didn't stare the way other humans would, with a certain level of disgust and an uncomfortable sort of intrigue, as if they wanted to imprison and study me.

Our branches were personal to us. Nobody else touched them or they risked losing their hands. I hadn't thought about killing her or relieving her of limbs, though. As soon as she'd touched them, holding me to her, I'd been consumed by her scent, her taste, the sounds she was making.

The intensity of her energy as she came for me was nearly enough to knock me on my ass. It was a far cry from anything I'd ever felt from her- or anyone. It was just as tangible as her anger, but more pleasurable even than her pain and fear.

Then, of course, she ran from me. I imagined she was disgusted with herself for allowing a beast to touch her. Something inhuman, so different from her. It was weak for me to lose my grasp on my concealment.

Even with all of that, she'd completely shattered under my touch. That alone should have given me a fraction of power over her. Instead, I'd been hiding away in the greenhouse since six A.M., relishing the pure energy of my plants. At this rate, training her would take so long that every rose would be dead before she could even get close to besting me.

Who was I kidding? There was no way she'd ever get there and it wasn't because she was weak. It was simply that she was human. This entire thing made less sense daily. Curse Riniya for playing such a game because she was incapable of winning in any other way.

The thought of my sister made me feel tense, as it generally did. It had been so long, but no amount of time could wipe her imprint from my mind.

Brushing a finger over a bright yellow petal, I let out a long breath. If I failed, I had no idea what would happen. There was a certain connection between our realms still and it was impossible to know how much of ourselves we'd retain if we lost that. The idea of being cut off from this sort of energy, the purity and warmth of it, brought with it a fear greater than any I'd ever known. I didn't think life would be worth living.

"What are you up to?"

I drew my hand back abruptly. "Must you ruin every place of peace that exists for me?"

When I turned around, Kiera was looking around the greenhouse a little awkwardly. Her hands were in her pockets and her lips were set in a tight line.

"I apologize. What are you doing up here?"

She looked at me, but didn't meet my eyes. "Just wandering. I thought you might want to train."

"There's this strange feeling in my mind that tells me I might end up with a blade through my gut again."

She laughed a little, then cleared her throat. "Well, if you get stabbed, that just means you're losing your touch."

"I suppose you're right. Let's go, then."

As I extended my arm, I remembered that she'd never accepted before, so I pulled it back. When she settled her hand around my elbow, I felt frozen to the spot. Unsure if I should address it, I simply walked with her toward the training room. It was uncomfortable and my heart was racing madly.

Once we stepped into the room, I pulled away from her. "Grab your sword."

She did as I instructed, weighing it briefly before pointing it toward me. The smile she gave me made my brow tighten.

"Get ready to have your ass handed to you, Reynaeros."

I froze with my dagger raised. "Why'd you say that?"

"Because I'm going to kick your ass."

"You said my name. My full name."

"Oh. Well, you don't like my nicknames, so-"

"Call me Reyn."

Her mouth opened, then closed. Without responding, she held the sword up in a defensive position and took a step forward. From her training with Rathiain, she'd learned better footwork and even the way she held her weapon betrayed slightly more expertise.

I took a large step to the side, then bounced off that foot to spring forward. Instead of jumping out of the way like she would've before, she pivoted, making me narrowly miss her.

"Nice," I commended. "You're improving."

"I dare say your brother is a better teacher."

"And who do you think trained my brother, little rose?"

"Mm. Maybe he honed his skills without you. It's not like he hasn't had time."

"All the time in the world couldn't make him stronger than me."

"Oh, yeah? I think you're overconfident."

With a smile, I funneled energy through my feet into the floor. It traveled through the wood, taking on a life that was connected to my own. Two vines burst from the floor in front of her and she darted out of the way, but there were two more waiting behind her that wrapped around her legs. As she stabbed at one, the other dragged her down to the ground.

While she struggled, I fostered a hollow trunk that sprang to life beside her. The vines gripped her tightly and dragged her inside of it, then the opening grew together, leaving only a small space for her to see out of.

"Let me out of here," she shouted.

I stood in front of her, staring through the hole. "You have to yield, little rose."

She set her jaw. When she started pounding on the wood, I fought the urge to laugh. Her sword lay on the floor a few feet away, so she had no other defense.

A pain ignited in my chest, making me hiss. I dropped my hold on the tree, allowing the side of the tree to open. She pounced on me, knocking me off my feet. I held her to me as I fell to keep her from hitting the floor, then grunted at the impact.

I caught her wrist before she could stab me with her dagger. She wrestled against me, refusing to release her grip on it. Sitting up, I twisted her arm behind her, narrowly blocking a blow from her other fist.

"What sort of blade did you use?" I demanded.

"Just a dagger."

Tightening my grip on her wrist, I forced her to drop it. My brow furrowed as I looked at the blade. It was just an ordinary, steel weapon, yet the blow had felt powerful, as if made by something from my world.

Entangled Realms

She shoved at my chest and I locked a hand around her throat before flipping her onto her back. She swore, kicking out at me with no real direction.

"Yield."

"No," she gritted out.

"Such a stubborn little rose."

Her face began to turn red, but she still didn't concede. I didn't know how long it took for humans to run out of breath. Judging by her weakening movements and the unfocused look in her eyes, I determined that it wasn't very long.

"Yield," I repeated.

Was she going to let me knock her out? It was needlessly obstinate. Either way, she lost.

With a growl, I released her and leaned back on my heels. It took her a few minutes to steady her breathing and for her color to return to normal. Holding a hand to her throat, she glared at me.

"Are you trying to get yourself killed?"

The corner of her mouth twitched. "You didn't kill me."

"In a true battle, I would have."

"Good thing we're just training then. Besides, you could probably use the practice, considering you'll be killing me when we actually do fight."

"It doesn't have to result in your death."

"Come on, Reyn. If I'm meant to bring you to your knees, I assume you have to give it your all. Otherwise, you could just yield right off the bat and voila, the curse is broken."

It wasn't worth it to argue with her because she was right. Voicing my doubts about the entire thing was also pointless. Truthfully, I thought it would be best to cease this whole thing and focus our energy on determining what else it could mean.

Lyndis' words echoed in my mind, as clear as the day he'd locked us in this place.

The key lies within the only one that can contend with you. She will present a challenge that no other could and she must bring you to your knees. This is the only way for you to be free.

It felt like such a clear instruction, but I should've known it would be a riddle of some kind. I prided myself on being intelligent, but I saw things at face value. Ascertaining a hidden meaning behind words wasn't something I was good at.

"Come on, fairy boy. I'm never gonna get good enough to bring you to your knees unless you actually train me."

I watched her bounce back and forth on her toes. She put her fist in her palm with a mischievous look on her face. Getting to my feet, I held her sword out to her.

"I suppose we'll have to keep training then."

There was a heavy thump as the man in the ring slammed his opponent's head against the ground. I heard his skull crack, then the scent of blood floated up to me. Turning away from the fight, I motioned Chester over.

"What's up?"

"Do you know where Kiera is?"

"Let me ask Portia."

His eyes glazed over for a moment, then he blinked. "She's training."

It was impossible not to be impressed by how hard she'd been working. I didn't have the heart to tell her it was pointless. It seemed to be one of the things holding her together.

"Send for her."

His eyes widened slightly, but he just inclined his head slightly and stepped back. As I waited, my fingers tapped rhythmically on the arm of my chair. This seat had always been comfortable; I'd ensured it. Now, it might as well have been a concrete slab. I'd have to get a better one.

When the doors opened, I kept my gaze studiously fixed on the fight. Kiera's scent reached me just before she stopped beside me.

"What's so important?" she asked a little breathlessly.

"Come here."

She rounded the chair to stand in front of me. I spread my legs, latching onto her wrist to pull her between them. Her eyes narrowed, but she didn't protest, which made me smile a little.

Putting my hands on her hips, I trailed my thumbs over her pelvic bones. They felt sharper than they had a few weeks ago.

"Did you need something?"

"Yes," I replied, pushing a hand underneath her shirt. The skin of her stomach was soft and slightly sweaty. My heart sped up at the contact.

She took a step back and I tightened my grip. With a hard tug, I forced her closer, her knee landing on the chair between my legs. Gripping under her thighs, I adjusted her so she was straddling me, and my hips moved to seek her warmth.

"I, uh, what is..."

"I thought you might want to watch the fight."

She glanced over her shoulder. "This isn't the way to watch it."

I chuckled, moving my hands around to her ass. She sucked in a sharp breath when I squeezed it tightly. Having her so close, being able to feel her heat and smell her, was stripping me of any control I might have been clinging to.

It was pointless to bring her up here, but if she was going to continue invading my mind, I had to sate it somehow. My mouth watered as I thought about all the ways I could do that.

"Alright." I turned her around, settling her in my lap.

She was tense, her back straight as a rod. As I stroked up and down her thigh, she relaxed the slightest amount. When she leaned back against my chest I tucked my nose into her hair and inhaled deeply.

Fully expecting her to freak out, I slipped my hand into the front of her pants. Even when she tensed, she didn't protest, which emboldened me to move further. When I brushed over her clit, she jolted.

Dipping my face into her neck, I grazed her with my natural teeth. She tilted her head to allow me access. I dragged my tongue up to her jaw, then pushed a finger inside of her. Her wetness made my dick harden more and I was sure she could feel it.

Pulling her sleeve down to expose her shoulder, I kissed it gently where there was a lingering bite mark from the attack. The sight of it infuriated me, awoke the same sort of desperation I'd felt when I set off to hunt them down.

Settling my teeth over the spot, I sunk them into her skin. She immediately tried to pull away, letting out a pained cry, but moving only made it hurt worse, so she stilled completely.

"Reyn, stop."

Pulling free of her, I ran my tongue over the marks, making her jolt. I kissed it softly as I lengthened my finger inside her. Curling it inward, I felt the softer flesh that made her squirm when I stimulated it. After a few of those movements, she relaxed and her breaths became heavier.

As her energy shifted with her pleasure, I closed my eyes and nuzzled into her neck again. My dick was throbbing and it didn't help that every time she moved her hips, she rubbed against it. I swore in my language, arching up to seek more of her.

She adjusted her legs, planting her knees on either side of me. My breath caught when she stroked me through my pants. Freeing my dick, I shuddered at my own touch. I wasn't sure if I should turn her over and fuck her right here or take her somewhere else. Maybe she didn't even want to do that. I wasn't sure if I would accept that, actually; not at this point.

My stomach lurched when she shimmied out of her leggings, then settled back against my chest. With one hand, I rubbed my tip against her, moaning at the wetness there. Putting a palm against her collarbone, I pulled her tighter against my chest, pressing my face against her neck as she lowered herself onto me.

"Fuck, little rose," I gritted out.

It was an effort to keep from pushing the rest of the way in. I hadn't been with someone in this position, but I assumed it meant she wanted to control this. Right now, I couldn't bring myself to give a shit.

Slowly, she slid further down. Every inch was more torturous. My concealment was slipping and no matter how tightly I held to it, each time she moved I lost it all over again.

Once she'd taken all of me, I arched up, desperate to feel more. She lifted nearly all the way off, then dropped down again. My head fell back at the blinding sensation. With her taking control of it, all I could do was focus on how she felt.

As she continued to ride me, I explored her body. I'd never paid much attention and what I had seen of females didn't impress me much. They were smooth and their skin was plain. Their eyes stayed one solid color with no movement to betray their emotions. They always had brown or blonde hair, for the most part. They just weren't anything special.

My hands covered her breasts and I paused. She was softer here, more malleable. When my fingers passed over her nipples, she made a little sound and her pussy rippled. With a growl, I tightened my grip and dove into her neck, desperate to have all of her.

My lips and tongue traveled over every inch of her that I could reach. I tasted her skin; the sweat, her soap, and *her*. I didn't know if every human's skin was different, but I was intoxicated by hers. All of my senses were overwhelmed by her and it heightened my pleasure immensely.

For seven centuries I'd been fucking the humans of this realm, but that was just sex. It was a task with a goal that left me feeling pleased for a short time. Before I'd come here, I hadn't experienced sex, really. It didn't really count, in my opinion.

This was something else entirely. It was emotion, connection, an all-consuming amalgamation of everything our bodies had to offer each other. It felt as if our energies were melding, both of our pleasures seeping into the other.

What was happening right now was the most powerful thing I'd felt in my life and I was utterly terrified by it.

Gripping the back of her neck, I pushed her forward. She put her hands on my knees, arching her back as I thrust upward. I slid a finger on either side of her clit, stroking, then pinching slightly. She made a choked sound, her grip on me tightening.

"Oh, god," she breathed.

Up to this point, I hadn't allowed my barbs to release themselves for fear of her changing her mind. Now I let them free, gasping when they latched on. With my concealment mostly stripped, my dick was in its natural form and the way her ridges rubbed against the corrugated surface pushed me closer to the edge.

"What the fuck," she whimpered.

I stilled. "Am I hurting you?"

"If you find a moral compass right now, I will stab you again."

Fuck. I resumed at a faster pace, growling as I neared my release. Her pussy gripped me so hard I couldn't control the sound that came from my throat. Wrapping an arm around her, I held her to me tightly, keeping myself buried deep as I came harder than I had in my entire long life.

I was still catching my breath when she lifted off of me and stepped into her leggings. My mouth opened, but I couldn't think of anything to say as she retreated through the doors. Dropping my head back, I seriously contemplated reevaluating my entire life based on that mind-blowing encounter.

Entangled Realms

This was supposed to sate me, get her out of my system. This time, I couldn't even try to lie to myself. I wanted her now more than ever.

Madilyn DeRose

Chapter 36

Kiera

Rolling onto my other side, I had the strong urge to break things. I'd been lying here for hours without being able to fall asleep. The throbbing of my pussy continued to remind me of what had happened up on that platform, no matter how much I tried to forget about it.

Distract him and make him trust me. That was my plan. The only way I would be able to land a killing blow was to catch him off guard. As much I hated the idea, I used the only advantage I had. Me.

I wouldn't say that plan backfired, but it didn't turn out how I'd expected. Mentally, I'd prepared myself ever since I left Riniya's realm. I knew it was going to be uncomfortable and dredge up all of my trauma, but it was worth it if I was able to get rid of him and earn my freedom. Then he'd made me cum so hard, I worried my thoughts would never catch up.

To be fair, I didn't realize he'd been hiding the details of his equipment. I didn't see it, but I felt it. That motherfucker was textured, as I imagined a knotted branch would be, but it was smooth like a normal dick. Those ridges stroked me in a way that made my eyes roll back in my head.

Add in the animalistic way he'd fucked me and it was a recipe for a big ol' orgasm sandwich. It wasn't what I'd expected to happen and I still felt disgusted with myself for touching him at all, but if I was going to get some really incredible benefits out of this deal, who was I to complain? Silver linings and all that, even if it was more likely to be some weird trauma bonding bullshit.

Psychological phenomena aside, nothing had changed about my plan. I'd confirmed that the blade Riniya gave me affected him more than a normal one. It had almost gotten me caught, but some sleight of hand and batting of my eyelashes secured my successful deception.

It was clear that he'd been incredibly affected by our sex earlier, so I was feeling more confident than ever. I didn't know how long it would take, but I would be getting out of here. I would spend the rest of my time on this Earth free of this beast and his court of nightmares, even if I didn't have much time left when I finally made it out.

Deciding it was no use, I got dressed and headed for the training room. A sound from the pool room drew me in that direction and I was surprised to find someone swimming there.

"Rath!" I shouted with my hands cupped over my mouth.

He put his feet down, the pool water coming up to the top of his chest. "If you want to talk, you're gonna have to get in."

I stared at the water, my nose wrinkling. "Nevermind. It's not that important."

He threw his hands up in exasperation. A wave leapt out of the pool, drenching me from head to toe. I stood there with my mouth open, looking down at myself. His laughter echoed in the room and the sound of it made it impossible to feign rage.

Stripping out of my shirt and pants, I slid into the shallow end in just my bra and underwear. He sped over to me, taking me in his arms. I screamed, trying to get free of him, but he held me tightly all the way to the other end. When he let go of me, I didn't release my death grip.

"Come on, ma belle," he laughed. "The water won't hurt you."

I rolled my lips inward to hide the way they trembled. His head cocked, then he wrapped me in his arms again, keeping me secured against him.

"You fear the water."

"No."

"Admitting fear is not a weakness."

Clenching my jaw, I leaned my head on his shoulder. He began to wade through the water slowly, back and forth, then in a circle. He hummed softly as he moved and it somehow helped me to relax slightly.

While he continued his water dance, I studied the marks on his skin. They looked like tattoos, but up close and with my hands on him, I found that they were raised. It was like there were taut wires beneath his skin and I wondered if it was translucent since I could see the darker color of the cords.

"When you're with me, the water can't hurt you. I wouldn't let it."

Tears pricked my eyes and I kept my face buried. "That's kind."

"Is it kind to simply not be cruel?"

"It depends on the context. For example, am I being held prisoner in a place that has hurt me more than anything else?"

"Hm."

He brought us to a shallower section and set me on my feet, then leaned his elbows back on the edge.

"You put on quite a show last night."

My face heated. "People could see us?"

"No. Reynaeros put everybody to sleep."

"He what?"

Entangled Realms

"Spores," he said, waving a dismissive hand.

"So, how'd you know?"

He smiled conspiratorially. "Spy plants."

I laughed. "I don't know if I want to know."

"My brother put one in your room, so I've been petty. There may be about seven so far in various places."

My lip curled. "He was watching me in my room?" Suddenly, I felt even more disgusted by what happened the day before.

"I don't think it was in a gross way. He worries, but he's too proud to simply ask how you are."

"Well, I'd be a lot better if he wasn't watching me sleep."

"But you're so cute when you're snoring." He made a ridiculous snoring face and I swatted him in the chest.

"Don't tell me you're spying too."

"Nah. Unlike him, I'm not afraid to approach women when I'm feeling horny."

"Jesus." When I thought about it, I cocked my head. "Is it weird if I ask how that works?"

"Well, ma belle, when a mommy tree and a daddy tree love each other very much..."

"Okay, smartass. I mean the..." I waved a hand in the general direction of his crotch.

Leaning further back on his elbows, he raised a single brow. "The barbs."

"Yeah, those."

"Just an evolutionary mechanism to ensure procreation. It's not necessary anymore, unless... Well, as long as she doesn't want to escape, there's not really a purpose to it. For us, it's become a sort of possessive act. It marks you as ours."

"So, if you bear another one's... imprint... you can't be with anyone else?"

"You can, but the man would know because he'd feel the marks. Then that person would likely be burned to ash."

"How would you know who it is?"

He laughed a little and rubbed the back of his neck. "Unless you have quite a bit of influence, you wouldn't be able to find out, but if you really wanted to, it can be figured out. Think of it as a fingerprint. They're all unique."

A laugh bubbled out of me. Putting a hand to my mouth, I took a calming breath.

"So, since Reyn is this big, important figure, he could have all the men present their dicks to determine who did it."

"Basically, yeah."

"That's weird as hell."

"And your males' smooth cocks are weird to me. Perspective, ma belle."

Even though I despised those barbs and what they'd done to me, I couldn't deny that it was different this time. He hadn't let them out until nearly the end, but when he did, they sunk inside me and felt... stimulating. When he moved inside of me, they tugged at my walls almost painfully, but not quite. Combined with his textured dick, I found myself nearly begging him to keep going. It was shameful.

Clearing my throat, I casually let myself float on my back and thought about how to broach the subject I'd come here for.

"So, this curse."

He groaned. "Ask Reynaeros, Kiera."

"No. He's a pooper."

"Fine. Begin your incessant questioning, you infuriating creature."

"Gross. Now you sound like your brother."

"Go on before I decide to drown you."

My stomach lurched automatically. "What happens if you don't break it?"

"Then we're stuck here forever."

"Is there a time limit?"

He was quiet, so I chanced a glance at him. With one finger on the surface of the water, he was swirling it around absently.

"Yes, there is a ticking clock."

"How long?"

"It's not exact."

"You don't have any idea?"

"Whenever the last one falls. Next question."

"The person who cursed you. Why didn't they just kill him?"

"They can't."

"Why not?"

"Kiera, it doesn't matter. It just is and the only thing we can do is try to beat it."

"What would happen if they did kill him?"

He stopped his swirling and met my eyes. "I don't understand."

"I mean, if they got impatient and just wanted to ensure he wouldn't come back. If they found a way to do it, what would happen to the curse?"

"She can't kill him. Interfering with the terms of magic like that would have dastardly effects on her."

"Oh. Okay. Couldn't they get someone else to do it or does that still fall in the no-no pile?"

His stare intensified. "Where are these questions coming from?"

"I'm just curious. I've had a lot of time to stew on it all without anyone willing to give me answers. Besides, you should want to know every possible outcome."

With a sigh, he returned to making his little whirlpool. "It's impossible to know what would happen. It could shut the passage, solidifying our place here, or it could shatter it by taking one of the anchors of the curse out of the equation. Both options need to be avoided at all costs."

"It could give you a chance to get home."

"Without him, it is not my home," he replied angrily. "I would be forced to kneel to a madwoman or take the throne, both of which I will not do."

"I'm sorry. I didn't mean to..."

"It's fine."

He pulled himself from the pool, glancing down at me briefly before heading to the exit. I didn't know if what he'd told me helped or not. They seemed to know precious little of the details. Killing Reyn could mean hurting the others, but it would free me, Lucy, and Collie. We were prisoners too.

In the end, what was the greater good? A year ago I'd reevaluated a lot of things in my life and I'd decided I was going to be selfish and put myself first. In my world, the greatest good was finding a way to be free, so that was what I would do.

Chapter 37

Kiera

Rising on my toes, I reached as far as I could. My fingers brushed the spine of the book, making it move even further away from me. I wanted to scream and stomp my foot, but that would probably make me fall off of this ladder, so I refrained.

Moving it would be the ideal situation, but I couldn't figure it out. When I pushed on it, the thing didn't budge. I assumed there was some sort of mechanism that would do it, but the more I looked for it, the less capable I felt. I'd been so close to grabbing the book the first time, then I'd pushed it further away.

With a growl, I began to climb down, resigning myself to the fact that I wouldn't be able to read the one that I wanted. There were at least a thousand other books in this place, but that was the second to the one Reyn had me read the other day and I was dying to dive in head first. Whatever crack the author imbued in those pages was addictive.

Something touched me from behind and I screamed. Arms pinned mine just before I was pushed against the bookshelf. A body pressed against my back, then sharp teeth grazed my neck.

"Don't be an asshole," I grumbled.

"Where have you been the past two days?" he murmured against my skin.

Jeez. Had I effectively made him pussy-whipped? That was my intention, I guess, but this was just weird. One dope sex session and he was all up in my business.

"I've been around. Shouldn't you know everything that goes on in your domain?"

"I'm not omniscient, Kiera."

"Well, that's a relief. I do need to find a way to serve the coup de grace and all that."

"You're not meant to kill me," he chuckled.

"Just almost kill you."

"Precisely."

"Maybe you can let me go now, so that I can read my book."

"Luckily for me, you have no book."

"Yeah, your ladder situation is flawed."

"Mm."

He reached up and something sprung from his skin, climbing up the shelves. It wrapped around the book and brought it down, hovering in front of me.

"That's still disgusting."

"Are you sure?"

The vine suddenly sunk into the front of my pants, making me rear back. He kept me pressed against the shelf, not allowing me to escape the creepy plant currently flicking my clit.

"I think you want to see what else I've got up my sleeve."

"I'd prefer it if you left me the fuck alone so that I could read."

"Well, I can't do that. You have a tendency to go wandering, causing problems and banging on walls."

"I'll bang your head into a wall," I muttered. An unattractive sound came from my throat when his vine slithered inside of me. I was simultaneously disgusted and not wanting him to stop.

He put his hands under my shirt, exploring my body. Squeezing my breasts, he brushed his thumbs over my nipples, sending a shock down to my core. I pressed back against him, craving more.

His hard dick poked against my ass, filling my head with thoughts of it inside me. It was absolutely unhealthy that I was enjoying this, but it was better than having to suffer through it to make it to the end. I could deal with the repercussions when I was home. Preferably after a couple bottles of wine and a long cry.

Kissing a path from my shoulder down my back, he knelt in the grass and pushed my pants down. He brushed his thumb over a spot on my side before biting into it. I swore and tried to kick him, but he wrapped something around my legs to keep me in place. This was the second time the motherfucker had chomped me like a shark and I was decidedly not into it.

When he released my skin, he licked the spot, then kissed it. Goddamn weirdo.

The restraints on my ankles tightened, then tugged on me, pulling my legs further apart. I latched onto the shelf as best I could so I wouldn't fall. It felt like I was about to have a skiing mishap and involuntarily do the splits.

As soon as that split tongue attacked my clit, I no longer cared about the uncomfortable position. He palmed my ass cheeks, spreading me open. While he was gripping me, I felt his fingers lengthen, reaching between my legs and sinking inside of me.

"Fuck," I whimpered.

My body shuddered, my legs weakening as all of my muscles contracted. His tongue traveled back, tasting every inch of me. When he dipped it inside, it felt like he twisted it and I thought I might literally die here in this magical library.

Straightening, he grabbed my hips and pulled my ass back. His dick rubbed against me, the barbs grazing on my skin. They were leaking, spreading something wet over me. With both of our lubricants, he sank inside of me easily, pausing when he was buried all the way.

His fingers dug into me as he began to move back and forth. When he pulled out, he pushed me forward and when he thrust into me, he yanked me back. The force of it was jarring, his texture creating blinding sensations. His barbs sunk in and I hung my head, my fingers tightening on the shelf.

Something that looked like ivy spread over my thighs. It traveled between my legs, then covered my labia, tightening so that I was completely open. Something- another plant, I assumed- began to softly stimulate my clit. It was so gentle, I wanted to beg for more, but I clamped down on my lower lip.

Reyn angled his hips so that he was hitting my g-spot, building up a fire in my core. It was almost too much. I wanted more and less all at the same time.

When he sped up and tightened his grip on me, his barbs latched onto me more firmly. I jolted, releasing the bookshelf and thrusting my arm forward involuntarily. Books tumbled to the ground around us and I could only hope they weren't old or valuable.

A fierce cry tore from my throat, echoing through the library. It seemed to bounce off the walls for a long time, though it could have just been that the sound went on for that long.

"Little rose," he growled, then his own language rolled off his tongue, the ethereal sound reverberating through the room.

Warmth filled me just before he stopped moving. He dropped his head into my neck, breathing heavily. My heart was racing and I wanted to get out of this position so I could return to my room with the book, but he was clinging to me and his barbs were still attached, so I was well and truly stuck.

The door opened, the creak sounding loud. "Oh, Christ," Portia squeaked, grimacing before backing out of the room.

Great. That was just what I needed. I'd learned that her and Chester shared everything, which just meant more people would be wondering about what was going on. I didn't want to draw too much attention to this or it could make everything more difficult.

Oh, god. I suddenly wondered what they would do when I accomplished my task. It hadn't been a concern of mine, but it was possible they would want to retaliate. One of them might go so far as to kill me.

Reyn's teeth grazed my neck lightly, making me shiver. "You appear lost inside your head, little rose."

"Yeah."

"Will you share your thoughts with me?"

He pulled free, the vines and ivy letting me go as well. I pulled my pants up and cleared my throat.

"No. It's not important."

I headed to the door, ducking my head. If I ran into Portia in the hall, filled with Reyn's cum, I might consider leaping from the roof.

"Kiera."

I paused at the door, gritting my teeth. He came up behind me, making me tense.

"You forgot this."

He reached over my shoulder to pass me the book I'd come here for. I took it, tucking it into my chest.

"Thank you."

Without another word, I pushed through the door, walking at a normal pace until I reached the stairs and confirmed that I was alone. As soon as I reached my room, I dropped into my bed, pulling the covers over my head to block out the light. A migraine was setting in and I just hoped I could fall asleep until it passed. It rarely worked, but I'd be damned if I didn't try.

The headache stuck around for longer than usual. Light made it infinitely worse, so I kept my curtains drawn and walked around in the dark when I needed to go to the bathroom. I even showered in the pitch black, which was both terrifying and relaxing, like a sensory deprivation chamber.

When I wasn't bumping into things in the dark, I was sleeping. Fitfully, but it was better than nothing. Portia came in a couple times to bring me food and I barely paid attention to her. It was clear she was worried, but I assured her I was fine. Eventually, Chester arrived to interrogate me, but when I said the same thing to him, he left with a frustrated huff.

When I dozed off again, I found myself deep in a dream that I'd rather wake up from.

A knock sounded on the door, making me groan. They'd only been gone for a few hours and I couldn't imagine they were done already. It was their anniversary, after all. That was the reason we were in France and since they hated letting me out of their sight for long, I'd been dragged along.

I couldn't say I was mad about being here, but it was weird to watch my parents act like newlyweds. They'd always been disgustingly in love. It was everything I could ever want for my future, not that I'd be lucky enough to have it.

"If you cut your tour short because you missed me, we're gonna have a talk about loosening the reins."

I stopped with the door halfway open, looking at the stranger. He was a small man with beady eyes and a large bald spot. From his apparent nervousness, I wasn't sure I trusted him, so I kept a tight grip on the wood, ready to shut him out if need be.

"Can I help you?"

"Yes, mademoiselle," he said in a heavy French accent. "Tell me. Are you Kiera Beaufort?"

"Yeah, unless I'm under arrest or something."

He didn't crack a smile, which made something curdle in my stomach.

"May I come in, mademoiselle?"

"No, I don't think so. Stranger danger, you know?"

"It is about Monsieur and Madame Beaufort."

It felt like he'd punched me in the gut. Wordlessly, I opened the door further to allow him in. He took a seat at the table and waited for me to do the same.

"What happened?" *I asked barely above a whisper.*

"There was an accident."

"I, uh, are they... Where are they? I need to see them. What hospital were they taken to?"

There was sadness in his eyes as he stared at me. I shook my head, getting up and pacing toward the window. Staring out at the vineyard in the distance, my vision began to blur. A sharp pain erupted behind my eyes, making me hiss and put a hand to my head.

"Perhaps you should sit."

"*I don't want to fucking sit.*"

The pain intensified and I hit my knees. This couldn't be true. They'd been gone for a few hours and it wasn't very far away. What were the odds something would happen so quickly?

A hand touched my shoulder, which just made the tears flow faster. I shook my head back and forth, willing this to be a dream or some sort of hallucination. That was something that could happen. Whatever it was, I didn't want to be in it anymore.

"Tell me," *I whispered.*

"A witness said they swerved to avoid an animal in the road. Their car went into the lake. They were unable to get out of the car."

"The lake? The only one around is down the road."

"Yes. They were headed back here, we assume."

Hurriedly, I pulled my phone from my pocket and unlocked it.

Mom: *Get dressed, ma belle fleur. Your father and I can't stand it if you don't come see the roses with us. This may be the only time we're here together.*

"No, no, no, no," I wailed.
The physical pain was nothing compared to what was happening inside my mind. They'd been coming back for me. If I'd only gone with them from the start...
"No, no, no. No, I can't. Please tell me they made it out. Please."

"Little rose," a deep, gravelly voice said, breaking through my dream.
Curling in on myself, I squeezed my eyes tightly shut, hoping he would go away. The bed dipped behind me, then a hand brushed over my arm, up and down. My shoulders shook and I was too weak to stop my emotions.
"Little rose. What has happened?"
"Just go away," I croaked. "I don't want you here."
"You're distressed. I could feel it from upstairs."
"Go away."
Clearly he'd gone deaf in his old age because he scooted closer to me and wrapped an arm around my middle, flipping me around to face him. I tried to squirm free, but he tightened his grip, pulling me against his chest.
"Leave me alone," I pleaded, my voice cracking.
"It's impossible when your energy won't leave me alone, so just shut the hell up and go back to sleep. Perhaps your dreams will not be as frightening."
"I wasn't dreaming."
"You were talking in your sleep. Begging for something. What were you seeing?"
"If I agree to sleep, will you stop asking questions?"
He was silent for a moment before stroking a hand down my back. "Okay."
Being in his arms like this was uncomfortable, which made it nearly impossible to relax. His touch made me a little nauseous when I had time and silence to think about

it. Apparently, the only time I could stand him was when we were having sex, which was incredibly, grotesquely ironic if you asked me.

Life was short. I knew that better than most people. You only live once, so having a few good orgasms before you died didn't seem like the end of the world, so long as I didn't have to talk to him after.

Chapter 38

Reynaeros

Now that Kiera was asleep again, her emotions were more tolerable. Before, I hadn't been able to read a whole sentence because they were attacking me so fiercely. Even though she argued about it, she appeared to be sleeping quite peacefully in my arms.

It was strange for me. I'd never laid beside someone like this, nor had I 'cuddled' as humans would call it. Tightening my arms around her, I inhaled her scent. I wouldn't even try to deny that I enjoyed the closeness.

Truly, I was tired of denying many things. She kept running from me and I had been doing the same much of the time, but I couldn't take it anymore. Something about this human had crawled under my skin and taken root, entangling with my own, and no matter how hard I tried, cutting her out was impossible without harming myself in the process.

As I ran my fingers through her hair, I allowed myself to imagine the possibilities for but a moment. It was pointless to dwell on it. A soul as beautiful as hers could never feel anything but disdain for a beast such as me. She didn't even know my greatest shame. It would solidify everything she believed about me.

And so, with her scent strong in my nose and a tightness in my chest, I pressed a kiss to her temple before getting to my feet. I allowed spores to release from my hand, the effects quickly making her fall into a deep enough sleep that she would not be plagued by whatever haunted her.

I felt lost in my head when I returned to the library. My book was lying on the arm of the chair, but I knew I wouldn't be able to lose myself in it right now. I'd been consumed by a weakness that I didn't know what to do with.

The door opened and I raised my gaze to Rathiain for only a moment. Sinking deeper into my seat, I tried to ignore him, hoping he'd get the hint and leave me alone. My little brother never did what I wanted, though.

"What has you looking so melancholy, Reyn?"

My lip curled. "Do not start calling me that."

"You allow Kiera to say it."

"It was part of our deal."

"Mm. Delusions can only be lived in for so long."

Leaning my forehead on one hand, I let out a dry laugh. "I believe I may feel affection for her."

"Is that so?"

"It's ridiculous. She is human."

"What does it matter?"

"For one, she is not a part of our world. If... When we break the curse, I will leave her."

"She could come with us."

"There's no point even thinking about it, Rathiain. She would never return such feelings."

"You don't know that. Considering all the places you've been fucking, I'd say she's already come a long way."

"Tell me this," I said, leaning my elbows on my knees. Do you think she could ever forgive me?"

He stared into the fire, appearing lost in thought. "I think there are some things, regardless of which world you're a part of, that can surpass a great many things. If there was not great power in love, there would not be so many tales and songs dedicated to its effects. People have killed, died, and betrayed for love. It may be a long shot- a very long shot- but I do not think it's impossible."

His words made my stomach churn. "It's just a passing fancy. It will fade with time."

"Stop being needlessly obstinate. You've been alive long enough to know better. In all your centuries, you've never felt this, right?"

"I've never felt anything resembling it. Truthfully, I did not think myself capable after... Everything."

"Then take a chance."

"But the curse. This could be a risk to our chances of breaking it."

He rubbed his jaw, then met my eyes, the blue swirling gracefully.

"You know as well as I do that it cannot be so straightforward. She will never contend with you in battle."

"I've determined this, but I don't know where that leaves us."

"I have never experienced it, but many of the strongest and smartest of men have been bested by one thing. Perhaps it is love that shall bring you to your knees, brother."

My brow furrowed as I watched the flames leaping in the grate. It sounded simple, yet it might be more impossible than our original sentiment. If he was correct, I'd been tested when I met Kiera and I'd failed miserably many times over. Had I been so lost to the darkness of my mind that I'd destroyed my people's chance of returning home?

"She will never love me."

"If you're simply going to give up, then maybe you don't deserve the emerald throne."

"Since you apparently consider yourself so wise, perhaps you can share the secret to redemption."

He smiled as if amused. "It's simple, but you're going to hate it."

"Go on."

"Groveling, Reyn. You're going to have to grovel more than anyone in history."

🌷 🌷 🌷

"This is so freaking dramatic," Kiera grumbled as I led her by the elbow. She put her hands in front of her, as if I would let her run into something.

"I have a question, Kiera."

"It's very likely I won't answer."

"Do you ever just shut the hell up?"

She tried to stop, but I pulled her along, even as she grumbled under her breath. She must have been the most problematic creature I'd ever encountered.

When we entered the kitchen, I drew the leaves away from her eyes. She blinked in the light, then looked around in confusion.

"Uh, are we making sandwiches?"

"No. Better. We're making coffee."

I gestured to the espresso machine on the counter. It was supposed to be the best in the industry.

Her brow furrowed. "So, essentially, you're giving me a job."

"That's the stupidest thing you've ever said."

"Well, one time I explained to a blind date that they never tell us if Westley regained all fifty-one of the years stolen from his life. He could literally have only a few years to live his happily ever after."

When I raised a brow, her cheeks pinked. Clearing her throat, she joined me in front of the machine, running her fingers over the shiny metal.

"Alright. You're not giving me a job as the castle's barista. What is this for?"

"It's for coffee, clearly."

She looked at me pointedly. I pulled my lip between my teeth, trying not to smile.

"Do you remember the drink you made me when I visited that book store?"

"Obviously. It's in my top ten worst days."

"Hm. What's number one?"

"Meeting you."

Rolling my eyes, I detached the four portafilters and set two in front of her. She picked one up, studying it like it held a secret.

"We're going to have a contest to see who makes the better cup."

"You're joking."

"No."

"What's the point?"

"Fun, Kiera. Have you heard of it?"

"I don't like you this way. It's like you learned your sense of humor by doing a deep dive into Reddit overnight."

"I don't know what that is, but I should probably be offended. Regardless, we're doing this."

"You know I'll just vote for my own, so it's not really a contest."

"We're not judging them, obviously."

"This is stupid."

"You're right, but I don't particularly care. Get to work."

She sighed, but grabbed some of the ingredients that were set out on the counter. As I worked on my own masterpiece, I glanced at her out of the corner of my eye. Her body was relaxed as she worked and she was chewing on her lip while she concentrated.

When the espresso was brewing, she turned to me with crossed arms. "How do you know how to make coffee?"

I matched her pose. "I was around before espresso and there's precious little to do around here. I have learned many things."

"Like what?"

"Cooking. Art. Music."

"Music, huh? Big fan of Eminem, I bet."

I smiled. "Tell me your favorite song."

Her nose wrinkled. "No."

"It won't hurt you to share it with me."

"Actually, it will completely taint it. I won't be able to stomach hearing it again."

Pulling out my phone, I turned on my own playlist, then set it on the counter. She looked from it to me, seeming conflicted.

"I never imagined you doing normal things."

"Let me guess. You assumed I spent my days thinking of new ways to torment humanity. Perhaps coming up with recipes that feature babies and puppies."

She laughed, then put a hand to her mouth, wiping the smile off her face. "Something like that."

We both finished making our drinks and set them on the counter. Before she could start saying something snarky, I planted a hand on the small of her back and took her hand in mine, pulling her flush against me.

"What-"

"Shush. Remember what I said about shutting up?"

"You're rude."

"Yes, but I can also be nice."

She followed my steps surprisingly well, her body lithe and her movements graceful. Her fingers stroked the side of my neck, making my heart thump harder.

She looked up at me as we danced and it was impossible to miss the tight set to her jaw. It made me want to plant kisses along it until all of her tension faded away. I'd never even kissed someone, outside of the ones I'd left on her body. The thought of it made me feel a little nauseous.

Moving my hand from her waist, I cupped her neck, using my thumb under her jaw to tip her face up. There was a fire in her eyes that I couldn't identify, but it made me want to experience more. Whether good or bad, I wanted to feel what she felt.

There was a burning need inside me to understand her, to learn exactly what brought her joy and what pained her. More than anything, I wanted to know the agony that seemed to permanently twist her energy into such a harrowing state.

"Why are you looking at me?"

"I think I find you beautiful," I admitted.

Her eyes widened before her lip curled. She wiped the expression away quickly and averted her gaze.

"I thought humans disgusted you."

"They do."

"Hm."

Tightening my grip on her, I leaned down, which made her tense. Our lips were so close, I could feel her warmth, taste her breaths. I was overcome with a sort of desperation that pushed me to close the distance between us.

She turned her head away before our lips could meet. Leaning my forehead against hers, I closed my eyes.

"I'm sorry," I murmured.

"Why would you do that?"

"You are not unintelligent, Kiera."

When she pulled away from me, I let her go. She put a few feet between us and glared at me.

"You may think I'm weak, but I'm not going to let this Stockholm shit win."

I couldn't help but laugh. "Stockholm? Is that what you think this is?"

"Obviously. It's textbook trauma bonding."

"You have no trouble taking pleasure from my body, but this is somehow different?"

"Yes. It's too much. I thought I could... No, take your manipulative bullshit elsewhere. I won't fall for it."

"You may justify your feelings in whatever way you see fit."

"Feelings?" she scoffed. "I don't have any feelings for you."

"Is that why you gave me a nickname?"

"I gave you that because you have a pretentious mouthful of a name. It's a tragedy, really. Did your mother hate you?"

"I would have asked her, but she died before I could speak."

Her jaw ticked. "Hm. She probably couldn't stand to look at your ugly face anymore."

"That's quite harsh."

"Compared to what you've done?"

I dropped my gaze for a moment. When I returned it to her, she'd wiped every trace of emotion from her face, pulling on a sort of mask.

"What would you have me do?"

"You can legally change it."

"Not about the name, Kiera. What must I do to earn your forgiveness?"

She stared at me for a solid minute, not once looking away from my eyes. It was like she was stripping me down to my barest threads. I felt vulnerable, igniting a fear that she would see every one of my shames hidden beneath the surface.

"You can't," she said finally.

I deflated. "Kiera."

"I can't do this. I shouldn't have done any of this. It was stupid."

"Don't leave," I implored as she made her way to the door.

"Go to hell, Reyn."

Voices came from the cafeteria, then Rathiain and Lucia entered the kitchen. She looked around awkwardly while my brother raised a brow.

"I'm assuming your weird contest didn't go well," she noted.

Gripping the edge of the counter tightly, I hung my head. "All I'm doing is humiliating myself. We're never going to break this damn curse."

"Just give it time," Rathiain suggested.

Madilyn DeRose

With a roar, I swept my arm over the counter. Glass shattered and the metal of the machine collided loudly with the brick of the fireplace.

"Damn," he muttered. "I was excited for an afternoon caffeine fix."

Chapter 39

Kiera

Getting Reyn to trust me and finding ways to effectively distract him were one thing. What was actually happening went far beyond any of that. He'd flipped it around on me, finding a way to play me in return because he thought I was weak. I may have been his favorite option for getting his rocks off, but we were not about to cuddle and kiss just because we had good sex.

He had dropped off the next two books in the series I'd become addicted to, which gave me a way to avoid him for a little bit. It was easy to sink into that world. The antagonist was a man with so much internal pain and concealed anger. I identified with him and I had to wonder if that was why Reyn had chosen to show it to me.

I hated how much he saw through me. He could somehow sense energies, which made it impossible to hide. It was the perfect ability for someone that spent their life manipulating others.

Turning Riniya's dagger over in my hand, I watched the emerald glint in the sunlight. I didn't know how I was going to accomplish this. If I could track him down and stab him right now, I would, but he wouldn't be in the right form. I needed him vulnerable, yet getting him to that point resulted in things like coffee competitions and dancing in the kitchen. It made me nauseous.

Even though I wanted to stay in bed today, I knew it was a bad idea to let myself stew. Regardless of what I did, it would be a bad one. There was a stiffness in my muscles and I felt like I hadn't slept in days. No matter what I tried to distract myself with, there was one thing on my mind.

Slipping into some socks that would make my steps nearly silent, I cracked my door and looked both ways. I hurried to the staircase, carefully walked past the training room, then paused in the grassy foyer.

The green doors to my right drew my attention. He could be in there right now, reading or god knows what else. There could be someone else bound by vines and pressed against the shelves for all I knew. The thought made me step toward it, but I stopped myself.

Turning in the opposite direction, I entered the red room. It looked the same, except there was a rose on the floor, its petals half wilted. There were seven still on the bush and I wondered what the significance of this place was.

"Riniya?" I called softly.

There was only silence around me. I half-expected her to show up behind me like before, but nothing happened. There should've been a handbook on how to reach someone in another realm. I had no idea what had brought her here the first time. Maybe it was a coincidence running into her.

I had no idea what I was supposed to do. More than anything, I wanted this thing to be over, but I was starting to think I wasn't capable of it. The idea of stabbing him to death was like a wet dream, yet the softer he became, the more it felt like attacking someone without cause. I had plenty of cause, so I was clearly going mad.

If I kept trying and he continued seeking forgiveness, I didn't know what would happen. Realistically, it would probably get harder. I knew I would never like the guy, but I didn't think anybody was completely immune to manipulation in a situation like this. Being around him was humanizing him and it was sabotaging my plans.

Crouching, I picked up the flower, turning it over in my hand. It was larger than any rose I'd seen and the petals felt thicker, stronger. There were thorns at the base of it, circling the entire thing. It was oddly intriguing to see a flower that was both beautiful and threatening.

I reached out to one that was still attached to the bush. At my touch, it fell to the ground and I gasped.

"What the hell are you doing?" a panicked voice asked from the doorway.

I straightened, turning to look at Reyn. The look on his face made my heart beat faster. His chest was rising and falling rapidly, but it was the visible branches and shifting color of his skin that made me step back. His appearance kept going back and forth, human to monster.

"I'm sorry," I said quickly. "It just fell when I touched it."

"Get out."

When I didn't move, he stepped toward me, grabbing my arm roughly and thrusting me toward the door. I cried out at the pain from his tight grip. Looking up at him, I sucked in a sharp breath at the raging green colors in his eyes.

"Reyn, I-"

"Get out!" he shouted.

Turning around, I sprinted out of the foyer. I passed Rath in the hallway, but ignored him when he tried to talk to me. I didn't stop running until I made it to my room. Shutting the door firmly behind me, I sunk to the ground, dropping my face into my hands.

Recently, I'd been seeing a side to Reyn that humanized him. Now I was reminded of why I had to follow through with my plan. What I'd seen in his eyes today wasn't just anger, but vengeance. He was seconds away from striking me down or worse.

No matter what pleasantries he managed to muster or what kind façade he put on, he couldn't erase what he really was. Beneath it all, he was a murderer. A rapist. A kidnapper. A beast. I couldn't allow myself to forget that.

I would seek retribution for myself and for all the other women here. I'd avenge Riniya, along with anyone else he might have hurt in his long life. He would not be getting a happy ending.

Swinging the sword in front of me, I smiled at how smooth the motion was. It no longer wobbled in my hand and it felt like there was more force behind my blows. Humans should really go back to using weapons like this one. There was a certain beauty to it, like it was an art.

I heard Reyn come in, but I didn't acknowledge him. I wasn't sure exactly how to approach the situation, so I was going to let him lead. All I had to do was get close enough to him so that he would let down his guard. After the situation in the red room, I might've lost some of our previous momentum, but I was sure we'd get there again.

"You're doing well," he commended.

"Thank you." I smiled at him over my shoulder, then swung the sword again.

He moved around me, then my blade collided with another. His was fancier, with an emerald jewel in the hilt. As I looked over the length of it, I thought it looked exactly like the dagger Riniya had given me, but much larger.

"Where'd the fancy sword come from?"

"A chest that was put away long ago."

"Sounds mysterious," I taunted as I began to circle him. He stayed in place, but turned his head to watch my movements.

"I have many secrets, little rose. Perhaps you'd care to learn some of them."

"Can they be used against you?"

"Without a doubt, but that's what keeps things interesting." I was behind him now, but it sounded like he was smiling.

Humming thoughtfully, I pressed the tip of the blade to his back. He turned his head, then held up his hands as if to surrender. Before I could get too cocky about it, brown cords shot from his fingertips. They wrapped around the blade and yanked it to the side. I nearly fell over from the force, but managed to right myself.

"This is pointless. I'll never beat you."

"You're right."

My brow furrowed. "Then why are we doing this?"

"You seem to enjoy it and I enjoy watching you get excited about violence."

"Are you trying to flirt with me in some weird tree person way?"

He smiled, revealing a row of sharp teeth. They still unnerved me, even when I spent time with Rath. I had two permanent bite marks from this asshole's chompers.

"My brother thinks I should have patience," he drawled, coming to stand in front of me. He trailed a finger from my jaw down to my collarbone.

"Patience for what?"

"To earn your affection."

I resisted the urge to grimace. "Is that what you're trying to do?"

"Yes, but I've come to the conclusion that it can never happen."

"Hm."

It was difficult to keep my expression neutral, especially when he was staring so intently. I wanted to walk away, but I had a mission to accomplish.

"I have a proposal," he went on.

"I'm waiting with bated breath."

"You clearly cannot tolerate me unless I'm making you cry out in pleasure."

My cheeks heated and he licked his lips. When he stepped closer, my stomach clenched. I could smell that strange scent, a mixture of tea leaves and peaches.

"Perhaps we can continue our physical relationship and forgo everything else."

"You want to be fuck buddies?" I laughed.

"Sure."

"And what am I getting out of this?"

"Well, it's in the name. We fuck. It's a win-win situation."

I hummed thoughtfully. "A situationship. Okay, but what's the point?"

"The point is that I enjoy your body for some unknown reason and I find myself thinking about you when I should be sleeping."

Dropping my gaze to the ground, I bit the inside of my cheek. "Okay. I guess that's something we can do."

"If I get home, you will be free of me and if the last rose falls before I can break the curse, perhaps I'll release you."

My head shot up and I immediately locked eyes with him. "Really?"

"There will be no reason to have you here."

"If you're sure I can't beat you in battle, there's already no reason."

"We'll see."

"How long is left?"

His expression darkened. "I do not know. Days. Weeks."

"Sounds like a plan, then."

His eyes widened. "You're agreeing?"

"I literally win in every scenario. I'd be stupid to refuse."

The smile that took over his face was bright, almost childlike. It drew attention to his sharp, ethereal features. He looked so young, yet he was apparently over a thousand years old. I'd always had a hard time imagining living a full human life, let alone as many years as he'd been around.

"In that case..."

When he stepped toward me, I instinctively moved back. The way his eyes lit up made my stomach feel like it'd been shaken aggressively. As he unbuttoned his shirt, I allowed myself to admire the sharp planes of his body.

When in Rome, I guess.

Chapter 40

Reynaeros

"Are you purposely fucking in every place I put one of those plants?" Rathiain groaned before dropping onto my bed.

My lip curled when I looked at where his shoes were touching the blanket.

"What better way to inform you that I'm aware of your sneaky shit?"

He laughed. "Maybe just tell me. Or remove them."

"This was more fun. You've played your little games with me for centuries. I thought it was time to get back at you in a way."

"So, you've developed a sense of humor."

"I've always had one. I simply forgot what it felt like to live until now."

He raised a brow. "Interesting."

"Don't start this again."

"Why did you make that strange agreement with Kiera?"

"It doesn't matter."

"It does."

With a sigh, I sat on the edge of the bed. "She will never care for me, but I can't stand the idea of not being able to be around her."

"But you lose her in the end if she does not come to love you."

"Yes. It's what must happen. Regardless of the circumstances, she will age and die. Keeping her here and allowing my feelings to fester would only make that loss harder. So, I will enjoy her body and bring her all of the pleasure I can, then I will allow her to live out her short human life as she sees fit."

"Damn. You've got it bad."

"Fuck off."

"What about what happened in the rose room?"

My stomach clenched at the memory. "She doesn't realize what she did. I just hope it didn't speed the process of the others."

He ran a hand through his hair, his expression appearing pained. "It's so close now and I feel almost... afraid. I cannot bear the idea of never seeing home again. I've run away from the thought for so long, but now I can't."

"I know, Rathiain. Perhaps..."

"What is it?"

"If Riniya will allow you and the others to return-"

"No," he interrupted firmly. "That's not an option."

"You could return home. My fate is all but sealed, but it doesn't have to be that way for you."

"She would not allow it anyway. She takes issue with me as much as she does with you."

"You do not want her throne."

"But I could take it and that's enough for her. She holds something over the both of us anyway. If I went back, she would only reveal the truth and ruin me."

Shaking my head, I tried to think of something that would spare my court from this fate. They would have to bow to Riniya if she allowed them to return. It was unlikely, but not outside the realm of possibility. Rathiain was right, though. She wouldn't tolerate his presence.

"The others, then. I will try to get them home."

"I don't think they'll want to leave you either."

"It's not going to be up to them. I won't subject them to this."

"Then you must win her over, Reynaeros."

"I can't. She has made it very clear."

"You need a gesture. Something grand."

"There's nothing I could give her. I don't even know her."

"So, get to know her."

"That's not part of our arrangement."

"I don't give a fuck. Sprinkle in a question here and there. Find a way to get her to talk to you. I'll dig into her life, if that helps."

Rubbing my jaw, I considered it. "She won't be happy if I learn things through nefarious methods."

"She'll never know. Plus, I'm the one being nefarious and she doesn't loathe me."

"Alright, but I don't think it will do any good."

"You'd be surprised. Friends with benefits often develop feelings for each other."

I snorted. "Not when they've wronged the other as I have."

"At least you can say you tried. If I end up stuck here with you, I will accept that, but only if you did everything in your power to prevent it."

"Then that is what I'll do."

"Plotting and scheming, huh?"

We both jumped to our feet and faced the door. At the same time that I wrapped a vine around Riniya's neck, Rathiain brought water to his fingertips. I knew from experience that he could fill her lungs in a matter of moments.

Riniya clutched at the vine with narrowed eyes. "Release me."

"I told you that I would kill you. You should know to heed my warnings."

"You cannot hurt me, Reynaeros. You know what happens if you do."

Tightening the vine, my lip curled. "It might just be worth it to see the life drain from your eyes."

"If he doesn't, I will," Rathiain chimed in. "It's been a long seven centuries, you traitorous snake."

Even though her life was in our hands, she smiled. "Perhaps you should pay more attention to the snakes within your court."

I narrowed my eyes. "What are you talking about?"

"You're so focused on winning her over, that you haven't considered she might be working against you."

"If you've gone near her, Riniya..."

"Don't be silly. I am not allowed to intervene. If it were me, though, I'd be plotting your downfall with every breath I took in this place."

"She is not you."

"What is the saying in this realm? 'Hell hath no fury like a woman scorned.' Do you think she would ever forgive your wrongs against her? I would not."

What was in her eyes made my stomach churn. Knowing it was useless, I uncoiled the vine and dropped onto the bed. Rathiain looked down at me briefly before turning to Riniya again.

"You've come to stir up dissension. I think it's time you leave."

She cocked her head. The gesture made her look more like our father. I grimaced at the thought of her resembling him in any way. He was a better person than she could ever hope to be. The black sprouts swaying in her palms were enough to solidify that point.

"Do you really wish to stay in this place, Rathiain? Perhaps our brother had a point before."

"I would never bow to you."

"Do you know what happens when that gateway is sealed?"

He shifted on his feet. I sat up straighter, my breaths coming quicker.

"We will be stuck here. It's not difficult to understand."

"Cut off from the energy of our realm," she droned, reaching out to touch the leaves of one of my plants. It immediately shuddered, then curled in on itself, the green darkening and a horrid stench filling the room.

Clutching the blanket on either side of me, I averted my gaze. It couldn't block the way its energy felt, though. I felt its pain, the manipulation of its life energy. Then it was nothing.

"That is what will happen to you."

"You're lying," Rathiain spat. "You couldn't possibly know that."

She laughed. "Look at that rosebush. Why do you think it is dying? It is not compatible with this world. When you can no longer feed off the energy from our realm, everything you are now will change."

He looked at me with a desperation that made my chest ache. "Leave, Riniya."

When she opened her mouth to speak, I built a thick wall of branches in front of her. They continued growing, pushing her out of the room. Once her energy disappeared from the realm, I closed my eyes and pinched the bridge of my nose.

"Reynaeros..."

"I don't know, Rathiain. Everything is speculation right now."

"So, it was Kiera's energy that made the flower fall, as we theorized."

"Yes. It exists between our worlds. The energy here is what's killing it and she embodies what this world is made of. Her energy could kill it in a matter of minutes."

"Shit. We need to move more quickly."

"I'll do what I can."

He nodded before heading toward the door. The branches opened inward, allowing him to pass. Once he was gone, I dropped onto my back, staring up at the plants on the ceiling.

This entire thing was my fault. Riniya took issue with me and everyone here would pay for it. It didn't matter what I did or did not feel for Kiera at this point. I had to do everything in my power to earn her forgiveness and pray to the gods that Rathiain was right about how we could break the curse.

If I had to let her kill me in order to save them, that was what I'd do. My brother would step up and take the throne if that happened. There was no way he'd allow her treachery to win, even if it meant claiming the thing he'd never wanted to be associated with.

Hopefully it wouldn't come to that.

🌷 🌷 🌷

As I flipped through the folder Rathiain dropped off, I found myself enthralled in a way I hadn't expected. Kiera's life wasn't extraordinary and there wasn't anything decidedly unique about it, but I knew that in some way every single thing in here brought her to where she was today.

Her parents died six years ago when she was only nineteen. To me, that was the natural progression of things, but in a human life, nineteen is an arguably young age to go through it. For her, it was probably a formative event. Maybe that was why she harbored so much anger and pain. From what I could see, they had been very close.

They'd been in France for her parents' twenty-fifth anniversary, which they'd apparently made into a family vacation. Three days in, her parents' car had ended up in a lake. Was it wrong for me to be grateful she hadn't been with them? I didn't really care if it was.

"Heavy reading?" Chester asked from the doorway.

I raised my gaze to look at him. "You've been absent lately."

He clenched his jaw, glancing around the room absently. When I laughed, his eyes widened.

"Lost in the human, I'm assuming."

He spluttered. "I, uh, if you..."

"Relax. There's not much else to do around here these days and we never know how much time there is."

He moved to stand in front of the desk and leaned his hands on it. "Has anything happened?"

"No. There are seven flowers still alive."

"Yeah, but we have no idea what that means."

"Dwelling on it doesn't do us any good. It's not something you should worry about anyway. I'm doing what I can."

He turned his head in an attempt to read the paper in front of me. After a moment, he chuckled and swiped a hand down his face.

"I should've thought of this. I assume she doesn't know."

"No and it's going to stay that way." Studying him, I leaned back in my chair. "Maybe her friends could help."

"God damnit, Reynaeros. Don't ask me to get in on this game of yours."

"It's not a game so much as a... match."

"I thought you were getting hot tips from Lucy."

My lip curled. "She's irksome and I have no interest in getting closer to her. After that awkward lesson she gave me in oral pleasure, I loathe even seeing her in passing."

"You could have asked me for a rundown."

My eyes widened, the corner of my mouth lifting. "I thought you hadn't been involved with the humans."

"We've been here for seven centuries. Why would you think that?"

"I suppose I just haven't taken the time to wonder all that much."

"I would ask if you still need assistance, but you appear to be doing quite well in that department."

"Yes. If only her mind would cave to me as much as her body does."

"Romantic words can go a long way. Trust me."

"I have none of those."

He gave me a pointed look. "You have a library full of books. Some of these you wrote yourself. I have a hard time believing you can't come up with something."

My heart beat unevenly as my stomach rolled. "I have not thought of courting a woman for a millennium, Chester."

Putting a hand over mine, his eyes softened. "Do not allow that to have an effect on what you have here. I know you are afraid, but this could be good for you. Sure, you hurt her and there is much you must do to earn her forgiveness. It was your own pain that twisted you into that beast and it's time for you to heal from it."

"Let's just hope I can heal her from myself as well."

"What can I do to help?"

Picking up the paper in front of me, I passed it to him. "Have Rathiain check this out."

He hummed thoughtfully. "If it pans out, it may award you some points with her."

"That is if she doesn't attempt to kill me again for looking into her past."

"She does not have the means to kill you. A day healing in bed is all you have to worry about."

"That and my ego."

Chapter 41

Kiera

Lucy and Collie were chatting animatedly at their usual table. I wasn't sure why they even ate in here, but most days I could find them here for lunch and dinner.

"Hey," I greeted, taking the seat across from them.

Collie smiled at me, looking cheerier than usual. "You've been a hard person to find lately."

"Usually I'm training."

"I thought that whole thing wasn't happening."

I shrugged. "It helps my mind. What else is there to do?"

Lucy hummed thoughtfully. "From what I hear, you've been getting up to a lot."

Rolling my eyes, I sipped on my water. "It's a pastime. I'll have to agonize over my poor moral compass when I get out of here."

"Out?"

"Yeah. If they go home, apparently he'll release me."

Neither of them looked as excited as I felt about it. Cocking my head, I tried to read what was on their faces.

"I'm sure he'll release you too," I assured them.

"Right," Lucy said with a little laugh. "Did you eat?"

"Yeah." I took a long drink of my water, keeping my gaze on the far wall.

"I have something to do," Collie announced, getting to her feet. "We should have a movie night soon."

"That sounds fun. I vote for The Princess Bride."

"That old thing?"

"It's a timeless classic. Don't hate on it."

She snorted. "Fine, but I'm picking the next one."

After offering a little wave, she hurried out of the cafeteria. I stared at the door as it closed, wondering what could be so important in this prison. Maybe she was super excited about one of the puzzles she'd undoubtedly completed at least once already.

"Spill the beans."

Turning to Lucy, my brow furrowed. "What?"

She nodded toward my cup. "That isn't food."

"I'm glad you know the difference."

"You can't fool me. I've been lying about this same thing for as long as I can remember. Are you..."

"No," I said quickly. "I'm just not hungry."

She chewed on her lip. "Kiera, I'm worried about you. I hardly ever see you eat and you've lost weight. The other day when I went to your room to find you, I heard you throwing up."

"It's been stressful here."

"You can talk to me, you know."

Swallowing, I wrapped a loose strand around my finger. "Seriously, Lucy. I'm perfectly fine. Usually I just eat in my room or on my way upstairs."

"Alright," she said, sounding uncertain still. "Do you want to hang out?"

"Actually, I want to practice my knife throwing. You could join me."

"That's alright. It's nice not having to fight anymore and if I never had to participate in violence again, it would be too soon."

I laughed as I stood. "I hear you. At least you're more than capable if the need arises."

"Kiera." Stopping halfway to the door, I raised a brow at her. "Grab something before you go. For me."

Grinding my teeth, I nodded and swiped a banana from the bar. She smiled at me, which I couldn't help but return. As soon as I made it to the stairwell, I stared at the fruit in my hand. Just looking at it made my stomach clench uncomfortably. It rumbled loudly, but with it came a wave of nausea.

"You'll attract a beast with that thing."

"Apparently I have," I muttered.

Reyn appeared at the top of the stairs, his arms crossed over his chest. We'd been fucking a few times every day and it was hard not to appreciate his body at this point. Even his face was beautiful, but there was a lingering uneasiness when I looked at that part of him. It reminded me of exactly who he was and made me question why I was even allowing this much contact between us.

Part of me worried that if I refused, he would just force me again. I didn't know how much of it had to do with that, but I also had no interest in thinking about it too much. This thing was simple. We had sex. We went our separate ways most of the time. Eventually, I would be free. That was all there was to it.

"I'm going to train," I said, trying to make the warning clear in my tone.

He smiled, then licked his lips. "There are many things we could practice, little rose."

"No. Knife throwing only."

When I reached the landing, he looked at me with unmistakable hunger in his eyes. I swore just before he latched onto me and pressed me into the railing. With a shuddering breath, I glanced over my shoulder, the height making me a little woozy.

"Are you afraid?"

"Of you? Never."

The corner of his mouth lifted. "That's encouraging."

"It's not because I don't see you as a threat. I just think I could take you if I needed to."

"Is that so? Maybe we should put it to the test."

I opened my mouth to respond, but his lips brushed mine. Turning my head, I tried to even out my breathing. He'd tried to kiss me a couple times and I never let him. He didn't make a big deal about it, but I'd hoped he would get the hint.

He pressed his lips to the side of my neck for a long moment. When his sharp teeth grazed me, I sucked in a sharp breath. Goosebumps rose across my skin and he ran his fingers over them.

"Why does this happen?"

"Uh, I don't really know. Sometimes it's when we're cold."

"Are you?"

"No."

"Mm. That was quite unhelpful."

"You don't get goosebumps?"

Pulling back, he raised an arm in front of him. "My skin isn't like yours."

"It looks the same. Even Rath's is similar."

"In appearance, it may seem so. Our makeup is entirely different, though."

I trailed my fingers over the markings on his skin. Rath's were raised, as if there were taut cords underneath. I wondered if Reyn's were the same way. In his human form, they were in the shape of leaves, vines, and flowers, but I didn't know what they actually looked like.

"Can I see?"

His body tensed. He was looking at the ground and I could see his jaw working. Putting a hand on his cheek, I waited until he met my gaze.

"Are you ashamed of what you are?"

"No, but humans never react well to it."

"I haven't insulted Rath for the way he looks."

"He is comfortable in his body."

My brow furrowed. Before I could delve further, he pushed my pants down and dropped to his knees. Lifting one of my legs over his shoulder, he went straight for my clit with his tongue, then closed his mouth around me and sucked on it.

He didn't always lose his grip on his concealment, but his branches seemed to make an appearance every time. I was glad for it because they offered the perfect thing to hold onto while he ripped my soul from my body. It must not have hurt since he didn't get angry or try to stop me.

Wrapping my fingers around them, I moved my hips to find more friction. His tongue pushed inside of me, the two sides twining together, making a shape like one of those twisted donuts. They'd never been my favorite, but they might be when I got out of this place.

He groaned against me, the vibration making it more pleasurable. When he returned to my clit, my legs began to tremble. He tightened his grip, then lifted my other leg over his shoulder. I had a minor freakout, but he was managing to hold me in place against the railing, so I relaxed after a moment.

My cry was seemingly endless in the stairwell. Not for the first time I worried that I would snap the branches in half or rip them straight from his head. He licked the length of me one more time before setting my feet back on the floor.

Biting my lip, I looked up at him. His mouth was wet and he wore a smirk as he returned my stare. Putting a hand on his chest, I pushed him backward until he hit the wall, then dropped to my knees, immediately going for his pants. His eyes were wide, but after a moment he helped me free his dick.

I hadn't done this since that day in the training room. This entire time, I'd been greedily taking my own pleasure, which was the point, but I had the strong urge to do this. If he could make me fall to pieces so easily, I wanted to have the same power over him.

Taking it in my hand, I licked up the underside of his shaft, making his breath catch. His palms were pressed back against the wall, his knuckles turning white. Raising my gaze, I found him looking down at me, but he averted his eyes quickly.

Wrapping my lips around the tip, I moved my tongue in a circle, then took him halfway. He pushed forward, but I moved back so that he couldn't get what he wanted until I was ready. His head thudded against the wall and I smiled around him as I pulled back. When I didn't do anything else, he looked down at me with a furrowed brow.

"Kiera."

"That's my name."

His eyes narrowed. "What are you doing?"

Licking my lips, I met his gaze. "Maybe I want you to ask for it."

"You already know that I want it."

"Mm." I licked the tip of his dick, making his fingers stiffen on the wall.

"Fine. You want to be problematic. Suck my cock, Kiera."

"Beg."

His eyes were so wide, it was an effort to keep my laugh at bay. As his gaze traveled absently around the room, I waited for him to decide. I would've paid an asinine amount of money to be privy to his thought process right now.

Finally, he looked down at me again, his jaw tight. "Please."

I stroked him once with my hand. "Is that what you consider begging?"

"Fuck," he said, his breath shuddering out of him when I licked up the underside of him. "Please, Kiera."

I took him in my mouth, but only to graze my teeth across his length. Once I pulled back, he threaded his fingers through my hair and tightened his grip, tipping my head back.

"Please," he said firmly.

Smirking, I teased him with my tongue. The growl that rumbled out of him made goosebumps rise on the back of my neck. He wrapped my hair around his hand until it was painful.

His green eyes were thrashing as he stared at me. "Kiera."

"Yes?" I asked innocently.

Moving his hips forward, he pressed his dick against my lips. "Suck my fucking cock before I make you."

My core throbbed at his words. There was no point arguing, so I sucked him down to the base, gagging when he hit my throat. His lubricant seeped into my mouth, something that had freaked me out the first time I'd done it. The liquid was thick like lube and had an almost earthy flavor, but in a pleasant way. Like a potato.

Snorting a laugh, I nearly choked on him. Ignoring my outburst, he used his grip on me to shove me further down. I gripped his thighs, glaring up at him. He was staring up at the ceiling, but I saw the way his lips curled upward.

Hollowing my cheeks, I moved back and forth quicker. The tips of his fingers pressed into my scalp, tightening then releasing. I felt his dick shifting, the ridges becoming firmer. It was such a strange thing and I kept expecting it to be rough, but it was soft, almost like skin, and it felt thicker.

His other hand joined the first, gripping my hair softly. I stared up at him as his body shuddered. He had his head resting against the wall and his lips were slightly parted. With his eyes closed, he didn't know I was watching him. It felt like a vulnerable moment; one he wouldn't know I'd witnessed.

He pursed his lips just as his grip tightened. A soft whimper came from his throat. The sound didn't feel like it belonged to him, a man so rough and powerful, nor did I think it would be downright sexy. I clenched my thighs when it came again, then he swore in his language.

Entangled Realms

The vast amount of cum he released didn't surprise me as much as the first time, but I wasn't used to it. I had to swallow a few times before he was finished. Dropping my gaze from his face, I pulled off of him slowly.

When I stood, he slid his hands to the sides of my neck and pulled me close. My heart leapt, thinking he was going to try kissing me again, but he just pressed his forehead against mine as he breathed heavily.

"Come to my room," he murmured, his lips brushing my nose.

My heart was hammering madly. "I need to train."

"There's no need."

"I want to."

"Then we can train together later."

Shaking my head, I pulled away from him and took a big step back. His arms dropped to his sides. It looked like he wanted to say something, the intensity in his eyes burning into my soul.

With a forced smile, I ducked my head and all but fled through the door. I made a beeline for the training room, not checking to see if he was following. I had no idea what I'd do if he was.

Thankfully, when I got to my destination, the door shut behind me and didn't open again.

Well, that happened. Mission successfully accomplished and weird, awkward look in his eyes avoided. Gold star.

Chapter 42

Reynaeros

"Why are you a grump?"

"I'm not a grump," I snapped.

Lucia's eyes widened, then she laughed. She hopped up on the counter, continuing to watch me as I made an espresso. It was annoying and I considered throwing the shot in her face. I was interested in seeing how much heat human skin could withstand.

"Let me guess. Your girl isn't as easy to win over as you thought."

"I told you I'm not trying to win her over."

"Oh, please. She's got you in a fucking chokehold, Lee."

I growled, my grip on the glass making it begin to crack. "Do not shorten my name."

"Kiera did."

"And she got her ass fucked for pissing me off. Is that what your goal is?"

Entangled Realms

She looked a little scared, but rolled her eyes. "You're not going to do that. But, you've just outlined exactly why you're having a hard time with her."

"What, pray tell, should I be doing then?"

"A date."

"A date?" I repeated incredulously.

She gestured around the kitchen. "They say the way to a man's heart is through his stomach, but true intellectual's know women love to eat. Cook for us and we'll be like the little squirrel that comes around after you start feeding it."

She put her hands up in front of her and made a sound I assumed squirrels made.

"That's ridiculous."

"It's not. Plus, she's lost weight since she got here. I'm worried about her."

"She has been training a lot. It's natural."

"No, I don't think it's that."

My head snapped up and a wave of fear overcame me. "Is she ill?"

"No. I don't know. She said she's stressed."

"I will cook for her," I decided. "She will eat even if I have to force it down her throat."

"Well, don't do that. It sounds like you've forced enough down her throat."

"I have not forced it," I muttered.

"Whatever. Just cook her favorite food."

Pouring the last shot into the mug, I tried to think of what that could be. Was I supposed to ask her? If I did, she'd probably laugh in my face or lie to me like she had about her name when I met her. Griselda. She was ridiculous.

"You're smiling."

Smoothing my expression, I finished making the drink and strode toward the door.

"Don't be here tonight," I said.

"You sure you don't want a buffer?"

"I'm sure that I don't want to deal with your bullshit anymore, Lucia."

"I'm the one that had to sit down and tell you how oral works like it was the birds and the bees talk."

"What do insects have to do with sex?"

She pursed her lips on a smile. "Someone must've thought they were connected."

"Bees and avians shouldn't be involved in sex. It's a recipe for disaster or inflamed skin."

Her laugh was still audible as I made my way through the cafeteria. As annoying as she was, she seemed to be a good place to go for ideas when it came to Kiera. If it wasn't for her, I wouldn't have made it this far. Even if this whole thing ended up being a failure, I felt grateful to have the chance to spend the moments I had with her.

I'd never been given the chance to feel affection for someone. Even if I had been, there were things that prevented me from wanting such an experience. It aroused something uncomfortable in me every time I considered it. Until Kiera.

That feeling still tried to take over, but when I was with her, it was as if she silenced it. Perhaps that was simply what happened when you cared for someone. They became the embodiment of comfort, light, and safety. Those were all things I felt when I was with her. For her, though, I was the complete opposite.

My stomach clenched. For her, I encompassed my relationship with Riniya.

The mug shook in my hand and I took a deep breath, forcing myself to continue to her door. I couldn't lose myself right now. Past shames had no place in my future. That was what I imagined Rathiain would tell me if he were here.

I knocked on Kiera's door and waited. With every second, I felt a stronger urge to bolt. This had seemed like a normal enough thing to do. Sweet, even. Now, I was feeling humiliated and vulnerable.

Finally, the door cracked and Kiera peered out. I immediately felt rage when I saw how pale and sullen she looked. Without waiting for her to invite me in, I pushed open the door and strode inside.

"What is wrong?"

She crossed her arms over chest. "Nothing's wrong. Why are you barging in here like this?"

I looked around for anything out of place. The window was still intact and I would've known if the plants had to attack anybody. I didn't sense any other energies, either.

"Your appearance alarmed me."

She scoffed. "Thanks. Remind me not to let you see me in the morning if I'm so ugly when I wake up."

The idea of waking up beside her made me feel nervous. "Don't be dramatic. I didn't say you're ugly."

"Essentially."

"Why were you sleeping? It's nearly noon."

"I'm allowed to have a lazy day, you know. Or is that something you're going to take away from me?"

Shaking my head, I set the cup on the nightstand. "I brought you coffee."

Her eyebrows went up. "You... Brought me coffee."

"That's what I said."

"Why?"

"Because you enjoy coffee. The other day, you said you missed drinking a quad shot every day."

Eyeing the cup, she rubbed up and down her arms. "Is it a quad?"

"Yes, though I can't understand how you can withstand so much caffeine."

"I'm immune. Did you poison it?"

I reared back. "Of course not."

She cracked a smile as she reached for it. I breathed a sigh of relief when I realized she'd been joking. The change in her expression helped to dispel my worries about her state.

"Wow. It's good."

"I told you I know how to make espresso."

"Honestly, I didn't believe you."

"I'm offended," I said with a laugh.

After another sip, she set the cup down and swallowed. She'd gone pale again, but when she sat on the edge of the bed, she offered me a small smile.

"Thank you, Reyn. This actually helped today."

Sitting beside her, I turned my body to face her. When I took her hand, she tensed, but didn't pull away.

"If I ask you something, will you be honest with me?"

"Uh, I don't know. That sounds foreboding."

"I don't see how."

"Because it's coming from you."

I tried not to frown. "What's your favorite food?"

Her face was extremely blank. I didn't know exactly how human bodies worked, but I'd heard of something called 'going into shock' and wondered if my question was shocking enough to cause that. After a moment, she dropped her face into her hands and laughed.

"That wasn't what I expected," she said.

"Some might call me unpredictable."

Looking up at me for a moment, she let out a breath. "You're bringing me coffee, telling jokes, and asking questions about me. What's going on?"

"The coffee made your day better, jokes make you smile sometimes, and everything about you intrigues me."

"Oh."

"Will you answer the question or do I need to go kidnap another one of your friends and torture the information out of them?"

Her eyes widened, a hint of panic shining through. Brushing her hair behind her ears, I smiled at her.

"Another joke, little rose."

"Right. That one was harder to discern."

Stroking her cheekbone with my thumb, I looked into her eyes. She kept them averted, but I studied them nonetheless. They were redder than usual and her skin appeared darker underneath them.

"I will go."

Forcing myself to pull away from her, I stood and headed to the door. I was halfway down the hall when she called my name. Turning, I looked at her form leaning against the frame.

"Grilled cheese."

"What?"

"My favorite food."

I laughed. "Are you serious?"

"Yes, but not the basic shit. At least three different types of cheese and I want grill marks on that son of a bitch. Maybe bacon."

"You're strange, even for a human."

I continued on my way, my mind turning with possibilities. She could have her grilled cheese, but bacon was not happening, no matter how cute she might be.

"Wait!" she called. "Why do you need to know?"

"No reason."

I heard her growl, then her door shut firmly. The pulse of her anger was so familiar at this point, I was happy to feel it take the place of the despondence she'd emanated before.

Somehow, I'd managed to get an answer out of her. I feared that might be the easy part. If I had to lure her into dinner with me under false pretenses, I had no qualms about that.

Madilyn DeRose

Chapter 43

Kiera

Griselda,

Please do me the honor of joining me for a meal. You will be both the main course and dessert, naturally. I'm already imagining having you spread out on the counter as my own personal entrée. In this dress, I can continue tasting you as often as I'd like without having to remove it.

Rhinoceros

Putting a hand over my mouth, I tried really hard not to laugh, but it was impossible. I was nothing less than shocked that he'd written those words on paper. I planned on memorializing them. Maybe they'd end up all over the Internet when I got out of here, simply because it would ensure they lived forever.

Portia had dropped off a rectangular box with a bouquet of roses and the note. It was ridiculous, but being devoured by Reyn was something well within the bounds of our agreement. The things he could do with that tongue...

Pulling the dress out of the box, I couldn't help but gawk at it. I wasn't nearly wealthy enough to know how much things like this would cost, but I imagined it was well above my price range.

It was a tight-fitting floor-length yellow dress with a plunging neckline. Around the middle, it cinched tighter and had gold accents. His statement made more sense when I saw the slit in each side, each one coming up nearly to the hip. It would, in fact, be incredibly easy to gain access to what lay within.

After I put it on, I couldn't help spinning around a couple times. It didn't flair out like a ballgown, but it was still satisfying. It was something I imagined one of James Bond's women would wear to a secret, high class club. They would undoubtedly garner the attention of every man and woman in the place.

I wouldn't look quite as ravishing in it, but when I'd applied my makeup and styled my wavy hair in a high ponytail with a few strands out to frame my face, I thought I looked pretty. Brown hair and brown eyes might not have been the most exciting combination, but I'd never been self-conscious about my appearance. They were the same as my mom's and I wore them proudly, as if I carried her legacy in those colors.

A knock at the door made my heart speed up. I didn't think he was going to collect me, like some gentleman caller. We might need to have a conversation to clarify the nature of this relationship.

Smoothing down the sides of my dress, I took one last look in the mirror. When I opened the door, I grinned.

"Rath. I thought you were out of town."

He returned the smile and held out a hand. I took it, letting him lead me down the hall.

"It was just a quick trip."

"Is it weird if I say I'm glad?"

"Aw. Did you miss me, ma belle?"

"You're more fun to hang out with than your brother."

He chuckled. "Reynaeros can be fun. He used to..." He trailed off, looking to the side.

"Did he get grumpy in his old age?" I teased.

"Something like that."

"I feel like I'm missing something."

Finally, he looked at me again, smiling in a way that housed less happiness. "Sometimes things change us. I'm sure you know that."

Dropping my gaze, I took a deep breath. "I do."

"Hey, cheer up." He squeezed my hand. "It'll be a good night."

My nose wrinkled. "It's weird that he sent you to get me for... this."

"I told him he should do it himself, but he's quite busy."

"Busy with what?"

"Dinner, of course."

Before I could respond, he led me through the kitchen door. My mouth dropped open at the sight before me.

There were various food items spread out over the island and pans on the stove. It smelled incredible and made my stomach growl. The food wasn't what made my mouth water the most, though.

Reyn was standing at the island chopping something, which I couldn't even focus on long enough to identify. He was wearing a black button up with the sleeves rolled to his elbows, showcasing the winding marks on his skin. The top two buttons were undone, giving me a view of part of this chest, and his hair was up in a neat bun that made the sharpness of his jaw stand out.

There was a towel resting over his shoulder and when he saw us, he used it to wipe his hands. When his gaze met mine, I thought I might actually throw up.

Fuck. This wasn't the plan. I didn't even think we were actually going to eat. Not food, at least. He was cooking for me. What the fuck was this?

Entangled Realms

Rath's touch disappeared and before I could protest, he'd backed out of the room. I turned back to Reyn, feeling panic rising at an alarming rate. I felt like a rat caught in a trap, yet I couldn't decide whether to flee or accept whatever fate awaited me.

Reyn leaned his hands on the counter and I watched the muscles in his forearms flex. My mouth, which was incredibly wet before, felt dry as the Sahara.

"You look beautiful."

Rolling my lips, I glanced around the room. "Uh, thanks."

"Edible might be a better description."

"Okay."

He was staring at me, but I studiously avoided looking at him. After a while, he rounded the counter, making me take a step back.

"What's wrong, Kiera?"

"I don't... I think I'm going to return to my room."

He pursed his lips, then something changed in his expression. Before I could make a break for it, he closed the distance between us and put his hands on my waist. Turning us, he pressed me back against the counter, one hand coming up to the side of my neck.

"No."

"No?" I repeated, the strength returning to my voice.

"You don't get to run."

"I'm not running. I just don't want to do this."

The hand at my waist moved to my stomach. "Your stomach is growling, so eat with me."

"It's not a good idea."

"It's just dinner, Kiera. I told you we'd have a meal in the letter."

"Sure, but I didn't think it involved actual food."

"Mm." He slipped his hand into the slit of my dress, trailing his fingers over my hip. "We'll get to that as well."

"Let's get to it now, then we can go our separate ways."

"You're quite ill-mannered, you know. One might think you were raised in a barn."

I rolled my eyes. "I'm not the beast here."

He groaned, dropping his forehead to my shoulder. "You infuriate me."

"Good. I'll just go, then."

He grabbed the backs of my thighs and lifted me, making me shriek. I twined my arms around his neck so that I wouldn't fall as he carried me to the other side of the island. Setting me on the counter beside the cutting board, he resumed his chopping.

I set my jaw, wanting to get out of this kitchen, but I knew that he would stop me. He wasn't exactly one for allowing a woman to choose, after all.

Swinging my legs back and forth, I watched him slice a cucumber into perfectly even pieces. There was no reason to be impressed. He probably learned by chopping up bodies or something grotesque like that.

When he held a piece up to my mouth, I pursed my lips and looked down at the floor. In my peripherals, I saw him shrug. Discreetly glancing up at him, I saw him pop it into his own mouth. I'd never seen him eat anything before and it shouldn't have made my core throb to watch his jaw moving like that, but I found myself clenching my legs together.

This was ridiculous. At this rate, I would end up like Lucy, trying to claim that this whole ordeal wasn't that bad. Worse, I might even start to enjoy the guy's company. I was currently watching him eat a piece of cucumber and I was ready to jump his bones.

It was just about sex. Obviously, my body was starting to react to him because we'd been trading orgasms like Pokémon cards. Emotionally, I still hated him and that would never change.

He transferred everything to a salad bowl and tossed it expertly a few times. I continued to watch him as he prepared various other things that I didn't actually look at. He left the kitchen a few times, then returned to stand in front of me, laying his palms on the tops of my thighs.

"Will you join me?"

Entangled Realms

"Do I have a choice?"

He hummed thoughtfully. "No."

Dropping to the floor, I marched past him into the cafeteria. One of the tables was set up nicely with a tablecloth and two places set across from each other. I took one of the seats, immediately pouring myself a glass of wine and draining it.

My eyes widened when he set a grilled cheese sandwich on my plate. It was fancier than any I'd made before. Even the bread looked incredible and, just as I mentioned the day before, it had grill marks. Along with it, there was a salad and some sort of bisque that smelled incredible.

My hand shook slightly as I poured myself another glass. This one I decided to take more slowly, the memory of the last time I'd been drunk around him coming to the forefront of my mind.

After taking my first bite of the sandwich, I couldn't help but look at him. He was leaning back in his seat with his wine glass in his hand. There was a vacant look in his eyes as he swirled it around. When he saw me watching him, he took a long drink.

"What is it, Kiera?" His tone had more of a bite to it than before.

"Uh, this is really good. Like, really good."

"I'm glad you enjoy it."

No, I couldn't start feeling bad that he looked so despondent. It was probably my fault. He'd done all of this for some reason and I was stomping on it like a petulant toddler. Did I care? No, of course not.

"It'd be better with bacon," I muttered loud enough for him to hear.

The corner of his mouth twitched. "Living things should not suffer for temporary enjoyment."

"If I eat bacon all day, the enjoyment isn't temporary."

"Your life would be."

I shrugged. "It's short anyway."

We returned to eating in silence. Every second that it was quiet, my stomach tied itself in tighter knots. I didn't know what he expected from me and I had no idea what I expected of him. I had so many questions I wanted to ask, but I wasn't sure I wanted the answers, nor did I think it really mattered.

Draining my glass, I stood abruptly. He looked up at me, his brow furrowing. The green of his eyes was moving, but he appeared to be keeping a tight hold on his control.

Shaking my head, I rounded the table and dropped into his lap. He slipped his hands inside my dress, gripping the underside of my thighs as I rose on my knees. Cupping either side of his face, I pressed my forehead to his and looked into his eyes, which were becoming more chaotic by the second.

There was a question in his eyes that I wasn't prepared to answer, so instead I reached down to undo his pants. As soon as I got his dick out, I lowered onto it. His barbs locked into place and I moaned at the strange sensation of them tugging on me as I rode him.

His grip on me was bruising, but I didn't feel afraid of his touch. Multiple times now he'd literally sunk his teeth into me, which I knew would leave a mark forever. *He* would leave a mark on me forever. It might have concerned me if I didn't know that soon enough I would be free of this place. What happened while I was here didn't ever have to see the light of day, so I was going to unapologetically take what I wanted.

Something grew from his body and began to stimulate my clit. I dropped my head back, increasing my speed. His lips pressed against my neck before he sucked on my skin.

I came undone, my walls shuddering around him and making him suck in a sharp breath. When my rhythm faltered, he used his grip on my legs to move me up and down his length. It didn't take long for him to find his own release, the swear that left his lips echoing in the large room.

Before he could get weird and sappy, I got to my feet. "Thanks for dinner."

I hurried to the door, throwing it open in a rush. It suddenly slammed closed, blocking my path.

"No."

"What the hell?"

Reyn moved between me and the door. "Every time we do this, you run away from me."

"That's how this works. The deed is done. Now we go live our lives until the next time."

"No."

Narrowing my eyes at him, I tried to go for the other door, but he shifted so his body blocked both. With a growl, I crossed my arms over my chest.

"What is your deal, Reyn?"

"Our night isn't finished."

"We both finished, so I'd call it good."

He gave me a pointed look. "Come with me, Kiera."

"Where?"

"Just trust me."

"That's a lot to ask."

"I know."

He held his hand out to me and I eyed it warily. His fingers twitched, but he continued to wait for me to decide. Finally, I sighed and took it. A smile broke out on his face and his eyes settled into a calm, beautiful forest green that I couldn't tear my gaze away from for a few moments.

Oh, god. This couldn't be good.

Madilyn DeRose

Chapter 44

Kiera

I was extremely nervous as I walked with Reyn along the street. He'd led me outside to a nice motorcycle- a fucking motorcycle- and we'd driven into the city like two normal people going for a night out on the town. It was ridiculous.

To be fair, I'd always wanted to ride on one, but I certainly wasn't going to learn and I didn't know anybody that owned one. The whole time, I had to scrunch up my dress and hold onto it so I didn't end up dead, but overall, the experience was pretty incredible.

Now, back on my feet and a little breathless, I trotted along in the sneakers Reyn had mysteriously pulled out of a little compartment. I wished he would've brought a jacket for me or given me the chance to grab one because it was cold enough to make me shiver every couple of minutes.

"Where are we going?"

"I know that patience is not something you possess, but you could at least try."

Rolling my eyes, I rubbed my hands up and down my arms. He turned to me and frowned. Grabbing my wrist, he detoured to the right and pulled me into a store.

"What-"

"Pick a coat."

Glancing around, I determined that this place was nicer than I would've chosen. We were in the middle of the city, not too far from my apartment, but in the area with the fancy shops and nice restaurants.

"I don't have any money."

He looked at me like I was an idiot. With a huff, I browsed the racks quickly, settling on a simple black zip-up jacket. After he bought it, I slipped my arms into it, sighing contentedly at its warmth. He stepped in front of me and zipped it up, then stroked the sides of my neck with his thumbs.

"Better?"

"Yeah."

With a curt nod, he started down the street again. Now that I wasn't focused on warming myself up, I was feeling even more anxious about this. When he directed me into a dimly lit restaurant, my heart threatened to burst straight out of my chest.

We'd already eaten, so this made no sense to me. Maybe he was bringing me here for dessert. If baking was outside his realm of abilities, I might have to give him shit about it until his face took on that pinched look.

I came to an abrupt stop when I saw someone sitting at a booth in the back. The rest of the restaurant was empty, save for a waiter standing behind the bar. When Eli looked up from the table, his eyes widened.

He met me halfway, pulling me into a hug and lifting me off the ground a little. Tears were already racing down my cheeks, no doubt leaving my makeup a mess. It didn't matter, though. He was here and he was okay. There'd been a constant part of me that worried Reyn hadn't actually followed through with his end and it felt like a giant weight had been lifted from my shoulders.

"Oh my god," I cried into his neck, clutching him tighter. "What's going on?"

"I don't know. Someone called me and asked me to come here to meet you. I thought it was a trap or some money exchange thing, but you're here."

Pulling back, he gripped my shoulders and looked me up and down. After he helped me out of my coat, his eyes softened.

"You look gorgeous."

"It's just a dress."

"Fuck the dress. I'm talking about you."

Smiling at him, I wiped at my nose. "Are you okay?"

"I should be asking you. I tried to get someone to go after you." His voice cracked, a tremble beginning in his lower lip. "I really tried, Kiera, but nobody would listen to me. They all thought I was crazy."

"It's okay, Eli. I'm okay."

"Are you sure? You look thin and..."

His gaze traveled to where Reyn was sitting in a booth. His legs were stretched across it as he leaned back against the wall. There was a book in his hand and he appeared to be paying attention to nothing else.

"Is he hurting you?" Eli asked, dropping his voice.

I opened my mouth, but quickly realized that I didn't know how to answer. For the entirety of my time in that place, I'd been fighting so hard to keep myself grounded. Now, with Eli here and feeling like part of the real world again, I had no idea what to think. It all felt like an uncomfortable, jumbled mess in my mind.

"No," I said finally. "He's fine."

It didn't look like he believed me, but he just led me over to the table and pulled a chair out for me. When he settled across from me, we clasped hands and both laughed a little.

"I missed you so much," I said.

"Me too. I've been worried sick. I didn't know what to do and I feel like I've just been going through the motions. Work, home, sleep, eat. That's it."

"I'm so sorry."

"Don't you dare apologize. It's not your fault. You saved me, Kiera. I literally owe you my life."

Waving a dismissive hand, I leaned back. "Telling myself that you were okay was what got me through the first couple weeks."

"Kiera, you're a prisoner. We have to find a way to get you out."

Glancing quickly over my shoulder, I leaned closer to him over the table. "He's going to let me go soon."

"And you believe that?"

"Not really, but I have a backup plan. It won't be long."

"Let's just get you out now. We can catch him by surprise."

"No." His eyes widened at the forcefulness of my tone. "We can't beat him like that. Just trust me, Eli."

"I hate having you here right now when I know that you're going to return to that place and be a prisoner again."

"It's not bad anymore. We... Have an arrangement."

"An arrangement?"

My face heated. "It's not important."

"Oh, don't tell me you've succumbed to some Stockholm shit."

"I have my wits about me, Eli. I'm making sure I stay aware of everything that's happening and I'm not letting myself forget the bad things."

He studied me for a long moment before nodding. "Fine. I still hate this, though. I feel useless."

"You're perfect, as always."

The waiter came over and filled two glasses of wine for us. I thanked him awkwardly and drained mine immediately. Maybe it would help me to sort through my scrambled thoughts. That or I could just get drunk enough that I didn't care for a little while.

Was this what trauma bonding felt like? I thought I had a tight grip on my sanity, but I was willingly sleeping with the enemy. As much as I told myself it was simply the best option out of the other possibilities, I was enjoying the sex. Was that allowed if I didn't catch feelings?

Ugh. Feelings. That was the biggest leap I could take. There was nothing redeemable about the man over there.

Turning a little, I looked at him again. He appeared so content as he read and every trace of emotion was wiped from his face. There was a glass of wine in one of his hands and when he took a sip of it, I licked my lips.

"Kiera."

Tearing my gaze away from Reyn, I looked at Eli. He was barely concealing his concern and it was beginning to irritate me.

"Stop acting like I'm delicate."

"How else should I act?"

"Maybe just enjoy being with me right now."

"There's a possibility I won't see you again and that's a looming threat in my mind. I swear to god, if you don't get out of there soon, I'm going to rally everybody I can to come save you."

"Eli, stop. Anyone you bring there will just be killed."

"And you expect me to be okay with you going back?" he nearly shouted.

There was a sound from the other side of the room. Glancing over my shoulder, I saw Reyn sitting up straighter. He looked like he was still reading, but I didn't think he actually was.

"Things are worse," Eli said, softer this time.

Looking down at my hands, I shook my head. "No. It's fine."

"Kiera, I can see it. Have you been eating?"

"When I can."

"Shit. You need to get out of that place or it'll kill you."

"I'm going to. I'll do whatever it takes."

"Promise me."

Meeting his brown eyes, I reinforced my resolve. "I promise I'll do whatever it takes."

"Good. Now, let me tell you all about Grayson's ridiculous antics while you've been gone. He asks about you every day."

The thought made me want to throw up my wine. The last thing I needed when I got back home was Grayson accosting me. I might not even return to the coffee shop, actually. We'd see how things were when the time came.

Madilyn DeRose

Chapter 45

Reynaeros

As I pulled the bike close to the entrance, I felt a wave of nervousness wash over me. I wasn't sure why. Maybe it was owing to how quiet Kiera had been since we left the restaurant. She hadn't said a word as we walked down the street, even when I'd asked her if she was still cold. She'd simply shaken her head and studied the buildings around us.

When she swung her leg over the side, I latched onto her waist, pulling her back down, but facing me. I removed her helmet and tossed it to the ground, taking her face in my hands. Her eyes were red and there was a tight set to her jaw that I'd learned meant she was trying to conceal her emotions.

"Tell me what's wrong."

"Nothing."

The way her voice cracked made me think otherwise. I'd hoped seeing her friend tonight would bring her joy, but it seemed to upset her. It felt like every time I thought I knew what would mean something to her, I ended up being wrong. This time I'd made it worse.

Slipping my hand into my pocket, I felt the little box there. It was entirely possible another attempt to please her would only increase her distress right now. Pulling my hand free, I stroked her jaw, wishing she could see me as someone worthy of releasing her tension around.

Leaning forward, I kissed her forehead. With her scent in my nose and the taste of her so close, I wanted nothing more than to bring her pleasure. It seemed to be the only time she relaxed around me. The energy she emitted while I was inside her was so pleasurable to me, it made it difficult to hold off my own orgasm for long.

"I've upset you."

She shook her head, keeping her gaze down. "I'm fine."

"I hoped you would be happy to see your friend. I apologize for making your night worse. Things here are different and I'm not sure how to live in this world."

"You've been here for, like, seven hundred years."

"And not once has somebody captured my attention enough to make me want to truly live in it."

Her shoulders shook a little and I pulled back, tipping her face up to me. There were a few tears on her cheeks, the sight of them making me feel angry.

"Tell me what I can do, Kiera."

Finally, she met my eyes. As usual, I had a difficult time deciphering what I saw there. Her energy didn't feel the way it usually did when she was angry. There was something else there. A sort of sadness, but different. I wished she would tell me what it was that plagued her mind.

The tips of her fingers traced over my cheekbones. I stayed as still as I could, letting her explore without breaking the moment. She watched my eyes as they began to shift and I wished I had better control of them. Out of everything, they were the most difficult to conceal.

Her thumb brushed along my lower lip from one side to the other. I took it between my teeth, biting down gently, then closed my lips around it. Her brow furrowed and her chest began to rise and fall more noticeably. I worried I'd frightened her, but she withdrew her hand and suddenly her lips were against mine.

Some instinct drove me to thread my fingers through her hair softly. I had no idea what was supposed to happen when two people kissed, but just having her like this made me feel content. When she opened her mouth more, I did the same.

The kiss was slow; sensual in a way that made my dick harden. I wanted to push her back and drive myself into her, but I couldn't stand the idea of our mouths being separate from each other. The desire I felt was entirely new to me. It told me to own her, protect her, never let her go. The closeness that would have made me uncomfortable with anyone else felt exactly right with her.

"Kiera," I murmured against her mouth. "Come upstairs with me."

She pulled back, putting two fingers over her lips. I reached for her, but she quickly hopped down from the bike and the next moment, she was gone. I was still staring at the door she'd disappeared through, as if she might suddenly reappear and ask if I was coming. I knew she wasn't waiting for me, though. She ran again, which was getting really old, but I didn't know what to do about it.

I pulled out the little box from my pocket and flipped it open. It was impossible to read her and even harder to determine what would piss her off. This felt like my olive branch, but if I was wrong, it could completely destroy any headway we'd made.

No wonder humans complained about dating. They lived such short lives that if it was anywhere close to this, I'd opt to be alone. Considering what this woman was igniting in me, though, maybe that was just wishful thinking.

Entangled Realms

"How are things with your human?" I asked Chester.

He immediately froze with his mug of tea halfway to his lips. I couldn't help but laugh.

"I did say you could pursue her. There's no reason to act strange about it."

"That doesn't mean I don't have a lingering fear you'll change your mind."

"I won't do that."

Finally, he smiled. "Collette is a very deep person, though she may not seem so on the outside. I enjoy her company quite a lot. It's just..."

"What?"

"I fear getting too close."

"You think she won't feel the same way," I guessed, my own heart echoing the sentiment.

"No. I just don't know what happens if- when- we break the curse."

"Bring her with you."

His eyes widened. "Is that an option?"

"I don't see why not."

"Well, the others, for one. Aerranata was not known for being accepting of things beyond the norm."

"It has been centuries and when we return, I will change that. For you, for Rathiain, and anybody else that needs it."

He nodded slowly. "If she does not want to leave this place, I could stay here."

This time, I was the one caught off guard. "You would not come home?"

"If we break the curse, the gateway will remain open. I can come and go as I please."

Tapping my fingers on my desk, I considered his words. I'd never imagined that any of us would want to remain here once the curse was broken. We all wanted to return home more than anything. The idea of Chester not being at my side while I ruled made my stomach constrict.

"It's your decision," I told him after a few minutes.

"Really?"

There was such a note of excitement in his voice that I smiled at him. Only Rathiain and I knew that if we failed to break the curse, it could be catastrophic for us. I wanted the rest of them to remain hopeful, even in the case that they were sealed in this realm forever. If they knew there was reason to fear more than just banishment, they would spend what could be their last days living in fear.

It was my burden to bear. Mine and Rathiain's, though I would take it from him if I could. He'd been subject to enough fear in his life and I hated the idea of him surviving this long only to face such consequences because of me.

Our time was quickly dwindling and with Kiera's habit of walking away from me, I couldn't adequately guess which direction things were going in. There were times I saw something different in her eyes; something that didn't speak of hatred and a wish for my death. Whether she chose to keep denying it or not, it was there.

I wondered if it was something I could build up, like the plants I fed to foster their growth. If she'd allow me, I would nurture her and do anything she wished until she found it in her heart to care for me. After that, even. I'd never stop, so long as I was able to dispel her negative energy and earn the occasional smile, as I had a few times over the past couple weeks.

She was my little rose and I needed her to bloom. I had no desire to clip her thorns. For her, I would gladly bleed so long as it pleased her. Until the day I returned to the earth, I wished to have her in my arms, no matter how sharp she was.

This morning, I'd found only three roses still on the bush. Now, more than ever, I had to move quickly. It was too early, but I didn't have a choice. I needed to bare my soul to her and give her the chance to accept or refuse me.

Chapter 46

Kiera

"Popcorn!" I announced, dropping into the spot between Collie and Lucy. They plunged their hands into the bowl immediately. "Okay, greed is one of the seven deadly sins, isn't it?"

"I'm not afraid of hell," Lucy garbled around a mouthful.

"We're already in it," I agreed with a laugh.

Neither of them responded and just then the movie started. I was filled with a childish sort of excitement, just as I always was when I watched The Princess Bride. Sure, it was a bit dated and cheesy, but there was something about it that I loved.

My mom and dad used to hide our VHS copy of it because I watched it so often and they grew tired of it. All I had to do was put on my best puppy dog eyes and my dad would cave, though, which my mom would scold him for. She could never be very convincing about being angry with him. They had that sort of love that poets spoke of. It was pure and most people never got the chance to see it, much less experience it for themselves.

Pulling my knees up, I wrapped my arms around them and perched my chin on top of them. There was a throb behind my eyes that made looking at the TV painful, but I refused to let it ruin this for me. Chester had gone out to buy this movie for us just so we could have a movie night and if I missed it, I would literally scream.

As I watched them run into the forest, I thought of my day with Rath in the woods. It had been the first happy moment I had in this place. I hadn't even been afraid of him without his concealment. He was a good person, or whatever he was, and something had told me I could trust him.

Riniya's words came to my mind again. If what she said was true, I couldn't trust Rath, no matter what I'd felt that day and every one since. He was on the side of the monster, which meant he was one as well.

Was Reyn a monster? Everything in my head was getting more jumbled with each passing day. When I'd kissed him on that motorcycle, it was strategic. I wanted him to drop his guard, give me an opportunity to kill him when his concealment fell away. If I continued this way, I was certain I could get him to trust me enough to do that.

Even thinking about it made my stomach feel acidic. That kiss had turned into more than just a peck. It morphed into passion, a connection that made me feel... safe.

Fuck. Eli was right. I was in way over my head.

"If we could leave, how soon could you be ready?" I asked suddenly.

They both looked at me. Their silence made me uncomfortable and I wondered when they'd last felt hope about such a thing.

"We can't leave," Lucy said. "So, why does it matter?"

"If we could," I repeated firmly, glancing between the two of them. "I have a plan and I don't intend to leave you guys here."

"A plan? What plan?"

"It doesn't matter."

"Yes it does. If we're involved in the escape, we should know the plan."

"She's right," Collie chimed in. She was wringing her hands in her lap, clearly uncomfortable and probably scared.

"I don't know the exact details yet," I admitted. "But I'm going to do it tomorrow. I need you both to have anything packed that you need and make sure the others aren't around. Can you do that?"

They hesitated, then finally nodded. Satisfied, I settled deeper into the couch and threw a handful of popcorn into my mouth.

We were getting out. It was now or never and the latter was not an option.

🌷 🌷 🌷 🌷

It wasn't safe to use the special dagger while I was training, so I practiced with a regular one. It was lighter, but I figured the extra weight in the other one might help me land a more solid blow. The dummy was smaller than Reyn, but I repeatedly stabbed it in the spot Riniya had shown me. I didn't quit until I was able to hit it exactly the same every time.

I was panting and sweaty, but my confidence was soaring. As long as I could get him to let down his guard and drop his concealment, I was sure that I would be able to accomplish this. Riniya deserved it. I deserved it. Hell, women everywhere deserved it.

To ensure I wouldn't back out, I'd dropped off a note to his door telling him I was going to stop by later. We hadn't seen each other since that stupidly hot motorcycle kiss and I hoped the couple days we'd gone without sex would make him that much more at risk to cave to me.

He was easier to manipulate when his brain was sex addled. Any time I came onto him, he was like putty in my hands. How I'd managed to make him so thirsty for my pussy was beyond me, but his need for release worked in my favor.

All I needed to do was shower, so I headed out the door. When I reached the stairwell, I collided with a body. It was like a heaping serving of déjà vu when I looked up into Rath's blue eyes. This time, he didn't use a plant to keep me from falling; he simply grabbed onto my biceps and righted me.

"Sorry," he said with a laugh. "I tend to space out when I go for a stroll."

"A stroll in the stairwell?"

"Too many places outside would require me to hide myself."

"Right. Well, I need to hit the shower."

"I'll walk with you."

"Okay," I agreed uncertainly.

My duplicitous plans had me feeling all sorts of anxious. Did he know something was up? Were they onto me? Maybe he was going to drown me with his water powers. God, at this rate I was going to throw up before I even made it to Reyn's room.

"You're quiet today," he noted.

"Sorry. Just lost in thought."

"Care to share some with me? I'd love to get out of my own head for a moment."

"Actually, I think I'd like to hear what a powerful, water-bearing prince has to feel melancholy about."

With a laugh, he threaded his arm through mine. "Just the future. Or lack thereof."

"What do you mean?"

"We do not know how much time we have or what happens when it runs out. I can face many things with courage, but staring uncertainty in the face is something that frightens me."

"Yeah," I agreed softly, my own thoughts getting away from me.

"I was thinking about the rest of the court. There used to be more of us, you know."

Entangled Realms

Pulling myself out of my head, I looked up at him. "More?"

"Yes. Many more."

"What happened?"

"Some simply left when they lost hope. We lost others in 1589."

"Lost?"

"We were not careful enough about our inhuman nature. Humans feared what we were and attacked us."

My brow furrowed. "I've stabbed Reyn a bunch of times, so I know you're not easily killed."

"Fire. They set our castle ablaze and not everyone escaped in time. It was catastrophic for all of us. Mostly for Reyn."

"But it wasn't his fault, right?"

"Of course not. He bears the pain of his people, though. That is what a lord does."

I tried to ignore the pattering of my heart. "Why are you telling me all of this?"

We stopped in front of my door and he looked at me intently, as if he was searching for something. I shifted on my feet, forcing myself to maintain eye contact.

"Maybe I'd like you to know that you do not understand him."

"There are a lot of things I don't understand about him."

"Exactly. What I'm speaking of is not surface level, though. He has made many mistakes, but most have been born out of his own pain. It does not make it correct, of course. I think that you know something about pain, Kiera, though you won't share that information with any of us."

"None of it matters," I said dismissively.

"How does it not?"

"I have to shower, Rath."

He rolled his lips. "Alright. If you're available tomorrow, may I come see you?"

"Yeah, of course."

His stare made me want to turn tail and run. I'd never been great at lying, but over the past few years I'd become decent at it. That was what happened when you had secrets to keep.

He bent down to press a kiss to my cheek, then headed down the hall. My eyes burned as I watched him go. He didn't deserve to lose his family, but neither had I. Sometimes we didn't get a choice. At least the person I was going to kill deserved it.

My parents were the best people I'd ever known and the universe took them from me in a cruel twist of fate. Now, I was the one holding life in my hands and I would not screw it up. I deserved to live out the rest of my days away from this place. That's what they would want for me.

Chapter 47

Reynaeros

When I received her note, I couldn't contain my excitement. Waiting around all day had been torture and I hadn't been able to force myself to do anything. Once I heard a knock at my door, I leapt to my feet and rushed to open it.

"Kiera," I greeted, trying to calm myself down.

She offered me a smile. "Hey, Reyn."

"Come in."

As soon as she'd removed her shoes, she looked around the space as if she hadn't seen it before. I followed her gaze, wishing I knew what was going through her head as she studied each plant.

After a minute, I could no longer stand it. I stepped in front of her and took her face in my hands, tilting it up to me. As soon as my lips touched hers, I felt the anxiety of the past few days begin to fade away. I'd been searching for some way to rid myself of it, but it seemed all I'd needed was her.

She pulled away and raised her brows at me. "You're, uh, chipper. What's going on?"

"I'm simply happy to see you."

"Oh. Okay."

"I'm making you uncomfortable."

I took a step back, but she grabbed my wrist. It was difficult not to smile at the fact that she wanted me to remain close. The way she stood awkwardly was strange, but this was new territory for both of us.

"Should we..." She went for my shirt, attempting to pull it over my head.

I grabbed her wrists. "Wait."

"Why?"

"This isn't the only thing I want to do."

"What else, then?"

"I would like to have a conversation."

She looked at me like I'd sprouted a new branch. "A conversation."

"Yes. It's when two people speak to each other."

"Yeah, I know... Oh, you're being sarcastic. That's different."

The look on her face made me want to find a way to make her smile. She must've been just as nervous as I was. Since she was the one that arranged for us to spend time together, I assumed she would be more comfortable.

"Sit down."

I guided her over to the bed and she sat on the edge, folding her hands in her lap. Reaching into my pocket, I brushed the little box with my fingers.

"There's something that I want to talk about."

"Reyn, I didn't really come here to talk."

"I know, but it's important." Taking a deep breath, I locked eyes with her. "Something has changed between us."

The words I'd been going over in my head for two days were escaping me in this moment, but I decided I'd just come up with something as I went.

"When you first came into my club, I knew you were special, but I didn't realize the extent of it. At first, I thought it was because you were meant to be my contender. When it became clear that it was impossible, we tried to determine what else it could mean. In the end, though, I've found that this thing isn't simply about breaking a curse. Not completely."

My heart was racing, making me feel breathless. It was embarrassing, but that was a part of it, I assumed. Baring your soul came at great risk and I just had to soldier on.

"The more time I've spent with you, the more I've come to understand you, though I know I haven't even scratched the surface. I know I have wronged you beyond repair and I don't know how I can fix that, but whatever you need, I will do it. You've taken over my thoughts, little rose, and when you are not near, it feels as if all oxygen has been sucked from the air."

She'd gone pale and her knuckles were white from clasping her hands so tightly. Kneeling in front of her, I took her hands in mine and brought them to my lips.

"What are you saying, Reyn?"

"Isn't it clear? If you would let me, I would care for you."

"You can't be serious."

I opened my mouth, but couldn't think of anything to say. She yanked her hands away from me and stood. As she paced in front of the balcony windows, she put a hand to her forehead and I tried to read the situation.

"You can't be serious," she repeated with a dry laugh.

"I'm beginning to wish I wasn't."

"This is impossible. I don't believe it."

Summoning my courage, I came up to her again and took either side of her neck. I pressed her against the glass, watching a flush rise on her neck as her breaths quickened. I dropped my forehead to hers, breathing in her air.

"In my world, committing yourself to a person is no idle thing. It is what I wish to do with you."

"You agreed this would only be sex," she said weakly.

"If only it were that simple. I want you for more than just sex, my little rose. Imagining a world without you is too much for me to bear."

"I don't know what you want from me, Reyn."

Pulling back, I stroked her jaw with my thumbs. "You, Kiera. I just want you."

Her brow was tight and there seemed to be a multitude of emotions warring behind her eyes. Her energy felt very strange, but I didn't know if it was good or bad. Perhaps it was conflicted, just the way she appeared.

"No."

She spoke so quietly, I almost didn't hear her. My thumbs paused as I stared at her.

"No," she repeated more firmly, turning so my hands fell away.

"No?" I repeated. The word itself felt like it could cut straight through my chest.

"No, I don't care for you."

"I don't understand. We have become closer, shared pleasure with each other. You kiss me now and it was your idea to see each other tonight. Does that mean nothing?"

"I've made the best of a bad situation. That's all it is."

"That's not true," I insisted. "You're hiding from what you feel."

"How could I do anything but hate you?"

I took a step back as if she'd shoved me. "You hate me."

She nodded. Her nostrils flared and I saw her eyes become wet, but she didn't shed a tear. Standing taller, she crossed her arms over her chest. My concealment was failing with the intense pain of my emotions.

"No matter what you think you feel for me, I will always just be your prisoner."

"You would not be a prisoner. I'm asking for you to be my equal. Perhaps my mistakes were what brought us to this place. This is a different sort of connection than I have ever felt, but you are saying you harbor none of the same feelings."

"It doesn't matter because I don't want you, Reynaeros."

I flinched at the use of my name. "You don't want me," I repeated. Even though she'd said it more than once, I was having a hard time letting it truly sink in.

"No."

She headed toward the door, crouching to grab her shoes. The roots under my skin were stretching, trying to burst free. I flexed my fingers, trying to keep them caged.

Shaking my head, I approached her. "You're lying."

She huffed. "I'm not. You need to accept that I don't feel anything for you."

"How?"

Straightening, she looked into my eyes. "You hurt me."

"I know and I told you I'm willing to do whatever it takes to apologize for it."

She let out a dry laugh. "It's not only me you've ruined, Reyn."

"I... Do you expect me to apologize to Lucia and Collette? From where I'm standing, they seem to be doing just fine."

"Fuck you. You don't get to have me. You don't deserve it."

"What can I do?"

"Nothing!"

Pushing my hands through my hair, I tugged at the strings. "I can't see how there's no way for me to make this right."

"You've never imagined having to answer for the things you've done, have you?"

"Before you, no."

"Sometimes there's nothing you can do."

"That can't be, Kiera. I can't imagine losing you."

There was a sort of desperation taking over. It had me considering dropping to my knees and begging. If that was what she wanted, I would do it.

"Does it hurt?" she asked.

"Yes."

"Good. I hope you agonize over it every night. Remember every scream. Every plea. And remember what you see in my eyes right now as I look at you."

Narrowing my eyes, I stepped closer. She kept her position as I studied her, but she was gripping her arms tight enough to redden her skin. Her denial was beginning to make me angry. It was senseless and born out of pure stubbornness.

"Let me tell you something, Kiera. I've become quite attuned to your energy and I may not understand it much of the time, but I can see when you possess a different sort of fear. You want me to look into your eyes. Let me tell you what I see."

"Reyn-"

"It's not just resentment. There's fear about what you feel for me. You may deny and fight it like you do everything else in your life, but I see it. I see you. You're tired, Kiera, and I want to help you carry every burden that weighs you down.

"You're right. I've hurt you, but let me tell you what I want to do now. I want to hear you scream again, but not because I'm causing you pain, but because I'm giving you so much pleasure that you know no other sound. I want to bend you to my will until your body learns to only ever respond to my touch."

Taking another step, I dipped my head until our lips were nearly brushing. She trembled as she looked up at me.

"What I will not do is accept cowardice from a woman that has proven to be the bravest person I've ever met in this realm and all others. If you consider that ruining you, then I will gladly turn us both into rubble so long as we go down together."

Taking a deep breath, I closed my eyes and let my concealment fall away entirely. I heard her gasp, but I didn't dare to look at her. If it was fear in her eyes, I didn't know if I could bear it after everything else that had happened tonight.

The vulnerability of this moment made me want to run away. I thought about the blanket on the bed and wanted to crawl under it, pull it over my head, and never look at anyone again. This form held all the worst of me. My memories, my shame, my weaknesses, and failures. It was the person I hated to be. I would have killed this form if I could.

This form held the most beastly parts of me. She thought she'd seen the worst, but she had no idea what I'd done in this body. Few people did.

She touched my cheek where it was wet and I felt myself shaking a little. It was humiliating. This entire thing was a mistake. Shaking my head, I took a step back and started to turn around.

"Reyn, look at me."

"I can't."

"Please look at me."

Opening my eyes, I stared at one of my plants in the corner before turning to her. There were tears on her cheeks too and my stomach constricted at the thought of making her afraid. When I looked into her eyes, though, there was no fear.

She reached up to stroke my cheeks, then trailed her fingers down my neck. I let her pull my shirt over my head, her eyes roaming over every inch of me. When she put her hands on my chest, I let out a shuddering breath at the feel of her touch on my true skin.

"Are you horrified?" I asked quietly, dreading her answer.

"Of course not."

In that moment, I felt everything more powerfully than ever. She was touching me, looking at me, and she was accepting me. I wanted to keep her forever. Whatever it took, I would make her believe how fervently I desired her forgiveness because I could no longer fight the intensity with which I adored her.

She was mine and I was hers. That was all that mattered.

Madilyn DeRose

Taking her face in my hands, I pulled her into a kiss that was meant to convey exactly what I was feeling. When she kissed me back, I felt hope sprout in my chest.

Chapter 48

Kiera

As we kissed, I tried to forget everything that was muddling my mind. It was easy when I was lost in him, but it kept coming back, prodding at the edges of my sanity.

I ran my hands over his chest again, mesmerized by him. There was a raised, branch-like protrusion where a collarbone should be, extending from one shoulder to the other, then down his sternum. His neck was corded, but still malleable enough that he felt like a person. All of his skin was that same pale, smoky green color I'd seen a little bit of before.

There was a thicker, plate-like covering that was a darker green in some places; his knuckles and a spot below the raised area on his sternum. That must have been where his heart was hidden. I ran my fingers over it curiously and felt movement behind it, but it wasn't like a heartbeat. It was like wind hitting a window during a storm.

I ran my hands up his arms, feeling the taut, raised lines where his tattoos were in his human form. Roots, maybe. That was what they reminded me of. There were smaller, more vein-like ones that extended from his hairline, down his forehead, and around to his cheekbones.

Pushing my hands through his hair, I found that the strands were thicker and silky. His lips were still soft and when he pushed his tongue into my mouth, it felt much the same as it did when he went down on me. It wasn't split, so I assumed he could just do that at will. It was a nifty trick.

Looking up at him, I was a little startled by the brightness of his eyes. Like I'd seen before, they were full of different colors, mixing and swirling together. Now, though, they were as bright as leaves in the height of spring. Even the darkest green of them shone in the darkness.

He was beautiful in the most dangerous, ethereal way. With all of the new parts of him combined with the branches on his head, he really did look like he was meant to rule some mysterious realm. It wasn't lost on me that this meant something to him. I didn't deserve it, yet I couldn't bring myself to turn him away now.

Rising on my toes, I kissed him again. He groaned, that familiar raspiness in his voice stronger in this form. When he lifted me, I wrapped my legs around him and let him carry me to the bed.

Setting me on my back, he crawled over me, not once breaking the kiss. He quickly removed my clothing and began to kiss my skin, starting at my lips, moving down my neck, then between my breasts. I arched into him, desperate for more of his touch.

His lips trailed over my stomach, then he bit down on my hip bone. I hissed and kicked out at him, but he held me down. When he was finished, he moved further down and sunk his teeth into my inner thigh.

"What the fuck?" I shrieked.

Brushing his thumb over the mark, he met my gaze. There was a little blood on his lower lip and I couldn't lie. It was pretty damn hot since I knew it was mine.

"Now your body belongs to me alone."

"Because you bit me?"

"You'll only ever bear my mark, my little rose."

Staring down at the bite mark, it hit me and my mouth went dry. He'd been making those marks since we started fucking after the attack. I didn't look at my body much anymore, but I remembered what I'd seen in the mirror that first day.

Sitting up, I pulled him to me, kissing him so hungrily that we were both breathless. The scent of him was stronger in this form and with everything else going on, it felt like he filled all the space around me. I was consumed by him and it filled me with a visceral sort of fear, one I'd never known.

I pushed on his chest until he laid back. Climbing into his lap, I rubbed myself on his shaft, letting his lubricant combine with mine. The ridges and knotted parts of him felt so good on my clit that I could've finished like that.

When I looked at him, he had an arm behind his head and he was smirking at me.

"What?"

"I'm just watching you."

"Don't do that."

Sitting up, he wrapped his arms around my waist. "And why not, my little rose?"

Instead of answering, I shifted my hips so that his head slipped inside me. His mouth dropped open at the sensation. When I'd worked him all the way inside me, he let out a shuddering breath.

"Do you know you're infuriating?" he murmured against my cheek.

"You've called me worse."

"Mm." He gripped my hair tightly, tipping my head back. "It's a good thing you're beautiful, even if you are quite sharp."

"I have a feeling you don't have an issue with thorns."

He smiled, his sharp teeth making him look dangerous. "For you, I'd grow a thousand thorns so that nobody could ever harm you again."

He held his hand between us, palm up, and three sharp thorns burst from his skin. Taking his wrist, I moved it to the side.

"That's still gross."

Tightening his grip on my hair, he let his lips brush mine. "I've lived a millennium without your touch and now that I've had it, I will never have enough. Now ride my cock, Kiera."

"Okay," I breathed.

His arms remained tightly around my middle and after a while, I felt that ivy-like plant spreading outward over my body. I wasn't startled this time, but it still made me nervous. Looking down, I saw that it was connected to both of us, keeping us connected everywhere we were touching.

"This is what it means to be mine, little rose. You are mine as much as I am yours. Nobody will dare touch you so long as I have breath in my lungs."

As my orgasm crested, he pulled me into another kiss. His raspy groan made goosebumps rise on my skin, then he swore in that beautiful language I didn't understand. Flipping us over, he hovered over me, brushing my hair away from my face as he stared down at me.

"Will you stay here tonight?"

My stomach bottomed out. "Here? In your bed?"

He smiled and the color of his eyes brightened. "Yes, of course."

"Why?"

"Is that a serious question?"

"Maybe?"

"I wish to explore every inch of your body in my bed and I want your scent on my sheets. Then, when our bodies are spent, we will sleep beside each other."

"For all I know, you sleep in a flower pot."

He narrowed his eyes. "We're literally in my bed."

"Maybe it's only for appearances and... activities."

"You're the only woman that has been or ever will be in my bed."

"I don't know."

"Asking was only a nice gesture. I'm not actually giving you a choice."

"I thought you were done with the rapey vibes."

"Is it the same thing if you're enjoying it?"

"Yes."

He shrugged. "Then I suppose I'll always be a beast."

With that, he thrust all the way inside of me. Apparently the case was settled.

Staring up at the ceiling, I listened for any changes in Reyn's breathing. He'd been asleep for a while, but I didn't know how his body worked. For all I knew, he was always sleeping with one eye open or something.

Maybe his plants were all little spies, like some hivemind where he was the mother ship. I didn't really know how that sort of thing worked, but it sounded complicated and problematic for me.

Slipping quietly from the bed, I tiptoed over to my shoes and pulled the dagger from under the sole. It felt heavy in my hand after practicing with the ones in the training room. If I was using it from above, the weight would be helpful, I imagined.

Returning to my place beside him, I rested on my knees and stared at him. He hadn't put his concealment back in place, making that darker, firmer part of his sternum easy to spot. It was like a beacon, drawing my gaze straight to the place he was weakest, even though it looked strong. That was probably why she'd given me this dagger.

I looked at the emerald on the hilt. Now that I was studying it, I didn't think it was any gem that I was familiar with. The color was paler, closer to the darker parts of Reyn's skin.

It began to shake in my hand and I gritted my teeth. This was it, the moment I'd been waiting for. It was why I'd been sleeping with him and trying to get him to open up to me. This was my one shot and if I didn't take it, I might not get another one. Further than that, I feared I wouldn't be able to take it if I got another chance.

Admitting it made me want to drive the dagger into my own heart. Somehow, even after everything he'd done to me and countless others, I'd softened toward this man. It was ridiculous and wrong.

He had manipulated me, planted some seed that would twist my thoughts. Maybe there were mind control spores he'd used on me or something. Whatever it was, I had to end it; cut it out before it could take root.

Poising the tip of the blade over his heart, I took a deep breath, then another. My hand was shaking so violently, I wasn't confident I would even hit my mark.

"Fuck," I hissed, dropping my arm back to my side.

At this point, I literally had nothing left to lose. If one of the others killed me for it, I wouldn't even be losing much time in the grand scheme of things. So, why couldn't I do it?

I stood, letting the blade fall to the floor. Hurriedly, I slipped into my shoes and rushed out of the room. My mind wandered back to my conversation with Rath, an idea beginning to form. Even if I couldn't make myself stab him, I wasn't going to give up. I had other things up my metaphorical sleeve.

There was no doubt I'd earn myself a place in hell before I died and I was okay with that. Life had been throwing shit at me for a long time. How much worse could that place be?

Chapter 49

Reynaeros

"What would you do for your brother, Reynaeros?"

"More than you would do, clearly. Why are you doing this, Riniya?"

She smiled in a way that made my heart race. "I'm taking what I deserve by any means necessary. Isn't that what you taught me?"

"In a completely separate context, Riniya. I wanted you to be strong."

"That's what I'm doing."

"This isn't strength. It's duplicitous nonsense. Plotting against your family." I scoffed. "I'm ashamed to call you my sister."

Her lip curled. "When I sit inside that great oak, you will pay for your words."

"You will never rule. It is my place, my duty, and my honor. It does not belong to you unless you wish to fight me for it."

"I will not do that."

"It is the only way to acquire a throne that does not belong to you. Come on. Fight me."

"Stop it."

"Fight me, Riniya!"

Black vines burst from the ground, making me stumble backward. I stared up at them as they rose high into the branches of the surrounding trees. Their leaves quivered and succumbed to the rot that spread to the rest of the plant.

My heart ached at the sight, combined with the pain of their life forces fading. My own plants unfurled, wrapping around hers and subduing them easily.

"You are weak. Even with your rot, you stand no chance against me. Give up this fight before I'm forced to send you back to the earth."

Turning around, I began to walk toward home. Her dark laugh made me pause, the hair on my neck rising.

"Rathiain will be ruined."

"Excuse me?"

"You know what I speak of."

Wrapping vines around her hands and her neck, I stood in front of her again, getting close to her face.

"Is that a threat, Riniya?"

She smiled, revealing her teeth. "What would you do for your brother?"

"I will not be blackmailed by you."

"Poor little Rathiain. You always doted on him."

Fisting my hands at my sides, I tightened the cord around her neck.

"I will simply kill you."

"And those in my circle will do just as I've instructed. It will ruin him. Let's not forget what you did."

"I have done nothing."

"Rumors can destroy dynasties, brother."

"What do you want?"

Jerking awake, I rolled to my side, curling up tightly. Her voice still echoed in my head, a constant reminder. My skin felt like it was on fire just from the memory.

Remembering that I wasn't alone, I reached out for Kiera, desperate for the comfort that she brought me. My hand met emptiness and I immediately sat up, looking around the room. She wasn't in the bed and her shoes were gone.

My chest felt emptier than it had when I woke from the dream. Why would she leave without saying anything?

The door slammed open suddenly, making me jump from the bed.

"Kiera?"

Rathiain stepped into the room, looking around frantically. "Where is she?"

"Who?"

"Kiera. Where is she?"

"I don't know. I was wondering the same thing."

His eyes landed on me and he froze, his eyes wide. Muttering a curse, I shifted the color of my skin, smoothing out the inhuman textures, and forced my branches to recede. He still appeared shaken, but moved on to search the room.

"She is not here, Rathiain. What is going on?"

"Lucia just sought me out."

My nose wrinkled. "I thought she had something with Brooks."

"Not for that. She gave me a warning."

"Well, don't keep me waiting."

He looked at me with a tight brow. The blue of his eyes was thrashing like waves in a storm.

"Why are you hiding something from me?" I asked.

He sighed. "She meant to escape."

"Escape? I don't understand."

Moving to the other side of the bed, he stared down at something. I joined him and my blood ran cold. He bent down to pick up the dagger and turned it over in his hand. I didn't need to look further to know what it was.

"Where could that have come from?"

"Only one place," he said.

"It wasn't Kiera. It couldn't be."

"Reynaeros."

"No," I shouted, grabbing the blade from him. "Even if it was, she did not use it."

"We need to find her. I don't think this is over."

"She won't betray us."

"She already has."

Swiping a hand down my face, I fought to control my anger. After everything that happened in the night, I couldn't believe that she would have plans to attack me. It was asinine. Nobody was that good of a liar.

Except Kiera was. Whatever plagued her mind was hidden so deep, even she was in denial about it. Her anger permeated her very essence. It didn't make for a person that could be trusted and I should have known better. She was working with Riniya and I'd invited her into my bed.

Putting a hand over my mouth, I fought the urge to be sick. I was overcome by so many emotions; rage, sadness, hurt, desperation.

"Let's just find her," Rathiain said softly, putting a hand on my arm.

I nodded and followed him out the door. "I'll check the library."

"Be careful."

Taking off at a run, I made it there in only a few minutes. As soon as I stepped into the foyer, I noticed something was different. I felt it. The plants were in pain.

I put a hand on the wall where there used to be a branch growing. It looked like it'd been sawed off. The thought of it enraged me.

I pushed into the library, looking in every direction. After confirming she wasn't at the window, it dawned on me.

"No, no, no."

As soon as I burst through the red door, I put my hands on my head. She was on her knees in front of the bush, the branch in her hand burning at the tip. When she heard me, she turned her head to look at me and I saw a deep sadness there.

"Kiera," I said softly, holding up a hand. "Talk to me."

She shook her head. "It has to be this way."

"Stop. Let's talk about this."

"There's nothing to talk about. You can't go back to your realm."

"You don't know what you're doing. My sister has clearly infected your mind."

She let out a dry laugh. "That's rich coming from the one that has filled my head with lies."

"Lies? Kiera, I have not lied to you."

"All of it is a lie!" she shouted before shifting the fire closer to the bush.

I growled, stepping forward, but I didn't know what to do. If she touched it, the bush would go up in flames immediately and I couldn't stop it. It was not of this world and fire was a phenomena that didn't exist in my realm. It took nothing for our forms to be engulfed in it.

Getting too close would only ensure my own death. I couldn't fight something like that. It was hungry and destructive.

"Please, Kiera."

"I'm sorry, Reyn."

As soon as the branch touched the leaves, they ignited. I rushed forward, not sure what I was going to do, but unable to just stand by and watch. My hand touched the flame and it ate at my skin, making me cry out from pain. It continued to travel upward toward my shoulder, the smell of my own body burning filling the room.

"Reyn!" Kiera shouted. "Oh my god."

I hit my knees, accepting that there was nothing to be done. Once those flowers were dead, it was over anyway. Maybe it'd be best to simply die before it happened.

There was shouting in the room, but I couldn't focus on it. Smoke filled the space, making it impossible to see anything. Something grabbed me, then water doused me completely, putting out the flames.

When I glanced around, I saw that we were in the foyer. Rathiain had his hands on his forehead as he stared at the ceiling. Kiera was huddled in a corner with her arms around her knees, tears streaming down her face.

I got to my feet and peered into the rose room. From what I could see, there was one left on the bush. The rest of it was dead, burned to blackness. Dropping my face into my hands, my shoulders shook.

"Reynaeros, there's still one," Rathiain said softly.

Shaking my head, I continued to laugh. My brother swore when he realized my state. Without looking at either of them, I marched into the library. Focusing my energy into regrowing my skin, I sunk into a chair beside the fireplace, the irony of it not lost on me.

I sensed her energy, but I didn't turn toward her. Using my vines, I brought over a bottle of whiskey, then took a long drink from it. The burn of it helped me to keep my head clear. By the time I was done with it, I intended to have a very muddled head.

"Why would you do that?" Rathiain asked from behind me.

She muttered something unintelligible. He growled, then something shattered.

"Why?" he repeated.

"Because I want to be free," she replied.

"Free? You would destroy our chance of returning home in the name of freedom? Forgive me if that doesn't make any sense to me, ma belle."

"Don't call me that."

"Oh, now you take issue with it? I suppose you've been faking our friendship this entire time, so it makes sense."

"I wasn't."

"You have damned us, Kiera."

"Enough," I said firmly.

"She must answer for this."

Standing, I turned toward them. "If you are to blame someone, blame me. I am the reason she wants us all dead."

Her brow furrowed. "I don't want you all dead."

"Just me, then, and in the process you are willing to kill everyone else." I breathed a laugh before taking another drink. "You had the perfect chance while we were in bed."

She gritted her teeth and averted her gaze. I closed the distance between us and grabbed her jaw, forcing her to look at me.

"You want to kill me, right? Let's fight, then. Or do you prefer to do it when I'm powerless? You enjoy the duplicitousness of it."

"No," she whispered.

"Come on, Kiera." I spread my arms wide. "Fight me."

She didn't answer, nor did she look at me. Rage rose in my chest at her cowardice. With a roar, I threw the bottle against one of the shelves, making her flinch.

"Fight me, Kiera!"

My concealment fell away abruptly, just as vines and trees burst from the ground. They were covered in thorns, my anger bringing forth plants with a matching energy. She was shaking as she looked at the chaos around us.

"You cannot forgive me, so kill me." I tossed the blade to the floor in front of her. She picked it up, running her finger over the gem.

"Go ahead, Kiera. I am vulnerable and I will not stop you."

"I don't..."

"Kill me!"

Gripping the handle tightly, she rushed forward and embedded it in my chest. I clenched my teeth at the pain, but it wasn't a fatal attack. When I pulled the blade free, I threw it across the room.

"You're weak."

"And you're a fucking rapist."

"Let's be done with this, Kiera. I've apologized to you and more."

"Not just me."

"The others do not matter to me."

"And Riniya?"

My gaze snapped to her face, my entire body going rigid. I felt the way my eyes thrashed at her words.

"What did you say?"

"Riniya. Did you apologize to her?"

Marching forward, I grabbed her by the throat and thrust her against one of the shelves. There was fear in her eyes, but she set her jaw and continued to stare at me. My brow furrowed as memories began to surface. Releasing her, I took a step back, taking her in one more time before I left the room.

What would you do for your brother, Reynaeros?

Chapter 50

Kiera

Rubbing my throat, I risked a glance at Rath. His jaw was set, his expression dark in a way that made him look dangerous. I'd never thought of him as a threat, but right now I saw exactly how formidable he was.

Whatever I'd seen in Reyn's eyes before he left was even more terrifying. It wasn't anger, though. It was something darker.

"Why would you say that?"

I looked at Rath again. "Don't try to defend him. I'm not interested."

"You know nothing," he spat.

"I know what he did."

He took a few steps so he was standing in front of me. "You know nothing." Shaking his head, he swiped a hand down his face. "I considered you a friend, Kiera. That was my mistake."

He began to head to the door, but I grabbed his arm. He yanked it away, whirling on me.

"What am I missing?" I asked.

"You listened to the words of someone far worse than the villain in your story."

"What'd she do?"

"Before she locked us in this place, she sought to control him."

"What do you mean?"

"She blackmailed him. I slept with men, which was not allowed in our realm. Everything is about procreation, furthering the species. So, she threatened me and my brother protected me."

"He gave her the throne so that she wouldn't out you?"

He laughed dryly. "No, Kiera. He gave her what she wanted, but she didn't ask for the throne. She took something that she could hold over him to destroy his chances of ruling. He knew what it would mean to do it, but he wanted to protect me. It wasn't just the once, though. He didn't know she would threaten him over and over and over."

My mouth felt dry as I listened to him. "How long?"

"Over a century."

I put a hand over my mouth, my tears spilling onto my fingers.

"When our father was on his death bed, she demanded that Reynaeros concede the throne to her, but he refused. I stood beside him and defended him, not caring if it ruined me. Of course, she had a backup plan and that's how we ended up here."

"I'm sorry, Rath. If I'd known..."

"You didn't care to, Kiera. He gave you the most vulnerable part of him. The part he despises so wholly that he hasn't worn that skin in seven hundred years, and you failed to see the significance of that. You've damned us."

Without allowing me a chance to respond, he left the room. I had no idea what I was supposed to do now or what I wanted to do. The new information didn't change anything Reyn had done, but I had sided with his sister with barely any hesitation, assuming Reyn had to be the monster she made him out to be. What did that say about me?

As if on autopilot, I walked back to my room. Lucy rushed out of her room and grabbed my wrist, pulling me to a stop.

"Kiera, are you okay?"

Shaking her off, I glared at her. "You betrayed me."

Her brows tightened. "I'm sorry. It's just that me and Brooks... I didn't know what would happen."

"Why would anything happen to him?"

"Because he heard Rath talking about the gateway. They don't know what happens when it closes."

"They'll be stuck here."

Her gaze fell. "They'll be cut off from their energy. It keeps them alive."

It felt like I'd received a third punch to the gut. "I can't talk about this right now."

She called after me, but I rushed to my room, slamming the door and bypassing the bed. My head was pounding incessantly and I wondered if it was possible for my skull to crack from it. I fell in front of the toilet and began to retch.

No matter what I did, I wouldn't be free. I didn't know why I thought it would be any different. It never was. My parents, Reyn, my own fucking head. They were all the things that destroyed me in one way or another.

There was no escape for me. I guess I just had to decide what to do until the inevitable caught up to me.

🌹 🌹 🌹 🌹

Sleep was impossible after everything that happened tonight. I kept tossing and turning. When I closed my eyes, I saw Reyn's face before he walked out of the library. It haunted me incessantly.

Throwing off the covers, I dressed quickly and headed into the hallway. I reached Reyn's floor just as Portia was stepping out of another door.

"Oh, Jesus," she hissed, putting a hand over her chest. "What are you doing, Kiera?"

"Looking for Reyn."

She pursed her lips. "He's not in his room. I don't think he wants to see you, if I'm being candid."

"I know."

With a sigh, she squeezed my shoulder. "Library."

I offered her a smile before taking off. As I pushed into the foyer, the scent of smoke reminded me of the horrible thing I'd done just hours ago. Taking a deep breath, I pushed open the library door and stepped inside.

Reyn was standing in front of the fireplace with a hand resting on the mantle and a glass of whisky in the other. He looked human again and after what Rath told me, the sight made me sad. I was under no delusion that he'd ever show me that part of himself again.

"Reyn."

His head inclined toward me just slightly. "Go away, Kiera."

"Can we talk?"

He hung his head, shaking it back and forth. "We're past using words."

"Then, can we fight?"

He turned to me, meeting my eyes briefly. After draining his glass, he walked toward me. My heart sped up as he closed the distance, but he passed me.

"Reyn, please."

He stopped with his hand on the doorknob. "You should leave."

"I don't want to."

"And why do you wish to talk now?"

"Rath told me."

His muscles tensed. "It was not for him to tell."

The rasp in his voice made my eyes sting. Moving closer to him, I touched his face. He grabbed my wrist, using it to push me against the door. Dipping down, he stopped just short of kissing me.

"You have no right to my past."

"I'm sorry. For all of it."

He dropped my arm, moving his hand to the side of my neck. I tipped my face up, brushing my lips over his.

"Leave." He stepped back, the distance making me feel suddenly cold.

"Reyn."

His fist clenched at his side. There was something gold in his hand that glinted in the light.

"What's that?"

"Something I sent Rathiain to find."

My heart sped up, but I wasn't sure why. "Show me."

He tossed it at me and I barely caught it. When I looked at it, I covered my mouth. A choked sob came from my throat as tears brimmed in my eyes.

"How?"

"You posted a reward for it after your parents' accident, but it was never found. I figured it was in the lake, so I sent Rathiain."

Even with my vision blurry, I stared at the gold pendant with a rose engraved on the front. Opening it up, I wasn't surprised to find the picture gone, but I didn't care about that.

Grabbing the back of Reyn's neck, I pulled him down to me. He backed me into the door again, one of his hands gripping my waist under my shirt and the other holding my neck. My tears breached our lips, but neither of us seemed to care.

"Why?" I asked against his mouth.

"You know why."

Pulling back slightly, he looked into my eyes. His were calm, a solid pale green that would've matched his skin if he was in his true form.

"I would love you, Kiera."

"I..."

"So, you must leave."

My brow furrowed. "What?"

"My feelings make me weak for you and I clearly cannot trust you, so you're free."

He released me and took a step back.

"Wait. I don't understand."

"I am freeing you. Go home and live your life in a way that will make you happy."

Something stung my wrist and I hissed. Looking down at it, I saw the rose scar flare red, then disappear as if it sunk into my skin.

"Reyn, let's talk."

His fists balled at his sides. They were shaking and I could see his lip trembling.

"Leave, Kiera. I do not want you here any longer."

"Please-"

What looked like bamboo shot up from the ground in a line from one end of the room to the other. It separated us, barely allowing me a glimpse of him as he returned to his place beside the fire.

"Reyn!"

I shook the plants, but they were solid. When I pounded my fists against them, it only hurt me. I leaned my forehead against them, letting the tears fall. He didn't look at me again or acknowledge that I was there. He simply stared into the fire and drank his whisky as if I didn't exist.

This was what I'd wanted. It was the goal this entire time. I should've been sprinting out of this place, but I couldn't stop watching him, wishing for one last look at his face.

It may have been minutes or hours that I stood there and nothing changed. Eventually, I accepted that he wouldn't look at me. It was time for me to leave this place once and for all. Judging by Collie and Lucy's attachments, I assumed I would be going alone. It felt like another blow.

This was the right thing. It was what I wanted.

I kept repeating those two lines in my head the entire way back to my room and every time they didn't sound quite right.

Chapter 51

Reynaeros

When Kiera finally left, I closed my eyes. A single tear rolled down my cheek before I reined in my emotions. That was all I'd allow myself. I was too raw right now, cut right open. Crying wouldn't do any good.

It was over. There was nothing else for me to do here. I had failed not only myself, but my people. My brother. I'd failed Kiera. The gateway would close and it was very likely we'd fade along with the energy of our realm.

Draining another glass, I stared at the flames. With a roar, I threw the glass into the fireplace. I dropped my face into my hands, taking heavy breaths.

"So, you're giving up."

I groaned. "Go away, Rathiain."

"No."

"You've had no issue running away for the past three centuries. You might as well have one last soiree off in France before we all turn to dust."

"She cares for you, Reynaeros."

Closing my eyes, I tried to block him out. His footsteps told me he had come closer and I wondered if I should make him leave the way I had with Kiera, though he had a better chance of fighting me.

"Stop being a coward."

Looking up at him, I raised a brow. "I am not a coward."

"You are. You're giving up."

"What would you have me do, Rathiain?"

"Talk to her. Make things right."

"It's too late. She's right. I wronged her and she deserves to return home where it is safe."

"But she cares for you. I know you were drawn to her for a reason."

"It doesn't matter."

"It's all that matters right now. It all means something and you're letting her slip through your fingers when you should be fighting."

"It means I am a lonely, cruel old man that saw an anger so deep it resonated with my own. In my madness, I had a desire to own it. Somehow, it led me to grow fond of her, but that's all it is. She will not and cannot put away her disdain for me and she is right in doing so. That's why I'm sending her home."

"Home? You can't do that."

"I can and I will."

"Try harder, Reynaeros."

"She won't let go of her disdain for me," I said firmly.

"Would you so easily pardon Riniya?"

I gritted my teeth. "That's different."

"Is it?"

"Yes. She took advantage of me for power. To control me and steal from me. She hurt people."

"And you did it for your own selfish pleasure. You got nothing from it but a moment's satisfaction and they got the shame you've been living with for a millennium. For what, Reynaeros?"

"Leave, Rathiain."

"Answer me! *For what?*"

"For reparation!" I shouted, rising from my chair and jabbing my chest with a finger. "To take back what she stole from me for a century. To share that shame with somebody else because I could not carry it alone. Feeling their pain, so similar to my own, but not my own. *Not my own.* That's all I wanted."

"And what happened when you fell for Kiera?"

"I didn't."

"Don't try to deny it now. What happened?"

With a growl, I looked at my brother. "I didn't have to replace my pain. She made it go away for every small moment she gave me. Her pain was so great that it overshadowed mine and I hated that, but then I found that her joy, her happiness, her bliss... They overshadowed both of our pains and with that I felt as one with her. Our darkness and our light. She split open my soul and with her departure, she will take it with her."

"Then get her back."

I sighed, suddenly feeling tired. "I can't. She doesn't feel the same. She can't."

"You don't know that."

"I know it more than anybody. She tried to fucking kill me today."

"And she failed. I don't believe it was simply an error. Her aim was poor and the tears she shed afterward did not speak of failure. They were guilt, heartbreak, love."

"See her home, Rathiain, and do not seek her out again."

He made a frustrated sound, but left the library. The room felt empty, devoid of life. This place had once been my refuge, the only piece of home I had left. Being alone here was my favorite way to spend my days. Now I felt lonelier than I had in an age.

It would have been better to have never met Kiera. Some would say it was best to feel love and lose it than to never feel it, but I disagreed. At least if I hadn't experienced the joy of her, I wouldn't feel empty now. I would've remained ignorant of what could be.

I wasn't human and I couldn't cling to some false hope that someone else would come along. That wasn't how it worked for my kind and I knew that nobody would ever compare to Kiera. Her soul was aligned with my own in a way I never knew I needed. I never thought I'd be able to accept someone's touch in my true form, but it had been easy with her. It had been everything.

Letting the anger take hold again, I flung my chair across the room, watching it shatter into splinters. It wasn't enough. I threw the other one as hard as I could, then followed it up with the table. Thrusting my hands through my hair, I dropped to my knees and let out a long yell. My hands hit the floor as I drew in shuddering breaths.

When that last rose fell, death would be a peace. It was better than living with this chasm in my chest. I could feel her energy getting further away and with every second, her imprint faded from this place.

"I'm sorry," I cried. "God, I'm so sorry. I failed. I failed. I failed."

Chapter 52

Kiera

The sound of Rath putting the car in park seemed loud to my ears. My heart sped up at the prospect of getting out and going up to my apartment. It was so final.

This was the right thing. It was what I wanted.

I wondered how many times I'd chanted that now. Not enough for it to stick, so I would have to keep going. Maybe I'd start writing it down like a punishment from high school.

"Here."

Rath held a phone out to me that I recognized as my own. I snatched it quickly and was surprised when I found it fully charged. Clutching it to my chest, I gathered the courage to look at him.

"I'm so sorry, Rath."

He offered me a kind smile. "I can't blame you given what you've been through."

"Will he be okay?"

"No. Not at all."

I sighed. "It's all my fault."

"We all failed in some way, ma belle."
"I wish I could fix it somehow."
"You could go back."
I shook my head. "No, I can't. I shouldn't be there."
"Are you afraid?"
"Yes."
"Is it fear from what he's done or from what you don't want to feel?"
"It doesn't matter in the end."
"You're both annoyingly stubborn and you think you can make decisions for each other."
"You wouldn't understand, Rath, but I need to be home now."
"Alright. We'll see each other again, ma belle. I have a feeling."
"Sure, Rath."
"Give it time. We'll figure this out and I'll take you for some awesome French crepes."
"It sounds lovely, but it's not going to happen, okay? Please forget about me."
"That'll never happen. You've made a mark here." He put a hand to his chest.

When I opened the door, he grabbed onto my wrist. I looked at him with raised brows.

"You should take this too."

I looked at the book he handed me. "What is this?"

"It's the last one."

"Why?"

"To understand him better. His pain."

"Him? Are you saying..."

"He wrote them, Kiera, and it's not all born out of fiction. I don't even know if he realizes it, but he wanted you to see him. He's never shared these with anyone else."

Before I could get too emotional, I stepped out of the car. He pulled away from the curb and I watched the car until the taillights disappeared. Holding the book to my chest, I looked up at the apartment building. It felt a little daunting to rejoin normal life after all this time.

I rode the elevator up, then stepped into the hallway. The familiar smell of cat piss assaulted me, but I smiled as I walked up to my door. I didn't know what I expected, really. Maybe I thought Eli would come running out of his room with a look of shock on his face, then we'd pop a few bottles of wine while we cried and laughed.

Instead, I was met with darkness and silence. I flipped on the light and looked around. It was exactly the same as always, but it felt colder. I wrapped my arms around myself and stepped into my bedroom.

Not knowing what else to do, I laid down on the bed and stared up at the ceiling. There was a yellowish splotch there that I used to study as I waited to get tired. The ceiling I'd been staring at for a month was in pristine condition and I'd resorted to counting the bumps on it, which usually just made me frustrated because it was impossible to keep track of where I'd been already.

Rolling over, I grabbed a couple of pill bottles from my nightstand. At least these would help me get through the days. Maybe I'd be able to eat again, though I wasn't feeling all that hopeful right now. That was the thing about my life. Regardless of what I did, it would always get worse.

My phone was full of texts and missed calls. The notification bar was so crowded, I ended up just clearing them all so I could tackle everything slowly. I didn't know if I would respond to everyone or what I was going to do about my job. I would have to come up with some sort of explanation that made sense and it just sounded like more trouble than it was worth at this point.

After sending a text to Eli, I returned my gaze to the water mark. It was actually sort of annoying to look at now. I wondered if I could just paint over it or if it would be too obvious and be more of an eyesore.

The back of my neck prickled and I sat up. There was a dark shape in the doorway, the pale hair standing out in the darkness. I turned on the bedside lamp and sucked in a breath.

"What are you doing here?"

"I was worried about you."

I snorted a laugh. "You're not funny."

Riniya smiled, revealing her sharp teeth. "Well, I'd say that's subjective, but you're right. I'm here because you failed."

"You lied to me," I pointed out.

"Oh, please. Don't lecture me on lying."

"I haven't lied."

She cocked her head. My lip curled when black tendrils sprung from her skin, waving like tentacles in the air.

"No, you just hide from everyone in your life and it will only hurt them more in the end. You're selfish. Is that not the same thing?"

"No."

"Tell me, *Kiera*." She stepped forward, her eyes locked on me intently. "Why are you so angry? Is it because mommy and daddy are gone? Or maybe it's in your own head."

My nostrils flared. "Fuck you, Riniya."

"Hm. You're as boorish as my brothers. It's a wonder you didn't end up attached at the hip."

"You tricked me into hurting them." I stood up, squaring my shoulders. She was taller than me, but I didn't feel the same sort of power emanating from her that Reyn and Rath had.

"It didn't take much for you to turn on them. Don't you see? You and I are the same. Two women who were denied power over our own lives from the moment we were born."

"I'm nothing like you. You're a rapist."

"I gave Reynaeros a choice, which is more than what you got."

"Blackmail and manipulations," I scoffed. "That's what cowards are made of. You were too weak to face off with him."

She pushed on my chest, making me drop to the edge of the bed.

"You've lost your mind to his charm. A few good orgasms does not an honorable man make."

Rolling my eyes, I looked at the wall behind her. "How do you know so much?"

"There are those loyal to me."

My stomach bottomed out. "A spy? Who?"

"Someone who sees everything."

"Why are you even here?"

"Well, I was going to kill you."

My breath hitched, making her laugh.

"Don't worry. I've changed my mind."

"Why?"

"I'm going to let you live because I'm merciful and killing you is pointless. Perhaps I pity you. Cutting such a short life shorter just seems cruel."

"Am I supposed to thank you?" I sneered.

"It certainly wouldn't hurt, but I don't expect manners from the likes of you. Do not seek him out again or I will change my mind."

"Since you seem to know everything, you can imagine that I don't care all that much about my life."

"I've done you the decency of warning you. This curse will become complete and I will not allow you to stand in my way. Take my gift or leave it."

Her skin bulged in that grotesque way, then she was gone, leaving behind the scent of rot. Tears pricked my eyes, all of my emotions swimming at the surface and feeling ready to burst free. Finally, I allowed myself to ask the question I'd been keeping at bay for a while now. Was this the right decision?

Clutching Reyn's book to my chest, I thought back to what Lucy said in the hallway earlier. If they didn't break the curse, their access to the energy that flowed through them would be cut off. They didn't know what would happen then. Would they become mortal or even die entirely? The thought made my breaths come faster.

He would have to deal with it alone, whatever happened. I'd left him to bear everything on his own, the way he had for too many centuries. Fuck, I should've stayed.

Getting to my feet, I pulled on my coat and rushed into the living room. The front door swung open, revealing a very panicked Eli. He immediately pulled me into his arms, holding me tightly enough to make it hard to breathe.

"Eli," I said, pulling back.

"Kiera, oh my god. I can't believe you're here. How are you here?"

"I just got dropped off not that long ago. Where have you been?"

"I was literally on my way to bust you out."

My eyes widened. "What? How?"

"After you left the restaurant, I didn't feel right about waiting for you to figure it out. It felt wrong, so I started trying to get someone to believe me again. The police kept acting like I was crazy, but then Grayson saw me there."

"At the police station?"

"Yeah. Apparently, his dad is the chief. He got him to agree if we could give him some sort of proof."

"Yeah, good luck with that. You'd never get close enough."

"Grayson did."

My blood chilled, the fear flooding my veins making me tremble. "Eli, tell me everything."

"He had people keeping an eye on the place. The fucker knows a lot of people. Yesterday, one of them took a video of someone leaving the warehouse. Someone... blue."

"Blue," I repeated, wanting to beat Rath over the head for being unconcealed where he could be spotted.

"Yeah, I don't know what they are, Kiera, but they aren't human. When Grayson showed his dad, he thought it was fake. Then some woman showed up today-"

"Fuck!" I shouted, thrusting my hands through my hair. "It was Riniya, wasn't it?"

"I don't know who it was. She looked like she was cosplaying, but once she made these nasty plants grow out of her body, Grayson's dad started shooting at her. She disappeared and he assembled a unit to raid the place."

"No."

"No?"

"Eli, don't tell me that's happening right fucking now."

"Well, yeah. That's where I was headed."

I swore, grabbing my keys from the side table. When I rushed toward the door, he grabbed my arm and spun me around.

"Kiera, what are you doing?"

"I'm going to warn him."

"That's insane. He's a monster and he deserves to be put down like one."

Rage unfurled in my chest. I yanked my arm out of his grip and stepped back, shaking my head.

"You don't know him. I can't let them do this. Either they'll die or he will and I won't accept either of those scenarios."

"He can't take out a whole team with automatic weapons, Kiera. If you go in there, you'll just get caught in the crossfire."

"Then I'll die."

"Kiera."

Ignoring him, I swung the door open, ready to charge in there like a woman on a mission. It would've been a badass rescue mission, but a shape appeared in front of me, then something struck me hard. I hit the ground, my head pounding.

Something latched onto my ankles, sharp tips embedding in my skin, and I screamed as it dragged me back into the apartment. I tried to find purchase on something, but there was only hard floor. Eli shouted behind me, then I heard a thud.

No. This couldn't be happening. I had to save him.

My eyes fluttered, the pressure in my head increasing. A dark shape crouched in front of me. My vision was too

Madilyn DeRose

blurry to make it out, but I saw blue eyes just before my head dropped to the floor.

    I had to save him.

Chapter 53

Reynaeros

It had been decades since I'd drank to excess. My body certainly wasn't accustomed to it, which made this experience that much more distressing. I was going through phases of finding the whole thing laughable or being so lost to my despair that I considered releasing the fire from its grate.

The door flew open and Chester appeared, looking concerned. "Your energy is all over the place, Reynaeros."

I held up the bottle. "I am quite drunk."

He set his jaw. "That's not the best way to deal with the situation."

"It's not the worst. I think I'm allowed a moment to grieve."

"We should be planning our next move."

Snorting a laugh, I brought the bottle to my lips. It winked out of existence, then appeared in his hand. I narrowed my eyes at him.

"There are no next moves, Chester. The curse can no longer be broken. Our chance has come and gone. You should be spending time with your woman."

"God damnit, Reynaeros. Counseling you is like beating a dead horse."

"That sounds grotesque. Why are humans such violent creatures?"

"We have killed our own on many occasions."

"Those that can fight. We do not harm those that are helpless and without the means to contend with us."

"Mm. If we're back to hating on humans simply to avoid our own pain, I think I'll opt out of this round."

"You sound like Rathiain. Where is he?"

"I have no idea. I haven't seen him since he left with Kiera."

"That was hours ago."

"I wouldn't be surprised if he has run off to another country. It is his way."

I frowned. "It is how he deals with it. My way has not been better."

Chester sighed. "Either go after Kiera or end Riniya."

"You know what that would do."

"So what? If you will not fight to end the curse, you might as well take your sister out while you have the chance."

Rolling my lips, I considered the two options. Ideally, I would have both, but if that wasn't a possibility, I wasn't sure which to choose. I was inclined to pick the one with the highest likelihood of success. Since I didn't have a way to get to Riniya, the choice was clear.

Narrowing my eyes at Chester, I crossed my arms over my chest. "That was a trick."

He smiled. It fell from his face, his brows pulling down. I watched something black push through his stomach, its rot spreading to Chester's skin. His concealment fell away just before he hit the floor, revealing the treacherous woman that had haunted me for a millennium.

She looked nothing less than amused. "I never liked him."

I stepped forward, glancing down at Chester's body. "How dare you come into my library and bring your corrupt energy with you?"

"He was spreading dangerous ideas, trying to make you run after the girl."

"It is not for you to interfere. It's against the parameters."

She shrugged. "Subterfuge. That's the thing about curses. There are loopholes if you're smart enough to find them."

"Just leave and let us expire in peace."

"It's so fun to watch you lose hope, Reynaeros. You had everything you needed right under your nose, but you were too arrogant and consumed with your own perceived plight that you couldn't see it until it was too late."

"There's still time," I mused, feeling a sense of satisfaction when her jaw ticked.

"Do you want to know something else about curses?"

"Not really, but I'm sure you'll tell me anyway."

"The closer you get, the faster they come to fruition. If you'd only given in earlier, you could have stopped it, but every moment she was in this place, the quicker those roses died. Inviting her into the library brought her even closer. That's why it's so satisfying. It's perfect for you because I knew that even if you did manage to acquire the means to break it, you wouldn't do it."

"Why tell me all of this now?"

"Because you've lost. She's gone."

Stepping closer, I pushed back my nausea. "At least she's far from here, safe from me and from you."

She threw her head back and laughed, making my stomach constrict.

"Oh, Reynaeros. I almost pity you."

"What are you on about?"

"You will not have her. She will be dead soon."

Rage forced my energy to burst forth, trapping her with my vines. Others grew all around us, reaching for the ceiling, then spreading outward until the entire room was encased in them.

"Did you just threaten her?"

She smiled. "It's almost ironic. You thought keeping her close to you was putting her in danger. Truthfully, it didn't matter either way. She's a pawn in a game she was never strong enough to play."

"I'm going to kill you."

Her eyes narrowed. "Killing me is only subjecting yourself to the same fate. Those are the rules."

I shrugged. "Then my life is forfeit. At least I will know that you will no longer be a plague on these worlds."

The flash of fear in her eyes solidified my decision. For too long she'd been a lingering shadow in my mind, the disgusting thing that dwelled and never let me close my eyes peacefully. For a short time last night, I slept without the imprint of her behind my closed eyes. As soon as Kiera left our bed, though, she returned. If that didn't tell me everything I needed to know, I didn't know what could.

Ebony plants burst from the ground, trying to choke mine. I could feel my weakness. It had been setting in since Kiera burned the other flowers. With only one left, the gateway was weak and my access to that energy was slim. It would be enough, though.

Thrusting my arms out to the sides, I released my form. I wrapped Chester tightly in a bundle of purple ivy, letting it cure the rot that had spread over most of his body. My skin shifted into a hardened plating that resembled human armor. I reinforced the area around my heart, then covered my knuckles with the solid surface before swinging at her.

The sound of my fist hitting her cheek was one of the most satisfying I'd heard in my entire life. The first, obviously, was the sound Kiera made when she climaxed. If I could hear both at once, I might be convinced there was a peaceful afterlife.

Her vines wrapped around my arms, tugging me back. While I was restrained, she managed to escape her bonds. She headed for the door and I let out a yell as I expelled thorns from my skin, shredding her plants.

"You're still so weak that you won't fight me."

Her skin rippled and bulged. I latched onto her, holding her to this plane. She struggled against me, but as quickly as she summoned her plants, mine subdued them.

"You're going to lose, Riniya, and when I take my last breath, I will finally feel peace because I will be free of you."

Her lip curled. "Release me, Reynaeros."

"Not until I watch the life drain from your eyes."

She growled, sending more of her plants toward me. I gritted my teeth as I fought them off with mine. It was draining me much quicker than it should have. I just had to finish it.

Pulling out the blade she'd given Kiera, I positioned it at her chest. Her breaths sped up, making me smile.

"You thought to have me killed with my own blade, Riniya? That's so dramatic."

I thrust it into her chest, feeling the pain of it in my own body. With effort, I broke through her plating. Her roots coiled inside her, trying to attack the blade. I persisted, sucking in a breath when I grazed her heart.

A scream drew my attention and she used my distraction to force me backward.

"No," I growled, reaching for her. She was already disappearing, though, fading into the other realm. I couldn't stop her because I didn't have the ability to follow her.

Slamming my hand into the wall, I let out a fierce yell. I raced into the hall to investigate the source of the scream. Looking out one of the windows, I saw a large crowd of people outside. They were shining flashlights in every direction and they had rifles.

"Fuck."

"You must be the beast that kidnapped my girl."

With a raised brow, I turned to look at the same guy I'd seen at the coffee shop when I visited Kiera. Grayson. He was wearing a red and black sweater and his dark hair was mussed back in a way that made him look like, for lack of a better term, a douchebag. I imagined making him spill coffee all over himself again, smiling at the thought.

"Your girl, huh?"

"Yeah. Where is she?"

My brow furrowed. "I sent her home."

His mouth opened, then closed. "I don't believe you."

"Maybe you should leave and check it out for yourself."

Raising his rifle, he kept his eyes locked on me. "Not until I've taken care of you."

I let vines push through my hands and wrists. They shot toward him, making him scream like a bitch. When he fired at me, I put an arm in front of me, reinforcing the skin so they didn't do much damage.

"You know," I drawled. "I've been working so hard on being an admirable person these past couple of weeks. I think it's time I released some of my rage."

Chapter 54

Kiera

The groan that came from me somehow triggered a pain in my head. I coughed at the scratchiness in my throat, then tried to swallow, but my mouth was dry. For a moment, I wondered if someone could die from having a dry mouth because it certainly felt like it.

"Kiera," someone hissed.

I opened my eyes, then closed them immediately. It wasn't very bright, but it felt like it. The dull ache turned into a sharp stabbing pain in my temples.

"Kiera," they repeated. I recognized the voice as Eli's which made me try to open my eyes again.

"Eli," I croaked.

Blinking a few times, I cleared some of the blurriness from my vision. He was sitting on the floor with his hands bound behind his back. I tried to move closer to him, but I found myself restrained in the same manner. Thrashing, I attempted to get free, but it just made the ropes dig into my skin.

"Stop," he hissed. "It'll hear."

"It'll- what?"

Suddenly, I remembered what had happened. I looked around frantically, trying to catch a glimpse of the person that attacked me. They definitely weren't human, which didn't bode well for us.

"Where is it?" I asked quietly. "Who is it?"

"I don't know. It... It looks like a tree, but not."

"It's a..." Rolling my lips, I realized I'd never actually asked what they were called. "A dryad."

His eyes widened. "Like, a fairy?"

There was frustrated growl from somewhere behind me. From Eli's expression, I assumed it was our captor. I was quickly trying to put everything together so I could come up with a game plan.

Riniya said she had someone on the inside that saw everything. I thought of the spy plants, my stomach constricting.

"No," I whispered to myself. With a sigh, I decided to just get the big reveal over with. "Well, you might as well show yourself, you giant fairy bastard."

Quick footsteps made my heart race. Eli shrunk back, looking at me with fearful eyes. The person that stepped in front of me looked so angry that I would have laughed if I wasn't so shocked.

"Portia," I said through gritted teeth. "You fucking bitch."

It was definitely her, though she looked a lot different in her true form. She wasn't as pretty as Reyn and Rath were, if I was being honest. Instead of the elegant root-like protrusions that wound around their bodies, she had, well, lumps. They were like the knots in a tree, but with the texture of her skin, they looked gross.

Her skin was more orangey, which didn't pair well with her blonde hair. The only thing that was still attractive about her was the color of her eyes. They looked like her brother's, but she didn't deserve them.

"She told you not to go back to him," she said, sounding annoyed. "You could have lived."

"You're not going to kill me, Portia. We're friends."

"Friends," she scoffed. "We barely know each other, Kiera.'

"Well, I was sort of in distress for the first portion of my stay. We could still get to know each other."

"I will not be here to fake a human life."

"How could you betray Reyn? Or Chester?"

Her tough expression faltered. Shaking her head, she drew a dagger from a cavity in her skin. It was an effort not to grimace.

"I was loyal to him for a long time, but I accepted that he would never be able to break the curse."

"So, you gave up on him."

"Do you know what I lost when I was banished to this place?"

I swallowed, trying to think of what I knew about her. "Reyn said you were married."

"Yes."

"He got to stay?"

"He did not work in the court, so he was not there the day Riniya placed the curse on us. I was forced to leave behind my two children. One was less than a year old and the other was barely five."

"I'm sorry," I said softly. "It's not his fault, though."

"It doesn't matter. I've lived seven centuries without them. I have missed their entire childhood, their marriages, the births of their own children. You must understand. I cannot be stuck here when the curse takes root."

"She offered you a place in your realm, didn't she?"

"She did."

"And you trust her? Portia, she's a liar."

She shook her head, tightening her grip on the handle. "All leaders lie, Kiera. It is how they remain powerful."

"They don't all rape their brothers."

Her eyes widened. "That's ridiculous."

"It's true."

After a moment, she shook her head. "It doesn't really matter in the end. I must return home, regardless of who is in power."

"How could you abandon your brother?"

"Stop talking."

A horrible realization dawned on me, bringing with it a wave of nausea.

"Vera's brothers," I whispered. "Reyn said a human couldn't have broken that window…"

She glanced at me for just a moment before dropping her gaze. "It's time to end this once and for all."

When she approached, I kicked out at her. "You're a monster! Why would you do that to me?"

"You weren't supposed to fucking forgive him after that Clearly, you're too stupid to reason with."

She grabbed my feet, trying to keep me from striking her. Expelling two weak-looking vines from her hands, she wrapped them around my ankles.

"Leave her alone!" Eli shouted.

Portia crouched beside me, poising the knife at my throat. My lip trembled and a few tears slipped free, but I maintained eye contact with her, refusing to make this easy for her. Her brow furrowed, but she pressed the blade in. I hissed at the sting and felt blood roll down my chest.

Gritting my teeth, I prepared for the inevitable. I wasn't well-versed in modes of murder, but I thought having your throat cut was one of those deaths that was painful, but relatively quick. There were worse ways to go, I guess.

Since I was a child, I'd thought a lot about death. When I was too young to have such thoughts, I did anyway. It was a part of my life that I couldn't escape. There was fear for a long time, but at a certain point you realized that accepting it was the easiest thing to do.

This was different. Even though I knew it was about to happen, I wanted to keep fighting. The survival instinct was no joke, apparently. I thought about the pendant around my neck and wondered if she had fought. It would have probably been better if she died on impact, but I liked the

Entangled Realms

idea of her having a chance to fight, even if she didn't win in the end.

A wet choking sound brought my attention back to the present. Portia dropped the blade, reaching for her throat. Water was spilling out of her mouth and she was convulsing. After a minute, she fell onto her side, spasming a few more times before going still.

I stared at her with wide eyes, feeling the beginning of a breakdown setting in. It was extremely late for this sort of a reaction, considering all the other things I'd endured recently, but it was on the cusp nonetheless.

Eli shouted and shrunk back. I followed his gaze, feeling such a wave of relief that I began to sob. Rath crouched in front of me and untied my hands before pulling me into his chest. I wrapped my arms around his neck, burying my face against him.

"It was her," I cried. "She was trying to sabotage us this whole time."

"Yeah, I'm putting that together."

"How did you know?"

"I didn't. I was actually on my way here to yell at you and tell you that you're an idiot."

"Are you still going to do that?"

He pulled back to look at me. "Do I need to?"

I shook my head. "We need to get back. There's going to be an attack."

He swore before pulling me to my feet. I untied Eli and grabbed his hand. He planted his feet, looking back and forth between us.

"He's one of them."

Rath held a hand out. "I'm one of the good ones. Nice to meet you. I'm Rath."

"Your name sounds scary on its own."

"Not that kind," he replied, rolling his eyes.

"We don't have time for this," I growled, taking both their hands and dragging them after me. This time, Eli obliged, though he still looked like he might throw up.

We piled into Rath's car and he took off at a highly illegal speed. As soon as we pulled off the road toward the building, dread coiled in my stomach. There was smoke and the sound of gunfire.

"They can't all be shooting at Reyn," I said, glancing at Rath.

"No. There are others here now."

"Others?"

"I called for them a couple days ago since we knew there wasn't much time. Even though they left, they are loyal to Reynaeros and if things were to end badly, they wanted to stand beside their lord."

"How many are there?"

He put the car in park and we all leapt out. "Thirty or so."

"That's great. That gives them a chance."

He didn't look like he agreed, but I didn't let it dash my hopes. In the chaos, it was difficult to navigate through the building. It was dark with flashes of light and the occasional flashlight beam. I couldn't tell friend from foe and I knew there was a high likelihood I'd get shot.

Someone grabbed my arm and I screamed. I was whirled around and I saw blue eyes that glowed in the blackness.

"Don't run off," Rath growled.

"Sorry."

He kept hold of my arm as we made our way to the other side of the fighting ring. When we reached the door that led into the hall, he pulled me to a stop and went inside first. It was light in there, so I saw when he motioned me forward.

Eli was holding onto my shirt from behind and I could hear his panicked breaths every time silence fell. I wished I could comfort him somehow, but I was just as terrified. Besides, there were no soft words that wouldn't be a lie. We were walking into a den of lions with barely our wits about us and only one person to protect both of us.

"I wish I had a gun," I whispered.

Rath snorted a laugh. "Your trigger happy ass? We'd all have a bullet in us before we reached the next corridor."

"You'd be fine, though."

"Not with the gateway nearly closed. Everything is taking more effort."

I looked him up and down. He appeared fine, but I didn't know enough about them to be able to recognize a problem. The idea of Reyn getting attacked in here and his body being vulnerable made me want to take off to find him.

A flashlight appeared around a corner, immediately followed by gunfire. Rath put up an arm and a wall of water appeared to block the bullets. He pushed it outward, slamming it into the officer. I heard the impact; more like I heard the snap and crunch of his bones breaking from the force of it. He hit the ground in a crumpled heap and didn't move again.

Rushing forward, I struggled to pull the strap over his head and wrestled the rifle out from under him. Holding it against my chest, I grinned at the guys. Neither of them looked pleased, but I felt better now that I at least had a chance to protect myself.

"Do you know how to use that?" Eli asked as we stepped into the stairwell.

"Nope, but I have a foolproof plan."

"And what's that?"

"Point. Pull the trigger. Pew pew. Dead."

He sighed and in my peripherals I saw him shake his head.

"Do you know where Reyn is?" I asked.

Rath held his hand out and his skin rippled like water. "It's hard to pinpoint exactly, but from the direction of his energy, I'd say the library floor."

When we reached the next landing, the door burst open. Five people with rifles and body armor came through shouting orders. I couldn't make anything out, but one of them gestured at the floor while the others pointed their weapons at us.

I looked at Rath and he gave me the slightest nod. A second later, water was falling from the ceiling. It knocked two of them down, but the others rolled out of the way. With their distraction, I raced up the stairs, taking them two at a time. By the time I reached the top floor, I was fighting for breath, but I didn't stop.

It was quieter up here, which might have been a good sign, but I wasn't so naïve. Holding the rifle up, I turned one way, then the other, my heart racing with both exertion and fear. If he was weak to bullets right now, I had to be careful. Moving my finger off the trigger, I positioned it to the side to be safe.

I made it to the foyer, my eyes going wide when I saw how many plants there were. They had huge, sharp thorns and a few dripped a liquid that was steaming. Some were more like sharp spears that protruded from the ground.

Moving into the library, I turned left, then right. It was even worse in here. There were black vines everywhere, but they looked dead. I recognized Reyn's extensive network of plants covering the walls and ceiling. They were moving and as I watched, one of them branched off and headed directly for me.

Holding my breath, I waited as it stopped in front of me, tilting as if it was studying me. My finger twitched, but I refrained from pointing the gun at it. The tip of it opened into something resembling the end of an octopus' tentacle. It latched onto my shoulder and I gritted my teeth. It wasn't painful, but there were soft, teeth-like things that felt like they were licking my skin.

When it released me, it returned to the ceiling. I continued searching the room, but there was no sign of Reyn. My gaze landed on a long, rolled up lump of purple ivy. I crouched beside it and nudged it with the barrel of the gun. Running my fingers over it, I parted it and gasped.

"Chester," I whispered, brushing his cheekbone.

He was in his true form, but was easily recognizable. Sniffling, I straightened and took a step back. It wasn't the time to get sentimental; not when I still needed to find

Reyn. The thought of him being in a similar state made me feel lightheaded.

    I headed out of the room, knowing only one other place I could go. Putting my hand on the knob, I took a deep breath before pushing open the red door.

Madilyn DeRose

Chapter 55

Reynaeros

A bullet grazed my arm, making me swear. This fucker in the red sweater was getting on my last nerve. It should have been easy to get rid of him, but I was feeling weak. Less energy was coming through the gateway, confirming what I already feared. We were out of time.

Even though it would soon be over, I had no intention of letting this man or his army beat us. If we were to return to the earth, it would be on our own terms and in peace. I owed my people that much.

"Aren't you supposed to be some big, strong beast?" he taunted.

I could hear him approaching steadily, unhurriedly. Soon, he would round the corner and be on me again. I moved back quickly, slipping through one of the doors before he could see where I went.

Harnessing as much energy as I could, I let thin, spindly vines crawl from my body and across the floor. They slipped beneath the door, making a web in the hallway. Grayson shrieked as they attacked him and the sound of gunfire echoed off the walls.

Leaving the room, I turned just in time to see him fleeing around the corner. It was funny that he acted so tough when he thought he had the upper hand, but was so quick to run. I would have laughed, but I wasn't exactly in the mood.

My biggest concern right now was protecting the rose. If they got to it, my entire court would be lost in seconds. I needed to buy them any time that I could. For what, I didn't know, but I refused to just let it all go without a fight.

Barging into the red room, I breathed a sigh of relief when I saw the plant was still alive, although I used the term loosely. It was in a sad state and I could feel the weakness of its energy. There was hardly a connection to the world it belonged in and it was withering with the absence of it, just as I was beginning to.

Reaching out with my mind, I tried to determine who was still in the building. Waves of confusion overcame me as I sensed more of my kind than I'd expected. It made me feel warm to realize that they'd come back here. It was where they belonged at the end. With their own kind in my court.

My heart began to race when I sensed Rathiain's energy. He was most likely to be able to help me with the human teams. Even if we were both weakened, together we could get rid of them.

Panic took the place of my relief when I was struck by another familiar energy.

"No," I choked out before turning to rush out the door.

I didn't even make it over the threshold before guns began firing. Since they'd seen me, they would be able to see the door, which fucked everything up. They couldn't get to the last rose.

As soon as they funneled through the door, I kicked through the far wall, drawing all of their attention to me. I ducked through the hole I'd made, glancing back to make sure they were following. I formed a wooden shield behind me to block the continuous smattering of bullets and continued through another wall.

"Stop!" one shouted. "Surrender now or you'll be taken down."

I snorted. "Overconfidence is a weakness that can get you killed."

Turning around, I expelled a host of spores in their direction. They skidded to a halt, their eyes widening. The three at the front breathed them in, their bodies spasming when they infected their lungs. After entering their bloodstream, the spores attacked the humans' cells and twisted them to match their own energy.

Those behind the men screamed when vines burst through their skin. The plants tore through them, diving in and out until the humans were nothing more than pulp spread across the floor, then they turned on the other officers. The gunfire started up again as they tried to defend themselves from being slaughtered.

"Gasmasks!" someone called.

They all pulled them over their faces, then resumed their fight. When they'd killed off the plants, they marched toward me and I led them further away from the gateway. Letting them get a little closer, I grinned before propelling a thick branch in their direction. It shoved them against the outer wall, which I turned to rubble so that they went tumbling over the edge.

"You can't have her!" Grayson shouted.

I turned in every direction, but didn't spot him. His energy was coming from the next room over, but he must have been hiding somewhere in the wreckage.

"Are you going to fight me or continue being a pussy?" I asked.

"Let her go and this can all be over."

"I told you she isn't here."

"You're lying. Where are you keeping her?"

"Jesus Christ. Why don't you call her and confirm for yourself?" When he was silent, I couldn't help but laugh.

"Oh, you don't have her number. How many times must you be rejected before you accept that you're not wanted, Grayson?"

With a not-so-fierce cry, he stepped into view on the other side of a wall I'd demolished. He drew his arm back, then threw something toward me before ducking back into his hiding spot.

"Motherfucker," I muttered, rolling away from grenade and throwing up as strong of a shield as I could. The explosion still rocked me, making my ears ring and my head feel hazy. Who the hell was this guy?

Blinking, I tried to refocus, but my vision was blurry. I barely managed to evade the bullets that came my way. More men with rifles filed through the hole in the wall, aiming at me as they approached. It was hard to tell if there were a lot of them or if I was seeing double. Regardless, I was in a bind and I hardly had access to any energy.

"Give it up," the weasel went on.

"Has she ever let you touch her?" I asked, leaning back against the wall as I eyed the guns aimed at me.

Grayson narrowed his eyes. "For your information, we were planning a date before you kidnapped her. Now, I'll have to put her back together after all the trauma you caused her."

"Trauma," I scoffed.

"Yes, beast. Trauma. It might actually work in my favor. Knight in shining armor is one hell of a way to win a woman over."

My lip curled at his insinuation. He looked smug about it, as if he had already won.

"Put your hands in the air," one of the officers shouted.

"No," I said simply.

"We will shoot."

"Wait," Grayson interrupted. "We need to find out where he's holding Kiera."

"We can search the place when the threat is eliminated. Step back."

"I'm handling this."

"Step back," the man repeated. "You don't have authority here. You shouldn't even be involved in this."

"My father-"

"I'll make sure he loses his fucking job if you don't let me handle this."

Grayson let out a frustrated sound before taking a few steps back. He clutched his rifle tightly, glaring at me while he waited. God, I wanted to rip the petulant look off of his face. Tearing off all his skin was an option. He dared to think he could touch Kiera and that was enough to make me fucking murderous.

"Put your hands up," the officer repeated.

Cocking my head, I did as he said. When he stepped forward, I released millions of spores, the sheer number of them making the room cloudy. I rolled to the side just before they began firing, then focused my energy into building a cocoon around myself to ward off the bullets.

I had no idea what would happen next, but I'd hold them off for as long as I could. While they were in here with me, Grayson couldn't go looking for Kiera. With the amount of energy I was using to keep my shield in place, I couldn't reach out to feel for her, so I could only hope she wouldn't come this way.

Rathiain would keep her safe. Well, he'd brought her here, so maybe I was wrong about that. God damnit, why had he done such a stupid thing? If by some miracle I didn't die here, I was going to have his head.

Still, there was a selfish part of me that was overjoyed that she chose to return. Feeling her energy again, even for a brief moment, eased the ache that had formed in my chest once she left the building. If that was all I'd have of her before I became part of the earth, it would be enough. I'd cling to it until my last breath.

Chapter 56

Kiera

Taking a deep breath, I pushed open the red door and took a step inside. It was darker in here and I could still smell smoke from the fire I'd set. The rosebush was mostly charred with only a small patch still alive. The lone flower made guilt rise in my chest.

The room, once only a small square, now opened up into another. A wall had been completely demolished and there was a trail of plants leading through it, which gave me the information I needed.

Stepping over the rubble, I squinted my eyes. It was dark and there was stuff floating in the air. It made me cough and my throat burned. Putting a hand over my mouth, I stumbled backward, running into a wall.

A large shape appeared through the haze, its limbs gnarled and twisted. The skin was a burnt orange and it had a head of black hair. Reaching out, I tried to form words, to tell it I was a friend, but it just made me cough more.

A rough hand came around my throat, taking away my air. I clawed at it, but it was stronger than me. Tears began to trail down my cheeks as I realized this was it. I'd failed and because of that, I would never know if Reyn was okay. My death meant nothing to me, but the thought of him departing this world because of those who sought to save me was unbearable.

Reaching up, I wrapped my fingers around the locket at my throat. At least I'd see her again. It was a long time coming and there had been many times I'd wished for it to speed up. Not now, though. I just wanted one more minute. Just one more.

The pressure around my throat disappeared and I hit my knees, drawing in gasping breaths. I didn't feel like I was getting any meaningful oxygen and every time I coughed, it felt like I was suffocating all over again. There was a sound like someone shouting, but my ears were ringing.

Something waved in front of my face and I looked up into the violet eyes of my attacker. They were holding a gas mask out to me that I recognized as the ones the officers were wearing. I took it and pulled it over my head, settling it on my face. After securing it, I took in a long breath, finally feeling like I wasn't about to die.

"I almost killed you," a gravelly voice said.

"Why didn't you?" I rasped.

They pointed at the necklace. "Rathiain told us about you. He said you were the one and that we would recognize you by the rose locket. Apparently, we needed a warning because if we so much as disrespected you, Reynaeros would have our branches."

I laughed a little, putting a hand over my chest when it pained me. "Where is he?"

"I came here to figure that out, then you showed up. These are his plants."

Nodding, I got to my feet and situated my gun. "Let's go."

"It's not safe for you, my lady."

"I don't care. I won't leave him to get hurt here."

They stared at me for a moment, then made a sound like a sigh, only it sounded more like wind whistling through the trees. Jerking their chin, they led me further into the space. Their fingers lengthened into sharp spears and they held them up in front of them as they walked.

Gunshots up ahead made me break into a sprint. There was another broken wall and I leapt over the bottom part of it, landing in a room with better sight distance. The outer wall was gone, letting in enough moonlight to give me a decent view.

There was a group of officers, all with their rifles raised. They were aiming them at an ivy barrier, which already had quite a few bullet holes. Without hesitation, I gripped my gun tighter and fired.

It didn't have as much recoil as I expected, but regardless, I ended up missing. I'd never shot a gun before; there had never been a reason to. Trying again, I thought I hit someone in the leg, which was better than nothing. At least their focus was no longer on Reyn, but with their weapons aimed at me, I was beginning to see that I hadn't thought this through.

"God damnit," my new companion grumbled.

"Please tell me you have some cool nature ability that will take these guys out."

"If I had the strength, we might have a chance, but you're in a better position with that gun. Reynaeros' spores aren't getting through the masks and I don't know what he has left."

Bouncing up and down on my toes, I tried not to let the panic take over. I could feel the agitation rising, threatening to send me into a spiral.

"Get on the ground!" one of the men shouted.

What looked like sharp wooden darts shot toward the group. One of them took a shot to the neck and dropped to his knees as he tried to stop the bleeding with his hand. The rest immediately began firing.

"No!" I screamed. My companion made a pained sound and dropped to the ground. I stared down at them in horror before firing at the group again.

"Wait!" someone yelled just before they peppered me with bullets.

My mouth dropped open when Grayson rushed into the room. He was wearing a gas mask, but his hair and red sweater were recognizable immediately. He was holding a rifle in the air as he approached the group and stopped in front of them.

Who the fuck gave this guy a gun? That was the most asinine idea in the world.

"She's the one we're here to rescue."

"She shot at us," the guy in front argued.

Grayson looked at me briefly. "She's been held prisoner here and is traumatized."

"Fuck you," I called, taking aim again. They responded by matching my position.

"Hey, hey, hey. Relax, baby."

"Don't you dare tell me what to do. Put your gun down."

"Why don't you come with me? We can figure all of this out."

"Tell them to stand down," I demanded, aiming at his chest. The thought of ripping holes in that damn sweater brought me more excitement than I cared to admit.

"Alright," he said softly, glancing at the officers. "We can all be reasonable here. Guys, let's put down our weapons."

"No," the one I assumed to be the leader said. "This is my call. We are not surrendering."

"He killed at least ten of us," another guy chimed in.

"He won't hurt you if you let me talk to him," I said, glancing at Reyn's wall. "Let me go to him."

The lead officer shook his head, tightening his grip on his weapon. "Get on your knees and slide your gun over."

Gritting my teeth, I tried to think quickly. Truthfully, I had no idea what to do. I was feeling desperate, but I didn't trust them and I especially didn't believe Grayson would be open to discussion.

"Okay," I said sweetly. "I'll do that as a show of good faith."

Slowly, I got down on one knee, never taking my eyes off of them. Knowing it would probably be the last move I ever made, I pulled the trigger, waving the gun back and forth, not aiming at any one of them in particular. They dove away, trying to evade the chaotic pattern of bullets. While they were occupied with taking cover, I darted behind a large piece of concrete from one of the destroyed walls, putting my back against it as I peered around it.

A roar came from behind the ivy wall just before it burst outward. As Reyn began attacking the nearest officers, I started shooting again, trying to go for the ones furthest from him so I didn't accidentally hit him. Grayson scurried away, no doubt scared off by an actual fight.

After the last one hit the ground, I locked eyes with Reyn. He was in full form, his branches and white hair standing out in the dimly lit room. His eyes glowed and thrashed with whatever emotions he was feeling. We only stared at each other for a moment before we rushed toward each other.

My arms came around his neck and he lifted me a little bit off the ground, burying his face against my skin. My body shook with the tears I could no longer hold back and I thought he was trembling as well.

"What the hell are you doing here?" he asked sternly.

"I heard what was going on and I had to save you."

"Save me?" he repeated with a dry laugh. "I'm better off here than you are."

"I don't care. I just... I couldn't... Reyn, I..."

He shushed me, running his fingers through my hair. "It's okay. Everything will be okay, my little rose."

Pulling back, I looked him up and down. There were various splotches of blood on him, but I had no way of knowing if it was his. Overall, he looked okay, albeit tired.

"The curse," I began.

He put two fingers over my lips. "Don't worry about it."

"But we have to do something. How do we break it? I'll do anything."

His eyes softened. "It's too late for that."

"No. It can't be. What do I have to do?"

Pressing his forehead against mine, he let out a long breath. "It's impossible, Kiera."

With a growl, I shoved at his chest. "Don't do that shit. Tell me the truth."

He opened his mouth, then shut it before abruptly turning toward the collapsed wall. Grayson was standing there with his gun raised, his chest rising and falling rapidly.

"Let her go," he demanded.

Reyn put an arm out, using it to wrap a vine around me and pull me backward.

"No," I cried, trying to dislodge it.

"Don't worry, Kiera," Grayson called, again butchering my name. My lip curled as he readjusted the gun.

"Grayson," I warned.

"He's a monster. I understand that you're confused-"

"You don't know anything! Don't you dare hurt him."

I struggled against my bonds, barely managing to get a grip on my gun. When I pulled the trigger, it clicked, but nothing happened. With a frustrated shriek, I continued to thrash.

"Kill him," I shouted to Reyn.

His body was tense and I saw his fists ball at his sides. I stared in horror, the reality of the situation setting in. He was spent and he was directing his energy toward keeping me out of harm's way.

"No," I cried. "Let me go, Reyn."

Ignoring me, he shifted on his feet, then rushed forward. Grayson began firing and Reyn ducked out of the way. He managed to grab hold of the gun, trying to wrestle it away. I felt hope spring up in my chest as he pushed Grayson back a step.

As if in slow motion, Grayson dropped one of his hands, the change in his resistance making Reyn stumble forward. He pulled a pistol from his side and aimed it at his chest. I heard myself scream as if I was floating outside my body. The sound was drowned out by the clap of the gun firing, followed by eerie silence as the bullet tore through the air. It found its mark, shattering the plating on Reyn's chest and sending splinter-like shards flying in every direction.

With the impact, the vines around me loosened and I shoved through them. I sped into a run, charging directly for Grayson. He turned to me at the last moment, his eyes going wide, then I collided with his chest. His arms came around me, holding me to him as we tumbled over the side, plummeting toward the ground ten floors below.

Something wrapped around me from behind and Grayson's face contorted before he released me. The world went dark, but I knew I was still conscious. We stopped moving abruptly, the force making my head whip forward. I reached out, but met something solid and rough.

There was a sliver of light and I hooked my fingers through the space, trying to pry it open. With a cry, I managed to make a gap big enough for me to squeeze through. Crawling out on my hands and knees, I glanced around.

I was on the ground in front of the warehouse and Grayson was lying a few feet away, his neck positioned at a grotesque angle. There was blood seeping from his head, mixing with the rainwater that was pooling around us. I turned around, then slipped in the mud as I scrambled forward.

"Reyn," I rasped, putting my hands on his chest.

His body shifted back to normal, the wood he'd encased me in becoming arms and his torso flattening again. When he looked like himself again, his gaze landed on me. His brows furrowed as he reached for me.

"Kiera."

I took his hand, holding it to my chest. "You have to heal yourself, Reyn."

"You're okay."

"Of course I'm okay."

"She said you were going to die."

My lip trembled and I brought his hand to my lips. "I'm alive. Please, you have to heal yourself."

He shook his head. "I don't have enough energy. My access to it is almost gone."

"You said you can use the energy of anything that's alive. Use mine."

"It doesn't work if I can't combine it with my own."

"It has to. Just try."

"It's over, Kiera."

My tears spilled over onto our entwined hands, mixing with the rain. He looked up at the sky and smiled.

"I love the rain. It's more beautiful than the sun."

I couldn't help but laugh through my tears. "I think so too."

"Isn't your kind all about kissing in the rain?"

Leaning over him, I pressed my lips to his. He tangled his fingers in my hair, holding me to him. When my emotions were too strong to hold back, I dropped my face to his chest, trying to memorize the feeling of him stroking my hair.

"I know that nothing I ever do will overshadow all the ways I've wronged you, Kiera. In your eyes, I will always be a beast because it is what I proved that I am."

"Don't say that."

"My greatest regret is making you think the worst of me. I only wish I'd been given time to continue trying to prove myself to you, even if it was futile."

"There's time."

"It's close. I can feel it."

"Don't stop talking to me."

His lips pressed against my temple. "Earning every single smile from you brought me more joy than I've ever felt. Each one has overshadowed this horrific shame I've shouldered my whole life. I'm so sorry that in my own despair I passed that feeling onto you. Breaking this curse involved a test that I failed. This is my punishment. For everything that happened here and there."

Lifting my head, I looked at him sternly. "It wasn't your fault, Reyn. She's the villain here."

He offered me a soft smile. The hand at my face felt different and I pulled back, taking it in my own. As I watched, the skin began to harden, the roots underneath flattening. Terror gripped me, but he shushed me and pulled me against him again.

"It doesn't matter whose fault it is. We're each the villain in someone else's story, regardless of what we might have done to remedy our mistakes. She is mine and I am yours."

My body shuddered as I watched roots crawling outward from his body, sinking into the earth. They seemed to be spreading endlessly, creating a structure that would be strong and undoubtedly beautiful.

"Kiera," he said softly, the grittiness in his voice more prominent.

I looked at him as he raised his hand in front of me. A thin vine sprung from his skin, then a rose unfurled. It was full of thorns and was a deeper red than any other I'd seen. When I took it, his arm fell into the mud and his eyes fluttered closed.

"No." I shook him, digging my fingers into his chest. "No, Reyn. Wake up."

A sound drew my attention and when I looked up, I saw Rath standing there. He dropped to his knees, clutching at his stomach. His skin was changing the way Reyn's had. The look in his eyes made me sob harder. It was sadness, but also acceptance.

"He loved you, Kiera. As did I and the rest of our people if they'd been given the chance."

"Please don't leave," I cried.

"We don't have a choice, ma belle. You will live and maybe you'll have more than only bad memories of us."

"No, I won't live."

"Quiet now. It's time for us to return to the earth. We will always reside in this soil. Long after your kind destroys this place, we will remain."

He laid beside his brother and closed his eyes, more roots spreading outward, entangling with Reyn's.

"No!" I screamed. "Reyn, no. Please. No, you're not my villain."

The rain fell faster, as if it too was mourning the loss of the men before me. It didn't matter that it was cold or that I was sinking into the mud. It could swallow me whole for all I cared.

Chapter 57

Kiera

"Kiera."

Eli's voice made me jump, but I shook my head.

"Kiera," he repeated.

Ignoring him, I climbed on top of Reyn, straddling him and burying my face in his chest. I couldn't catch my breath with how violently I was sobbing. Everything I should have admitted before was attacking my mind, reminding me that this was my fault.

"You're not my villain. I thought I wanted to go home because I had this plan for my future, but I was wrong. Whatever time I have left, I want to spend it with you. You're not my villain, Reyn. I forgive you and you made me fall in love with your fucking fairy ass, so you're not allowed to leave me."

With a scream, I beat my fists on his chest. Eli grabbed me from behind, trying to pull me off of him. I latched my arms around Reyn's neck, holding myself to him.

Pressing my lips against his neck, I inhaled the scent that had become so familiar. It was stronger when he was in this form and I wanted to somehow bottle it so it would never be lost to me. It was what I wanted to smell when I took my last breath.

I continued kissing him, moving up to his jaw, then his cheekbones. When I reached his lips, I cupped the sides of his face, allowing myself to savor the feel of him one last time. I tasted my tears as they breached our mouths and tightened my grip on him.

Eli touched me again and I shook my head. Hands settled on my sides, then one traveled to the back of my head. Reyn's lips moved and I gasped, my eyes flying open and meeting his green ones.

"Oh my god," I croaked. "Y-you're alive."

His brow furrowed and his eyes traveled up to the sky, then back to me. "What'd you do?"

"I didn't do anything."

Sitting up, he tightened his arms around me. I felt ivy spreading over my body, then plants burst from the ground. Flowers, shrubs, and trees taller than the buildings around us. Putting his palms down on the ground, he closed his eyes and I felt some sort of pulse.

Rath sat up abruptly and groaned. "What the fuck? Am I hungover?"

"You're alive," I said before a laugh escaped me. "How is this possible?"

Reyn's hands tangled in my hair. There was an intensity in his eyes, the green swirling beautifully as he stared at me.

"You broke the curse."

"I did what?"

"Holy shit," Rath breathed. He punched Reyn in the arm, grinning like a madman. "What the fuck did I tell you?"

"I don't understand. What does this mean?"

"It means I was right and you're in love with him."

"But... That doesn't make sense."

"You're the one that can contend with him, ma belle, and it wasn't just about him falling in love with you. The thing that brought him to his knees was being able to be loved. He never thought he deserved that."

"I don't," Reyn whispered, still staring at me.

Running my fingers through his hair, I dropped my forehead to his. He tightened his arms around me before pulling me into a kiss so deep, I almost thought it was enough to put all of the broken parts of me back together.

"I will grow with you," he murmured against my lips.

"Um, that's sweet," I laughed.

He grinned. "It is what we say to the one we commit ourselves to."

"So, it's like saying, 'I love you.'"

"Yes. It's better, in my opinion."

"Mm. Well, I don't have plant parts that burst out of my skin."

"Pity."

"So..."

We all turned to Eli, who was standing awkwardly with his hands in his pockets. Rath cocked his head, seeming to study him.

"Did you have more to say, human?"

Eli looked a little panicked to be addressed. "What happens now?"

Reyn pulled me to my feet and wrapped his arm around me, keeping me snugly against him.

"Now, I kill my sister."

"That sounds dangerous," I said.

He snorted. "Hardly. Now that the curse is broken, we can hunt her down in our realm. She is no match for me, let alone Rathiain and I together."

"And me."

I put my hands over my mouth as I watched Chester approach. He was still in his true form, but he looked significantly better now.

"Thank god," Reyn breathed. "I thought you were dead."

"I think I might have been, or close to it. You sent a shit ton of healing energy to all of us. Some did not awaken, but many have."

"Then we have an army," Rath said, clapping his hands together once.

"We must prepare."

Reyn pulled me along with him toward the warehouse. As I watched, it began to stitch itself back together, but instead of metal, it was made of wood. Eli looked just as mesmerized as I did. I knew we'd need to have a really long talk about everything, but right now I was just glad we'd made it through the attack alive.

Hopefully the same would apply to this next part.

🌷 🌷 🌷 🌷

It was strange to see them all preparing to essentially go to war. While they were obviously different from us, I'd only ever seen them do mostly normal things, like read books or have mundane conversation. Now, they were growing weapons, detaching them from their bodies, and strapping them in easy to reach places.

All of it was a stark reminder that they were decidedly not human. Reyn told me they were called Cresceterraent, which I decided sounded too much like a cross between crustacean and croissant. I was just going to call them Dryads or fairies and he would get over it.

My head was aching as I watched them, but I refused to take my eyes off of Reyn until he left. I wanted to go with him, but that was obviously a stupid move. It would give him a weakness and Riniya would surely latch onto it. I didn't want anything to get in the way of him tearing her into pieces. He deserved that much.

I continued to focus on the short-term goal because allowing myself to think about the future filled me with anxiety. We would deal with it all after he took back their realm. I didn't know what would happen then, but again, that was a problem for future me.

Entangled Realms

Eli joined me as I slumped against the wall. He took my hand, squeezing it reassuringly.

"I still have no fucking idea what's going on, but I'm confident they'll be okay. Your dude is pretty terrifying."

I smiled. "He sure is."

"And you're positive this isn't Stockholm?"

Shrugging my mouth, I turned toward him. "Maybe. Who knows? It feels right and recently I decided I was going to start taking what I wanted. This is what I want."

"Alright, then I guess I'll support you. I would say that I'd kick his ass if he hurts you, but..."

Leaning my head on his shoulder, I tried to rein in my emotions. It felt like that was all I'd been doing since I left the apartment. I'd been so good at keeping them at bay since I was young, but right now I felt like I'd been split wide open. It didn't help that there was that shadow looming over what would happen with Reyn and I.

"Ma belle," Rath called, jogging over to us. "You better not run away while we're gone."

"I'm sure you'd be able to hunt me down."

"You're right, but it would be tedious." His gaze traveled to Eli. "Don't put any ideas in her head."

He spluttered for a second. When Rath grinned, he breathed a laugh and relaxed.

"If you haven't noticed, Kiera does what she wants regardless of anyone else's opinion."

"That's why she's a match for my brother. Stubborn fuckers."

He was shoved out of the way by Reyn, whose gaze was locked on me. I could see the war going on behind his eyes, so I stepped forward and wrapped my arms around his neck.

"Promise me you'll be safe," I murmured in his ear.

"Of course. I will come back to you, little rose."

"I'm holding you to that."

He pulled back with a smile. "You may hold me to it forever. Once I return, I don't intend to leave your side for years. Decades, even."

My gaze dropped to the floor. "Good."

He put a finger under my chin, tipping my face up. "Not as a prisoner."

Rising on my toes, I kissed him, holding the sides of his neck tightly. It was an effort to let him go, but eventually I did. I looked around at the group of them, all in their true forms and undoubtedly lethal.

"You should go before I get emotional."

"I expect to find you in my bed when I return," Reyn called as he joined the others.

Smiling at him, I leaned back against the wall. I wrapped an arm around my middle, blowing out a long breath as I watched him. Their skin bulged in that way I'd seen Riniya's do, then they were gone.

Immediately, I sunk to the floor, pulling in a gasping breath. Dropping my hands, I tried to support myself as I retched, even though there was nothing in my stomach except bile. Eli crouched beside me, swearing as he gripped my shoulders.

"What's wrong with her?" I heard Lucy ask. She and Collie came into my peripherals and dropped beside me.

"I'm fine," I rasped.

"They'll be okay," Collie assured me, rubbing my back.

Moving into a sitting position, I leaned against the wall. My body was shaking as I clutched my stomach. The light was too bright and now that they were gone, I couldn't ignore the pain. Eli stroked my back and I wasn't sure if it was more for my comfort or his own.

"Kiera, what is happening?" Lucy demanded.

With a dry laugh, I looked at them. A single tear escaped, rolling down my cheek and dropping onto my hand.

"A cruel twist of fate. That's what it is."

Chapter 58

Reynaeros

My first breath of Aerranata air felt like it expelled centuries of pain. I could see that it affected the others in much the same way. If we didn't have a mission to complete, I would have taken time to bask in it, but the longer we waited, the more likely Riniya was to enact some game to throw us off.

"Chester."

He came up beside me. "What do you need from me?"

I put a hand on his shoulder. "Are you up for this?"

His eyes darkened, but he nodded. "I will deal with my sister's death when this is over."

I nodded. "Take half of them with you and seek out Lyndis. I don't want him to have a chance to cast any of his magic. We don't know if Riniya is aware of what happened yet, but I'm willing to bet he is."

"Understood."

He signaled to some of the others and they marched off in the direction of Lyndis' burgh. I hoped they would find him there quickly and this thing wouldn't become too complicated. I was dying to return to Kiera already.

Jerking my chin, I led the group toward what used to be my home. I felt nervous as we drew closer to it. It might be the same or Riniya may have completely destroyed it. Seven centuries had passed since I'd last been here. A lot could happen in that time.

Rathiain held his arm in front of me and sniffed the air. I sensed the energy and drew out one of my spears. From what I could tell, there was more than one, but it was hard to determine if they were friendly or not. After a few minutes, they came out from behind the trees.

"Makala," I sneered, eyeing the violet-skinned man.

"It's been a long time since your energy rang through this place, Reynaeros."

"Perhaps you should bow," Rathiain said casually, flipping a weapon over his knuckles expertly.

"To whom? Our sovereign is not here."

My lip curled. "Then tell me where she is."

"Where she belongs. Unless you are to defeat her, I owe you no allegiance."

"She did not take the throne from me. If you'd like to stick by her side, then so be it. Your body will become one with the earth."

More soldiers revealed themselves, their numbers nearly doubling ours. It wasn't ideal, but now that we were in this realm, we could fight at full power. Most of them were not part of the royal guard when I was pushed out of this place and I doubted they were as well trained as mine.

"Alright, Makala. You've made your decision."

Dropping to one knee, I placed my palms flat on the grass, drawing in an energy purer than I'd felt since I last stepped foot here. The trees around us bent to my will, their branches coming to life and lunging for anyone close enough. Their roots moved beneath the earth, making the ground rumble.

Most of them were fighting at close range, their abilities not as powerful as mine. Only Rathiain stayed by my side, his mastery over the water creating geysers that took out some of our enemies. A projectile came directly at me and I manipulated my energy, binding it with the roots just below me. Bark sprung up in front of me, blocking the weapon's path.

Getting to my feet, I flexed my fingers, the surge of nature's energy tingling beneath my skin. The raw power of it excited me, reminding me why I, not Riniya, was destined to rule this place. Her energy had been twisted by the vileness of her mind, turning everything she touched to rot. It could be powerful, but it was no match for the purity of life energy.

Makala was the most formidable of our foes and he was overpowering two of my own. I marched toward him, sending vines out to lock around his wrists. Thorns sprung from his skin to slice them off, but I'd already reached him.

Locking a hand around his throat, I completely encased his arms in a strong bark that he wouldn't be able to break through.

"There's a reason the realm isn't entrusted to just anyone," I told him. "The one who rules is the first to march into battle for their people. Tell me. Where the fuck is Riniya right now?"

"Safe from you."

"Safe," I scoffed. "She is a coward that sent you out here to die. She knew what your fate would be and used you as a means to prolong the inevitable. That is no leader."

"I know what you did, Reynaeros. You don't deserve the throne."

His words made me flinch. Clenching my teeth, I took a deep breath.

"Her lies will be wiped from this place with her death."

Shoving my hand through the plating on his chest, I grabbed the bulb that hummed there and yanked it free, severing it from his root system. He went limp in my grip, his skin darkening and becoming brittle. I dropped him, summoning plants from the ground to drag his body under.

Rathiain cut down the last of the soldiers, but I didn't feel relieved. This massacre was senseless and if I would've had the chance, I would have determined which of them even wanted to be here. I was sure some of them would have sided with me. Because of Riniya, our own people had departed this world.

We continued on our way at a quicker pace. I had no doubt that she would try to send others if I gave her the chance. She would not come out to face me, so I would drag her out by her hair for all to see the treacherous coward that she was.

When the city became visible, we all stared at it for a long moment. The trees stretched high into the sky; higher than any in Kiera's realm were capable of. Winding staircases led to the tops of them and others brought you deep underground. Houses made of various plants made up the lower portion of the city and set into the hillside was the giant oak, its trunk spanning half a mile in each direction.

Opening my palms, I released the energy I'd been holding onto. We entered the city, marching through the winding streets, gasps and whispers following us. Most of them got down on a knee and lowered their heads. Others appeared unnerved by our presence.

Climbing a large staircase, I found myself in a courtyard of stone. It was so familiar to me, I was overcome by emotion. Memories surfaced of running through the gardens and learning to harness life energy. Rathiain loved to douse me with water every time I was deep in concentration.

He laid a hand on my arm, drawing me out of my thoughts. I turned to the others, clearing my throat.

"Stay out here and keep watch. I don't trust that she won't try to box us in."

Nodding at Rathiain, we both headed for the giant double doors. I brushed a hand over the etchings of vines, then pushed them open. Striding into the massive circular room, I found Riniya sitting on my throne surrounded by not only ebony vines, but also trees and flowers. The scent was strong, nearly enough to make me gag.

"Get your ass out of that seat," Rathiain demanded.

"Actually, I'm quite comfortable," she returned, feigning confidence. The way her fingers gripped the armrests betrayed her unease.

"You know that you can't win," I pointed out, moving further into the room. "Why try to save face now?"

"You know, Reynaeros, I'm surprised you would even come here."

"Why is that?"

"In doing so, you have left your woman to suffer alone."

My lip curled. "Don't attempt to threaten her again."

"I've never threatened her. There would be no point."

"Enough with your games," Rathiain spat. "Let's get to the fun part where I watch our brother bury you."

She stood, her vines moving with her. "I have a better idea."

"This should be good."

Crossing my arms, I waited for her to go on.

"Banish me."

I laughed. "What?"

"Send me to another realm and lock me away. I won't be able to interfere over here."

Rathiain hummed thoughtfully. "Nope. That's not how this works."

Riniya looked at me, raising a brow. "Does he make all of the decisions now?"

Rolling my eyes, I took another step toward her. The putrid plants moved to block my way and I used my own to subdue them. She watched me approach, only the twitch in her fingers betraying her fear.

"Why would I allow you to live?"

"Because I'm your sister."

"That means nothing to me. Try again."

"There's been enough death. Vengeance doesn't change what has happened thus far. Don't you think your people will respect a show of mercy, especially after you've been gone for so long?"

Cocking my head, I pretended to consider it. Closing my fist, I dropped a vine from the ceiling and coiled it around her neck, lifting her until she was on her toes. Rathiain took over destroying her plants, leaving her defenseless.

Getting close to her face, I steeled myself against the automatic nausea that threatened me with her closeness.

"Try harder, Riniya."

She bared her teeth. "I will destroy this city and everyone in it."

"Excuse me?"

"My plants are spread wide, a vast web underground. All I have to do is give them one command and they'll burst forth, turning it all to rubble. They will choke out the roots of the four corner trees. When they fall, there won't be a single person that escapes."

Rathiain swore. "If we kill you, they die along with you."

"Not in time to stop it," I said.

He looked at me. "You can't seriously be considering letting her go."

Riniya's lips curled upward. "He doesn't have a choice."

I released her, making her nearly fall to the ground. Once she'd stabilized herself, she rubbed at her throat and adjusted her clothes.

"See, brothers, I may not have the same strength you do, but clearly I'm able to outsmart you at every turn. You never think far enough ahead, whereas I always have a backup plan."

"I think we'll take our chances," he replied, looking at me expectantly.

When I gave him a small shake of my head, his mouth dropped open. I stepped closer to Riniya, then locked a hand around her throat. She clawed at me, but her fight just made this whole thing sweeter.

Leaning forward, I got close to her face. "Do you know what I see when I look at you? A scared, insignificant little girl. You desired power from the start because it was the thing you knew you would never have. Our mother died giving birth to you and none of us blamed you for it, but you convinced yourself that we did. You turned yourself into a victim and based your entire personality around it."

"Let me go, Reynaeros."

"You've been rid of me for so long that you've forgotten the reason you resorted to trickery. As soon as I stepped foot in this city, I wove my own network underground."

Flexing my wrist, I allowed my plants to attack hers. There was a rumbling beneath our feet, then we were surrounded by complete silence. She grimaced at the loss of her leverage.

"Without your rotten webs, you have nothing. You're not nearly strong enough to contend with me, Riniya. That's why you threatened our brother. That's why you needed something to hold over my head. That's why you tricked me and cast that curse. Everything you've done to me, I have overcome. Now what do you have?"

Rathiain was bouncing up and down beside me. I couldn't help but smile, his excitement mirroring my own. Riniya's copper eyes were becoming muddled with brown, the colors mixing violently.

"Is there anything you want to say to our sister, Rathiain?"

"Just one thing." He stepped closer. "Fuck you. I'm going to chuck your body into another realm so it doesn't taint our beautiful forest."

She bared her teeth at me again. "I can save her, you know."

"That's enough."

"Fine. Go ahead and kill me, Reynaeros." When she smiled, I tightened my grip. "At least I'll die knowing that after all of your efforts, you still won't get your happy ending."

Tired of her games, I crushed her windpipe before plunging my dagger into her chest. The same one she'd intended for Kiera to kill me with. I was a sucker for a good full circle moment.

When she went limp, I tossed her body carelessly to the side. It collided with the wall, making a satisfying crunching sound. I hit my knees, drawing in my first free breath in a millennium. It felt damn good.

Chapter 59

Reynaeros

"What do you think she meant about your happy ending?" Rathiain asked as we stepped into the hallway.

"She just wanted to have the last word," I assured him. "She probably thinks I'll fuck it all up."

"The jury is still out on that."

"I would burn myself to ash before I allowed anything to hurt that woman. She belongs to me."

He clapped me on the shoulder. "Look at you. Kiera has domesticated you."

"I miss when you spent three centuries in France."

We turned the corner and nervousness swirled in my gut as I looked at my bedroom door. There shouldn't have been a reason to feel this way, but regardless of what I told Rathiain, I did fear that I would somehow screw it up. Further than that, I worried about our future. She was mortal and I still had another millennium to live, at minimum.

It was possible that the energy in our realm would extend her life. There was just no way to know yet. When we got there, I could have one of our doctors take her blood and see how it reacted. Maybe we could get a better idea of how long I would have with her.

The door opened and Lucy's blonde head appeared. When she saw us, she pursed her lips.

"Why the hell are you in my bedroom, Lucia?"

"I was with Kiera," she said softly.

"Has she been overly concerned?"

Chewing on her lip, she glanced from me to Rathiain. "She's just resting."

"There's something you're not saying."

"You should just go be with her. She misses you."

Staring at her for another moment, I nodded. Rathiain took her by the arm gently, a question in his eyes. She nodded and followed him down the hall. When they disappeared, I took a breath and entered the room.

It was dark in here, the first light of dawn barely starting to peak over the horizon. Kiera was lying in the bed with the blankets pulled up and I couldn't help but smile at the sight of her there. It fell from my face when I felt her energy. I didn't know how to interpret it. There was something akin to sadness mixed with a duller version of the anger she usually bore.

Slipping out of my shoes, I climbed in beside her, wrapping an arm around her middle. Dipping into her neck, I inhaled her scent and moaned contentedly.

"Reyn?" she asked softly.

"Yes, little rose."

Turning in my arms, she smiled at me. I reached out to tuck a strand of her hair behind her ear. Her skin was pale, but I didn't know if it was whiter than usual. Lucia's strange reactions might have been making me paranoid that something was wrong.

"Are you alright?" I asked.

"I should be asking you that. What happened?"

"Riniya is dead and her body has been discarded in another realm."

She laughed a little. "The bitch deserved it."

"Mm. Now answer my question."

Her gaze fell. "I'm fine."

"You're lying to me."

Running her hand under my shirt, she leaned forward to kiss me. My body responded to her touch immediately and I rolled her onto her back, hovering over her. Our tongues met, igniting a fire in my veins.

"This feels like a deflection," I said.

She shook her head. "I just need you right now."

Pushing aside my concerns, I pulled her shirt over her head and bit down on the skin of her breast. My tongue circled her nipple before I pulled it into my mouth, sucking on it gently. She arched into me, her nails digging into my back.

When I'd removed her pants, I dropped between her legs. The scent of her had become something I craved and her taste nearly drove me wild. Branching my tongue in two, I pinned her clit between them as I sunk two fingers inside of her. She settled her legs over my shoulders, allowing me better access.

Pulling my fingers free, I brought them to her lips, spreading her wetness on them. She grabbed my wrist and took them into her mouth, the sight making my dick throb. Moving forward, I explored her mouth with my tongue just as I pushed inside of her.

She moaned against my lips, then sucked in a sharp breath when my barbs settled into place. They gripped her tightly, as if they somehow recognized that she was mine. I was overcome with a sort of possessiveness that was new to me, but had been growing for longer than I would have admitted.

Sitting up on my knees, I brought her feet up to rest on my shoulders and fucked her harder. She clutched the sheets tightly, a shrill cry escaping her as I reached a place deep inside of her. Turning my head, I bit down on her ankle, struggling to hold off my orgasm as her pussy gripped me tighter.

Pulling free of her, I turned her onto her knees. Leaning over her back, I settled my lips at her ear.

"Do you remember the last time I had you in this position?"

"I try not to."

My laugh earned me one of her murderous glares. I nipped at her ear lobe before sitting up and slapping her ass hard.

"I'm going to take all of you again, my little rose."

She tensed. "What if I say no?"

"That's not one of the options."

She groaned, dropping her head onto the pillow. "I hate you."

"You've stabbed me on quite a few occasions. Your words hardly wound me."

I locked my barbs into place inside her pussy before lengthening one of my thorns and rounding it out. After stroking it a few times, I spread the lubricant over her asshole. She was rigid and clutching the sheets, but at least she wasn't crying this time.

Unlike the first time, I wanted her to enjoy this, so I worked myself inside of her more slowly. Once I was inside, I gradually expanded the protrusion, letting it stretch her out before I pulled nearly all the way out. I rubbed my hand up and down her back a couple of times, then pushed inside again.

She let out a grunt. "Reyn, I don't know."

"Relax."

With a growl, she dropped her forehead again, but did as I said. After a few more strokes, she was noticeably less tense. Reaching between her legs, I circled her clit as I found a rhythm. The double stimulation was so incredible, I knew I wouldn't last long like this.

"Fuck," Kiera squeaked when she convulsed around me. "God, Reyn."

"You're mine, Kiera."

"Yes."

"Tell me."

Entangled Realms

"I'm yours."

Slamming into her harder a few times, I gripped her hips so tightly, I was sure she'd bruise. Pulling free, I collapsed onto my back and breathed heavily. She rolled toward me to lie on my chest and I wrapped an arm around her, leaning down to kiss the top of her head.

Suddenly, she sat up straight and drew in a sharp breath. My brow furrowed as she launched herself out of the bed and rushed to the bathroom. When I heard her throwing up, I joined her. Standing in the doorway, I watched her, not knowing what I was supposed to do.

"Kiera, what's going on?"

She flushed the toilet, then put a hand over her forehead. I went to turn on the light, but she shook her head.

"Please don't."

"Why?"

"My head."

Dropping to my knees, I cupped her face. Her eyes were red and I was certain that she looked paler than usual.

"Tell me what's going on. Why was Lucia here earlier?"

"We were just talking. Can we go to sleep? I'm tired."

Picking her up, I carried her into the room and set her on the edge of the bed. My agitation was mounting and I didn't want to lash out at her, so I began to pace.

"Kiera, after everything we've been through, I don't like that you're lying to me."

"It's not important."

"Like hell it is. I just killed Riniya, secured my realm, and I want you to be by my side, but you're hiding things."

She dropped her gaze to the floor. "Reyn, I can't rule with you."

I came to a halt. "What?"

"You heard me."

"What the fuck is this?"

"It's just the truth. I'm human, Reyn."

"I don't care about that. Even if I only have fifty years with you, I want them all."

"You won't have that long."

"The average human life for a woman is nearly eighty years. I Googled it."

She smiled slightly. "You Googled it?"

"Of course I did."

"That's cute."

"You're far from eighty, so that gives me some time and when we get to Aerranata, it might be different."

She shook her head and I felt her energy morph into something angrier. Even though I'd grown used to it before, I hated to feel it return now.

Crouching in front of her, I took her hands. "You're angry."

"I'm not."

"I can feel it, Kiera. You're angry, but also so full of pain that you don't know what to do with it. Tell me."

"I don't want to talk about this right now."

"Why are you angry, Kiera?"

"Stop, Reyn."

"Why the fuck are you angry, Kiera?"

She jumped to her feet, pushing me backward. "Because I won't live!" Her shoulders shook and the life seemed to drain out of her. "I won't live, Reyn."

My blood ran cold. "I don't understand."

"I'm not going to live. I was never going to live."

Chapter 60

Kiera

There was pain in my head, my stomach, and basically everywhere else in my body. It had been progressively getting worse, but I always had something I could focus on to distract myself from it. It was a looming threat at all times, but I'd learned to deal with it. Now, it was out in the open and it didn't feel like it belonged. I wanted to shove it back in that little box I'd locked it in at some point.

What was worse than me having to deal with it was the look on Reyn's face as he processed what I'd said. I wanted to comfort him, but I had no idea what was going on inside his head. The only reason I knew he was distressed was because the colors in his eyes were thrashing more violently than I'd ever seen.

Finally, he lifted his gaze to mine. "No."

Shit. Denial. I should've known he would immediately resort to trying to fight it.

"There's a bomb in my head and it will kill me, Reyn."

"No," he repeated, stepping forward and taking my face in his hands. "I won't lose you."

"It's not fixable."

"What is it?"

"Technically, it's called craniopharyngioma. It's a tumor in my brain."

"Can't they cut it out?"

"Not without significant risks."

"Then take the risk."

I breathed a dry laugh. "Reyn, I've been living with this since I was eight. The risks were... substantial. We decided not to take them and now it's too late. It's too big."

"Kiera, no. I won't accept this."

"You have to. I've had seventeen years to deal with this shit, but I didn't expect some fucker with branches growing from his head to come in and rattle everything I'd come to terms with."

"How long?"

My lip trembled and he ran his thumb over it. "A year ago, the doctor gave me twelve to eighteen months before it started to shut my body down."

Stepping back, he put a hand over his mouth. Whirling around, he grabbed the dresser and threw it across the room. I tensed, closing my eyes as a tear rolled down my cheek.

Anger.

I opened my eyes, watching as he paced the room. He thrust his hands through his hair, gripping it so tightly I worried he'd rip it from his scalp.

"Reyn."

He shook his head and continued walking back and forth aggressively.

"Reyn."

"Riniya knew, didn't she?"

"Yeah. Her plants sensed it or something creepy like that."

He lifted me into his arms and headed for the door. I held onto his neck, not sure what he was doing, but I didn't think arguing with him would do much at this point. When he brought us into the library, I looked around curiously.

The plants were gone and everything seemed to be back in its rightful place. It must've been nifty to have magic.

He set me gently in the chair by the fireplace. I brought my knees up, perching my chin on them as I watched him search the shelves.

"What are you doing?"

"Looking for something."

"I can see that."

He grabbed one of the books and came back over to me. "We have doctors. They can do something."

"I don't think your plant doctors can do anything the ones here couldn't do."

"You don't know that. Our bodies are intricate. The pathways in our brains are significantly more complicated, as are our root systems. Someone can fix it. I don't care what I have to do."

Bargaining.

I didn't bother arguing with him. He had to work through it and no matter what I said, he would do whatever he wanted. Soon enough, he'd realize that it was no use.

A sound drew my gaze to the doorway. Rath was standing there, his brows pulled down and his hands in his pockets. The way he looked at me told me Lucy had told him everything. His eyes moved to his brother, who was frantically looking for another book, and the despondent expression intensified.

He came up behind me and kissed the top of my head. It was clear that he was under no delusions, but he joined his brother anyway.

"What are we looking for?"

Reyn stared at him for a moment and I saw those emotions threatening to break free. Turning back to the shelf, he gestured aimlessly.

"I have over five thousand books from both of our realms. There is something here. I just know it."

Sinking deeper into the seat, I let my mind wander to the last time I'd watched two people go through these phases. Even once my parents reached acceptance, I knew they'd never let go of hope. On their anniversary, they took me with them to France because they couldn't stand the idea of me being alone for a week. My mother worried so much that she was convinced something would happen to me while they were gone.

In the end, they were the ones that departed this world first. At least they didn't have to see me slowly wither away. I knew that things would only get worse from here as the tumor began to affect my faculties. I'd already been hit with blurry vision a few times. My headaches were so bad, I experienced them more often than not. I couldn't even keep food down.

Maybe this entire thing was some big, elaborate hallucination because the tumor was compressing my frontal lobe. That would be a funny twist.

🌷 🌷 🌷 🌷

I woke with a start and saw only darkness. At first, I thought it was something going wrong with my vision, but then I saw a pale sliver of moonlight shining on the wall.

"Reyn?"

He pulled me against his chest and nuzzled into my hair. "I'm here, my rose."

Snuggling into him, I let out a contented hum. "How did we get in bed?"

"You fell asleep in the library and I carried you here."

"You're staying, right?"

"Yes."

"Good. We haven't slept next to each other yet, so I should probably warn you that I kick a lot."

He stroked down my back. "You won't hurt me."

Lifting my head, I frowned at him. "Stop being so serious."

His eyes were red and the green was still, but it didn't strike me as calm. I'd never seen him look so tired and I hated that I was the reason for it.

Depression.

"Don't be sad because of me."

Entangled Realms

"I'm sorry," he said softly. "We're going to Aerranata in the morning."

"Why?"

"To see a doctor."

I let out a sigh. "No, Reyn."

"Just one," he insisted. "Rathiain and Eli headed over there tonight to brief him."

"Eli went?"

"I think they're fond of each other."

"Weird."

"He'll be prepared when we arrive and we can get more information."

I shook my head. "There's nothing anyone can do."

"It could be different there. The energy is purer. It could help to heal you."

"I don't want hope, Reyn. I gave it up a long time ago because it hurts more than knowing I'm going to die."

He flinched. "You're not going to die. I won't allow it."

"You can't beat everything. This isn't a fairytale."

"Will you do this for me, Kiera?"

Looking into his eyes, I couldn't get past the sadness there. It was unbearable. Even though it was the last thing I wanted to do and I knew it would only hurt me more, I nodded. He smiled, then leaned forward to kiss me.

"I'm going to prove you wrong, my little rose. Then, we will live a long and happy life together among the trees. You will see."

Settling against his chest again, I kept a firm grip on my sense of reality. I couldn't start to hope again. When my parents were here, I held onto it simply because it made them happy. The weight of losing them and that hope all at the same time nearly killed me.

We'd go to Aerranata and they would determine that nothing could be done. Then, Reyn would have to accept it. Whatever time I had left, I wanted to spend it with him, not with a bunch of doctors doing tests. That was the one thing I never wanted.

Chapter 61

Reynaeros

Kiera was trying to put on a front, but I knew she was doubtful. She looked around in wonder at my world and smiled at me every time I looked at her, but I saw through it. Not only did she have no hope, she also did not feel well. I kept trying to carry her, but she wouldn't allow it.

She and Eli chattered excitedly as we entered the city. I led her up the steps into the great oak, then down the hall to what would be our room. The doctor was already inside with his tools and instruments set up. She looked terrified as she stared at everything.

I stroked the back of her neck. "Do not be afraid."

"I'm not."

Smiling at her show of courage, I directed her to sit on the bed.

"You must be Kiera. I'm Elleer."

"It's nice to meet you," she replied. "I appreciate that you're doing all of this."

"I would do anything for Reynaeros. I took care of his father in his last years."

"Oh. Wow."

"Your human friend, Eli, allowed me to explore his brain last night."

Her mouth dropped open. "You explored his brain?"

"He put this fibrous root in my head," Eli said with a shudder.

"It's very small," Elleer assured her. "I'm very dexterous with it."

Kiera had a lingering expression of uncertainty as she listened to Elleer explain what he learned about the human brain. As I'd told her, it was simpler than ours, which I was confident meant that fixing what was in hers would be possible. Humans used machines connected to electricity, but we didn't need any of that. What we had was connected to us and was more trustworthy.

"Will you lie back so I can explore your brain and see where the problem is?"

She glanced at me and I climbed onto the bed behind her, having her lean back against me. I stroked my hands through her hair repeatedly, nodding at Elleer.

"Will it hurt?" she whispered.

"Not one bit."

She gripped my thighs tightly and closed her eyes. A small fiber sprung from Elleer's finger and floated through the air. It went up her nose and his eyes glazed over a little as he directed its energy.

A few minutes later, the fiber returned and he looked at me. I gritted my teeth, but stroked down Kiera's arms reassuringly.

"See? It didn't hurt."

She let out a heavy breath. "It was terrifying, though."

"You couldn't even feel it."

"Yeah, but I knew it was there."

"You're quite dramatic."

"I will stab you again."

"Put your thorns away, my little rose. You can show me how sharp you are later."

"Ugh, is that a sex thing?" Eli asked, his nose wrinkling.

"How would that be a sex thing?" Kiera laughed.

"I don't know how plant-human relations work."

"You and Rath look pretty chummy."

Rathiain's eyes widened and Eli looked at the ground. The corner of my mouth lifted, but I couldn't muster up more than that.

"I'll be right back."

"You're leaving me?" Kiera asked, looking panicked.

"Don't worry yourself. I have some things to take care of. I've been gone for seven centuries, remember?"

"Okay. Just don't stay gone too long."

"Never."

I moved into the hall and Elleer joined me a moment later. We began to walk toward the main room and with every second, my anxiety heightened.

"Tell me."

"I don't know how to get to it," he admitted.

"You said their brains are less complicated."

"They are, but everything is tightly packed. I could easily damage something."

"We have to try something."

"Does she agree?"

"It doesn't matter. She does not get to simply give up."

He sighed. "I can try, but if I fail, she will die. If I don't try, you can take whatever time you have with her."

"I don't accept either of those outcomes," I said firmly.

"You may not have a choice," he replied sadly. "Tell her what her options are. When you've decided, let me know."

He headed out the front doors and I had the urge to break something. This was not how things were going to end. I had endured too much to have the one good thing in my life ripped away from me so suddenly. If I had to put her to sleep and allow the doctor to operate without her consent, I would do that and live with the consequences.

"What'd he say?" Kiera asked when everyone had left that evening.

Leaning back against the headboard, I crossed my ankles. "He'll operate if it's what you want."

She stared at me intently. "What are you leaving out?"

"Nothing."

"You didn't let me withhold the truth."

"He doesn't know if it will work, but he'll try."

Setting her mug on the nightstand, she laid back and pulled the covers over her. When she turned away from me, I wrapped an arm around her and kissed her neck.

"Don't hide from me."

"I'm not hiding."

Her voice shook and I could feel her body trembling. It pained me to know I'd distressed her, but I refused to back down. This wasn't something that would simply work itself out.

"You're upset with me."

"I told you I didn't want hope."

"You act as if we shouldn't have any."

"This isn't any different than the decision I made before. I'm not taking the chance."

"You will die otherwise."

"I will die either way."

"You can't know that."

"You're not stupid, Reyn, nor are you a blind optimist. You're simply refusing to accept this."

"Yes. I refuse to accept it."

With a growl, she threw the covers off and stood. I followed her into the hall.

"Don't walk away from me."

She whirled around. "You can't decide my future for me."

"I am protecting you."

"No. You're in denial. It's easier if you just skip to acceptance."

"Then I would be giving up like you."

"This is my fight."

"You're not fighting!"

She set her jaw, looking to the side. I cupped her face, staring down at her watery brown eyes.

"Fight, Kiera."

"I can't," she whispered.

"You marched into my club and killed a woman for the first time in your life in order to save Eli. You barely flinched. When I took you prisoner, you banged on the walls and stood up to me, even though I could have killed you. I did worse and you still fought me. You have fought all the way here. Why stop now?"

"I'm tired, Reyn."

"I don't care."

"Just let me die the way I want to."

"No. Fucking fight, Kiera."

I brushed away her tears with my thumbs. Looking up into my eyes, she finally nodded. I was filled with both relief and fear for what this meant, but I just pulled her into my chest, giving myself a moment before I had to be strong for her again.

"This time, we're fighting together, my little rose. I will grow with you and nothing is allowed to stand in our way."

Chapter 62

Kiera

As much as I wanted to fight against it, there was a kernel of hope growing in my chest. Maybe it was just Reyn's confidence rubbing off on me. He seemed so certain that this would work, even though the doctor was clear about it not being a foolproof plan.

Even if I didn't die, there was a high likelihood I'd end up with some sort of deficit. Blindness. A loss of speech. Hell, I might not be able to do anything on my own anymore. Was that worth it? I'd never thought so, but I guess if it meant I could be with Reyn for a little while longer, I would accept it.

Gripping Eli's hand, I pulled him down to me. "If I don't make it, you'd better grow the balls to ask Rath out."

He laughed and shook his head. "You want those to be your last words, Kiera?"

"No. My last words are that you and Rath have to make sure Reyn doesn't lose it."

"I don't know if that's possible."

"You can't let him lose himself again. To become what he was."

"I'm pretty sure he only changed because of you."

I shook my head. "He's damaged, but he's not bad. I know that you can't see it because you don't know him. All you've seen are his flaws and maybe you still think it's some sort of Stockholm Syndrome, but it's not. I'm not looking past his flaws. I never have. I just found the beauty within the beast. Don't let him lose that part of him again."

Pressing a kiss to my forehead, he blew out a breath. "I'll do my best. You know what I think, though?"

"What?"

"You're going to be here to keep him in check yourself. There are no other options, Kiera."

Sniffing, I nodded. Rath came up to me and kissed my forehead next. "You're too strong to let this beat you, ma belle."

They both shuffled out and Reyn cupped my face. I could tell he was trying to keep his emotions hidden, but his eyes always betrayed him. The colors weren't thrashing. Instead, they were moving languidly, as if they were dancing together, becoming one.

"Is there a ballroom here?"

He breathed a laugh. "Yes. Why?"

"I want to dance with you when I wake up."

"Then we will dance, little rose."

"Forever. Promise me."

"Forever, Kiera."

🌷 🌷 🌷 🌷

Surgery was weird as fuck. One second, I was staring at Reyn's pale green eyes and the next I was waking up. It felt like I'd just had the best nap of my life and I almost wanted to sink back into it.

"Little rose."

Blinking, I turned and found those beautiful eyes, wide and locked on me. He immediately kissed me, smiling against my lips.

Entangled Realms

"You made it."

"Did he fuck anything up?"

"No. You're perfect."

My grin was nearly painful. I couldn't believe it. For seventeen years, I was waiting for that bomb in my head to kill me. Now, it was gone. It didn't feel any different, but I guess I wouldn't really know.

"You were right," I laughed.

"I told you I would be."

"I'm not gonna lie. I didn't believe you."

"You'll just have to learn to trust me."

"How long do I have to wait to leave the bed?"

Elleer appeared at the side of the bed. "Why would you have to wait?"

"Uh, usually after surgery you have to wait a while. Healing takes a while."

"The energy here nurtures your body. You might react a little more slowly than us, but as long as you're not off fighting battles, you should be just fine."

"Wow. That's incredible."

Reyn held a hand out to me. "Come."

"Where are we going?"

"You wanted to dance."

"Now?"

"Why not?"

"Fuck it, I guess."

Even though I was wearing jeans and a boring t-shirt, I let him lead me down the winding halls. There was a set of ornate double doors with vines and flowers etched into it. He pushed through it into a circular room with sparkling lights and a gold floor. I looked around with wonder, hardly able to believe what I was seeing.

Gripping my hand tighter, he spun me in a circle. I stepped into his chest, settling one arm around his neck.

"Can I be honest?"

"Always."

"I don't know how to dance."

He smiled. "I'm not surprised."

"Are you calling me uncouth, Reyn?"

"Perhaps, but we'll change that. You are going to be ruling an entire realm, after all."

My stomach constricted. "I didn't give myself time to process all of that."

"You'd better start processing. Your duties begin today." When my eyes widened, he laughed. "I'm kidding. Although, we could make your regency official."

"Are you going to crown me or something?"

"Better."

He spun me and when I faced him again, I put a hand to my mouth. He had dropped to one knee and was staring up at me with the brightest green eyes.

"You're joking."

"Don't ruin this."

He opened a wooden box, revealing a delicate ring with a thin, winding band. Nestled at the top of it was a green stone like the one in his dagger.

"When did you have time to get something like this?"

"I made it the moment I realized I wanted you to rule with me."

"When was that?"

"Before I took you to that restaurant."

"That's insane. You know that, right?"

"Have you ever known me to be entirely sane?"

"Good point."

"Kiera, I never thought I'd be doing this. Even now, I wonder if it's just a dream because I don't deserve it. In our short time, we've weathered some of the worst storms, but we made it out of them because we did it together. I want to grow with you and one day I want to die with you. Will you accept me as yours?"

Pursing my lips on a smile, I pretended to contemplate it. He narrowed his eyes.

"Don't even think about it."

"Yes, Reyn. I'll fucking grow with you or whatever."

Straightening, he lifted me and spun me around a few times. "We'll have to work on your dancing skills, my little rose."

"We can do it every day."

"Forever."

Madilyn DeRose

Epilogue I

Reynaeros

Swiping both my hands down my face, I tried to clear my head. I was more tired than I'd been in an age and my thoughts were a jumbled mess. With each passing second I hoped that I would wake up, but I knew this was reality. I didn't want to be a part of it anymore.

"Her energy feels calmer," Rathiain said from beside me.

"I flooded her with the purest energy from the earth. Whatever she is seeing in her mind is peaceful. Happy. I know that much."

"Good. It's a small comfort, but it'll have to do."

"I don't understand. How did it come to this?"

"We knew it was a long shot, Reynaeros."

Gripping Kiera's hand, I looked at her still form. She looked beautiful, peaceful. It was impossible to imagine that she might not wake up again. I wouldn't see her smile or hear her laugh. Even when Elleer warned me it might not work, I didn't allow myself to consider the possibility. I couldn't bear it.

"I shouldn't have convinced her to do this."

"You wanted to try. There's nothing wrong with that."

"We could've had time together. Even if it was only months, it would've been me and her. That was what she wanted and I took it from her."

"Take solace in the fact that she won't know. Right now, she's somewhere happy and she has no idea it isn't real. Even if you had months together, she would be decaying. She'd be in pain. Maybe this is a mercy."

Our hands grew wet from the tears that fell from my eyes. I gripped her tighter, staring down at our fingers. If I hadn't come into her life, she would be spending her last days at home, even if she was in pain. It should have been her decision, just like everything else should have been. She had a plan and I'd come along to ruin it.

"Keep feeding her energy," he said. "Elleer said it could still help."

As much as I wanted to hope, I was quickly losing the strength to hold onto it. Regardless, I did as he said. If she had even the slightest chance, I would do everything in my power to get her through this.

The door slammed open and hurried footsteps approached. A shape appeared in my peripheral, along with labored breathing.

"No," Eli choked out. "No, this isn't right."

"Eli," Rathiain said softly.

Eli shoved him away and took Kiera's other hand. "No, no, no. You're supposed to live, god damnit."

"Take him home, Rathiain."

Eli shoved me and I got to my feet, vines beginning to push through my fingertips. Rathiain stepped between us, holding up his hands.

"Don't do this here. Not now."

"This is your fault," Eli shouted.

I narrowed my eyes. "I'm trying to save her."

"If you hadn't kidnapped her, she would be home. Even if she died, she would have been better. Happier. She would've been with people that love her."

"I love her."

"I'm sure whatever abuse you put her through only hurried it along."

Stepping forward, I bared my teeth at him. Rathiain huffed and grabbed Eli's arm, hauling him toward the door.

"This is disrespectful to her. Both of you need to get your shit together or take this elsewhere. Then you can do whatever the fuck you want."

Dropping to my knees again, I laid my head on Kiera's chest, listening to her heart. If it stopped, I decided I would take her into the forest and join her in the earth. For me, there was no other option.

It infuriated me that Riniya may have been right. I might not get my happy ending, even though I'd fought so hard for it. Maybe, in the end, my darkness had spread too far, permeating everything around me.

I faulted her for letting the rot take over her essence, but I was hardly any better. In my despair, I'd been twisted into something ugly. A beast. Kiera's despair had turned her into something pure and beautiful.

She was right before. This wasn't a fairytale. Beast and beauty did not get to coexist. Our entangled realms were not compatible in life, but in death, our souls would rest beside each other.

At the end of it all, it was more than I would have asked for a year ago.

Opening the locket resting at the hollow of her throat, I tucked a picture inside it from our first night here.

I brought more energy into my hands and pushed it into her. "Forever, my little rose. I promised you forever. In life and in death."

Epilogue II

Kiera

"Forever, my little rose. I promised you forever."

Warmth flooded me, almost feeling like it was burning through my veins. My heartbeat sounded loud in my ears and there was pressure in my head. Groaning, I reached up to touch my temple.

"Kiera."

Reyn's voice made me open my eyes. "Reyn."

"Jesus. You're awake. How?"

"What do you mean? Isn't that what happens after surgery?"

His eyes were wide, the green beginning to swirl and darken. "You... You were dying."

"Yeah, I've been dying for a long time."

"No, you weren't supposed to wake up. Elleer said removing the tumor put too much stress on your brain and you slipped into a coma."

I scoffed. "Pretty sure the guy should have his medical license revoked."

He laughed, putting a hand over his mouth. "You're going to be okay."

"It appears that way," I said with a smile.

After a while, Elleer showed up and did his weird nose to brain excursion. It turned out that once the swelling went down, my body was able to stabilize itself. Apparently, the energy in this place might have made enough of a difference to keep me alive.

When his expression grew solemn, I felt like my hopes were going to be dashed again.

"What is it?"

"It's just something I noticed while testing your blood earlier."

"Go on."

"The energy from your world will continue to make the tumor grow."

My brow furrowed. "But you removed it."

"The majority, yes, but it will regrow."

"Fuck. Does that mean we'll have to do it again?"

"It's likely. You said it took something like seventeen years, so it's possible you'll have quite a while until it becomes a problem."

"What if we close it?" Rathiain asked suddenly.

Reyn turned to him. "The gateway?"

"When we were on the other side, the energy from our realm was cut off when the gateway closed. It should work the same way and if that connection to her world is what causes this, we can shut it down."

"Chester was going to stay there with Collie," I pointed out.

"He'll have to come back. I have no doubt she'll follow."

My heart raced as I considered it. If it was closed, I would be stuck here. I wanted to be here with Reyn, but the idea of never being able to go back was terrifying.

"Would it work?"

Elleer looked thoughtful. "Probably."

"I'm willing to take that chance," Reyn said.

"Then I guess I'm in agreement."
"Are you sure?"
I squeezed his hand. "Forever, remember?"

🌷 🌷 🌷 🌷

Wiping at my nose, I lunged for Eli again. He laughed and squeezed me tight.
"You're going to be happy, Kiera."
"But I won't have you. Can't you stay?"
"What would I do here? I'd just be a human among a bunch of tree people."
"We're not tree people," Reyn grumbled.
"They're fairies," I whispered loudly.
"For fuck's sake."
Rathiain came up beside me with his hands in his pockets. "You could stay, you know. Nobody would mind."
Eli chewed on his lip, then shrugged. "The coffee shop would probably go up in flames without me. I also have a date with some guy on Friday."
"No fight clubs," I said sternly.
"No fight clubs."
He smiled, then held an arm out to Chester. He was making one last trip to help Collie prepare and bring over whatever she wanted to keep from home. Lucy was also moving here with Brooks, so in a way, it would be like old times.
Stepping closer to Rath, I pinched his arm.
"What the fuck?"
"Stop being a pussy, Rath."
"I don't know what you're talking about."
"Yeah, you do."
He bit his lip, staring ahead of us. "Fuck it."
Marching forward, he grabbed a wide-eyed Eli and pulled him into a kiss. After a moment, I had to look away because it was getting pretty steamy for a first kiss in the forest.

Madilyn DeRose

Threading my arm through Reyn's, I turned us around and headed back toward home. Touching the locket at my throat, I opened it up, feeling a little twinge of sadness that the photo of my mother and I was no longer there. In the end, though, it was the memory of her that mattered most.

Reyn pulled me into his side and kissed the top of my head. "You look happy."

"I am. I can't believe everything worked out the way it did. It's almost too perfect."

"Just like you."

"You're too sweet to me these days. You're supposed to be a beast."

He bared his teeth at me. "If that's what you want. Run, my little rose."

"Ah, fuck."

Taking off into the forest, I couldn't help but laugh. It was far from the ending I'd expected, but being chased by Reyn wasn't the worst way to live my life considering I knew exactly what would happen when he caught me. A day ago, I would've insisted it was impossible to feel this blissfully happy. Once again, I was glad to be wrong about something.

I screamed when I was swept off my feet and deposited on the ground. He dove into my neck, grazing me with his teeth.

"I'm fucking starving, Kiera."

He had my pants off in record time and immediately dove between my legs. I gasped at the sensation of his split tongue on my clit. Grabbing onto his branches, I held on for dear life as he devoured me like a man starved.

This is what it is to be happy.
-Sylvia Plath, The Bell Jar

Entangled Realms

Books By This Author

Mature Books 18+

Hemlock: *Malefic Bloodlines Book I*

San Francisco is widely known as a hub for technology, sky-high rent prices, and a great night life. Underneath it all, it's also home to a coven of vampires that have learned to blend in flawlessly. With two powerful leaders keeping things running smoothly, nobody could pose a threat to their way of life. The best threats, though, came from the inside.

The only thing Lock loved more than blood was power, which was why he'd been planning a flawless coup d'état for over a decade. Nothing would get in his way. When vampires suddenly start going feral in the streets, it's bound to complicate things. Lock is nothing if not imaginative, though. He isn't afraid to paint the city in red, as long as he gets what he wants in the end.

When he meets Sam, he finds that what he wants might become more volatile than he expected. Killing her would be the smartest move if he wants everything to go according to plan. He refused to throw away a decade of planning for some redhead with a bad attitude. San Francisco would be his, even if he has to kill everybody that stands in his way

Belladonna: *Malefic Bloodlines Book II*
Releases December 1, 2023

After everything that happened over the summer, Hemlock and Samara spent some much needed time together as they navigated the new aspects of their relationship. Now that she has been filled in on the truth, he hopes she'll make the decision to change sooner rather than later, but every day he grows more concerned about her decision.

While she's battling with the implications of ending her mortal life, a threat looms in the distance, seeking to draw Lock out of his comfortable tower. When the mysterious drug that turns vampires feral pops up in Seattle, he must once again try to unlock its secrets and uncover the mastermind behind it. If he can't unravel it all, both his coven and his mate could become casualties in the game that's been set in motion.

This whole thing seems to revolve around him, but then, perhaps it goes even deeper than that. A horned villain hiding in the shadows might offer the greatest challenge he's faced yet. As the most powerful vampire in existence, though, he shouldn't have anything to fear.

If only his mate would finally give up her mortality and fight alongside him. That would make things a hell of a lot simpler.

Faded Pages: *From Yesterday to Always Book I*

If someone ever needed a picture to conceptualize the term 'emotionally volatile', I'd be the one screaming, "I volunteer as tribute." I was a mess, I couldn't keep a 'real job', and I was prone to angry outbursts at the slightest provocation. I had five mental diagnoses under my belt that all simultaneously tried to sabotage me. That's right; I made the DSM-5 my bitch. Although, it could have been the other way around.

TLDR; I was problematic. Toxic, if you believed every one of my exes. I wouldn't, though. Clearly I wasn't in the business of picking winners.

Sure, I was pretty enough and I worked out, but if we were looking at the whole picture, I was not a catch. Men didn't want someone difficult like me. They didn't have the patience or the will and I didn't blame them. A boring relationship with a guy that tolerated me was the best I could hope for. That was exactly who I'd been with for the past two years; a boyfriend that was kind of an asshole and barely acknowledged my existence.

Then... he showed up. Two years and an ocean had separated us, but now he was back and it seemed like he was on a mission to pull me back into his orbit.

Not happening. None for me, thanks. Okay, maybe a bite. Just one, though. I swear.

Sentence Redacted: *From Yesterday to Always Book II*

Sometimes to understand the story, you have to go back to the beginning. Read between the lines. Evaluate all of the pieces to see how they fit together.

Instead of standing my ground when I came face to face with my own version of the devil two months ago, I ran away. Healthy? No. Effective? Temporarily.

Facing my past was a battle I had no interest in fighting, but it was stupid to think it'd come to anything else. I took what I wanted, claimed the love that I'd finally let myself believe I deserved. I forgot that things don't work out for people like me. We don't get the boy and the house and the good life. We're the scraps. The leftovers that someone else already chewed up and spat on the sidewalk.

Jaden did that. He really did a number on me; he managed to top all the other trauma I'd endured in my life. Now he was here, living in the love of my life's house. Breathing the same air, in the same city, looking at the same moon I did every night.

So yes, I ran, but I couldn't stay gone forever. Alright, Portland. What new horrors do you have for me this time around?

Blurred Lines: *From Yesterday to Always Book III*
Releases January 1, 2024

Em, Alden, and Kade have spent the last six months navigating their relationship together. After seemingly endless twists and turns, it feels like things will finally work out for them.

There's just one thing they can't forget, no matter how much they'd like to. Jaden is a looming threat, even though he's been silent ever since Halloween. They're not stupid enough to think he'd give up on Em, so all they can do is wait for him to make his next move. The situation is taking its toll on all of them; Em's state of mind is trending downward, Kade's mysterious past is threatening to drown him, and Alden feels responsible for holding all of them together.

When Em receives a mysterious gift, she starts a game Jaden set up just for her. She could never say no to a good old-fashioned puzzle. What happens when she reaches the finish line, though?

Sometimes things aren't always what they seem, but does it change anything in the end?

New Adult Books

Brimstone

A new world might've sounded like some futuristic dream, but in reality, it was the old world that had everything they could ask for. The one I was born into was barren, dangerous, and barely holding onto some semblance of peace between humans and what they not so affectionately called witches. Starvation, death, sickness, and lack of resources were our reality. The war made it that way and another one would probably destroy the entire planet.

I loved a good book as much as the next person, but this wasn't fiction. This wasn't a fairytale. I wasn't the proverbial hero of some story. I was a runaway, a disgraced son of non-magical parents, a veiled shadow within the human world. This was life and death; blood and ash; love and loss. I could not be responsible for it. This blood would not be on my hands.

Timefall

Madilyn DeRose

Releases December 15, 2023

At some point in the near future, I was going to lose all of my friends. It was inevitable, really. That was the sort of life my fortune cookie foretold or whatever. While everyone else wanted to be a doctor or an astronaut, I always found comfort in a good heist movie. I was never very sociable and according to other people, I was kind of weird. The only people I was really close with were my brother, Blaise, and my best friend, Brandy.

Now, he was gone and she was a couple months away from marrying a straight edge millionaire. Me; I was a thief. Not the kind that stole one shoe from Walmart. No, I got my hands on things that were a bit more valuable. My life was about intricate surveillance, burglary, and grand theft auto when I was feeling ballsy. I was good at what I did, but I hadn't made my big break yet. That was about to change.

When I learned about a fancy lab with mysterious inventions, I set my sights on it. What I found there was far above anything I'd imagined. I mean, time travel was the stuff of science fiction. With top secret documents and one of their devices in hand, I was going to be a billionaire very soon. Well, that was the plan. Note to self: don't mess around with a device that could send you hundreds of years into the past. Second note to self: make sure you don't have a straggler when you head back to your own time. The guy definitely wouldn't fit in and he'd probably cause all sorts of problems.

Hell, at least he was really damn hot. And straight, of course. It's possible he's a homophobe, if we're being honest. My main concern was getting him home. What else could go wrong along the way?

Made in the USA
Columbia, SC
11 January 2024

3d231700-16b7-41d7-a9a2-0b4e7ba6f813R01